Edie

Bob Bancks

Published by Bob Bancks
Blue Grass, Iowa
www.iowafarmboy.net
bob.bancks@gmail.com

Edits by Misty Urban
Cover and Interior Design by Emily Heim, Expressions by Em

ISBN: #978-1-0818246-3-1

DEDICATION

This novel is dedicated to my loving wife Jane. Not only does she edit my writings, but before retiring from farming, she became a skillful tractor driver and excellent swine manager. She did this plus all the many household duties most farm wives accomplish. She is truly a champion among working women.

TABLE OF CONTENTS

CHAPTER 1: HERE'S EDIE

Pete McKillip was the only student in second grade at Patterson School #4 until a cute little girl arrived in March. She was Edie Mae Mohr, a small girl with long dark pigtails and an infectious smile. Her father had just hired on at the McKillip Farm. She and her older brother, Ralph, started on the first day of March. In farming, the first of March was moving day or changing job day.

The pair swelled the one room school to fifteen. Pete soon found out Edie was a tomboy. She could run faster than most boys and she could hit a baseball. She wasn't afraid of frogs, toads, or snakes. She would rather play boys games instead of girls She was smart, too. She excelled in arithmetic and science. She didn't have much time to become acquainted with her school mates because school was out the middle of May. The boys worked with their fathers on their farms. Even eight-year-old Pete helped with chores. The same was true for the girls. There was plenty of gardening and house chores to be done. Fortunately, there was also plenty of play time. There were days Pete would have his dad ask Edie's father, Frank, if Edie, as everyone called her, could come over and play. Edie, Pete, and his little sister, Susan, would play for hours in the woods near Pine Creek. During a slow time in July, Edie was at Pete's three or four afternoons a week, because Edie's grandmother was in poor health. Her mother, Hattie, had to spend entire days helping care for her. On those days Edie came early in the morning with her father and stayed all day. Pete's mother, Alma, grew fond of Edie. Edie was always willing to help set the table and clean up afterwards. She never complained about being the hired hand's daughter. She appreciated the hand-me down clothes from Pete's older sister, Mary. Edie idolized Mary, who was a quiet, tall, thin, blond girl. Alma said she was the spitting image of her grandmother, Rebecca McKillip. Mary loved Edie because she was always happy.

1

One day in late June when the Mohr kids were there all day, the men were cultivating for the last time and the house chores were finished. Alma suggested they all go to the creek for a picnic. The McKillip children were excited since they knew it meant splashing in the cool waters of Pine Creek. Clara, the eighteen-year-old hired girl, was asked to come along.

"All right, girls get your swim suits on. Boys, you can just wear pants, no underwear," Alma ordered.

All the girls giggled except Edie. She looked down at the floor. She began to cry and said, "I can't go because I don't have a swim suit."

Alma replied, "Oh, pshaw, you're right, Edie. Let me see. I know. Mary, you go and find an older undershirt of yours and maybe some old panties. We must fix little Edie up. We wouldn't want her to miss out on the fun."

In just a short time, Alma had Edie dressed.

Alma commented, "If it weren't for your pigtails, I'd swear you're were a boy, Edie, and a very cute one, too."

Edie smiled her biggest toothless smile. She was going to the creek.

The gang clambered into the buckboard and headed for the creek. Alma parked the wagon under a big oak tree. The boys jumped out and were splashing around almost before the buckboard had stopped. The place Alma had picked was called "the pool." It was where the water made a small waterfall because eons ago a layer of limestone formed over the sandstone. The force of the water cut into the sandstone bottom and made a pool about fifty feet across, which varied from shallow to maybe five feet deep. It was almost always clean because of the falls.

It wasn't very long before the three boys were downstream chasing minnows and frogs. They were floating hickory nut shells as tiny boats. The girls waded in slowly. It was Alma who surprised everyone. She had secretly donned her swim suit and was ready for the fun. She splashed into the deepest part. Clara followed right behind. Alma grabbed Susan, while Clara grabbed Edie. They pulled both girls into the deeper water. Susan screamed, but Edie laughed. Clara threw Edie up and over her head. Edie dove head first into the water. She came up sputtering.

She called, "Clara, help me. I think I just lost my pants."

Clara quickly turned around to see Edie's too-big shorts floating away. Mary reached out and retrieved them.

"I bet you're glad the boys are downstream, aren't you, Edie?" she said with a smile. Mary helped Edie ashore and quickly replaced the naughty shorts. She tightened the belt some more and said, "I guess you are not as big as we thought."

They played for about an hour. Alma and Clara left the creek and set up the picnic. Alma called the boys. Soon everyone was enjoying peanut butter and jelly sandwiches along with lemonade. The group returned to the homestead just as the men were coming in from the field.

On Mondays, Edie was needed at home. It was wash day. Tuesday and Thursday afternoons were free, so Edie walked over to the McKillip's after she had finished her chores. Pete and Susan each had a Shetland pony. When Susan wanted to play dolls, Pete and Edie would ride the ponies all afternoon in the spacious pastures.

Pete was interested in the Native Americans who once lived in the Pine Creek valley. His grandfather and father had found many arrowheads near the creek. Pete had searched many times but only found a few. Edie loved to search the creek banks with Pete. One afternoon she spotted a white stone high on the exposed bank. It was too high to reach from the creek bottom, so she scurried around the edge to a low spot and ran to the top of the bank. She lay down on her tummy and reached as far as she could, but still her arm was too short.

She called, "Pete, come hold my legs. I think I found an arrowhead."

Pete hurried up the bank. He grabbed Edie's legs as she worked herself further down the dirt bank.

"Got it!" she yelled. "Pull me up."

Pete tugged and tugged. He couldn't pull Edie back.

"I can't do it. Can you push with your hands?"

"No, I don't want to lose the arrowhead."

"But my feet are slipping on the grass and I can't pull any harder."

"Okay, I'll brace myself against the bank. See if you can get a better footing."

"Okay, ready?"

"No, don't let goooooo . . ."

Edie slipped over the edge and went head over heels down the bank into the creek. Pete scrambled to the edge and peered over. He could see Edie lying in the water. Her face was smudged with mud, her dress was dirty, but she smiled and held up the precious arrowhead.

She hollered at Pete, "Look, I still got it!"

Pete hurried down to have a look.

Edie washed the stone in the water. It was about five inches long with notches on the bottom where it would have been tied to a shaft.

"It's a spearhead. Boy! It's a beauty." He looked at Edie and asked, "Are you okay? You look a mess."

Edie looked at her dress. She was soaked to the skin. Pete got out his hankie and wiped the dirt from her face.

Edie grinned and said, "What'll your mom say?"

"It won't be my mom. What will your mom say?"

"I don't know, but I got the arrowhead."

"We'd better get home. I'll go get the ponies."

The pair rode back to Pete's. Alma gasped at the sight of Edie, then started to laugh. Pete's tomboy friend looked like a clown with her muddy face, one pigtail hanging in front and one in back, and her soaked muddy dress.

Alma said, "We can't send you home like this. I'll see if I can find some clean clothes of Mary's for you to wear. Say, what happened? Just how did you fall into the creek?"

Edie reached into her pocket and pulled out the perfect spearhead.

"Wow, that's a nice one. Is this what you were after when you fell?"

"Yes. Mom let me explain." Pete answered, "I was holding onto Edie's feet, but I slipped on the grass. I didn't mean to let go."

"That's quite a story, but I'm glad you still have the spearhead. I'll have Clara help you clean up. You're going to need a bath. Pete, you go to the kitchen and get Clara. Edie let's go out to the wash house and get you out of these clothes."

Clara drew some water and partially filled a washtub while Alma helped Edie undress. The water would be cool, because there was little hot water left in the heater. Edie sat in the middle of the tub while Clara washed her hair and back. Pete stuck his head in the door and asked, "Is Edie okay?"

"Pete, get out of here, can't you see she's bare, for Pete's sake!" scolded Clara, then she started to laugh at what she said. Edie giggled, too, and Pete disappeared. Alma came in with an armload of clothes. She helped Edie dry and dress into some of Mary's clothes.

"I'll wash your clothes and have them ready for you when you come again," Clara told Edie.

"And I'll drive you home and explain to your mother," added Alma.

The next Tuesday, Edie's mother answered the phone. It was Aunt Helen calling.

"Mother is ill," Helen told her sister. "Could you come over and sit with her, Hattie?"

"I could in the evening. I have to stay here and be with Edie and Ralph in the daytime."

"I have meetings to go to, and a tea tomorrow. I just don't have time. Certainly, you could change your schedule a bit, Hattie. Maybe take your children with you."

Hattie sighed. Aunt Helen had no children; she didn't understand or didn't want to understand anything about raising children. Her rich sister couldn't be bothered with taking their mother to a social event.

"I suppose I could stay for a day or two. Maybe Mrs. McKillip could keep Edie and Ralph. I know Frank won't be able to take off any days. This is a busy time on the farm. He's working long hours."

"I suppose he is working overtime and his boss needs him now. After all, he is only a hired hand," Helen quipped.

Hattie rolled her eyes again. "I have to go, Helen. I will find time to take care of mother. You have your fun. We'll get along."

"Well, you don't have to get huffy," Helen replied.

Hattie had had it. She slammed the ear piece on the hanger. Her uppity sister was always belittling her and Frank. Because she was fortunate to marry a rich banker from Tipton, she felt she was much better than Hattie.

As soon as she hung up she called Mrs. McKillip.

Hattie stated, "Mrs. McKillip, my mother is very ill and I must go over and stay with her for a couple of days. I need to relieve my sister."

Alma answered, "Oh my, is there anything I could help you with? And please, call me Alma."

"Okay, Alma. Yes, that is the reason I am calling. Could Edie and Ralph stay at your home for a night or two? I could send them over early in the morning with Frank. I think they will be okay until he gets home. I must leave right away."

"Listen, Hattie, you go right ahead. I'll send Clara over to sit with them. In fact, I think they should come right back with her. Have them pack their night clothes. Say how are you getting to the station?"

"Oh, thank you, thank you, Alma. You're a godsend. I'll get the children packing right away. To answer your question, I'm walking to Pleasant Prairie."

"Walking! That's a long way. I'll have Clara drive you there."

When Clara arrived, Edie and Ralph were waiting by the door. They piled into the Buick and delivered their mother to Pleasant Prairie before going to the McKillip farm. Pete, Susan, and Harry were waiting. They already had plans for tomorrow. That evening after supper, Alma read to the gang. The sun was disappearing over the ridge and the lightning bugs filled the air.

"How about we see who can catch the most lightning bugs?" she asked.

"Yes, yes," was the answer from all six children.

"Okay, here's the rules. First, everyone must wear their nightie or pajamas. So, everyone, go and change. I want you ready for bed right after. Clara, you go fetch six or seven fruit jars."

"I'll fetch seven. I want to be included," said Clara.

"Okay, but then you must put on your nightie like the other girls."

"Will do. It will be cooler than this housedress."

Alma cocked her head. Bruce sat in his rocker enjoying the scene. He was wearing just his overalls and undershirt and no shoes.

"I think I'll put on my nightgown also. You won't mind, will you, Bruce?"

Bruce shook his head. Seeing his wife in her nightgown was always his pleasure. In fifteen minutes, all members assembled on the porch. Each was given a jar. Bruce was to keep time. Twenty minutes would be the time limit. Alma would be allowed to help Susan.

Bruce called out, "One, two, three, go."

Everyone scattered. It wasn't two minutes before Clara and Alma got rid of their dressing robes. They ran around in just their nighties screaming and laughing like the kids. It was dusk anyway, so who could see what they weren't wearing.

Bruce started the countdown with thirty seconds to go. When he hollered, "Stop," everyone gathered on the porch. The count was on. Pete had 12, Edie, 11, Ralph 15, Harry 16, Mary 21, Clara only 10. Susan and her mother won the contest with 25 bugs. Everyone kidded Susan and Alma saying they should have to divide their catch.

The game was over, it was time for bed. Even though the McKillips had a big house, they also had a big family, including Clara. Susan and Mary already slept together. Ralph would sleep with Harry. That left Pete and Edie. Alma thought, "What should I do with Edie?" She could sleep with Clara, but everyone knew Clara snored something awful.

She didn't have to ponder long because Pete piped up and asked, "Can Edie sleep in my bed?"

"Well, I don't know. We'll have to ask Edie," was his mother's answer.

Edie joyfully chirped, "I'd love to sleep with Pete. I like Pete."

Alma looked at Bruce. He just shrugged his shoulders and said, "Why not, Alma? They're only eight years old. What harm can there be in that?"

So, Edie was Pete's guest, she and Pete slept in the same bed. In the morning, Alma looked in on the pair and smiled. Edie was sound asleep with her arm over Pete's shoulder. Edie had kicked off her sheet, revealing a bare behind. Alma gently pulled the nightie down and covered the little girl. She made a mental note for Edie to wear some underwear tonight. The next two days went fast. Gramma Ida recovered. Edie and Ralph returned home to a normal life.

In August, it was threshing time. Bruce McKillip farmed many acres. He had his oats and wheat threshed by a custom crew. There would be 15 to 17 men for dinner at noon and for lunch at three.

The custom operators provided three men, one for the steam engine, one for thresher maintenance, and one for general operations. Bruce had to provide thirteen others. These men were his four hired men plus neighbors. His neighbors depended on him to help them later at their farms. Even the boys got involved. Pete was a water boy. He rode his pony around the field furnishing water for the men. Harry and Ralph were also water boys, plus they would tend to the teams when the horses got thirsty. Once the horses were satisfied, Harry or Ralph were allowed to ride them back to the field. Horses were still used in the field because they were slower and would stop when ordered. Sometimes the drivers on tractors didn't hear the orders from men pitching up the oat shocks. Gas-powered tractors were used to haul threshed grain to the corncrib with bins overhead. The McKillip farm had an inside bucket elevator to help with the unloading. It was powered by a small gas engine. Another luxury in the crib was a lift to raise the wagons. This meant the men did not need to shovel the oats from the wagon box.

Feeding this hungry crew was quite a task for the women of the farm. Alma had Clara, but she needed extra help. She hired two neighbor ladies plus Hattie and Gertie Hahn, one of the other hired hand's wives. She was a hoot. She could tell the funniest stories. She helped Mary with the potatoes, while Edie and Susan set the table and pushed all the chairs around.

When the men arrived for dinner, it was mayhem. Clara and Mary served the big bowls of mashed potatoes and green peas or beans. Alma carried the huge platter of meat. Hattie brought in the gravy boats. Next Mary and Clara poured water and iced tea. While they were pouring, the younger men smiled and eyed the young women. Clara was eighteen and looking for a man. She was a very nice young woman, but a little plump and not the prettiest. She flirted with the unmarried men. Mary was only thirteen and a very pretty, tall blond for her age. Romance was just becoming a fancy of hers and boyfriends were not her priority.

After the meal, there were dishes to wash, tablecloths to take care of, and lunch to fix for the men. This was the same routine for four days.

The weather was pleasant the first three days with highs in the low eighties and low humidity. It was the last day which was uncomfortable. The wind was out of the southwest. It came roaring out of Kansas and Oklahoma with temps in the nineties and high humidity. The men needed extra water. The horses were also thirsty and were watered in the field. At noon the men were glad it was the last day at McKillip's. They needed a break.

The women were also glad. They worked just as hard as the men, preparing the meals, washing the dishes, and preparing the lunch for the afternoon. As the morning progressed, the women's crew were wiping brows with aprons and skirts. The McKillip's had electric fans, but the heat from the ovens overwhelmed their breeze. After the men finished their meal, the women and girls could eat. They sat at the end of the extended table.

Edie looked at Mrs. McKillip and asked, "May Susie and I go to the pool in your creek? It sure would be cool."

Alma smiled at Edie, pondered, and said, "I suppose, if your mother approves and one of the older girls goes with you."

"I'll take them," piped up Clara, "if Mary will go, too."

Mary answered quickly, "Yes, I'd love to go. It will sure be cooler there than here. It'll be fun with just us girls."

"Remember there are extra chores tonight because the men will be late breaking down equipment."

Clara replied, "I'll help with the milking."

Edie chimed in, "I can milk, too. I can help my mom with our cows."

"Let's see. If the lunch is fixed, Gertie and I could deliver it. If Edie could stay, Hattie, you could leave at two. I'd bring her home later. Clara could take the girls down in the auto if you are back by five."

The girls all agreed. They hurried through their dinner and began making lunch sandwiches. At three, Clara drove the girls to the pool. The water was smooth with some oak leaves floating on the surface. Water spiders skated across like they were on ice. Edie and Susan, being barefoot, were out of their dresses and quickly waded in up to their knees in the cool water. Mary and Clara laid the towels out on the shore. They had to pin hair, remove shoes and stockings, then skirts and blouses, and finally, under slips.

Edie said, "Mary, you know if Susie and I take off our underwear and go wading bare, we wouldn't get our panties wet. What do you think? May we go bare?"

Mary paused.

"Clara," she said, "Edie has a good point. Our underwear is going to be wet. Do we go back in just our dresses? There will be men around."

"I hadn't given that a thought," Clara answered. "I know. Let's all not wear anything while we are swimming."

"You mean you and I go naked, too?" asked a shocked Mary.

"Sure, there're no men around and it's called skinny dipping. I read about it in one of my women's magazines. I'll do it if you will?"

Mary thought a minute, then a big smile appeared on her face. This was so devilish.

"Okay. Let's do it. Edie and Susan, come here. We're going swimming bare. So, we'll have dry underwear to wear back to the house."

Susie asked, "You mean we can go swimming nakit?"

"Sure," answered Mary, "but the word is pronounced naked. There are no boys around."

It didn't take Edie long to strip. She splashed into the water up to her waist in a flash. Her long pigtail touched the water. Susan followed behind. Mary, although willing to be nude at first, was reluctant to strip completely. She hesitated in the shade before entering the pool. Her long, slim body shivered as she waded in. Clara undressed and plunged in. The girls played and splashed. The water was cool.

It seemed like they had just gotten in when Mary asked Edie, "Will you go to the car and check the time? I sort of want to stay in the water."

Edie laughed and answered back, "Gee, Mary, are you afraid a boy might see you? There are no boys around here. I'm not afraid. See."

Edie sprinted out and checked Alma's watch.

She announced, "Ten to five. Five more minutes and we have to get out."

They all dunked each other one more time and got out. They toweled dry, then redressed. Only their hair was still wet when they reached the house.

"Where's your wet underwear?" asked Gertie.

"We don't have any. We went skinny dipping," blurted out little Susan.

"You did!" exclaimed Alma. "Well, was it fun?"

"Oh, yes," replied Edie, grinning ear to ear. "Clara said it would be all right. She did it, too."

Alma looked at Clara and said, "Well, Clara, what do you have to say?"

Clara looked down at the floor and replied, "I didn't think it was wrong. There weren't any boys around. I thought keeping our underwear dry was better than not wearing any home."

Alma smiled and said, "It's okay, Clara, I just wish I could have been there. I haven't gone skinny-dipping since I was a kid."

Everyone was relieved.

School started after the Labor Day holiday. Edie and Pete worked well together in third grade. She was good in arithmetic. He was good in reading. The teacher on busy days let Edie and Pete help the younger students with their lessons. If they were finished quickly, all five students could go outside and play while the upper grades held their classes. In the winter months, the teacher let them play simple cards games in the corner of the room if they were quiet.

The summer between third and fourth grades Edie and Pete's play routine changed. First, there were fewer days to get together because they each had more responsibilities. Edie helped more in the garden and became the official milkmaid in the evenings.

Pete had more chores. He was limited to hunting eggs, feeding the chickens and ducks, and fetching the cows, because of all the hired men. Edie and Pete had some time together on Thursday and Saturday afternoons. Being nine years old matured them both. They would ride the ponies, Mr. B and Knucklehead, to the creek, but once there it was either just sit and talk or fish for minnows or small bullheads. If they caught any, they would unhook them and throw them back. It was something to pass the time on a summer's day.

On one of these fishing adventures in July, Pete and Edie got to know each other better. It was hot. They decided to go barefoot so they could wade in the water. The creek was barely flowing. The pool looked inviting.

Edie asked Pete, "Do you think we could go wading in the pool?"

"We could try. I could roll my trousers up to my knees. You have a dress on, so you're okay."

They put their fishing poles down and skirted around the bushes to the pool. They held hands as they waded in. The water was bathtub warm. Edie bunched her dress high around her waist. Pete rolled his pantlegs to above his knees, but he was soon getting his pants wet.

"This isn't working," commented Edie. "You're getting wet."

"Yeah, I can't roll my pants up any higher. I wish I could take them off."

"You can if you want to, I won't tell."

"Will you take off your dress?"

"Sure, I'm not afraid."

Pete thought a minute. He had let his sister see him in his underwear, but never a stranger. Should he show Edie his underpants?

While he was contemplating, Edie pulled her dress over her head and hung it on a bush. She stood there in her panties and undershirt with a little bow in the middle of her chest.

"Come on, Pete. It is just you and me. I've seen Ralph in his underwear. Heck, I even have had to wash it."

Pete grinned and unbuckled his trousers. He took off his shirt and threw them on the same bush as Edie's dress. They held hands as they waded into deeper water. Soon they were thigh deep. They waded around the pool. It was no fun.

Pete said, "You know several times Harry and I go swimming here bare butt. It is fun. Of course, there is never any girls around. I bet you've never went swimming bare butt?"

"Yes, I have. In fact, it was right in this very pool."

"Really, when was that?"

"Last summer. It was the last day of threshing. Clara brought Mary, Susan, and me down here. You boys were busy, and Clara said we could go skinny-dipping. We went bare butt like you said. It was fun."

"Have you ever seen a boy bare butt?"

"Yes, I saw Ralph several years ago. He fell into a hog wallow. Mom made him take his clothes off outside. What about you? Have you seen a girl bare butt?"

"Sure, I've seen Susie several times. Mom bathes her in the kitchen sink at times. She likes to run around bare butt."

Pete looked at Edie and said, "Let's take off our underwear."

Edie paused. "Okay."

"Deal. You first."

"Nope, we do it at the same time."

"Okay."

Edie stripped her undershirt off. Pete stared at her. She looked no different than he did.

Edie put her fingers on the waistband of her panties and said, "On the count of three, one two three, down."

They both slipped from their underwear. They stared at each other. Edie started to giggle.

"What's so funny?"

"You."

"Me?"

"Yes, you, turn around."

"Okay, but then I get to see you."

Pete danced in a circle. Edie danced, too. She reached for his hand and led him into the pool. Soon they were splashing in the water. Being a naked boy or girl didn't matter. When it was time to go home, they sat on the grassy bank and talked while they dried.

Pete asked Edie, "You'll never tell my mom, will you?"

"No, never, but wasn't this fun?"

"Yeah. You're the best girl I ever met, Edie. I hope we are friends forever."

"Me, too. Now we better dress and get for home."

They gathered the fishing gear and rode their ponies home.

Gramma Ida required more care and Hattie stayed there overnight many times. Only twice did Edie stay at the McKillip's, and then she slept in Mary's room on some sofa cushions on the floor. One warm night, Mary woke up Edie and they quietly climbed through the window onto the porch roof, not wanting to wake Susan. They sat on a rug and watched the moon and stars.

The cool breeze blew under their nighties. Mary pulled her gown to her hips for more cooling. Edie mimicked her.

Mary said, "I'll tell you a secret, if you will tell me a secret. I wish Clara would leave so I could have her room. But she's not very pretty, so I suppose she'll be here forever. I think she'll be an old maid. Now you tell me a secret."

Edie thought a moment and said, "Okay, but promise not to tell. Pete and I went skinny dipping in the pool."

"When?"

"About two weeks ago."

"Was it fun?"

"Yes. I think Pete is cute."

Mary teased, "Naked or dressed?"

Edie rolled her eyes and replied, "Naked. You know he has a tiny wienie."

Mary about fell from the roof trying to stifle a laugh. They both giggled for another hour before returning to bed.

Despite Mary's prediction, Clara found a beau at a Spring dance. He was from Montpelier and ran the grocery store. He asked Clara if she wanted to work for him. Since he was a bachelor, she said yes. Soon they were married.

August was threshing time again. The crews arrived. Mary had to assume Clara's job load. Alma hired three neighbor ladies to help cook. Edie had graduated to potato peeler with Gertie. She also was the butter spreader on all the sandwiches for lunch. Hattie made pies. There was no mention of going to the creek on the last day.

BOB BANCKS

CHAPTER 2: SEAN ARRIVES

During the summer, Pete's father decided to open an old sandstone quarry located across the creek next to a seventy-foot bluff of sandstone. There were many farmer and businesses seeking good, economical foundation stone. Limestone was the stone of choice, but the limestone quarries at Montpelier and Buffalo were busy and couldn't keep up with demand. Bruce hired a quarry manager from Vermont to run the stone business. His name was Rafe O'Keefe, an Irishman. He and his wife, Irene, had one son, Sean, who was Ralph's age.

In September, Patterson School opened with three sixth graders, Sean, Ralph, and Harry. Mary was alone in eighth grade since her classmate Huey Kepper turned sixteen and no longer was required to attend school.

The kids giggled at Sean's brogue. He said the words farm, barn and car with a different sound. There was only one seventh grader, Lester Paul. He teased Sean about being from Vermont. That all ended when Ralph chose Sean for the baseball team. Lester chose Harry. The boys were chosen first, then the girls. Mary ended up on Ralph's team with Sean. The other eight kids were divided up, four to a team. Miss Lang, their teacher, would be the umpire.

Lester's team scored first. It was three to zero and recess was almost over. Miss Lang knew how important it was to be fair, so she extended the recess to allow the bottom of the inning.

Mary was up to bat. Lester pitched the ball as fast as he could, but Mary clobbered it over his head and into left field. Lester was upset. Next was Edie. Sean whispered into her ear, "Bunt it, Edie. There's no one covering first

17

base."

She bunted and beat the throw from Harry to Les, who ran to cover first base. Ralph hit the ball right to Harry, but he dropped it. Everyone was safe.

Now it was Sean's turn. Lester was determined to strike him out. No dumb Vermonter was going to hit his pitches. The first two were strikes. The third was a ball. Lester rubbed the ball in his hands. This was the big pitch. He would be Cy Young. He wound up and threw with all his might.

Sean swung the bat and connected. The ball left his bat with a whack. It sailed over the left field fence into the cornfield, a grand slam. Ralph's team won four to three. Ralph's team was at the plate when Sean arrived home. Edie gave him a hug, Ralph shook his hand and patted his back, the others cheered, and Mary, sweet lovely Mary, kissed him on the cheek. Sean turned a bright red. His face matched his red hair. Everyone laughed, including the teacher.

Even Lester had to laugh. He shook Sean's hand and said, "Nice hit. Next time you're on my team."

Fall arrived, and the quarry opened with five employees. Sean worked there after school and on Saturdays. On Saturday afternoons, Mary made extra sandwiches for the men picking corn. She saved a couple for Sean at the quarry. He would her meet by the gate and they would talk. Mary liked Sean very much.

The quarry prospered under Rafe's management. His only problem was Irene. She hated living in the country with no electricity. She complained all the time. She couldn't wait for Rafe to finish work on Friday so they could go to town. Many nights Sean was home alone. Mary would ask him to come over and play board games. She was certainly sweet on Sean.

January was very cold. The schoolhouse sometimes was chilly all day. In February, the flu bug hit Patterson School. The students passed it from one to another. Mary was the last to get the flu. Being the oldest student, the disease affected her more than the others. She lost weight and coughed often. Alma called the doctor. He claimed there was little he could do. He prescribed bed rest and plenty of fluids.

The next day, Mary had a rash on her legs and feet. Alma thought maybe there was a spider in her bedding. She changed the sheets and hung the comforters on the clothesline. Nothing seemed to help.

Late that night, Alma was awakened by Mary's screams. She rushed to her room. Mary was in great pain. She said her neck and head hurt something awful. When the pain hit, she arched her back and moaned. Her fever hit 102 degrees. Doctor Wilson came over as soon as he could. After he checked Mary, he motioned for Alma to speak with him in the hall. Alma called Bruce.

Dr. Wilson said, "I'm very sorry, but your daughter has meningitis. Right now, there is no cure. Keep her as comfortable as you can. I have some strong pain medicine to help. If she lives through the night and her fever breaks, call me. I might be able to help then. I'm very sorry."

Alma sat with her daughter all night. All she could do was wipe her brow and run her fingers through her golden hair. She prayed Mary would last until morning and her fever would break. Bruce came in to relieve her for a few minutes. She went downstairs for some coffee. When she returned, Bruce met her at the door. He held her close. She knew what had happened.

"No! No! No!" she cried. "I wasn't here to say good-bye."

"It's okay, Alma," replied Bruce. "She never opened her eyes. She just stopped breathing."

"I must see her. I must kiss her good-bye. Please let me see her, Bruce," Alma moaned.

Bruce let his wife into the room. He left her alone and went to wake Harry, Pete, and Susan. They needed to know the fate of their sister.

The funeral was held at Pleasant Prairie Presbyterian Church. The church was so crowded it overflowed into the basement. Alma made sure any of the students who wanted to attend had reserved pews near the front. Edie and Ralph were there. It was one of Edie's saddest days in her short life.

Pete missed the next week at school. When he did return, Edie hugged him. She helped him with all his missed work. Harry also returned. It was Sean who hugged him and talked to him privately. He knew Mary had feelings for him.

As with all deaths, the survivors must move on. Everyone did except Alma. She grieved at Mary's grave every day and wore black for sixty days. Bruce worried because Alma had lost a lot of weight. He asked the pastor to talk to Alma. His talks did help, but Alma never forgave herself for not being with Mary at her time of death.

Spring arrived. School let out in early May. Pete was now eleven. He begged his Dad to let him drive a tractor. Bruce started him driving the 5-10 Mogul on pull-up rope at the barn. Pete did a good job. He proved he was strong enough to drive a tractor.

In mid-July the second cutting of alfalfa hay was ready. It generally was not as heavy as the first. The first field was mown and a second field was ready. Harry and Joe did the mowing. Now the first field needed raking, but Frank and Tom were fixing fence in the hog pasture. Bruce had to run into town for some supplies. This left Vince, one of the five hired hands, to rake twenty acres of hay. The problem was he couldn't start until the dew was dissipated. Bruce needed another driver.

"I'll see if Ira can come over and rake," he told Vince, "We need to have it finished by noon."

Standing by his dad, Pete said, "I can drive the little Mogul. Let me rake. I know I can do it."

Bruce looked at his eleven-year-old son, then he looked at Vince.

"What do you think, Vince?"

"We need to get that hay raked. Maybe if he followed me around he could do it. I'd try to watch him. Why don't I make a couple of rounds with him just to get him started?"

"Okay, but Pete, if you get sleepy or the tractor is too hard to steer, you must take a break. Understand?"

Pete answered, "Yes sir, I understand."

Bruce smiled at his enthusiastic son. Vince gave him a wink. It would be a big step for the young lad. Vince cranked the engine and Pete hooked onto the New Idea side rake. Pete climbed up and rode with Vince to the field. The other rig was already there. Vince threw the rake in gear. They started around the field. On the second round, he let Pete drive. He instructed Pete how to drive with one wheel off the crop. He showed him how to roll the entire swath into a neat roll of fluffy hay. Pete drove with great concentration. They stopped before the third round.

Vince said, "I'll rake the third swath and you follow on the fourth. You just follow me around. When we to get the center, you let me finish. Okay?"

Pete nodded and answered, "Okay."

Pete followed a steady hundred feet behind Vince. Vince looked behind and gave the thumbs up. After several rounds, the job became routine. The tractor purred. The rake turned the hay into neat rolls. The sun grew warm. Pete's eyes squinted. He had to pinch himself to stay alert. Vince looked back less often. He lit his pipe and cruised around the field.

They were about two thirds finished. Vince made his corner and was making his next corner before Pete had made the first. Pete was very sleepy, but he was not going to let Vince know. His Dad had told him to stop when he got sleepy or tired, but he convinced himself he was neither. He cranked the steering wheel around to turn the tractor, but his sleepy hands slipped. Pete started to fall from the cast iron seat. He grabbed for the shifter. He missed. He tumbled head first behind the steel-wheeled machine. One of the lugs caught his pant leg and dragged him up over the wheel. He desperately grabbed the drawbar and screamed, "Vince! Vince!"

Vince was three hundred feet ahead and the noise of his tractor drowned out Pete's pleas. Pete's leg stopped at the fender. The lug tore his pant leg and ripped his shoe away. Pete fell on his head and was knocked out. The Mogul continued without Pete. The side rake caught Pete and rolled him several times before it spit him out. Pete was inside the swath of rolled hay. His leg hurt something awful. His back, chest and face were scratched from the rake's teeth as they spun over him.

Vince, at the other end of the field, looked back to see the driverless tractor crawling across the field. He threw his tractor into high gear and hurried across the field. The hay was flying, but he didn't care. His concern was Pete. He threw his Mogul out of gear and jumped off. He ran to where Pete was last on the machine. He heard a moan, then a cry. He scratched away the hay. Pete looked at him. His face was bleeding, and his leg was cocked back at a weird angle. He gently turned Pete on his back.

Pete stammered, "Don't tttellll Ddad . . . hhhhe'll bbbbe mmmmad."

"Don't you worry, son. It will be Vince he'll be mad at. Now can you sit up?"

Pete sat up with Vince's help. His leg hurt something terrible.

Vince said, "I'll try to pick you up carefully. Then we'll take you back to the house."

"Where's my tractor?" Pete asked.

Vince peered around the field. The tractor had plowed through the fence and was dragging netting through the corn field. He could see the tractor would soon be across the field and into a grove of trees. Surely, the trees would stop the errant machine. Right now, he had to take care of Pete. He unhooked his rake and lifted Pete onto his tractor. Pete winced in pain. Vince climbed aboard and placed Pete in his lap. He slowly drove home, thinking all the time of how he was going to explain the accident.

Alma was hanging out clothes when Vince arrived. She could tell by Vince's look there was something wrong. She saw Pete's body on Vince's lap.

She ran screaming," No! No! Not Petey." When she reached the tractor, she fearfully said, "Is he dead?"

"No, ma'am, he's just scratched up a bit and maybe has a broken leg. He must have fallen from the seat. I was ahead and didn't see him until I saw his tractor without him. I got there as quick as I could. I'm sorry."

"You shouldn't have let him drive all alone. He's just a boy." she scolded.

"I know, ma'am, but when he asked his dad, we just couldn't say no."

"Bruce let him drive? He should know better! Here, help me carry him to the house. I'll must call Dr. Wilson again."

Vince carried Pete inside and laid him on the couch in the kitchen.

"Do you know where Bruce is, Vince?" Alma asked.

"He went to Blue Grass. He should be home soon. Ma'am, if you don't mind, I better get back to my raking, and first I must find Pete's tractor. I think it's in the woods."

"Yes, you can go. If you see Bruce before I do, have him come quickly."

Vince was glad to leave. He didn't want to be there when Bruce arrived.

Alma washed Pete's face and arms. She removed his torn trousers and shirt. His back was a series of long marks from the teeth of the rake. When she tried to remove his sock, Pete cried out. She knew his leg was broken. Bruce arrived, but Alma didn't have time for a scolding. Bruce placed Pete and Alma in the back seat of the Buick. He sped to Hershey Hospital in Muscatine. It was two days before they could set Pete's leg. It was broken in two places.

The hay was made without Bruce's bossing. The runaway Mogul was not damaged except for some scratches on the paint. The tractor made it all the way to a small creek and became mired in the mud. The two fences were repaired. Farm life returned to normal.

Pete came home in a week. He had a cast from his ankle to his thigh. He hobbled around on crutches for several weeks. His best friend Edie came over as much as possible. They read books and played board games. One day she helped Alma lift Pete into the car and they drove to the creek for some fishing. Edie baited the hooks and cleaned Pete's line when he hit snags. Pete's mother sat by a tree and read. She smiled at Edie helping Pete. She knew Edie was good for Pete. By school opening, Pete was out of his cast, but he walked with a limp which would be with him the rest of his life.

BOB BANCKS

CHAPTER 3: CHANGING TIMES

Another year cruised by. The quarry was operating at a profit, but good stone was running out. Concrete blocks were becoming the rule for new foundations. A new company in Davenport was producing them by the thousands. Bruce and Rafe decided to close the quarry. The mine had grown to thirty feet high and one hundred fifty feet deep. There were several columns supporting the ceiling.

Bruce helped Rafe find a job at Huttig Button factory in Muscatine, where he soon became a floor manager. Sean's mother, Irene, was happy again. She had electricity and running water. She became a cook at a café downtown. Sean finished grade school at Franklin Elementary, and at the age of fourteen, he joined his father at the button company.

Edie's Grandpa Charlie died of a heart attack in January. Edie's parents moved Grandma Ida into their crowded little house. Grandma slept in Edie's bed. Edie slept on a cot in the corner of the bedroom. She soon discovered her Grandmother snored something awful. Some nights Edie would sneak downstairs and sleep on the living room sofa.

It was mid-February and a decision had to be made on Grandma's farm by the first of March. She could rent it to a neighbor or sell it. Grandma Ida and her two daughters held a family meeting. Aunt Helen pushed for her to sell the family farm. Hattie was against the idea. Grandma Ida wanted more time.

Helen became impatient with her mother. She said she'd give her mother two days before she would call an attorney. Grandma Ida scowled at Helen and said she'd be ready in two days.

The next morning, Ida asked Hattie if Frank would like to farm the home place. All she wanted in return was to live with Hattie. Frank jumped at the chance, but he had little money to buy seed. Uncle Bill, Aunt Helen's husband, came to his rescue. He told Frank his bank would loan him the money at a low interest rate.

When Frank told Bruce, Bruce said, "Frank, congratulations, you are starting up the agricultural ladder. You have been a good man. Maybe someday you'll be able to own that farm. If you need any machinery for the first few years, don't hesitate to come over and borrow something."

Edie knew it would mean a new school. She must make new friends and worst of all, she'd lose Pete. She also knew this was the way of farmers and she'd have to move. The first week in March they said goodbye to the McKillip's and moved to the Mohr farm just west of Melpine School. It would be a new chapter in their lives.

CHAPTER 4: MOVING TO TOWN

Sean stayed at the button factory for two years before he found work at Roach and Musser, a sash and door factory in Muscatine. It was farther away from his parents' home on East Hill. His ride to work took over forty-five minutes. He needed housing nearer the plant.

He found a widow, Mrs. Olga Kerchinske, who had an upstairs room available. She needed someone to help her occasionally. Sean became that person. It was within walking distance of the plant. Work was strenuous at Roach and Musser, but Sean didn't mind. He had slaved scooping shells in the button factory. Yes, it was sometimes dusty, but it didn't stink. Mrs. Kerchinske's home was along a plugged waterway nicknamed Sloughtown. Most people living there worked at Roach & Musser. The area was crowded, and more like Vermont, so he fit right in with his neighbors. When the weekend arrived, it was time to relax. The married men fished or clammed. The single men headed uptown to the many dance floors. It was at one of these dances Sean saw who he thought was an old friend. He approached the young lady and her girlfriend.

He asked, "Edie, Edie Mohr?"

Edie was shocked to see Sean. She gasped, "Sean! Sean O'Keefe why are you here?"

He smiled and replied, "To see you, I guess. You're just as lovely as I pictured you would be. How have you been and why are you here?"

Edie answered, "To meet you. No, really, I work for a family on Mulberry. My friend Louise brought me down here."

"Great! Do you come to the dance often?"

"This is my first time."

"I thought you'd still be in high school."

Edie looked at Sean then explained, "I attended high school for three years before my father decided I didn't need any more schooling. I'm sixteen and he expected me to go to work, find a husband, and raise a family. All I could find was a job as a cleaning girl and nanny for a wealthy family, the Roger Steinbeck's, who have two boys. They live on Mulberry Avenue. You know where the wealthy of Muscatine live. Guess what, they have running water and electricity. I love my job and the family."

"I hope you come here often. I'd like to see you again."

Edie smiled and replied, "I'd like to see you again, Sean. I get two Saturday nights off a month."

Sean danced with Edie several times. The local Moose Lodge generally had the best bands. The evening was winding down. Edie and her best friend, Louise, always walked together to the dance, but seldom walked home together. Louise always had some man take her home.

The band played their last set. Louise was asked by Ernie Plett if he could walk her home. Edie had no one. Sean asked Edie for the last dance and while dancing asked if he could walk her home. By the time they reached Edie's little apartment in the back of the Steinbeck's mansion, she was already in love. Sean was such a gentleman. When they reached her door, he held her hand and kissed it.

"I hope we can do this again, Edie?" he asked.

"Most definitely," she answered.

"Then how about tomorrow evening?"

"Oh, I have to take care of the young Steinbeck's, Jody and Steven. I'm free in the afternoon, though, if I can be back by five."

"Tomorrow afternoon it will be. I'll be here at one. Let's take the trolley out to Weed Park. I hear there is a band playing and an ice cream social. I'll make sure you are home by five."

"It's a date."

Sean left Edie standing at her door. She was floating on a cloud. She had an actual date, her first ever. Louise had many dates and bragged how they would smooch in the back of her boyfriend's fancy auto. She bragged about the auto as much as her boyfriend, as owning a fancy automobile was only for the rich. A lot of farmers drove Ford T's and A's.

The next morning Edie hurried through her chores. She made sure Jody and Steven were ready for church ahead of time.

Mrs. Steinbeck asked Edie if she would be going to church with the family. Edie declined.

"I have a young man coming to pick me up at one. We're going to Weed Park for the afternoon."

"You remember Mr. Steinbeck and I are meeting the Kline's for dinner."

"Yes, Mrs. Steinbeck, I will be back before five. Sean promised."

"Oh, the young man's name is Sean. Does he have red hair?"

"Yes, he does. His family is from Ireland, but he was born here in America. His grandfather emigrated here many years ago. He works at Roach & Musser. His father is a floor manager at Huttig Button."

"Well, he sounds like a nice young man. We need some good hard-working Irishmen to keep this country going. Have fun, Edie, I'll see you at five and maybe this Sean."

Sean arrived promptly at one. He wore a brown suit and a driver's cap. Edie was ready in her light blue dress with white lace circling the high-necked collar. They rode the trolley to the park and spent the afternoon listening to the band and eating ice cream.

On the way back, Edie was looking out the window when Sean slipped her hand into his. They held hands the rest of the way. Edie floated to her room after Sean left.

The romance continued. The pair went dancing on Saturday and spent summer Sundays at a park. In the winter they went ice skating on the slough or played parlor games with the Steinbeck boys. Jody and Steven soon discovered Sean could hit a baseball a mile. He played catch with the two youngsters. They loved it when he called on Edie.

Mrs. Steinbeck also was impressed with the Irishman. He was always clean and courteous. She watched as he courted her employee as she felt a need to protect this naïve country girl.

Mrs. Steinbeck's only fault with Sean was that he was Catholic. She knew Edie was a Methodist. One day she approached Edie and said, "You know your father will never approve of Sean because he is a Catholic."

"Yes, I realize that," answered Edie. "But I love Sean. If Daddy doesn't approve, I'll wait until I'm eighteen. Then he can't stop me."

"Okay, young lady, but don't say I didn't warn you," Mrs. Steinbeck replied with a stern look. She knew what was ahead for Edie. When she was younger, she had been in love with a Catholic man. Her father forbade her to see the young man again. He used his influence to make sure her beau lost his job and could not be hired in Muscatine. He had to leave town. She hoped Edie would not share the same fate.

That year Decoration Day fell on a Monday, so there was a three-day holiday. It was the day to remember those who had died in the Civil War and other conflicts the nation had become involved in. Edie would have four days off because the Steinbeck family was going to Des Moines to visit Mrs. Steinbeck's parents.

The week before, she and Sean made plans for him to spend the weekend at her home farm. On Saturday he'd ride the Interurban out to Melpine Station and walk to her place. He knew she needed to help her mother, but they could be together most of the day. Sean said he would help her father if he had any chores he could do.

Sean arrived at seven on Saturday morning. Frank was coming out the barn door.

"You must be Sean?" he asked the young man walking up the lane.

"Yes, sir," answered Sean.

"Edie talks about you all the time. It seems she thinks you are quite a nice young man. Say, didn't your father work for Bruce McKillip?"

"Yes, sir. He's working for Huttig Button right now as a floor manager."

"Good for him. I always liked your father. Tell him I said hi."

"I certainly will, Mr. Mohr. I came out here to see Edie today. I know she has many chores to do for her mother. I told her I could help you with something."

Before Frank could answer, Ralph arrived.

He extended his hand and warmly said, "Hi, Sean. Remember me? We were in the same class at Patterson School."

"How could I forget? We had some good times there. Man, you have really grown."

Ralph was 5'10" and about 220 pounds. He had the curliest black hair Sean had ever seen. When he smiled, he revealed a missing tooth in his lower row; otherwise he was a very handsome young man.

"You stretched some, too, Sean," Ralph replied.

Sean stood 6'0" and a lean 200 pounds. His hair was a bright Irish red.

Ralph turned to his Dad. "Dad, I need to get off early tonight. Ruth and I want to go to Credit Island in Davenport. They are opening the beach rides and the dance hall. Jim Clark and Florence Harding are going."

Frank answered, "Well, you know your mother and I are going to Tipton this afternoon. She wants to see your Aunt Helen because she is not feeling well. Someone should do the milking. Another thing--the chicken house needs to be cleaned and I want to finish planting the last field north of the creek."

"I can get the chicken house cleaned and maybe Edie will do the milking."

"You can't ask you your sister to do your job when she has company."

Sean spoke, "I know how to milk cows. I could help Edie."

Frank gave Sean a wary eye and said, "Are you sure? You're a city boy. How would you know how to milk?"

"My family lived near the quarry in Vermont. We had a small farm with chickens, two cows, and a few hogs. I learned to milk early. I had to milk the cows before I went to school. How many cows do you milk?"

"Twelve."

"That's six apiece. If Ralph and I get the chicken house cleaned and Edie agrees, he can leave."

"That's mighty generous of you, Sean. Let's go ask Edie." Ralph added, with a big smile on his face, "If it is all right with her, can I go?"

"Yes, I guess so, but you be home by midnight. I don't want you leaving Edie with chores in the morning."

"Right, Dad, I'll be home. Come on, Sean, I'll ask Edie, so we can get to cleaning out that chicken coop."

Dad added as he headed for the barn, "Now remember, you put the roost manure on the asparagus patch."

"Yes, sir, I won't forget."

"Then let's get cracking!"

Sean and Ralph headed for the house to clear things with Edie. She was just coming out of the wash house. She had a curl sticking to her forehead. Her hands were black from carrying coal to the water heater inside. Despite the black smudges on her skirt and blouse, she smiled at Sean.

"Hi, Sean. Sorry for my appearance, but Mom and I are doing the kitchen curtains and bedding before she and Dad take off. What can I do for you fellows?"

Ralph started right away. "Ruthie and I want to go to Credit Island in Davenport and Sean volunteered to help me clean the chicken house and he said he would help you do the milking, so is it all right for me to go?"

"Whoa, whoa, how do I know Sean can milk cows?"

"Oh, I can milk cows, Edie. I learned to milk as a kid."

Edie eyed the two anxious men. "I'll only agree if Sean agrees to stay and

32

help in the morning, 'cause I know you won't be in any shape to do chores."

Sean's eyes lit up. He smiled at Edie and answered, "I'll be more than happy to stay and help. You shouldn't be left alone out here on this lonely farm."

"You are so right, Sean. I'll need some protection from a strong Irishman," she answered with a coy smile.

The two men went to work cleaning the chicken house. Sean carried several buckets of the high nitrogen-content roost manure to the asparagus patch while Ralph drove the team and spreader to the pasture. Just before noon, Frank rode in with the corn planter and unhitched the horses. It was hot and dusty riding the corn planter. He headed to the house to clean up. Hattie, Edie's mother, met him at the door.

"You're not going to Cedar Rapids smelling like that. I just got the water heater fired up, so there may be enough hot water for a quick shower. The water is still warm. I'll bring some clothes down for you. Edie says she will finish the washing. I'm glad because I certainly don't want to do it on Monday."

Frank shook his head and reluctantly shuffled to the basement. He knew not to cross Hattie when she was in a hurry. When Sean and Ralph came in from the chicken house, Hattie had Edie put wash basins out on the bench by the shed for them to wash. Ralph was combing his hair when his dad appeared at the back door. He was all dressed except his shirt.

"Boy, don't you look swell. You'd better get that shirt on before you go inside. You know Mom's rules," Ralph told him.

"Yeah, I know. I just thought I could air dry a little more before I went in. How did you guys get along?"

"We're all finished, thanks to Sean's help. I'm going to check the horses after dinner, then I'm heading for Ruthie's and Davenport."

The three went in for dinner. Many farmers called the noon meal, dinner, instead of lunch because it usually was the biggest meal. They were just about finished when Frank looked at his watch and said, "We'd better get going, Hattie. The Plug stops at Summit at 1:30. Ralph, you get the T fired up. Mom and I will be there in five minutes."

"Wait a minute, Frank. Who's going to do the dishes?"

"I'll help Edie with the dishes, Mrs. Mohr. You and Mr. Mohr get going. Have a good trip and don't worry about a thing," Sean assured her.

Hattie gave Sean a wary glance, but she didn't have time for rebuttal. She put on her big hat and stuck a pin in her hair, then followed her husband out the door. She waved and called back, "Take care of Edie."

Sean and Edie finished the dishes. Edie wiped the same curl from her forehead.

"Let's go out on the porch and cool off. It's too hot and sticky in this kitchen. You know I have some washing to do yet."

"I'll help," Sean replied. "I know how to sort clothes and wash in a tub."

"We're modern, honey, we have a Maytag."

Sean followed her to the porch. They sat in the big swing and let the breeze cool them. They had barely settled when Ralph chugged up the lane. He dashed to the porch.

"You two okay?" he asked.

"Yes, why ask do you ask?"

"Because I stopped by Ruthie's and told her to be ready, I'd be there in thirty minutes. If that's okay with you?"

"Sure, go ahead. We're just cooling out here. " answered Edie.

"Thanks, Sis. I'm beholden to you."

Ralph hurried inside. When he returned, he was dressed in his going-to-meeting suit and new bowler hat. He was going to pick up Ruth and they were riding the Interurban from Pleasant Prairie to Davenport. He waved good-bye to Sean and Edie, as he chugged down the lane and turned left for Ruth's.

CHAPTER 5: THE STORM

Sean and Edie held hands and swung in the swing. They said little to each other. Finally, Edie announced, "Sean, I wish you would call me Edie. Edith sounds so formal and I am not that kind of a person. I'm a farm girl and not one of those uppity people on Mulberry. Just don't tell Mrs. Steinbeck I said that. She's very nice, but I know she feels she is much better than I. You know they drive a Buick like the McKillip's."

Sean looked at her, a little shocked, and said, "Well, Edie, it is. I'm glad you are not a formal gal. They can be so snooty."

Edie giggled. She turned to Sean and kissed him.

"I love you, Sean O'Keefe. We better get to work at the washing. If you change your outer clothes, I'll get them in with the last load. You do have other clothes, don't you?"

"Yes, I put them next to the sofa. I'll run and get them. Where do I change?"

"Right here." Edie kidded, she'd love to see Sean's muscles. "No, really, why don't you change in the wash shed while I hang the sheets. I promise I won't peek."

Sean was just buttoning his shirt when Edie opened the door. She swirled around the room. The work clothes needed to soak in an old tub first. The water needed changing and the tub wiped before the next round of wash. She and Sean spent most of the afternoon washing and hanging clothes out to dry. Being with Sean made a drudgery job enjoyable. It was almost four when they finished. Edie wiped her curls back from her forehead and said, "I'll make some lemonade before we start milking. Okay?"

Sean nodded. He followed her to the kitchen and chipped some ice from the icebox. They sat and sipped their drinks. The air was warm and sticky. The lemonades tasted delicious.

Edie groaned and said, "Well, I guess we'd better get to the milking. Those old cows won't do it by themselves. I'm going to put on my milking clothes, Sean. They are more fitting for the job."

She looked at Sean in his clean clothes. "You don't want to wear those duds to milk. I'll see if I can locate some overalls of my dad's. You two are about the same size. Maybe you'll have to lengthen the straps. You won't need a shirt."

Edie disappeared inside and reappeared in ten minutes. He stared at her for a moment. She was dressed in a colored peasant blouse with a scoop neck and matching gingham skirt which had been split up the middle and resewn. They were like a big pair of trousers. She had a large bandana wrapped around her head and some farmer work shoes on her feet.

"Here's a pair of Dad's overalls. You put them on and meet me in the barn. I hope the cows came home today so we won't have to go find them."

She noticed Sean's eyes as she spoke.

"You like?"

"Very much so."

"I like it, too. It is so much cooler. It doesn't do much for my figure though."

"Who cares?"

"Well, I know it will be hot milking those old four titters, so I might well be as comfortable as possible. You'll find out real soon, the old cows put out the heat. You can take off shirt. I don't mind."

"I don't have one on, remember?"

"Oh, that's right, I only gave you pants. Darn!"

Of course, the cows were still in the pasture. The lush green grass made them stay longer. It also made their manure very green and fluid. Milking became a dirty job for the first few weeks.

Edie let the cows into barn. She fed each one two scoops of ground corn meal and one small scoop of dried molasses. Sean did as he was told. He gathered up the milking stools and buckets. He grabbed a bucket and started on the first black and white cow. Edie started on the other end of the row. Sean was sweating profusely, his muscles glistened in the heat. Edie couldn't help but notice.

By the third cow, she was sweating profusely, too. She looked to see if Sean was watching her. He was not. He was behind his fourth cow already and filling his pail. Edie pulled her blouse sleeves down over her shoulders. It was much cooler. Sean got up from his stool and carried his bucket to the milk room where the milk was stored in ten-gallon cans. He didn't notice her until he came back. He did a double take when he saw Edie's bare shoulders. He stopped in his tracks to take a second look, just as Edie looked up. She saw him staring.

"You like what you see?" she asked.

"Of course, I haven't seen a woman's shoulders since my dad took me to a bar in Boston when I was a little boy. He had to go and recover my uncle from a brawl."

"And?"

"I was a little boy. All I remember is one of the ladies picking me up and planting a big kiss on my cheek."

"Good."

In another hour the pair finished the chores. Sean carried the milk cans over to the cooling tank. It would be Tuesday before the cream could be delivered to the creamery. They both were sweaty and dirty. Edie's blouse clung to her body.

"I need to take a bath immediately. I'll try not to take too much hot water," Edie said. "Then we can have leftovers for supper."

"I could stoke the heater right away and maybe we both will have plenty. Is the water heater in the basement?"

"Yes, right next to the furnace. Listen, I'll get some clean clothes while you stoke the fire. In the summer, we use wood for the heater. It burns faster. You'll find the wood behind the garage. In a few minutes the water will be warmed and we can shower. You can put on the clothes you wore when you got here, but you may skip the shirt. Mom's not home, and I don't care if you are wearing a shirt for supper. It's hot."

Edie dashed upstairs. Sean hauled some wood to the basement, which was divided into three rooms: the furnace and coal room, a large room with a sink, and a small room with the toilet and shower. He shoved some oak chunks into the heater. The fire flared. He went to retrieve his clothes from the entryway, and Edie met him halfway.

"I'll try not be long. You can stay here in the basement if you like. Did you light the lamp in the bathroom?"

"No."

"Okay, I'll get it. There's one for the big room also. It is very dark down here if the lamps aren't lit."

Edie disappeared into the bathroom. Sean waited in the larger room. He could hear the water run, then shut off. Edie sang softly behind the door. Then she appeared dressed in a light cotton skirt and blouse, her hair wrapped in a towel. On her feet were some knit slippers.

"I'll brush my hair out upstairs, so you may shower. See you there."

He showered and dressed. As he entered the kitchen, Edie was checking the icebox. Although her blouse buttoned to the neck, she opted to leave the top buttons undone. Her long brown hair flowed over her thin shoulders. She was now barefoot. She looked stunning.

"It's so warm. I think after we eat, we should go outside and swing some more. Do you think it will rain tonight? The laundry is still on the line."

"I don't know, but it should be all right for a while. The sun is still shining."

They ate supper and retired to the porch. The air outside was still. The breeze was softly blowing before they milked the cows, but now nothing. Edie made some lemonade and sat with Sean. She laid her head on Sean's shoulder. He moved his arm around her shoulder. They sat and watched the sunset.

The moon was half full and the humidity oppressive. Even though it was the last weekend in May, there were lightning bugs and no mosquitos.

"Sean, would you swing me in my old rope swing?"

"Sure, where is it?"

"In the oak tree. I think the board is in the garage."

Sean found the board and met Edie at the tree. He placed the board in the rope and Edie promptly sat down. Sean started pushing her. Soon she was going chest high. Her flimsy gown crept up her legs. She giggled as she arched back and forth. The breeze felt cool as it entered underneath her skirt. She laid back and tried to kiss Sean as she reached the apex of her arc. The moon faded behind a dark cloud. A flash of lightning streaked, followed by a clap of thunder that shook the sky. The clear sky darkened. The wind picked up.

"Sean, hurry, we a have to get the laundry in," Edie screamed as she leapt from the swing.

Sean ran to the wash house and grabbed the biggest wash basket he could find. He ran to the line full of whipping sheets and curtains. Sean grabbed the flowing sheets while Edie unsnapped the clothespins. He ran the first basket inside and returned to help catch the rest of the wash, the kitchen curtains and towels. The wind wrapped Edie's skirt around her legs. She was having difficulty walking.

The rain began to fall. One section of curtain escaped the clothesline and went flying off across the lawn. Edie chased after it.

"You take those inside, I'll run down the last piece," she called over the rising wind.

Sean was almost to the door when a bolt of lightning struck the oak tree where they had just spent some joyous time. A top limb exploded. He looked back into the yard. He saw Edie running toward him as the lightning struck again. The bolt was so bright it almost blinded him. The bolt exploded the water droplets with a searing, slashing sound. The thunder cracked with a deafening crash. Edie staggered and grabbed the clothesline pole, then collapsed.

"Edie, Edie!" he screamed as he ran to her.

The rain came down in torrents. Hail pelted the pair, followed by chunks of ice the size of eggs. Sean scooped Edie up and headed for the wash house. The hail grew larger. It pounded him as he carried his stunned girlfriend. One piece slammed into his right ear. Another smashed into his cheek. Several pelted his bare back.

Sean ran as fast as he could, holding Edie close to protect her from the falling chunks of ice. The wash house had the only open door. He placed her on the folding table, then pushed the door shut and latched it. The storm raged. Rainwater poured in under the doorway and ran across the floor. The hail had dropped the temperature by twenty degrees.

Edie was half-conscious and soaked to the skin. Sean considered his options. She was freezing. He had to get her out of her wet clothes. Spotting, the old wash tub, he turned the tub upside down and sat Edie on it, propping her head against the wall. Next he cleared the folding table, a three-foot by eight-foot table covered with oilcloth, used to fold the dry clothes. He found a bedsheet and covered the surface. Because Edie was soaked, he stretched a clean towel on top of the sheet. He rolled up a small towel for a pillow. Now the problem was getting her out of the wet dress and warmed. In one swoop, he picked her up and sat her on the table. She looked at him with questioning eyes. She was barely coherent.

"Edie, we have to get you out of these wet clothes. Do you understand me?"

Her eyes were open, but fixed in a stare.

Sean shook her gently. "Edie, you must get out these wet things. May I take them off?"

She shivered and nodded. The cooled air from the hailstorm had chilled her. She tried to balance herself and weakly began to unbutton her blouse. Sean put his arm behind her back to hold her up. With his free hand he undid the buttons. He slipped the blouse from her shoulders. Next he unbuttoned her skirt.

"You got to stand up, Edie."

She wobbled as she leaned against the table. Sean stripped the skirt to the floor and laid it on the back of a chair. It had grass stains from her fall and a small tear near the hem. Sean studied her for a moment.

Okay, Honey, you still are in very wet clothes. Now I can help you remove them or I could carry you to your room and you undress yourself. What do you want me to do?"

Edie again stared at him. She cocked her head as if she was thinking. The door rattled and blew open. A burst of wind roared in bringing another shot of rain. She shivered again, then she raised her arms to say take it off. He pulled her camisole over her head. She tried to cover bosom with her arms.

Since she didn't seem to want to talk, Sean pointed to her underpants. She questioned his movements. He undid his trousers and took them off.

He said loudly, "May I remove your underwear?"

She looked down and shrugged her shoulders. The cotton was clinging to her legs. Water was running down from her knees.

She gazed at Sean and said a slurred, "Yyyyyyeeess."

He worked her underpants off. He quickly grabbed a towel and wrapped around her bare body. He picked her up and laid her on the table and covered her with a curtain.

Now it was time for himself. He dropped his wet trousers and searched the laundry for some washed underwear. Sean wore undershorts which went to his knees. He had no extras for himself, so he borrowed a pair of Frank's.

Edie was shivering violently. Sean wasted no time and decided to carry her upstairs to her bedroom. The rain subsided a bit. He opened the wash house door. He picked her up and dashed across the open space, cradling her bare body close to his. It was a long way upstairs. He was puffing when he finally got there. Now what was he going to do? He threw the blankets back on one side, gently put her on the bed, then pulled the covers over her. She moaned again. He pulled a chair over and sat down beside the bed. He brushed her hair back from her face.

He would stay by her side and try to stay awake, but fatigue took over. He dozed on the side of the bed. Every time she made a sound, he awoke and patted her arm or face.

The night was long. At 4:30, with dawn approaching, Sean awoke. The rain had subsided. Edie was sleeping soundly.

He thought, *Someone must do the milking. I didn't hear Ralph come home. I guess it will be me.*

He tucked the blankets tightly around her body so she couldn't fall out of bed. Downstairs, Sean put on the same milking clothes. On the way, he passed a mirror. His reflection surprised him. His ear was bright red, and his right eye was almost swollen shut. He tried to turn to see his back, but it hurt too much.

Ignoring the pain, he headed to the barn. On the way out, he noticed a big limb lying on the ground. He wondered where the lightning struck. He walked over to where Edie had fallen near the flagpole in the middle of the lawn. The pansies around it were fried. The lightning must have hit the pole as she ran by. He picked up the curtain she dropped, hung it on the yard fence, and headed for the barn.

Around 6:30, Edie began to stir. She could barely move her arms. The blankets were tightly packed around her. She freed one hand, but she felt funny. Where were her shoulder straps? She lifted the blanket and discovered she had nothing on.

Where is my nightie? she thought. *Wait a minute, Sean's here. What happened? I remember seeing a flash of light. Where's Sean now. How did I end up in my bed naked? I must have really been dizzy if I forgot my nightie. Certainly, he didn't put me to bed. Gosh, I hope not. I wonder if Ralphie made it home. Maybe Ruth is here? She might of helped me in bed.*

She peeled back the covers and slid her feet to the floor. She stumbled to the closet.

Where's my blue dress? Where's my underwear?

She tip-toed across the hall to the guest bedroom. Sean was not there. His bed was not mussed. She crept down and looked into Ralph's room. His bed hadn't been slept in. She looked out her window and could tell someone was in the barn. She figured it was Ralph.

Sean must have gone home early this morning. Ralph is probably milking and chuckling all the time. That sneaky Ralph. I'll go right out and confront him. I'll give him a piece of my mind.

She dug out an old yellow pinafore which had beet juice on it and a white blouse with grease stain from when she tried to fix the motor on the Maytag. She dressed without underwear and stomped out to the barn. The top of the Dutch door was open.

"Ralphie! Ralphie! You no-good, low-browed skunk! Where did you put my dress and underwear?" she hollered at the top of her voice.

There was no answer.

She yelled again, "Ralph James Mohr, you come here right this minute."

"Ralph is not here," came a reply from a voice down several cows.

"Sean?" questioned Edie. "Sean, why are you here?"

"Because Ralph is in Davenport with his girlfriend."

"Well, how come I awoke in my bed with nothing on?"

"Because you were soaked to the skin and I had to do something. I asked you if I should remove your dress and you said it was okay. Don't you remember the storm?"

"I remember taking down the wash and running after a curtain, then a flash of light. That's all."

Edie unhooked the door and entered the dimly lit barn. She could see Sean's arm and leg underneath the next-to-last cow.

Sean peeked out and said, "You chased after the curtain. Lighting struck the flagpole right as you ran past. You were stunned. I thought you were dead. It began to rain and hail. I ran out and carried you to the wash shed. You were soaked to the skin and shivering. I knew I needed to get you out of those wet clothes. I asked first, then took off your blouse and skirt. You seemed to be dazed when I asked about your underwear. When you put your arms up, I pulled your top. It wasn't until I removed my trousers that I got you to understand you needed to remove your bottoms. I covered you with a towel and carried you to your bed. You moaned a lot. I stayed by your bed all night. I thought it was safe to leave and do the milking because you were sleeping so sound."

"So, you undressed me. You saw me naked. You carried me upstairs to my bed and covered me. I was naked all that time?"

"That's how it happened. Sorry if I upset you."

"Well, you did, Mr. O'Keefe. I don't cotton to boyfriends taking off my clothes and carrying me anywhere. I'll bet my dress is hanging on a hook and my underwear is under the bed. How dare you undress me? I don't know how you did it, but I also don't know how I didn't know about it. I think as soon as you finish chores and eat breakfast you should go home. Ralph will be here tonight."

She turned around and stomped out of the barn, never once looking directly at Sean. She slammed the door shut but it caught her skirt. She stumbled forward and fell into a mud puddle. The skirt made a ripping sound as it freed itself. It tore to her knee. Now she was madder than a wet hen.

"I might as well feed the chickens and hunt the eggs," she grumbled to herself as she stomped through the mud..

She went to the wash shed for the egg bucket. She spotted her blue dress neatly lying over the back of a chair. It had grass stains on the front and a small tear near the hem. Next to it was her underwear lying on the folding table. In a pile on the floor was Sean's trousers, shirt, and underwear. Evidently, he had been soaked, too. She started to mellow. Maybe Sean was trying to help her. It looks as if he was naked at some time, too. All kinds of visions danced in her head, naked girl, naked boy, in bedroom. Wow!

She grabbed the egg pail and walked to the hen house. She noticed several window panes were broken in the windows of the henhouse. Once inside she spotted a mass of red feathers in the corner. It looked like hens. Underneath the nests lay several dead hens. She panicked. If these old birds were frightened by the storm, what about the pullets in the brooder house? She put down the bucket and dashed to the small building. Sure enough, there was a large pile of dead pullets and cockerels stacked in the corners. The storm frightened the chickens causing them to crowd into the corners where they suffocated each other.

Her mother would be upset when she came home. Her chickens were her pride and joy. Edie would have Ralph bury the carcasses before her mother got home. Sean must have been right about the hail also. She mellowed some more. Maybe she would have to apologize, but he did admit he saw her naked. She thought about what she would tell her mother.

On her way back from hunting the few eggs in the henhouse, she passed by the garden. It was a disaster. The peas and beans were mowed to the ground. The strawberries were flattened to mush. The cherry tree had most of its fruit knocked to the ground. The storm was real. She probably was lucky to be alive.

She put the few eggs in the shed and was about to go inside the house when she saw the mud splotch on her skirt. Her blouse was muddy from her wrist to her elbow. She was a mess. She'd didn't dare wear it inside. She poked her head out the door. Sean was still milking. Slipping out of the skirt and blouse, she wrapped a towel around her body and ran for the house. She found some underwear in a basket and her mother's housecoat in the downstairs closet. She would dress properly after breakfast.

Meanwhile, Sean finished up. He carried the milk can to the cooling tank. He had planned to separate the cream, but Edie's tirade made him feel otherwise. He limped to the hog pen and slopped the hogs. The weather hadn't curbed their appetite. Several panes of glass were missing from its windows. He slowly walked across the farm yard. He hated to face Edie again. He went to the wash house and located his clean clothes. They were hanging on hooks and not on the floor. Edie had hung them up. This was a good sign. He washed his face and hands, then he looked in the mirror. His eye was almost completely swollen shut. His ear was bright red. It hurt like hell. He couldn't see his back, but it was becoming stiff. He knocked on the door.

"May I come in?"

"Sure, come on in," cooed a cheerful voice from inside.

He opened the door and found Edie standing at the cook stove with her back to him. He eased across the kitchen and sat.

"I trust you found your clothes."

"Yes, I did. Thanks for hanging them up."

Edie turned toward Sean and gasped.

"What happened to you?" she cried.

"I was hit by some of the hail while I was picking you up from the lawn. I'm sorry you got some grass stains on your dress. I'm sorry if I upset you. I thought I was doing the right thing."

Edie melted completely. "Oh my sweet, sweet Sean. Look at you. You're a mess. You protected me. You did the right thing, trust me. I'm sorry I chewed you out. I was so mad at Ralph I couldn't think straight. Ralph isn't even here. I know he never came home. His bed wasn't slept in. I checked. You hadn't slept' in yours either. I thought you had gone home. Boy, was I wrong. You eat your breakfast and I'll see if I can treat your face. Do you hurt elsewhere?"

"My back is really sore."

Edie went behind Sean and pulled up his shirt.

"Oh my God, you have bruises all over. Let me get some Epsom salts ready. You are going to rest."

Sean ate his meal and watched with his good eye as Edie worked. Her housecoat slipped open and revealed her underwear. He loved watching her.

She drew some water to wash his wounds and after he finished eating, she made him sit on a stool. She carefully washed his tender ear, then put an ice pack over the swollen eye. She helped him remove his shirt and began to apply the Epsom salt compresses.

Sean closed his eyes. The Epsom salts felt soothing. The ice on his eye was reducing the pain. His body ached all over, but Edie's tender touches made it tolerable. When he opened his eye, he found Edie had doffed her housecoat and changed into an old flannel shirt. It fit her better and showed more leg.

She worked silently, not realizing he was watching. A couple of times she leaned over him and her bosom almost touched him. At least, that's what he thought.

"Stand up," she ordered.

Sean struggled to his feet. She maneuvered around in front and unbuckled his trousers. They fell.

"Take off your pants."

"It looks like you already have."

"Listen, by the looks of your back, you must be hurting other places, too.

How about your legs?"

"They're fine," he said, and winced.

She noticed his grimace. She couldn't view his upper legs because of his knee-length underwear.

"Let me be the judge of that."

"No. I'm fine."

"Sean O'Keefe, you risked your life to save me from much pain, maybe worse. The least I can do is fix your hurts. There is no one around but you and me. Ralph won't show up until afternoon. Now, let me take a peek. You have some bad bruises on your legs. I want you to lie down on the sofa."

Sean complied. He was at her mercy. He laid down on his stomach. She applied some Absorbine Jr. to his bruises. It burned like fire. Sean moaned.

Edie knelt by his side and touched his arm as if to say, I'm sorry. Sean turned his head and opened his good eye. He reached with his finger to the top of Edie shirt. He gave it a little tug. The material loosened. He got a better view. Last night he hadn't noticed her breasts. This morning they looked wonderful. He could tell she was thin but strong. Her arms were tanned and not white. It showed she worked outside.

"What are you doing?" she asked.

"Trying to see what I missed last night," he replied with a smile.

"What do you mean by that? You saw me as naked as a jaybird."

"Listen, I was so busy trying to save you, I never noticed your lovely body."

"You say I have a lovely body? You must have seen something."

"At the time, you were all I was concerned about. I didn't care if you were man or woman, fat or thin. All I can remember is how smooth and white your skin was."

"That's all you remember? You did have a lot of hurts on your body and only one good eye. Maybe the pain was too great." She kidded, "Any other red-blooded man would notice something."

"No, I think it is the rush one gets from emergency situations. You are more concerned in saving a loved one's life than viewing her or him for other purposes."

"Did I just hear you say loved one?"

"Yes, Edie, I love you. I was scared you were injured or even worse. Your safety and health were my only thought. Now it is a little different."

"Gee, honey, May I call you 'Honey'? I'm really sweet on you."

"I guess so. It sounds like we both love each other. That's good."

"You're so much nicer then what I read in Mrs. Steinbeck's books."

"Mrs. Steinbeck's books?"

"Oh yes, she has a lot of books hidden from the rest of the family, including her husband. They are really racy. You know, naked women, naked men, skinny dipping, sex, etcetera."

"Really!"

"Yeah, she really surprised me. I found her reading in my room one day. She said it was the only place she could read in private. I asked what she was reading. She showed me and became a little embarrassed. She told me she shouldn't be reading such trash, but she liked them. She asked me never to tell her husband."

Edie eyed her Irishman. He was truly a great male specimen.

"Sean, my hero. Close your eye."

Sean complied again. He heard rustling and shuffling.

"Okay, you may open your eye now."

When he opened his eye, Edie stood in front of him in just her underwear. She was stunning. She seemed embarrassed, like he had been.

Sean rolled over and swung his legs to the floor. He tried to stand. Edie helped him up. She stood on her tip-toes and kissed him. She laid her head on his shoulder and grabbed one of his arms to guide it around her waist. Despite the pain, he held her. She felt so soft.

Edie stepped back and took Sean's hand. She smiled and led him upstairs.

Once in her room, she sat on her bed and said, "My bed still isn't made. Will it cause you too much pain?"

"With you in my arms, my pain disappears. What do you have in mind?"

"Oh, you'll see."

Edie sat on her bed. She turned and gazed at Sean.

"Is this how it was?" she asked.

"Exactly, and I kissed you on the forehead like this."

Edie moved to her knees. She closed her eyes and arched her back some. She wanted to mimic the girls in Mrs. Steinbeck's books. She thought to herself, *"Touch me, Sean. I want to experience the feeling."*

She held her hand out to beckon him. She felt his fingers touch her arm, then her shoulder. His touch moved to her face. She felt his lips kissing her forehead. She reached and touched his bare chest. She felt him slowly moving his fingertips over her body.

Sean was surprised and elated at this beautiful nymph beckoning him. He bent over and kissed her forehead. Sean noticed Edie's cheeks glowing. He placed his fingers on her arm and slowly moved up to her shoulder. He resisted petting the rest of her body. It was so soft and smooth. He placed his hand on her back and helped her lay full out on the bed. He slipped her brassiere shoulder straps from her shoulder, then caressed her bare skin. Edie closed her eyes. She sucked in her tummy indicating for him to go further. He stopped.

"Edie," he said softly, "This isn't right, you know it and I know it. Sex is for married people, not us. At least, not right now. Do you understand?"

Edie opened her eyes. She stared at Sean.

"You're right again, Sweetie. We will wait."

The spell was broken by the sound of a car coming down the road. Edie jumped up and ran to the window.

"It's Ralphie. He's almost to the lane. Hurry, we must get dressed."

Sean followed Edie downstairs. They giggled all the way down. She grabbed her clothes and headed back to her room. Sean pulled on his trousers. He just got his belt tightened when Ralph walked in the door. He took one look at Sean and said, "What happened to you, buddy? You look like you got into a fight with a bull."

Sean gave Ralph a wry grin and replied, "I got caught in the hailstorm. The chunks of ice were the size of eggs and they hit hard."

"Why were you out in the rain?"

Edie appeared from the staircase, "He was saving me. I was trying to retrieve a flying curtain and I was stunned by a lightning strike. Sean dashed out and saved me. He protected me with his body. I was stunned. I was so out of it he sat by my bed all night just to make sure I would be all right. I didn't realize he was injured so badly until this morning. To top it all off, he milked all the cows by himself in this condition."

Ralph looked at his sister and got a silly grin on his face.

"Say, if you were out in the storm, it had to be raining. Both of you had to be soaked. Did he put you in your bed in wet clothes? That's stupid."

Edie snapped back at her brother, "Are you insinuating that Sean is stupid?"

"No, but it is stupid to put you in bed in wet clothes."

"Well, I was not in my wet clothes."

"But, Sis, you just said you were unconscious. You could not have removed your clothes yourself. Sean had to do it." teased Ralph with a big grin on his face.

Edie knew she'd been caught. She glared at her brother, then at Sean. Sean shrugged his shoulders. He didn't know what her relationship with her brother was.

Edie sighed and said, "I'll tell you the truth, Ralphie, if you promise not to tell Mom."

"Promise. You know I won't tell, Sis. Look at the goods you have on me and my love life." Ralph assured her, "Now tell me the good stuff. You were naked, correct?"

"Well, Sean did save me. We were both soaked to the skin. He carried me to the wash shed. He removed my clothes, covered me with a towel, and carried me to my bedroom. My dress and underthings are still in the shed, if you don't believe me."

"So, Sean removed your clothes and carried you naked to your bed. He or you did not put any night clothes on you and Sean took care of you and nothing happened. What did he have on?"

Sean interrupted. "Ralph, she was unconscious. I was worried she might die. I would never touch your sister in that condition. To answer your question, I found a pair of underwear in the clothes basket to wear."

"I admire you, Sean. You're a great guy, but I still think you missed a great opportunity. Even though she is my sister."

"Jumping chiggers," exclaimed Edie. "What kind of person do you believe he is? We won't have any sex until we are married."

"Okay, okay, Sis. I believe you. Let's drop the subject. I didn't walk part way to Pleasant Prairie to discuss your love life. I left Ruthie in Davenport at her cousin's, so I could get home. I heard there was a tornado south of Blue Grass, the Interurban was shut down, and so are the phone lines. I thought I'd better get home. I thumbed a ride with a trucker to Blue Grass and walked the rest of the way. It looks like I made the right decision."

"On that point you are right. When I fed the chickens, I found several dead ones in the brooder house and some more in the hen house. The chickens suffocated themselves in a corner of the chicken house. Mom will be upset. Those chickens were her egg money. But she'll be more upset when she sees her garden. It's a disaster."

"I'll change clothes and take care of them first. How about the other animals?"

Sean spoke up. "I think the cows and horses are fine. Most of them headed for the shed when it started to hail. The ones in the pasture probably look like me. I'll help you bury the chickens."

Ralph replied, "You better sit tight. By the way you look, you got the worst of everything. Edie, you come help me and tell this man of yours to rest."

"Sure, just let me get into some chore clothes. Don't let Mom know I'm doing man's work."

Sean reluctantly rested on the porch while the siblings headed for the chicken houses. He wished he could hear their conversation because it probably was a lot about him.

Ralph found some old gunny sacks from the barn while Edie gathered some shovels. They went into the chicken barns and stuffed the dead birds inside the sacks. The dead birds required three sacks. The hole would have to be large.

"Where are we going to bury these chickens?" asked Edie.

"Let's go to the edge of the corn field. The soil is softer and there will be no roots. I'd like to see what the corn looks like anyway. If it is anything like Ma's garden, it will be a mess. Dad may have to replant. The alfalfa will recover, but the first cutting will be hell to make. I'm sure Dad will call as soon as the phone lines are back up."

Ralph and Edie dragged the full gunny sacks about 150 feet down the fence line before stopping to dig. Ralph marked out the size and they started digging.

Ralph watched his sister as she spaded the dirt. She was humming a tune.

"What's that song your humming?"

"Ragtime Girl. It's been around for a while, but it has a catchy tune. I've heard Mom sing it."

"Sis, you really seem happy. Did you and Sean have a good time?"

"What do you mean by 'good time'?"

"You sit together. Do chores together. Maybe do a little petting."

Trying to act annoyed, Edie answered, "Why, Ralphie, why would you think that? Sean is very pleasant to be around. He's kind and considerate. He is always a gentleman. He almost never swears. When he picks me up in town, he always meets Mrs. Steinbeck. He brings me home on time and he is great with the Steinbeck boys."

"But Edie, he's a Catholic. Dad won't allow you to marry a Catholic. In fact, I know, I dated Beverly Braun and he about threw us off the place."

"I know, but I love Sean. He said he would marry me. We discussed it this morning in my room."

"In your room? What, pray tell, was he doing in your room this morning. A little loving?"

Edie blushed. She had been caught again.

"I asked him to help me pick out a dress he liked. That's all."

"Nothing else."

"No. Now stop asking me personal questions."

"You didn't sleep together last night, did you?"

"No, I told you he carried me to my room and stayed there all night. He was worried about me."

"But you said he milked the cows, then came in for breakfast. Had you seen him before that?"

"Yes, I went to the barn to scold you for stealing my clothes!"

"Me!"

"Yes, you. I forgot Sean was here."

Edie continued with a repeat of the events which happened through the night up to breakfast the next morning.

"So, you and Sean were in just your underwear and nothing happened."

"Noooo . . . nothing happened."

Ralph detected some doubt in her voice.

"All right, spill the beans. You're not telling me everything."

Edie confessed everything, right down to the undressing.

"It just seemed the right thing to do. I wanted to give something to him and all I could think of was me. Heck, I wouldn't let Sean unbutton my blouse in town."

"What's town got to do with it?"

"I don't know, but in town there are lots of people close-by. Here we were all alone. You know how we run around in our underwear upstairs, both of us. You've seen plenty of me. This is different. Mom will kill me."

"First, our Dad doesn't need to know, neither does Mom. If you didn't have sex, it was just a, let's say, a revealing."

"Sean--what do you think he feels about me now? Does he think I'm some sort of a hussy?"

"No, but I bet he was smiling ear to ear when you took off your clothes. If he is like any other male, he likes to see scantily females. It is just natural."

"I hope you are right. Have you and Ruthie been, you know, intimate?"

Ralph paused and replied, "Yes, Sis, only once. It scared us until she had her period."

"Changing the subject. Isn't this hole getting deep enough?"

The hole was deep enough to bury the birds. Now it was time cover them with the same dirt they had just dug out. It was now eleven. The sun was warming the air. Although it was not as humid as the day before, the pair was still sweating. Edie's blouse with the long sleeves clung to her. Ralph removed his shirt. He wiped his brow and kidded his sister, "Why don't you take off your top and be cool?"

"No, it wouldn't be proper."

"Listen, I'm your brother, you're behind the barn, Sean cannot see you, of course he's already seen you with less, the neighbors cannot see you, so why not. You've got underwear on. I'm not going to suggest you take that off."

Edie thought a minute. Two days ago, she would have never considered it. But after Saturday night, her inhibitions were not as strong.

"No, I believe one man seeing me in my underwear is enough."

"As long as that man is Sean, Right?"

"Maybe."

It was eleven thirty by the time the pair got back to the house. The smell of food wafted from the kitchen. Edie burst through the door and found Sean at the cook stove. Sean turned and said, "I thought if you are doing man's work, I'd do some woman's work. I do know how to cook, ya know. It's some Irish stew."

The stew smelled delicious. When Ralph appeared, he couldn't believe his nose.

"Do you bake, too?" he blurted out.

"Yep, got a cake in the oven. You and Edie wash up. I'll have the table set when you get back."

Ralph looked at Edie. She looked at Sean. He was wonderful. They had lunch and decided to rest some before doing something else.

Sean announced, "A neighbor called and said the Declaration Day ceremonies in Blue Grass were canceled because of the storm. I guess you are free for the afternoon."

The telephone rang. Ralph answered it.

"Dad . . . yes, everything is fine here . . . we had some big hail . . . ruined Ma's garden and some of the chickens piled up in the brooder house and suffocated. There are a few panes broken out of the windows in the barn and hog house . . . The corn isn't too bad . . . . hay is flat . . . we're okay. Sean got hit by some hail, he's sorta banged up . . . it's a long story, Dad, I'll let Edie tell you when you get home." . . . . . Okay Dad, I'll be there, good bye."

Ralph returned to the table and said, "That was Dad. He'll be at Melpine

Station at ten. Mom's staying with Aunt Helen."

Edie replied with a smirk, "I figured as much. If we are going to be home alone again, why don't you call Ruth and see if she's home, then ask her if wants to come over and play Parcheesi or dominoes or some card game. Sean might be able to see well enough with his good eye."

"Good idea, Sis. Maybe she can stay over. I can take her home in the morning when I pick up Dad. I'll call her right now. It will also keep you from picking on Sean."

Sean chimed in, "She can pick on me all she wants."

"Yeah, I know how she takes care of you. I bet she is really smooth," kidded Ralph.

Ralph called Ruth. She was ecstatic. Her mother wasn't so keen on the idea, she'd heard stories of young couples staying overnight and no parents around, but Ruth convinced her that Edie would be there, too. Ralph was to pick her up at 6:30. Edie offered to fix supper for the four of them. The only problem was the milking still had to be done.

"Edie, can you help with the milking?" Ralph asked.

"What! How am I going to fix supper and milk? You've got to be kidding."

"Well, Sean can't help. He'd probably start on the wrong end of the cow with only one good eye."

Sean spoke up, "Hey, I did all the milking this morning alone. I must admit my back is much stiffer now than then, but I can do the cooking if Edie tells me what she wants and where the ingredients are."

"Okay, Edie, you show him where things are, then change clothes for chores."

"Boy, are you getting bossy," Edie shot back.

"If you don't help I'll never get the milking done on time. Besides I have to slop the hogs."

"I can slop the hogs," interrupted Sean, "and I'll wash up before I fix supper."

"Great, everything is set. Let's get going."

The trio went to work. Sean quickly fed the hogs. Edie changed her clothes and hunted the eggs before heading to the barn. Ralph had the cows stanchioned and fed. By six o'clock, Edie and Ralph were back at the house. Sean had a cobbler in the oven. The aroma filled the kitchen.

Ralph took one whiff and exclaimed, "Edie, this guy can cook better than you. He's a keeper." Then he changed his tune. "I should clean up first, so I can get over to Ruth's. I'll stoke the water heater and take a cold shower."

"You don't have to take a cold shower. I fired up the heater when I came in. Just don't take all the hot water," Sean told him.

"Boy, you are great. Thank you, Sean. Edie, I'll be as quick as I can."

Ralph headed downstairs. Edie went upstairs to her room. Soon he was back wrapped in a towel. He waved at Sean and headed to his room. Edie appeared at the kitchen door wearing a robe.

"How you are doing?" she asked Sean.

"Fine. Where's the black pepper?"

"Black pepper? Why do you need that?"

"I always mix salt and pepper with the flour when I do chicken."

"I think it's in the pantry, second shelf."

Edie disappeared through the basement door. Sean searched the pantry but could not locate the black pepper. He waited for Edie to reappear. He heard the water shut off. Edie poked her head inside the kitchen again.

"Any luck with finding the pepper?"

"No."

She shook her head and tiptoed in her bare feet to the pantry. She scanned the open pantry.

"I bet it is higher up. I'll get a stool."

"Here, let me lift you up."

Sean put his hands around Edie waist and lifted her high. The upward movement caused her robe to slip from her shoulders.

"Here it is," she exclaimed as she reached deep into the cupboard. When she pulled her arm out, a container of nutmeg followed and fell inside her sleeve. Sean let her down and took the pepper from her hand. Edie giggled and shook her sleeve to remove the small container. Her robe slipped from her shoulder to her elbow.

"Oops!" she said. This time she turned a bright pink. Sean just smiled. He had seen her bosom before. Edie readjusted her garment and skedaddled out of the kitchen and upstairs. She met Ralph halfway up.

"You'd better be fully dressed before I come back," he kidded, "or Ruthie will get the wrong idea about you two."

"Don't worry, big brother, I'll be dressed. Sean and I will be waiting."

Ralph waved at Sean as he disappeared out the door. Edie watched him leave from her bedroom window. She would have to hurry. The Watts farm was only ten minutes away by car.

She was still in her dressing gown, combing her hair, when she heard Sean coming up the stairs. He glanced through her open door, then disappeared into his room on the other side of the hall. He needed to change into a clean shirt.

Edie called, "Sean, could you help me?"

Sean came quickly. He did not have his shirt on yet. He answered, "How can I help?"

"Will you button the back of my blouse?"

"I'll try, but remember I have only one good eye."

Sean fumbled with the tiny buttons. The ones in the middle of her back were easy. It was the top ones and the very bottom ones which were giving him the most trouble.

"How do you button these by yourself?" he questioned.

"Mom usually does it and when I am at Steinbeck's, Mrs. Steinbeck or her housekeeper, Katy, help me. They are difficult. I wish men had to button these, then they wouldn't design these blouses."

Sean continued to struggle. Finally, Edie sighed and said, "You know, Sean, I think I'll put on my blue gingham dress. I can button it myself, so undo what you've just done."

Sean rolled his eye and attempted to undo his work. It was a good thing the undoing was easier than the doing. As soon as he had the last button through its hole, Edie slipped it off. Next, she unhooked her skirt and let it fall. She acted as if Sean was not there at all. She went to her closet and pulled out her dress. Turning, she realized Sean was standing behind her.

She asked, "Sean, do you like seeing me in my slip?"

"Yes, and I hope someday I can see you every day this way and maybe with less."

Edie ran and threw her arms around his neck and kissed him. "I love you, Sean. I hope I can accommodate your desires someday, but now git. Ralph will be back from Ruthie's and I won't be dressed. He'll tease me that you and I were messing around again."

"What do you mean, again?"

Edie paused. She turned away from Sean and said, "Well, he got me to confess about Saturday night. Don't worry, he won't tell anyone. I've got plenty of goods on him."

"Are you sorry it happened?"

"Heavens no, my big Irishman, I am a little embarrassed that I went that far. "

"Well, if it will ease your mind, I found you quite charming and beautiful. I love you, Edie."

They barely made it downstairs when they heard the model T chugging up the lane. Sean was starting to fry the chicken as Ruthie barged through the door.

"Boy, it smells delicious in here." She noticed Sean at the stove. "Does he cook, too?"

"Yes, he is a great cook and he can do washing." Edie glanced at Sean turning the pieces over in the pan. "And he does some nursing, too."

"Ralph told me how he carried you inside after being stunned by the lightning. How heroic."

"Did he tell you anything else?"
"No, just that Sean was badly bruised from the hail. Now that I've had a look at him. He is badly banged up. Was there more?"

"No, that's pretty much it. Did you see his right eye? Doesn't he look terrible?"

They sat down for a great supper cooked by Sean. After they ate, Sean helped gather the dishes.

"Come on, Sean, let's go outside while the girls finish the dishes."

Sean glared at Ralph and said, "No, you go outside. I'll stay here and help. I made most of the mess, so I feel I should help clean up."

Ralph shook his head and went out to the porch. Ruth stared at Sean. She couldn't believe her ears. He had just volunteered to wash the dishes. Her dad, her two brothers, all her uncles, had never volunteered to cook let alone, wash dishes. Edie caught her staring. She just smiled and pinched Sean on his side. She knew he was special.

When the dishes were clean and put away the two couples played Parcheesi and Kings on the corner. The evening disappeared. Edie could tell Ruthie and Ralph were itching for a little alone time.

"Ruthie," she asked, "did you bring some clothes to stay over?"

"Yeah, but where will I sleep? Sean is in the guest room."

Ralph piped up, "You can sleep with me."

"In your dreams," was the quick reply.

"You can sleep in my bed, and I'll lock the door to keep him away." Edie teased, "let's take your bag to my room. Maybe we can find something more comfortable to wear for the rest of the night. You look like you are poured into that dress."

"Be sure it's light and flimsy." teased Ralph.

The girls went upstairs. Ralph and Sean sipped their iced tea.

"Sean, do you really think you can marry my sister, I know you are a Catholic and all?"

"I hope so. She is a wonderful woman. It doesn't bother me if she is not Catholic. I love her for what she is."

Ralph chuckled a bit and said, "And she is a good looker, isn't she?"

"What are you implying? Ralph, are you saying my only desire is to have sex with your sister? No, sir, my good man, I would never impose myself on her if she was unwilling."

"But you will admit you saw her naked."

Sean was starting to become irritated by Ralph's questioning. He rose from his chair and glared at Ralph. "Ralph, I know what you're implying. Yes, we saw each other nude, but we stopped short of being intimate. We decided we should wait until we are married. Yes, I am a Catholic, it shouldn't matter. Now, I don't like your questions. Stop it right now before Edie and Ruth come down."

"Touchy, touchy," chided Ralph, "I'll tell you right now my father does not like Catholics dating Protestants, man or woman. He gets along with his Catholic neighbors, but just let one of their kids date someone other than a Catholic and he goes berserk. I know, I tried. I suggest you find a nice Catholic girl and have a dozen kids like they always have."

Their argument was cut short by Ruthie sauntering out on the porch. She had on a lacy knee length gown covered by a thin lacy peignoir. She sat next to Ralph. Edie followed her wearing a short cotton nightgown and barefoot.

"How 'bout you guys getting more comfortable?" cooed Ruthie.

"Sure," answered Ralph. In a flash, he removed his high collared shirt and shoes.

"How about you?" Edie asked Sean.

"I think I'll pass. Maybe it's time for me to go home."

"Home?" questioned Edie. "You can't go home now. Why?"

"I think I better not be here tomorrow morning when your father gets home."

Edie was astounded. She could sense Sean was very upset. His face was red and he was clenching his fists. She followed him as he went inside.

"What's wrong, Sean?"

"I like your brother and all, but I feel when your father and mother return they will have the same attitude as Ralph, so I'd better leave before I do something I regret."

"What? What did Ralph say something? I'll confront him if he said something bad. He doesn't control me. Did he say something about Saturday night?"

"Yes, sort of, Edie. He also told me because I'm Catholic I'd better not think of marrying you. If he feels that way, so will your father. I love you very much, Edie. I don't want to cause you any problems. I just feel we better cool it for a while. I can walk back to Muscatine or maybe I can catch the Interurban at Melpine Station. It should be running again. You should think it over, too. You could be shunned by your family. I have no family except my mom and she's in Boston dying, so it won't hurt me as much."

"No, no," cried Edie as she followed him to his room. "Please give me a chance."

"I am giving you a chance, Edie. A chance to think about our relationship. A lot of things happened this weekend. We probably became too close. Saturday morning was wonderful for me. I hope I haven't ruined your life. Maybe, like Ralph said, I should find some Catholic girlfriend."

"But I love you because you are kind and gentle. I don't care if you are Catholic or Jewish or anything else. I care for you because you are you. Don't you understand? We're made for each other."

Sean packed his bag. He refused to look at Edie. His leaving was the most difficult thing he had ever done, but he knew he had to go.

Edie was distraught. She didn't understand. Mrs. Steinbeck had warned her about the problem of dating a Catholic. She thought Mrs. Steinbeck was just over reacting. Evidently, Sean realized the problem was more of a barrier than she thought. She had to do something and something fast.

Sean straightened. He turned and looked at Edie. She had tears in her eyes. He couldn't help himself. Here was the only girl he truly loved. Just a few hours ago she was willing to give him everything and now he was walking away. He went to her and hugged her.

"Edie, if we are to be together, God will be with us. I will never forget you as long as we live. Now I must go."

"No! no! no! don't leave me. Please reconsider." she pleaded, "I want you. I know my Dad will kick me out, but I can find you. We can be together. I don't care what religion you are. Don't you love me?"

Sean gazed at her as if he was taking a long last look. He didn't answer. Then he picked up his bag, pushed past her, and disappeared downstairs. Edie crumpled to the floor in tears. By the time she recovered, Sean was almost to the end of the lane.

She dashed out of the house and across the farmyard, opened the barbed wire gate, and headed across the flattened alfalfa field. As she ran the through the field, the tangled stems tripped her. She fell, landing with one hand on a muddy gopher mound. She wiped her hand on her gown, but she could see Sean was outdistancing her. She knelt in the field and sobbed.

She knew he was gone. Her gown was alfalfa-stained and muddy. Her world was turned upside down. Slowly she rose. Her pain turned to anger.

"Damn you, Sean O'Keefe! Damn you Irishmen! Damn you, Catholic Church! Damn you all! I hope I never see you again," she screamed at his disappearing figure.

She stomped out of the field, crossed the farmyard to the front lawn, and stopped to peek around the corner to see what was transpiring on the swing. She didn't want to embarrass Ruth. Ralph, the jerk, she didn't' care about. She saw Ralph and Ruth engrossed in each other. Ruth had lost her dressing robe and was down to her nightie. Ralph had one of Ruth's shoulder straps off her shoulder. She was starting to slip her arm out. Edie stood quietly for a second. This could have been Sean and her. The couple on the swing were oblivious of her watching. As Ruth slipped her hand inside Ralph's trousers, her gown fell to her waist. Ralph was quick to fondle Ruthie's breast. Edie could take no more.

"Ralphie," she screamed, "You filthy pig, you no good piece of cow dung, you womanizer."

Ruth, surprised by Edie's outburst, quickly moved away from Ralph. She caught her gown before it fell off completely.

Ralph smiled at his disheveled sister and said, "Golly, Sis, what happened to you? Did your boyfriend leave?"

"You know very well he left, and you caused it. You had no right to meddle in my affairs. Sean is a better man than you'll ever be. Just because he's a Catholic doesn't mean he is no good. You and Daddy are tied to the same stick. You're prejudiced. You don't trust Catholics, Jews, or Black people. And as for you, Ruthie, the only reason my brother is even interested in you is because you have big boobs. I'd drop him as fast as I could."

"Whoa, little sister! You know as well as I, Pa will never let you marry a Catholic. You just find a nice Protestant boy somewhere."

He looked back at Ruth. "Don't believe what she just said. I don't date girls for their boobs. I really like you."

Ruth spoke up. "Ralphie, you just ruined your sister's life. I like you a lot, but I will not be just your cook, washer woman, and baby machine. Maybe we should cool it for a while. In fact, I do think we will cool it. I need to go home right now."

Ralph, shocked by Ruth's statement, rose and grabbed Edie by the neck. Edie squirmed and twisted away. He caught her gown and pulled her toward him. He raised his hand to strike her, but Ruth caught him.

He glared at Edie said, "You little imp, you know I'm right. The man's always right. You shouldn't talk to my girl like that."

Then he added, "Ruthie has the nicest tits I've ever see on a woman."

After that statement, he realized he had made a big mistake.

"Nice tits, huh! Well, that settles it. We're through. You find some other bimbo with NICE TITS! I'm going home."

Ruth stomped inside and slammed the door.

"Now look what you've done, Edie," Ralph scolded.

"Me! You started it. I'm leaving too. I don't want to speak to you again. You better get up early tomorrow because you're doing all the milking. That's what men do, right? You better not be late picking Dad up, either. You say women shouldn't drive. Right!"

Edie stomped inside. She shut the big door and locked it. "I'll let you in when I want to. You just swing out there and dream of Ruthie's tits."

It was after ten before Edie unlocked the door. She didn't say a word. Ralph went upstairs to apologize to Ruth. She had locked herself in Edie's bedroom. Ralph pleaded with her to come out, but her only response was, "I called my dad. He will be here at seven in the morning. Don't try and stop me."

The night was short for Ralph. He had many chores ahead and Edie would not be helping. Edie was up early also. She fed the chickens and hunted the eggs. She was working at the stove when Ruth came down.

"How are you feeling?" asked Ruth.

"Some better. I cried all night."

"I know. Remember I slept with you. I am so sorry, Edie. Sean was such a nice guy. I hope I can meet someone like him."

"I wish you well. I'm sorry if ruined your relationship with Ralph?"

"On the contrary, you opened my eyes to his motives. I think he has a lot to learn about women."

"You know, like father, like son. He's just how Dad treats Mom. I don't know how she stands him."

A horn honked outside. It was Ruth's father.

"There's my ride. I better be going, Edie. We'll talk someday."

Ruth left. Edie returned to the kitchen. She stoked the stove to warm the oven. Since her mother was not returning right away, she figured she had better bake a cake and maybe some cookies for her dad and brother. Tuesday, she would return to Muscatine and maybe, just maybe, she might see Sean again. She was putting the cake in the oven when Ralph poked his head in the door.

"I'll be in in fifteen minutes, lovely sister," he called.

He received no reply. Edie started to cook the bacon and eggs. She put the oatmeal into a pan of water to cook. Ralph entered the kitchen and sat at his place at the table.

"Sure smells delicious."

Silence.

"What are you going to do today?"

Silence.

"As soon as I finish, I'll go get Pa."

Silence.

"Look, Edie, I know you are mad at me, but it is for your own good. Marrying a Catholic just causes problems. Trust me."

Edie slapped his three eggs and four strips of bacon on a plate and set it down hard in front of him. Next, she spooned the oatmeal into a bowl. She went to the icebox for the milk. This she set just out of his reach on the other side of the table.

"Could you set that a little closer?" he asked.

She went behind him and tugged the tablecloth. The bowl and pitcher moved closer. Still she spoke no words but left him alone and went upstairs to make the beds. Ralph finished and followed her upstairs to change his clothes. He threw his dirties out in the hall. That was the last straw. Edie groaned and kicked his clothes down the stairs. She went to her room and sat on her bed and cried.

Ralph peeked in just before he left and said, "Sorry, Sis." She looked at him with eyes swollen and red. She stuck her hand up and flipped him a middle finger. He turned and slammed the door.

Since her mother would not be home until Thursday. she began the washing. She was on the second load when she heard the T chugging up the lane. She was wringing out the clothes when the door to the wash house darkened. It was her father.

"Ralph tells me your Irish boyfriend left."

Edie straightened up and answered, "Yes, thanks to Ralph."

"Daughter, you know you should have never started this relationship. You knew he was a Catholic."

"What is so bad about Catholics? Sean was much more a gentleman than Ralph ever will be, Dad. He was concerned about me. He washed dishes. He cooked dinner when I had to help Ralph milk. In fact, he milked all the cows himself the morning after the storm because I was sick. He did it when he was hurting more than me. Daddy, he saved me from serious injury from the hail. I was stunned by a lightning strike and he carried me inside. Is that so bad? Just because he is a Catholic doesn't mean a thing. He is just as good as any Methodist, probably better. I'll be glad to go back to Muscatine to get away from this farm and family who are so prejudiced."

"I suppose you think when you get to Muscatine, you'll look him up again."

"Might, but he told me we should stop seeing each other for my sake. He didn't want to cause me any trouble."

"Maybe he's smarter than I give him credit for. He realizes he shouldn't marry a Protestant. You know his priest will insist you become a Catholic and raise your children Catholic. You don't want that now, do you?"

"Right now, I don't know what I want. I know Ralph just ruined a wonderful weekend. I have to think about it some more."

"Edie, you are young. There are other men just as good. I don't want to forbid you to marry him, but if I must, I must. You should not see him ever again. Do you understand me?"

Edie didn't say a word. She stared at her father.

"Did you hear me, daughter? I will never let you marry a Catholic, whether it be that Irishman or any other Catholic. Do you understand me?"

"Yes, Father. And his name is Sean, not that Irishman."

Her father left. Edie continued most of the day doing the washing. She only stopped to fix dinner for the men. She sat down at four for ten minutes before starting supper. Her father and Ralph would be in at seven after milking. They would take showers and eat, then retire to the porch or parlor. She would wash the dishes by herself until nine.

While she worked, she heard her father on the phone. She could tell he was talking to her mother. It was a long conversation. It was nearly ten when she lay down on her bed. In the morning after breakfast, she would pack her things and have her father drive her to Melpine to catch the Interurban. Once in town she would catch the trolley to Steinbeck's.

The next morning was uneventful. Breakfast was very quiet. Her father told her to be ready at eight and he would drive her to Melpine Station. Her father said nothing all the way to Melpine. It was as she was getting out of the car when he said, "Now remember Edie, I said no Catholics, ever again. I forbid it."

CHAPTER 6: WRONG DECISIONS

Edie nodded and stepped from the car onto the station platform. She waved good-bye. Frank just moved a finger and drove off. An hour later Edie was at the back door of the Steinbeck home. She was so glad to be back and on her own again. Mrs. Steinbeck answered the door.

"Edie, we're so glad you're back. The boys missed you. They missed Sean, too. Is he coming up this weekend?"

Edie took one look at her boss and broke down crying. Mrs. Steinbeck grabbed her and held her.

"My dear girl, what's happened?"

"It's Sean," blurted out the distraught Edie.

"Oh, my goodness, is he hurt?"

"No, Mrs. Steinbeck, he's gone. My brother and he had an argument about Catholics. Sean is so nice, he didn't fight or anything. He just packed his bag and left. He told me I should find someone else. He didn't want to cause me any trouble. Mrs. Steinbeck, I love him. I don't care if he is Catholic. He is the gentlest person I have ever met. He saved me from getting severely injured during the hail storm. My dad told me good riddance. What am I going to do?"

Mrs. Steinbeck held Edie tight and said, "Edie, my dear, I, too, had a boyfriend, Earl, who was Catholic. My father would not have it. He tried to break us up, but when I wouldn't listen he used his influence at the bank to make sure he would not work anywhere in Muscatine. He was so powerful he made sure he never would work in the entire county. He moved to Davenport. We wrote back and forth for a while until father found out. He was so angry he sent me to a boarding school in Missouri. I never heard from him for a long while. Finally, after I married Sam and had the two boys, he contacted me. He was coming to Muscatine to buy some doors and windows from Roach and Musser. He asked if he could stop and see me. He said he was married and had four children. He lived in Chicago. I wanted to meet him, but thought it was not appropriate, so I wrote back saying I would be out of town on that day. I have never heard from him again. Edie, I love Sam, I love my boys, but I will always have a place in my heart for Earl. I often wonder what would have happened if I would have defied my father."

"Gee, that's sad, Mrs. Steinbeck. Do you think that will happen to me?"

"Only time will tell, Edie. If God wills it, you will know. Be patient."

Edie wiped her tears. She asked to freshen up a bit before she met the boys. When they saw her, they were excited. They knew she would listen to their stories and adventures. The boys loved Edie Mohr.

Two weeks flew by. Edie asked Louise if she had seen Sean. She claimed he was not at any of the dances. Edie left a note at his work for him to call, but he refused to acknowledge her notes. She asked his friends if he was still around and they told her he was at work every day. She had called her mother once but didn't see any reason to go home and face her Dad. Ralph stopped by with Ruth, one evening. It seemed they had reconciled. Ralph was different. He opened doors for Ruth, he made sure she entered his car with dignity, and he wasn't pawing her body.

The second time he visited, he was alone. They talked for an hour.

Ralph asked, "When are you coming home? Mom misses you."

"I don't know. Dad told me never to see Sean again. I haven't. Sean is surely keeping up his end of the deal. No one has seen him. I leave notes for him to call at the plant, but he doesn't. I just can't get him out of my mind."

"Yeah, I know what you mean. The night you and I had that fight and Ruth left. I didn't realize how much she meant to me. I realized I have been quite a jerk. I was becoming my Dad. You know like father like son. Luckily, after some flowers and some gut retching apologies, Ruth decided to give me another go. You probably won't believe me, but it has been fun trying to woo

Ruth. Yeah, we still do pet and kiss, but she and I agreed to no heavy stuff. Now I see a glow in her eyes when I visit. I think her mother likes me now."

"Great! I'm happy for you."

"So, will you come home sometime soon?"

"I'll think about it. Maybe Dad and I could be civil for a weekend."

Just before he left, Ralph touched Edie's hand lightly and said, "Good, Mom and I will be waiting."

The following Thursday night in rained. The next day Edie entertained the boys by showing them how to make mud pies. Of course, they were a mess when they were finished. She helped them bathe and change into clean clothes. Mr. Steinbeck came home early and took the boys to a baseball game in Davenport. Mrs. Steinbeck stayed home. Edie asked if she could get off early. With no children, Mrs. Steinbeck said okay.

Edie boarded the trolley and headed for the south end of town. As she neared the station, she noticed south end Muscatine was not as nice as Mulberry Avenue. The houses were neat, but small. Most had outdoor privies. The streets were mainly dirt and now muddy. On the corners were groups of men standing and smoking. She stepped from the trolley and cautiously walked toward the Roach & Musser plant. It was a little before five. The men would be quitting soon.

She stood across the street from an entrance. A man with a scruffy beard came up to her and asked, "Are looking for someone, Miss?"

"Yes, Sean O'Keefe."

The man put his hand on his whiskered chin and answered, "O'Keefe, you say? Let me see, he'd be at entrance number six, Miss. You go down two more doors. This is number four. I can walk you down. If you'd like."

Edie started to walk away. He followed. She went a little faster. He quickened his pace.

She turned and faced her follower. "Sir, thank you for your offer, but I can take care of myself."

"Oh, you're a smart little hussy from uptown. You think you're too good for us hard-working men down here. I think maybe you should come with me. I'll show you the way we live down here."

He grabbed her arm and started to pull her away from the plant.

"Please, leave me be, sir. I do not want to go with you."

The man laughed and held on tighter. He started to her drag her. Edie hit him with her purse. He laughed harder. He grabbed her dress and tugged at the neck. He pulled several buttons loose. She struggled even more. He put his hand on her chest and grabbed some fabric. His strong hand tore her blouse open. He leered at her underwear.

Edie screamed, "Help! Help!" A big ugly hand covered her mouth.

Several men showed up, but they didn't show any sign of helping. They cheered the man doing the stripping. Dragging Edie from the street and into an alley, one of them grabbed her light jacket and pulled it off. One grabbed her foot and pulled off her shoe. She kicked and fought, but the men held her tight. The first man tugged her blouse from her shoulders and down to her waist. Another tore at her skirt and ripped it off.

Edie kicked some more, but all it did was to expose her legs from beneath her slip. One of the men said, "I'll get her drawers, you take her top."

Edie felt her underwear being pulled off. Her top was not so easy for the men. One of them pulled out a pocketknife to start a tear. Two others grabbed it and tore it away. Now she was naked. Her first attacker started to unbuckle his trousers.

Suddenly, a wild, red-haired man came out of nowhere. He punched the man unbuckling his pants. He kicked two others. Fists and feet were flying. The fight fell into the street. Two men ran away. A third limped away holding his hand over his crotch. Another had a bloody nose.

The last man, the man who first attacked Edie, said, "O'Keefe, I'm sorry." But it was too late. A big fist caught him square in the jaw. The man fell over a garbage can. The red-haired man stood over him as he struggled to gain his footing.

"Get out of here and never come back. You're fired. If you don't believe me, I'm reporting you to Mr. Roach."

The red headed man turned and looked at the shattered young woman standing in the shadows trying to cover herself with her torn dress.

He went to her and said, "Miss, I'm sorry this happened, but you shouldn't be here by yourself. Some of these men are ruffians. They work all week and have all weekend to spend their pay. Most haven't had a woman for a long time. All they get is the girls in the back of the bars and that ain't much."

It was Edie who recognized Sean first.

"Sean, Sean, it's me Edie. I came to see you."

"Edie! Why? This is no place for you. Come let's go to my room. Quick, before those hoodlums come back."

Sean took off his shirt and wrapped it around Edie. They gathered her one shoe, one stocking, and picked up her scattered clothes. As he recovered her jacket, he noticed the gang he had just whipped was reforming. This time they would have clubs and stones. He would be no match for them. He rolled her clothes into a ball and swooped her up, carrying her down the alley toward his apartment. He could hear the gang shouting and cursing. When he reached the backyard where he was living, he saw his landlady dumping her dishpan water from the back porch.

He hollered, "Olga, open the door. I've got to get in."

Olga looked at Sean carrying a girl and a bundle of rags. She quickly turned and opened the door. She could see the gang turning in her backyard gate. She slammed the door after Sean. She didn't follow them inside, but she grabbed her broom and held it up as the five men approached.

"You boys had better turn around and head back before I call the cops."

"Now, Olga, you don't need to do that. We meant no harm. We were having some fun with the girl."

"Yeah, I bet. If Sean hadn't come along, you'd still be having fun, wouldn't you, and I know what kind of fun you'd have. You're just a bunch of hoodlums. You have your fun with those women down at the flop house. Now git!"

The ruffians dispersed. They threw down their sticks and stones in Olga's yard. She came down from her porch and hollered, "Oh no you don't. You pick up those sticks and rocks and take them with you."

She swung her broom at the last man and hit in him the head. Despite her small size, she had a lot of spunk. The men recovered their weapons and sulked away. Olga returned to her kitchen.

A distraught Edie sat on a chair. Sean had wrapped a blanket around her shoulders.

"My lord, girl. You're lucky to be alive. Where are your clothes?"

Edie pointed to the pile on the floor.

"Sean, do you know this girl?"

"Yes, Olga, she's a friend of mine. She works uptown and was trying to find me. She was alone, and the hoodlums took advantage of her. I got there in the nick of time. You see, they stripped her."

Edie's emotions started to take over. She began to sob. Her body ached and trembled. "I just wanted to see you, Sean."

"I understand, honey, but you can't be down here without a man. Young women are an easy target, especially those from uptown."

Olga raised her eyebrows and asked, "Did I just hear you call her honey?"

"Yes, Olga, we're more than just friends. Edie and I have dated several times. I thought we might get married someday until I found out from her brother her father didn't want his daughter dating or marrying a Catholic. Because I'm Catholic, I tried to break it off. I know families are important because I don't' have any brothers or sisters. I see my parents occasionally. They live on East Hill. I didn't want her to lose her family just because she thinks she loves me."

Edie blurted out, "But I do love you, Sean. It's my Dad who can't see it."

Olga replied in her Polish brogue, "That's the silliest idea I ever heard. I was Catholic and my husband was Lutheran. It caused some commotion at first, but my folks were still in Poland. My priest scolded me, but what does he know about true love? I changed. I know many who have turned Catholic. They have great families. I say it doesn't matter, as long you both are of the same faith. There are many roads to heaven and God doesn't care which one you take."

"I never thought of it that way. Maybe God does have a plan for us. You are very wise, Olga," said Sean.

Olga turned to Edie. "Now, young lady, we have to get you cleaned up and find you some clothes to go home in. Where do you live?"

"I live out by Pleasant Prairie, but I work in town as a nanny for the Steinbeck's on Mulberry."

"Steinbeck, Mulberry, Good land young lady, no wonder those hoodlums attacked you. They like nothing better than harm a girl from uptown."

Olga sorted through Edie's clothes. They were all soiled at different degrees. Her skirt and her jacket were just lightly soiled. Her blouse and underwear were the worst because the men had dumped them into a muddy puddle and stepped on them. Her under slip was torn badly. As for Edie herself, her legs and arms were splattered with mud.

Olga barked at Sean, "You draw some water from the cistern. Get enough for the washtub and the bathtub. You can wash her clothes on the porch while I give her a bath. I'll fire up the stove. You, young lady, will have to shed that shirt. I'll go get my housecoat for you to wear until the water is hot. Sean, no peeking either."

Sean smiled at his landlady as he went out to draw the water. Olga scurried into her downstairs bedroom. Edie sat and unbuttoned Sean's shirt slowly. Olga had ordered her to take it off, but Sean had not returned with the water. She stood and was about to shed his shirt when Sean opened the door. He had two buckets of water. He placed them on the stove.

"I'll be back with the cold, so don't take that shirt off yet," he said with a smile.

"I'm sorry, Sean. I didn't mean to bring you any trouble. I just wanted to see you," Edie told him with tears forming in her eyes.

Olga appeared and saw Edie with the open shirt.

"My land, girl, button up, Sean is still here. He'll see you bare. Here, put this on, "Olga ordered as she handed Edie her robe, "Sean, get out of here.

Bring me some more wood. The stove needs more. You'll need very hot water for her clothes. Did you bring in the tub?"

"Yes, ma'am, it's right behind the table."

"Okay, while we wait for the water to heat, I'm making us some coffee. Do you drink coffee, girl?"

"Her name is Edie, Olga."

"Okay, do you?"

"Not really, but I sure could use some right now. I'm becoming a little chilled."

Olga made a pot of coffee while they waited. Sean suggested Edie call Mrs. Steinbeck. It was getting dark and she might be worried. Edie agreed and went to the phone. It was mounted high on the wall. Edie stretched up. Olga's short house coat rose above her knees. Olga quickly rose and stood in front of Edie. Both Sean and Edie smiled at each other. Olga quickly brought a small stool for her to stand on. Edie gave the crank two healthy turns. The bells clanged.

"Hello, Central, would you connect me with the Samuel Steinbeck residence? Thank you. Hello, Mrs. Steinbeck, this is Edie. I'm all right . . . I'm at Olga Kerchinske's. She owns the house where Sean lives . . . I had a little problem with some men while looking for Sean. My clothes got dirty. Mrs. Kerchinske is washing them . . . She and Sean think I should stay here tonight . . . I'll be there in the morning . . . I know, Mrs. Steinbeck, I shouldn't have come down here alone. I won't do it again. Please don't tell Daddy."

Edie hung the ear piece up. Olga tested the water with her elbow. It was ready. Sean poured a bucketful into the tub. He took the other bucket outside to his tub. Olga locked the door behind him and pulled the curtains shut.

Edie chided her. "You don't have to do that, Olga. Sean won't peek."

Olga replied, "I'm not so sure. Men will be men. They like to look at young ladies. Especially when they are bare. Now you get in the tub and test the water."

Edie slipped out of the housecoat and stepped in. She grimaced and held one foot high. Olga poured in some cold water. Soon Edie was satisfied. She sat down in the tub. Olga dipped a pan in the water and poured it over her head. She grabbed the soap and washed Edie's back. Edie held her long hair up. Olga handed her some liquid soap for her hair. Edie enjoyed the attention. It had been a long time since she had a bath in a wash tub. Olga poured many pans of water over her head to rinse her hair.

"My, you have beautiful hair, Edie. I used to have beautiful hair like that, but that was years ago. Now all I have is this dingy gray. I wish I could afford to go to a salon like the rich women."

"Maybe I could wash your hair with some of Mrs. Steinbeck's shampoo. I'll ask her if I could buy some tomorrow. Now I better get out before I turn into a prune."

Edie stood up and Olga gave her a towel. She dried herself and put Olga's house coat on. Soon Sean knocked on the door. He had the washing finished. Olga knew Edie's clothes would not dry outside, so she hung them behind the cook stove.

"They should be dry by morning," she announced, "Now what are we going to find for Edie to wear until then? She can't go around just wearing my housecoat. I've got some old night gowns I haven't worn for years. Edie, come with me and you can pick something out."

Edie followed Olga into her bedroom. Olga opened her closet. It was packed with dresses and tops and skirts. Edie was surprised at the volume of clothes.

"Where did you get all these clothes, Olga?"

Olga smiled. "My first husband and I could not have any children, so we traveled a lot. He was a buyer for R &M. When he went on a business trip, I went with him. I accumulated a very nice wardrobe. He died in an accident at a logging camp in Wisconsin. My second husband worked for R & M as a floor manager. He had a drinking problem which finally killed him. All he left me was this house. But I still had all these clothes and nowhere to go. You may pick anything you want."

Edie picked through the closet. She laid out what she thought she needed to get through the night. While searching she found a very sheer negligee. She pulled it out and held it up.

"My, my, Olga, this is quite racy."

"Yes, I know, I had a good time with my first husband. He liked me to wear sexy things. Our home was out in the country and nobody could watch what we did. Here, try it on."

Edie slipped on the negligee. It was very revealing.

"It fits me to a tee. I wish Sean could see me."

Olga smiled and said, "I tell you what, if you and Sean ever marry, I'll give it to you for a wedding present. For now, you'd better wear something more conservative. You hurry and get dressed while I make up the upstairs spare bedroom."

Edie found a cotton gown and a slip that fit. She dressed and met Sean and Olga in the front room. They opened the windows to let the evening breeze in. They talked about Olga's varied life. She related her stories and how she met her misters. Her first marriage although childless was fascinating with her world travels. She lived in a middle-class luxury. Her second husband was not great. What he earned at work, he drank at the corner tavern. He did provide a house and money for food. Olga worked at Rinks' Grocery on Oregon Street. She still filled in there when they were short of help. It was Sean's income from her upstairs apartment which allowed her to live comfortably. Edie and Sean just listened to the older woman.

When the old clock struck ten, it signaled time for bed. Olga showed Edie her room. It was small with a sloped ceiling. The bed wasn't more than a cot with a mattress. There were hooks on the back of the door to hang clothes. Olga not only had her bed turned down, but there was a nightie lying on it and some worn slippers sitting on a small stool.

"I hope you like the gown I picked out for you. It's an old one but comfortable." she told her.

"I'll be fine, Olga. I think I'll make a trip to the privy before I turn in."

"I'm sorry I don't have indoor plumbing like you're used to uptown."

"Oh, Olga, I'm a farm girl. We didn't get indoor plumbing until four years ago. I know about outdoor facilities. It doesn't bother me."

Sean and Olga waited in the kitchen while Edie went outside.

Sean commented to Olga, "I'm amazed how well Edie is holding up after her ordeal this afternoon. I'm not a woman, but that would have drove me crazy."

"Me, too. I would have died on the spot. She's an amazing girl."

"That she is, Olga, that she is!"

Edi returned. She blew Sean a kiss when she was behind Olga's back.

Olga looked at Sean. She caught his eyes as Edie passed.

She said, "Now you two young'uns behave upstairs. I'll have no hanky-panky in my house. I'm right below Edie's room, so I can hear everything."

"Don't worry, Olga, we'll be good," Sean reassured her.

As soon as Edie disappeared upstairs, Sean headed to the necessary house. He knew Olga always liked to be last. By ten thirty, Olga turned out the lights. The only light in the house came from the street light just outside. The evening breeze softly blew the curtains. The only sound was the distant clang of the trolley bell, four blocks away.

The clock struck twelve. Edie screamed. "No! No! Leave me alone. Help! Help! Please, somebody, help me!"

Sean scrambled from his bed and ran to her room. Edie was sitting up, flailing her arms. Sean caught her arms and pinned them against her side. He held her close. Edie began to cry. She dug her fingers into Sean's arms. He tried to calm her. She was shaking so much it was difficult to hold her. Soon he could hear Olga coming up the stairs.

"My land, what is going on?" she said as she appeared in the doorway, her tiny bent body outlined by the light from outside.

"I think Edie just had a nightmare. I'll just stay with her until she calms down. I guess the attack was traumatic after all."

"My mother used to give me warm milk and honey when I couldn't sleep. It worked every time. I'll go down and fix some right away."

Olga hurried downstairs. Sean held his shaking Edie. She felt warm against him, so vulnerable, so alone. He knew she was the woman for him. Her father might not approve, but eventually he would win. He would never give up.

Olga returned with the warm milk. She whispered to Sean, "I put a little Jack Daniel's in it. Just don't tell her."

Sean nodded. He helped Edie sip the mixture. It seemed to calm her. Olga waited beside Sean. Finally, she put her hand on his bare shoulder and said, "I think she will be all right now. You stay with her till she is asleep. I'm going back to bed. If you need me, just call."

"Okay, Olga."

Sean caressed Edie's hair as he held her. The milk seemed to be working. Her grip on his arm lessened. He laid her down on the bed. The gown Olga had given her was old and thin. It was an expensive gown when it was new because there were lacy cutouts and trim. Edie's skin showed through the lace.

Sean studied her. She stirred a bit. He touched her hand, and she calmed. He was having a difficult time leaving her side, but he knew he shouldn't stay there all night. He pulled the light blanket to her chin and left. He made sure both doors were open. She was quiet for another four hours. This time she didn't scream, but he could hear her sobbing.

He tiptoed back, trying not to awaken Olga. This time he found Edie sitting on the edge of her bed, her head in her hands. Sean knelt in front of her.

"How may I help you?" he whispered.

"I don't know, Sean. It was so awful. What will I tell my Dad? He'll find out someday."

"You tell him the truth. The truth is always the best. He'll be angry, but he'll get over it. Just remember, I'll always be here for you. I'll support you. I'll do whatever you want."

"Right now, I want you to hold me. Would you sleep with me?"

"I can hold you, but I'm afraid Olga wouldn't approve of me sleeping with you if she found out. I love the old lady and I would not want to get on her wrong side. You saw how she stood up to those outlaws."

He helped her stand up and embraced her tightly. Her body was soft against his chest. He placed his hands on her back, so smooth and soft. She stood on her tiptoes, moved her arms around his neck, and laid her head on his chest. He lifted her, so she could stand on the bed. They stood face to face. Edie kissed Sean on his mouth and worked her tongue inside. Passion was starting to show. The cot creaked.

Did Olga hear it? They waited for a call, but all they could hear was the breeze rustling the leaves on the elm tree outside. Soon they heard Olga snoring. They were safe

Edie gazed into Sean's eyes. He gazed back. Edie was beautiful. Her hair hung over her shoulders and almost covered her bosom. He brushed her long hair from her chest behind her shoulders. Edie untied the satin bow on the bodice of her gown. The ribbon opened and revealed the curve of her lovely breasts. Sean was about to open the gap further when Olga's alarm clock exploded downstairs. They looked at each other and almost laughed. Olga's clock caught them in the nick of time.

"Tie up my gown so I can go downstairs first. I need to go to the privy anyway. While I'm distracting her, you can get back to your room."

Sean gladly tied the loosen satin ribbon and tiptoed to his room. She slipped into Olga's slippers for the trip outside. When she returned, Olga was at the stove fixing breakfast. Olga turned when she heard the door shut.

She took one look at Edie and exclaimed, "My land, girl, did you go outside just in that?"

Edie replied, "Yes, is there something wrong with it?"

"Girl, you're in the city now, not the wide-open country. People can see you in your nightie and that nightie is so thin you might as well be wearing nothing. Look at you when you stand in the sunlight."

Edie looked down at her legs. She was a bit risqué. If she was home, no one would notice.

"I'll try and remember next time." She smiled a guilty smile at the old lady. "I'll grab my clothes and head up to change."

"I heard some commotion upstairs around five. Was there a problem?"

"Yes and no. I had another anxiety attack, but it wasn't bad. Sean came in and calmed me. He stayed there until he heard your alarm telling us it was time to get up."

"Oh. I heard the bed creak, and thought maybe there was some trouble."

"Nope! It was just Sean. He stubbed his toe on the stool and fell against the bed. I didn't know he could cuss."

Edie went behind the stove and gathered her clothes. She was about to head up the narrow stairs when Olga called out, "You'll need some new buttons on that blouse. Leave it here. I'll see if I can find some in my sewing basket. You can wear my housecoat until then."

"Okay, Olga. I'll leave it on this chair."

Sean was coming down. She winked at him as they passed and mouthed, "I love you." Sean just smiled.

"Good morning, Olga," he said. "I hope you could get back to sleep after that little escapade last night."

"Oh, yes. Edie tells me you had to return a little later."

"Yes, ma'am, I just stayed there by her bed until dawn. I'm a little tired this morning."

His answer seemed to satisfy Olga. She returned to her task of fixing breakfast. Fifteen minutes later, Edie came down fully dressed except for her top. Her hair needed some more work, but without her brush and comb she was limited. After they finished breakfast, Sean and Edie washed the dishes while Olga sewed on new buttons. They didn't match, but they were better than no buttons at all.

It was time for Edie to return to the Steinbeck's and maybe go home. She thanked Olga for her kindness and hoped they would meet again. Sean decided he would ride the trolley all the way up Mulberry Avenue. He wanted to make sure Edie would be safe. As he walked her to the door of the Steinbeck home, Mrs. Steinbeck met them.

"Edie, Edie, I was worried sick. Sam was going to come and get you. He's heard terrible stories about young women walking alone in the south end. There are some men down there who prey on them. Thank goodness for your Sean. When you called and said he had taken you to his place, I was so relieved."

"It was so scary. Sean came to my rescue. I'm so glad he lived so close. The real reason I didn't come back was those men."

Mrs. Steinbeck gasped. "I knew there was something bad."

Edie continued, "They grabbed me and dragged me into an alley. Sean arrived. The man who was holding me dropped me. Unfortunately, it was right into a mud puddle. I was a mess. His landlady, Olga Kerchinske, washed my clothes—well, really Sean washed my clothes. Olga helped me bathe. I wore one of her nighties and a housecoat until this morning."

"Do you think you should go home? Sam took the boys fishing with one of his partners. They won't be back until late Sunday. Why don't you come back Monday?"

"Oh, thank you, Mrs. Steinbeck. I'll comb my tangled hair and go home. Maybe it's time I face my Dad. My brother told me, my mother is very depressed."

Edie hurried to her room to repair her unkempt hair. Sean waited at the door.

"You may come in, Sean. I won't bite," Mrs. Steinbeck told him.

"Thank you, ma'am. I thought I should make sure Edie gets on the Interurban properly."

"Sean, you are such a nice young man. Have you lived in Muscatine long?"

"No, ma'am, just six years. I worked at a sandstone quarry near New Era for Bruce and Pete McKillip. My dad managed the quarry. "

"Is your father still around?"

"Yes, he works at Huttig Button works. Mom cooks at a downtown café."

Edie came waltzing back into the room.

"I'm ready to go. If I hurry, I can make the ten-thirty car. Good-bye, Mrs. Steinbeck. See you Monday."

"Have a good time at home, Edie, and Sean, you can stop by anytime. The boys love you."

"I will someday. They are a sharp pair of young men."

Sean rode with Edie to the station. Just before she entered the train car, Sean told her he would be leaving on a long buying trip for the company. He was leaving Wednesday and would be gone for three months. His boss was sending him to Idaho, Wyoming, and Colorado. Edie didn't have time to comment for the Interurban was leaving. They kissed and the Interurban pulled away. Edie waved from the window for as long as she could see Sean.

She was lucky at the Melpine station, Mr. Watts was there picking up Ruth's cousin, Edna. He gave her a ride home. Her mother was surprised when Edie walked in the door. She hugged her and then held her away at arm's length. She noticed the buttons on her blouse didn't match. She said nothing. The pair chatted and prepared dinner for the men. Ralph was happy to see Edie at home. Her father welcomed her, but he said little. It was Saturday. The men quit early. The hay, what there was of it, was made, the corn had recovered and had been cultivated once. Ralph went to a dance in Blue Grass. Edie, Hattie and Frank sat on the front porch.

"How's your job going?" asked Frank.

"Oh, fine, Daddy. Sometimes it's boring and sometimes it is fun. The boys are such little devils."

They chatted about the neighbors and the relatives. Her father never asked about Sean. Edie wasn't about to bring the subject up. About ten, the mosquitoes drove them inside. Edie claimed she was tired and went to bed. Her parents followed a short time later. Ralph would wander home after midnight.

It was around two in the morning when Hattie heard Edie scream. It was a blood-curdling scream. "Stop, stop. Help me! Help me! Please someone help me!"

Hattie jumped out of bed and ran to her room. She found Edie sitting up, wringing wet with sweat. Hattie sat on the edge of her bed and held her. Her father and brother came to the door and stood watching. They, too, had been awakened by Edie's screams. Hattie looked at them.

"You two men go back to bed. I'll take care of Edie."

Ralph left, but Frank didn't leave, but stood just outside in the hall. He wanted to eavesdrop on Edie and her mother.

Hattie held her daughter and asked, "Edie, tell me all about this dream. What made your dream so scary?"

Edie quit sobbing and calmed down. She started telling her story.

"There were these awful men, Mommy. They grabbed me and pulled me into an alley. They pulled all my clothes off until I was naked. They were going to rape me. Sean came out of nowhere and beat them off. He saved me."

Hattie spoke quietly, "Where were you when this happened?"

"I was at the plant where Sean works."

Hattie realized Edie was not having a nightmare, but a recurrence of an actual experience.

"This really happened, didn't it, Edie? You were trying to see Sean after your father said you shouldn't. Did these men hurt you?"

"No, because Sean got there before they could. He carried me all the way to Mrs. Kerchinske's house."

Edie continued with the details of her ordeal. Her mother listened quietly. When she finished, Hattie hugged her daughter and said, "We mustn't tell your father. He would be very upset."

Frank quietly slipped back into bed before Hattie came. He pretended to be asleep. The next morning Edie was helping fix breakfast before getting ready for church. Her father sat down as usual and waited for his meal.

"Edie, you gave us quite a scare last night. Are you okay this morning?"

"Yes, Daddy."

"Did you go and see that Irishman this week?"

"No, Daddy."

Frank was quiet for a moment, then he exploded. "You're a liar. You did go see that Catholic. I know you did. I told you never to see him again. You disobeyed me. I'm right. Ain't I?"

Edie was shocked. She looked at her mother. Her mother was also aghast.

Edie started to shake. She had been the recipient of her father's wrath before. When she was a small child he'd spank her, right on her bare bottom.

She stammered, "Yes, Daddy, I went to see Sean."

"I thought so. You disobeyed me again. When will you ever learn? I think you need another spanking."

"No, Frank, she's a grown woman. You're not going to spank her. I forbid it."

Frank turned to Hattie. He was shocked at her response.

"Since when do you tell me what to do?"

"Right now, I guess. I will not have you striking your grown daughter. How did you know she was lying anyway?"

"I heard her tell you last night."

"You were supposed to be in bed, but you didn't go, did you? You spied on us. You ought to be ashamed of yourself. That's just as bad as lying."

"She lied to me and you know it."

"Yes, but you spied. It is the same."

Frank looked at Edie and said, "Edie, go to your room. I'll talk to you later. Your mother and I have to have an understanding."

Edie ran out of the kitchen and upstairs. She closed the door to her room and waited for the dreadful wrath of her father. She could hear a loud argument going on downstairs. Her mother, to Edie's knowledge, had never challenged her father. There was the sound of a crashing chair and a scream from her mother. Edie wanted to go down, but she knew she had to stay put, her Dad's orders. Next, she heard Ralph's voice hollering, "Stop it, Pa! Stop it!" It was followed by a slamming door. Edie watched from her window as her father stormed out to the barn.

"Edie, come down here. Take care of Mom," Ralph called.

Edie hurried to the kitchen and found her mother sitting on a chair. She had a bloody nose and blood dripped from a corner of her mouth. She held an ice pack on the side of her face.

"Pa hit her. You clean her up. I'll go out and talk to Pa."

Ralph never made it to the door because Frank stormed back in and upstairs. They could hear him grumbling and shuffling around upstairs.

"I'll try to talk to him. You take Mom into the front room," Ralph ordered.

Again, before he reached the stairs his father was coming down.

"Pa, stop for a minute. We need to talk."

Frank replied, "Out of my way. I'm going to Muscatine. I have some business to do. Sorry about your mother, I'll deal with her when I come back."

He pushed Ralph aside and hurried outside. He cranked the T and drove away. He wasn't going to tell anyone what he had in mind because they would stop him.

Edie cleaned up her mother. She and Ralph helped her to her bed.

"I'll take care of her from here," she told Ralph, "you go finish chores. We'll discuss this later."

Edie put a wet compress on her mother's face. She helped her change into a dressing gown and lie down. She knew she would have to act quickly to remove the blood stains from her blouse and skirt. All the time, she wondered what was going to happen when her father returned. This was not what she expected when she returned home. It was supposed to be a joyous time not a vicious family argument. She and Ralph were going to have to grow up today and take control of the family. Controlling their father would be a difficult task. His attitude and his ego made him the ruler of his family, but he could become a tyrant. She wondered what he had to do in Muscatine on such a short notice. She would have to wait until he returned.

Frank Mohr drove the T as fast as he could on Highway 22. It was the best gravel road to Muscatine. Entering town at the northeast corner, there was a six-block stretch of the highway shaded by towering elm trees. They were planted by Dr. Weed years ago, thus it was called Weed's Lane. He turned on Washington Street, which would take him across Mad Creek to Isett Avenue. Isett to Eighth, Eighth to Mulberry Avenue. Mulberry was the wealthy family's street. There were huge homes with large lawns. One even had a dance floor attached.

He pulled a piece of paper from his pocket. It read 1802 Mulberry Avenue. He pulled along the curb. The walk to the front door was wide. There were four steps to the porch which fronted the home, plus it went around the south side of the house. He rang the doorbell and waited.

A young lady came to the door. She asked, "May I help you, sir?"

"I would like to speak to Mr. Steinbeck."

"Mr. Steinbeck is not here, but Mrs. Steinbeck is. Would you like to speak with her?"

"Yes, I suppose so."

"May I tell her who is calling?"

"Frank Mohr, Edie Mohr's father."

The young lady disappeared and soon a tall stately woman came to the door. She seemed perturbed at the intrusion.

"Mr. Mohr, I'm Stella Steinbeck. My housekeeper tells me you would like to speak with me."

"Yes, I would. I'm Edie's father and I am here to inform you that Edie will not be returning to Muscatine for work."

Mrs. Steinbeck had a concerned look on her face as she asked, "Is Edie ill?"

"No, she is fine."

"Is there a problem with my children?"

"No."

"Then what is the problem?"

"I do not want Edie to live in this city any longer. There are people here who are a bad influence on her."

"Do you mean Sean? The nice young man she has been seeing?"

"Yes."

"I don't know why you feel that way, Mr. Mohr. He is a fine, hard-working, clean young man. He seems to treat Edie with great respect. I would be proud of my daughter if she dated such a person."

"I appreciate your comments, Mrs. Steinbeck, but this young man you think so highly of is a Catholic. I forbid my daughter or anyone in my family to marry a Catholic. Catholic's are heretics in my mind. My father was a Catholic. In fact, he was an altar boy. He told me the horrible things the priests did to him. He hated his church. That's why. Now, I would appreciate it if you could gather her things and I will take them home to her."

"I do not have time for that, but Katy can do the task for me since I must leave for church. I'll miss Edie. She is such a lovely girl."

Stella turned to go, then stopped.

"I'm wondering, Mr. Mohr, does Edie know you are here? Are you trying to break them up for your prejudices only?"

"That is none of your business, Mrs. Steinbeck. If you don't mind, I'll wait right here for her things."

"Mr. Mohr, I know you will not take my advice or any woman's advice. If Edie and Sean are truly in love, you will not be able to stop them. No matter how hard you may try. Good Day, Mr. Mohr."

With that, she turned and shut the door. Frank stood on the porch and waited. Fifteen minutes later, Katy appeared. She handed Frank a small box with Edie brushes, clothes, and cosmetics.

She tearfully said, "Tell Edie I'm going to miss her."

Frank only nodded. He took the box and headed to his auto. Soon he was out of Muscatine and driving up Highway 22 to home. It was about noon when he pulled up the drive. Ralph was on the porch. Edie was inside fixing dinner of fried chicken, mashed potatoes, and peas. She had her back toward the door when her father walked in.

He set the box he was carrying on the table and said, "Here's your things from Steinbeck's. You are not going to Muscatine again."

Edie turned. She saw the box. She knew what her father had just done.

She screamed, "You didn't?"

Frank answered with a snarl, "I did, and it is for your own good. Someday you'll thank me. Now I don't want you to go to Muscatine without me or your mother with you ever again. Do you understand?"

Edie was furious. She threw the spoon she was holding at him.

"How could you, Father? You have no right."

Frank ducked the flying spoon and raced to Edie. He grabbed her arm.

"I'll teach you to disobey your father. You do as I say. I have all rights until you are an adult and live in my house."

He backed her into the stove and placed her hand on the hot stove top.

Edie screamed a blood curdling scream. Ralph jumped up from his chair on the porch and raced into the house. He could smell the burning fabric and he saw his father holding a frantic Edie's hand on the hot stove.

"Pa! Pa! Stop!" he hollered. He dove at Frank, knocking him into the table. Frank tried to recover, but Ralph laid his shoulder into his body, knocking him to the floor. He held him down.

Hattie heard the screams and came downstairs to find the men wrestling on the floor, Edie holding her burnt hand.

"What's going on?"

"Pa held Edie's hand on the stove. He also held her against the stove. I could smell her dress burning."

Hattie ran to Edie, who was putting her hand in a pan of cold water. Her skirt was not burning but was badly scorched. There was a brown stripe across the back. It wasn't until later Edie discovered the back of her legs had first degree burns.

Hattie looked at her hand. "Rub some butter on it and wrap it in a wet towel."

Hattie turned to the men wrestling on the floor. She could see Ralph had the advantage and Frank was succumbing to his pressure. She put her hand on her son's shoulder and pulled, indicating for him to let his father catch his breath.

She glared at her husband and asked, "How dare you attack our daughter like that? What's come over you? You've taken this Catholic thing way too far. Get out! Get out right now! You can sleep in the wash house. You're not sleeping with me. I'll see that Ralph protects me from you."

"What do you mean? You can't kick me out of my own house!" It was the first Frank had seen his wife since he hit her. She had a black eye and swollen lip. She was in her nightgown and dressing gown.

"Your house! It's my house and my farm and you know it. Helen and I inherited this place. If Helen hadn't married a banker, she might have married a farmer and they would have been farming instead of us. You just remember that. When you come to your senses, we'll talk. Now I must take care of Edie. Get out of here."

Ralph helped his father up. Frank hobbled outside. He knew he was beat. This was the first time Hattie had ever crossed him, but he knew she was right. If it wasn't for her inheritance, he'd be working as a hired hand on some farm or in town. He'd follow orders and bed down in the wash house for tonight.

Everything calmed down the next day. Edie had to work with her hand wrapped in gauze. She was proud of her mother finally standing up to her father. It proved he was all bluff. Maybe someday his heart would soften.

Edie did her best to stay busy. Working at Steinbeck's was so much easier. She had her own life. Her mother allowed Frank to sit with the family for meals, but any time he'd tried to apologize, she'd point to her lip and bruised cheek. She was enjoying her new-found power over her husband.

Edie moped around after she realized Sean would not be back until

September. Her mother tried to console her. Ralph also tried to console his sister, while trying to run a conversation between his parents. The lack of Sean calmed Frank's rhetoric and hatred. He slept in the wash house for six nights before a rainy cold night drove him to beg to come inside. Hattie agreed, but made him sleep in the guest room where Sean had slept. It would be a long time before Hattie allowed him back into her bed.

CHAPTER 7: PETE RE-APPEARS

The Fourth of July holiday was on a Monday. It would be a three-day holiday. Ralph wanted Edie to come with Ruth and him to a Saturday night dance. She refused saying she would feel like a fifth wheel. Sunday morning everyone but Ralph headed for church services at Melpine Methodist. The pastor was in a patriotic mood. He praised the efforts of President Wilson for keeping the United States out of the terrible war in Europe.

In the afternoon, Aunt Helen and Uncle Bill dropped in unexpectantly. Ralph volunteered Edie and he to do the milking, so Frank and Bill could talk. Uncle Bill liked Frank for his farm business knowledge, but not his family management. He asked Frank if he thought tractors were the future of agriculture. Frank told him he thought tractors were here to stay, but it was a few years off. Most farmers couldn't afford to buy the machines. He suggested Uncle Bill's bank start becoming more liberal with their money and start loaning to farmers. With this war, there would be a need for more food. Bill agreed.

"I don't believe we can stay neutral much longer." Bill added, "The Germans have already sunk the Lusitania. Since then there had been five American ships sunk by the infamous U-boats."

The two sisters stayed in the kitchen and fixed a nice supper. It was nearly six -thirty when Edie and Ralph finished chores. They both smelled awful.

"You two hit the shower before you come to the table," ordered Hattie.

"I'm first," Edie called out.

She headed down the stairs. She was back up in a few minutes wrapped in a towel.

Aunt Helen gasped, "Don't you know your Uncle Bill is right outside, child? Get upstairs in a hurry."

Edie giggled a bit. Aunt Helen was always a bit of a prude. According to her, women were not to show their arms or legs. *No wonder they never had any children,* she thought. She dashed upstairs, not wanting to upset her rich aunt. She hurriedly dressed and piled her hair in a bun. At seven they all sat down for supper.

It was after nine before the relatives left in their Cadillac. Uncle Bill loved his expensive autos. He had to drive all the way to Davenport to purchase this one.

Monday dawned as a beautiful day. It would be the usual Fourth of July. It was also reunion day for the Mohr family at Weed Park. Frank was the youngest of six. He had three older brothers and two sisters. Most of their children were married and had children. Ralph and Edie were also the youngest of the cousins.

Grandpa Mohr went to the park early and reserved several tables and possibly a shelter. The rest of the family showed up after the big parade downtown. There were relatives everywhere, babies crying, little boys chasing little girls. The women busied themselves by setting the tables and spreading blankets on the ground. The men pulled up folding chairs and sat in a circle. It was after twelve before every plate was set. Grandpa said grace and the procession to the big spread began. First the children, then the few teens, followed by the men and last the women. In less than an hour, everyone was full. It was time to clean up the dishes and pack them away for the trip home. Maybe at four, there would be extra pie or cake.

Ralph and Edie were bored. The action in the park was down by the bandstand. Ralph told his mother he and Edie would be back to say goodbye to all the family. They wandered down to the bandstand. The Muscatine Municipal Band was playing marches. Ralph and Edie walked around until they spied a bench in the shade. They were still bored, but they could people watch.

"I wonder what Sean is doing today?" asked Edie of her brother.

"I'd say he is sitting in a bar sipping some whiskey."

"Sean doesn't drink alcohol. He told me it was killing his father."

"Listen, Edie, forget about Sean. I know he is a great guy, but you can't marry him. Pa won't allow it."

"Dad is wrong. He is old fashioned and prejudiced. I'll just wait until I'm older, then I can do what I want."

"Okay, Sis, but be careful and remember I warned you. Say, let's change the subject. I'm thirsty. How about a Coke? They have a lot of drinks over at the refreshment stand."

"Do they have sarsaparilla? I don't like Coke."

"I am sure they do. You stay put and I'll get some."

Ralph left Edie fanning herself as the day was becoming quite warm. She closed her eyes to relax. She didn't see the young man approaching her bench.

"Pardon me, Miss, but may I share this bench with you?"

Edie opened her eyes and there was a handsome young man dressed in an expensive suit. His dark hair was slicked down and he had a very nice smile.

She answered, "Why, yes." She eyed the man and was a little wary of him. She continued, "My boyfriend is getting some drinks, but there is plenty of room for all of us."

The man sat and commented, "Your boyfriend is a lucky guy to have such a lovely girlfriend."

"Thank you, kind sir."

"Pete McKillip is my name. What's yours?"

"Pete McKillip! The Pete McKillip from Patterson School?"

Pete stared at the young woman and exclaimed, "Edie Mohr! The Edie Mohr from third grade to sixth of Patterson School. Well, how about that. You look as cute as when you were my classmate, but now all grown up."

"You've grown some since I saw you last. How are you?'

Ralph returned and saw Pete.

"Pete McKillip, what brings you to the park?"

Pete looked up and replied, "Ralph Mohr, fancy meeting you here. I just sat down with your lovely ....ah....girlfriend."

"Girlfriend! She's my sister."

"Ralph, he already knows that. I just wasn't going to let any Tom, Dick, or Harry sit here."

The trio talked over old times for a while. It had been four or five years since they had seen each other.

Pete asked "May I change the subject? Are you going to the fireworks tonight?"

"No." they both answered.

Would you like to go tonight?" Pete asked.

"Sure," both siblings answered.

"Listen, if you can have your chores done by seven, I'll stop by and pick both of you up. Ralph, don't you date Ruth Watts?"

"Yeah."

Why don't you call her and see if she would join us? She lives on the way to town."

"Sounds peachy. Come on, Edie, let's ask Pa if we can go home early and start chores."

The trio headed back to the Mohr Reunion shelter.

Edie held back as Ralph approached her father. Her relationship with him was still cool.

"Dad, we met Pete McKillip over by the bandstand. He asked Edie and me if we wanted to go to the fireworks tonight. Is it alright for her and I to leave early and do chores. Edie said she'd help with milking."

"I don't care, but I don't want to leave right now."

"I'll drive them home right now, Mr. Mohr," said Pete.

Frank agreed. He would enjoy a vacation from chores, especially when he could visit with his family longer.

They walked to Pete's car about three blocks away. Ralph rode in front with Pete. They made it home in thirty minutes. On the way home, Ralph asked Pete to stop at Ruth's.   Her mother okayed the venture. Ruth would be ready at seven. Pete dropped off Edie and Ralph, then headed home.

"I'll do the hogs first. It's too early for the cows to come in. We'd have to drive them all the way. You do the chicken chores."

"I'll fire up the water heater before I start. That way we will have plenty of hot water for showers."

Edie stripped off her skirt and blouse. She stood in front of the mirror. If she wore her underwear she'd smell like the cows she would be milking. She stripped to the buff and pulled on just her skirt and peasant blouse. She hurried to the hen house and fed the chickens, hunted the eggs, and watered the pullets. She could see the cows starting to wander in from the pasture.

"I'll get the cows," she called to Ralph.

The sun was bearing down. It was humid and hot. Her blouse became soaked with sweat. It clung to her skin. The cows were not ready to be milked today.

"What a day to be stubborn," she said to herself. She pulled her wet blouse away from her skin to let what little breeze there was cool her.

The cows entered the barn. It was stifling. The cows kept swishing their tails to chase the flies. The ends on those tails were not clean. They were tainted with greenish brown manure. Her blouse and skirt were spattered and streaked. Ralph sensed her weariness as she leaned against the wall.

"Wow! I'll have to take a shower before I take a shower," she laughed. "Do you suppose the outside shower is warm enough?"

"I'm sure it is. Just don't use all the water. I need some, too."

Edie scurried out of the barn. She headed for the outside shower, as the men called it. It was a barrel perched on the roof of the wash house. A short hose with a trip valve was attached to a shower head. The shower taker stood on a wooden pallet. The site was surrounded by a bridal wreath hedge and two lilac bushes. This provided some privacy. Showering outside was a new experience for Edie. It was so much better than showering in the darken basement.

Ralph finished the chores and showered. He reached his room but knocked on Edie's door before entering.

"Are you decent?" he asked.

"Sure, I've got some clothes on."

Ralph opened the door to find Edie in her slip combing her hair. She glanced over at the door and could see Ralph wearing only a towel. He had a piece of tissue on his cheek.

"Did you cut yourself?"

"Yeah, shaving."

"You shave? Why you must have grown up right before my eyes," she said with a sparkle in her eyes.

"I wanted to tell you we have just forty-five minutes."

"I'll be ready."

Thirty minutes later Ralph hollered up the stairs, "You got fifteen minutes. Hurry up!"

"I said I'll be ready."

At five to seven, Ralph heard Edie coming down the stairs. His sister was dressed in a crisp white blouse with a dainty upright collar encircling her neck. Over the blouse was a blue check gingham pinafore. She had her hair piled on her head with a straw hat pinned snugly. She even had some lipstick on which she had to borrow from her mother's dresser.

"Wow! You look stunning. I wish we weren't brother and sister," he gushed.

"Thank you, dear brother. I hope Pete likes it, too."

"Oh, I'm sure he will," Ralph answered.

They heard a car coming up the lane. Pete was right on time. Ralph jumped into the front seat across from Pete. Edie crawled into the back seat. They pulled into the Watts farmyard five minutes later. Ruth came running out. She started to join Edie in the back seat when Pete said, "Ralph, why don't you ride with Ruth and let Edie ride up here with me."

Ralph thought a short minute, then agreed. He hopped out and crawled in the back next to his girlfriend. The couples arrived at the Muscatine river front around seven thirty.

"Let's go for some rides," said Pete.

They rode the carousel and the Ferris wheel. The fireworks would not start until nine o'clock. They visited the sideshow with the fat lady and the bearded lady. There were several booths giving out prizes if you won the game.

Ralph knew Pete from summer baseball. He was a left fielder until he broke his leg, when he moved to the pitching mound and found his position.

"Hey, Pete, why don't you win a bear for Edie. You're a really good pitcher. Why not knock those bottles into the next county?"

"Okay, I'll give it a try." Pete answered.

He fired two balls and every bottle, but one fell. He fired the last one and hit it squarely. The bottle fell. Edie won her bear.

Ralph was next. He tried three times before Ruth got her bear.

It was nearing nine o'clock. The fireworks would start soon. Pete walked over to the hotel. He came back with a blanket.

"Did you buy the blanket just for us?" asked Edie.

"No," Pete replied, "I have a friend who works there. He let me use it for tonight. I'll take it back later."

The two couples spread their blanket on the grass in Riverview Park. They sat down to watch the explosions. They stopped at Wintermute's ice cream shop for a malt before leaving town.

Ralph walked Ruth to the door. She gave him a peck on the cheek. No more wrap around hugs or deep kisses. Edie was amazed. The next stop was the Mohrs. Ralph was out in a jiffy. Pete ran around and opened Edie's door.

"Thank you for the nice time, Pete," Edie said.

Pete paused and asked, "Would you like to go to the Dance in the Woods over at Paul's timber? It's next Saturday night."

"Sure. I haven't been to a dance in a long time."

"Good. The only thing is that it is canceled if it rains. It's too muddy on the path back there. See you about seven."

The week was short. Edie told her mother of her plans. She gave her the okay, but warned, "Watch out for this Pete McKillip. I've heard stories about him and they are not good."

"Mom, I've known Pete since third grade. He's okay."

"Well, the ladies at church say he's likes to pet and has very active hands. They claim Carrie Fuller's her mother found both of them naked in the barn one night. I also heard stories of he and girl going swimming in the nude. There are other stories and none of them good. So be careful."

"Mom, Pete has money and a lot of girlfriends. Most of his escapades are rumors or men stories. All young guys like to brag. It's their nature. Don't worry I can defend myself."

Saturday afternoon at four a thunderstorm rolled through Muscatine County. It rained three inches in about an hour. Edie remembered Sean and the storm on Declaration Day. She had tried to forget him, but she couldn't. Pete hadn't called so she figured the dance was still on. She finished her chores and dressed for the dance. She was excited to do something other than sit home at night. Ralph was usually not there and her father just read the newspaper and grunted. Precisely at seven, Pete arrived in his maroon Studebaker Six. She met him at the door with a big smile.

"Sorry, the dance is canceled. I drove by the road to the woods and there was a sign saying it would be postponed until next week. I thought I'd come this far so why not go over and see Edie . Is that okay?"

Edie frowned. She was hoping for a dance or a ride in his automobile.

She answered, "Sure. Dad and Ralph are on the porch. I'll fix some lemonade and cookies. Go on out."

Pete went through the house to the porch. Edie and her mother fixed the drinks and cookies. When they got to the porch, they found the men engrossed in a lively conversation about tractors and cattle. The women put down the trays and found their place in the swing. They listened to the conversation. Pete was doing most of the talking.

"You know, McCormick has this new rig out. It's called a 15-30. That's fifteen-horse pulling power and thirty-horse belt power. It will pull a 2-14 plow like slicing through butter. My dad ordered three of them. McCormick also makes a 10-20 for smaller farms. I also read about a new company in Moline. They are working with a company in Minneapolis. They produce wheat country tractors and want to get into the Midwest market. You ought to get one for your farm, Ralph."

Ralph looked at his father. His father was smiling. Ralph said, "I don't know, they are pretty expensive."

Frank entered the conversation by asking, "What does your father think of the Wallis 14-30 machines? I heard they are quite reliable."

"Don't know much about them, Mr. Mohr. I guess they are okay."

Frank smiled at his son and said, "Well, I just ordered a 14-30 Wallis from Dickey's in Durant. It should be here next week."

His statement caught Ralph by surprise.

"You bought a tractor, Pa? I didn't know that."

"Well, I figured we'll be needing one soon when you are farming with me."

"That's great, Mr. Mohr. I'll bet if you have one, you'll get another. Horses are on their way out."

It was nine thirty before the men stopped talking. Edie and Hattie replenished the drinking glasses and the cookies several times.

Hattie rose from the swing and said to Frank, "It is time to go to bed."

Frank pulled out his pocket watch and replied, "It's only 9:45."

"I don't care. It's time to go to bed. Now come along. You too, Ralph."

"But, Mom."

"He came over to talk with you and all you men did was talk tractors. Now, come along. I am sure Pete must go home soon, too."

The Mohr men caught her drift and said their good nights. Pete rose to sit by Edie on the swing. He put his arm around her shoulders. Edie slid closer to him. He patted her arm and moved in to her face. Edie turned away.

"Not now," she told him. "This is only our first date."

Pete was dismayed but moved away. They sat and swung a bit. The conversation was awkward. Finally, Pete said, "It's late. I believe I should be going. I was going to tell you earlier, but I'm going on the show tour for my dad this Wednesday. I won't be able to go to the dance next weekend."

"Show tour? What's a show tour?"

"My dad shows cattle all over Iowa. He has a herdsman, but I help at the fairs. Dad just stands around and shoots the bull with the guys around the ring. That's how his sells his breeding stock. I go to Cedar Rapids' Hawkeye Downs, first, then to the Cedar County Fair, then the Mississippi Valley Fair, then we skip a week before the West Liberty Fair and finally the State Fair in Des Moines. I'm gone until after Labor Day. May I call you when I return home, okay?"

Edie gave him a sad pout, but answered, "Okay."

Pete gave her a peck on the cheek and headed for his car. Edie waved at him as he drove away. The next six weeks were going to be long.

The very next morning the phone rang. Hattie answered. "Yes, she is here. I'll go and get her. There's a phone call for you, Edie."

Edie hurried to the phone. Maybe it was Sean. "Hello, this is Edie . . . Oh hello, Mrs. Kautz . . . Yes, I took care of two boys in Muscatine . . . Mrs. Steinbeck . . . I'd be glad to, Mrs. Kautz. When do you want me to start? . . . Fifteen dollars a month would be fine . . . I can come Monday . . . I'll bring somethings for overnight. Thank you, Mrs.Kautz."

"Sounds like you just got a job," her mother said.

"Yes, it was Mrs.Kautz in Blue Grass. She needs me to nanny her two boys and one girl until school starts. I start Monday. Do you think Dad will approve? It's not in Muscatine. That's okay, isn't it?"

"Sure, honey, it will get you away from your father. I think he will approve. I know you will do fine. I won't need you until tomato time. We'll have all September for canning."

"Thank you, Mom. I will tell Dad at suppertime."

Frank whole-heartily approved. The Kautz family were well known in Scott County. He was hoping Edie could get a job soon, but he wasn't pushing because he caused her to be unemployed.

Monday, Edie rode the Interurban to Blue Grass. Mrs. Kautz, her family, Fred, Walter, and Gracie, met her at the station. They walked to their home. The Kautz home was huge. The Kautz's owned the lumber yard and several properties in town. They were wealthy. Mrs. Kautz showed Edie her room upstairs. It was next to Grace's. The boys had a room together. Mrs. and Mr. Kautz had a master bedroom in the front with a separate bathroom. They also had electricity and running water. It was just like the Steinbeck's.

The very next day, Mrs. Kautz had to leave. Edie was on her own. At first the boys were cool, but when they found out she could swing a baseball bat with power, she was okay. She split her time with the boys and Gracie. Gracie many toy dolls and a doll house, bigger than any Edie had ever seen.

The job went well. It was mid-August and the Mississippi Valley Fair started. Mrs. Kautz asked if Edie would like to go and be with the children. She didn't have to ask twice. Edie had never been to the big fair. They went on a Thursday, which was the cattle show. Edie took her charges around to the barns. She wanted to avoid the carnival rides as long as possible. They were walking through the big cattle barn when she heard someone call.

"Edie? What brings you here?"

She turned and there was Pete. He was dressed in brown show trousers, a tan cowboy hat, and a white shirt. He held a big black Angus steer.

"I'm taking care of some children. I thought they should see livestock. I want you to meet Fred, Walt, and Gracie. How are you doing, Pete?"

"Fine! We won Grand Champion at Hawkeye. Say, I'm home for a week. Would you like to go to the Ziegler Ice Cream Social in New Era a week from next Saturday?"

"I guess so. I don't work on weekends."

"Great! I'll pick you up at seven."

Saturday came quickly. Edie readied herself. She was sitting in the kitchen and promptly at seven she heard Pete's car pull up the lane. When they arrived at the church, she found the social was on the lawn. There were games and bingo. They had a small band in the gym. The Lutherans were much more liberal than the straight-laced Methodists. Of course, there was plenty of ice cream and cake. She and Pete danced and ate ice cream, then danced some more. They played a couple of games of Bingo. It was after ten when Pete suggested it was time to go home. He took a turn on the road before Edie's home.

"This isn't my road, Pete," Edie told him.

"I know. I'm just taking a different route."

She was about one-half mile from home when Pete pulled his auto into a field. There were trees bordering the fence. Anyone behind them could not be seen from the road.

"Should we be stopping in some farmer's field?" asked Edie.

"Don't worry, my dad owns this one."

He shut the engine off. Edie sat still.

"Let's sit in the back. There's more room," said Pete.

Edie complied. It would be nice to talk without a gearshift between them. Pete took off his jacket and started petting. Edie was very cautious. She played along for a while. They kissed. Pete's hands moved to her waist. He tugged at her blouse. She twisted away. They kissed some more. He began to unbutton her blouse. She pulled his hand away. He placed his hand on her knee. Soon he was bringing her skirt up. When the garment reached her knee, his hand slipped under her skirt. This was not going well. She pulled her skirt down. Pete wouldn't give up. He attacked her blouse again, this time with quick precision. He had her front unbuttoned in seconds. He had his hand inside and touched her bosom. Edie had had enough.

She pulled his hand out and said, "I think you have gone far enough, Pete. I'm not one of your bimbos. You keep your hands to yourself. I'm leaving."

She moved to the door and stepped out, slamming the door.

"Good night, Mr. McKillip."

"You're not walking home, are you?"

"I know my way home and I have two feet. I'll be fine."

Pete jumped out of the back seat and into the front. He pushed the starter button. Nothing happened. "Damn!" he said. The starter was stuck. He'd have to crawl underneath and hit it with a wrench. He opened the trunk toolbox, found a hammer, cussed some more, crawled under and gave the starter a whack. It took a couple of times to finally fix the starter. He backed out of the field and onto the road. He slammed the gear shift forward and roared down the road. Edie was just turning into her lane. Pete stopped and hopped out, not realizing there was a slight grade at the end of her lane.

"Wait, Edie. I'm sorry," he pleaded.

"Go away, Mr. McKillip. I can take care of myself. You go find some rich girl to fondle. This rural hick isn't what you need."

"But, please."

Edie stopped and turned toward Pete. He thought she might be weakening, but instead she said, "You'd better go catch your lovely car before it hits the culvert at the bottom of the hill."

Pete turned to see his Studebaker slowly rolling down the road. He ran to catch it. He hopped in and applied the brakes. He backed up to Edie's drive hoping to see her waiting, but she was gone. All he saw was a light in the window.

What Pete didn't see was Edie peeking out from behind the curtain. She watched him slowly back down her lane.

She thought, "*I like Pete as a friend. He has a sense of humor. He holds a nice conversation and is somewhat handsome. I know I'll get to go places with him I would never go otherwise because he has money. But mother was right about one thing, Pete does have active hands. He has been inside many girls blouses before. I could tell. I'll will be very careful of him until some other guy comes along or I find Sean.*"

Pete was out of the picture at least until after Labor Day. Edie was glad. The next Saturday was the Cedar County Fair. Uncle Bill and Aunt Helen invited Edie's family to visit. The men could go to the fair while the women would chat on the huge porch. Ralph and Ruth opted out, but Edie decided to go. She liked to explore Aunt Helen's big house.

They left home right after chores were finished and were in Tipton by eleven. Aunt Helen was busy baking pies. She welcomed the extra hands. Edie peeled potatoes and put them in a pan of boiling water. While she waited, Aunt Helen told her to look on the top shelf for some powdered sugar. Edie thought it odd for sugar to be stored on a top shelf when it was needed quite often in baking. She found no sugar there, but there was an envelope addressed to her. It was from Sean.

Aunt Helen smiled and said, "It came last week. You'd better go upstairs and open it. We don't want your father to know."

Edie rushed upstairs to one of the many bedrooms. She tore open the envelope. Sean started with flowery words and said how he missed her. It wasn't until the last paragraph he announced he wouldn't be coming home until October.

Edie sighed. She'd have to wait another month. Aunt Helen could tell the letter contained sad news. Edie told her, but Aunt Helen just smiled again and said, "You know, absence makes the heart grow fonder."

"I suppose you're right, Aunt Helen," Edie lamented.

"Now you better put that letter back where you found it. I'll keep them all for you."

"Thank you, Aunt Helen. You're a peach. How did Sean know your address?"

"My Bill knows Mr. Steinbeck. Mr. Steinbeck told my Bill, Sean had visited their place on Mulberry and asked for your address. He didn't know right off hand, so when he got home he asked me. I explained your problem with your father and I suggested we have Sean send his letters to us. I would find the proper time to give them to you."

"Gee, Aunt Helen, you're a peach. Thank You very much."

A month later, Pete called on Edie again. He knew if he was to win her, he'd have to go through her father and brother. He hadn't figured her mother out yet. Hattie met him at the door. She called Edie, who was working in the wash house canning beets. Edie came with her hands and clothes all stained with beet juice. She was surprised to see Pete.

She asked with a cold stare, "What are you doing here?"

"I've come to apologize for my behavior. I hope you will forgive me and give me another chance."

Edie stared at him. She didn't know what to say. She looked at her mother standing behind Pete. Her mother mouthed, "Be careful." Edie put down the rag she was holding.

"All right, but no more funny business or there never will be another time. Understand?"

"Yes, completely. Would you go with me to the last dance at Paul's Woods? I promise to have you home by ten."

"Okay, but you will be on probation."

The dance was fine. Pete was a gentleman, but as usual didn't dance much. Edie didn't care because there were others very willing to twirl her around. He only kissed her on the cheek when he brought her home.

He courted Edie, but he also courted her father. Frank thought he was the catch of the county. He was rich. His father was a big man in politics and Pete was not a Catholic. Frank would have given his okay at any time.

Hattie wasn't so sure. She knew Pete's father, Bruce, when Frank worked for him and he was a very demanding person. He worked everyone hard including his wife, who never looked happy.

Sean returned home on September 25, but he didn't call Edie. He wasn't sure for Edie's sake if he should try and contact her. He had heard through the grapevine that she and her father had had a big argument. Her father was dead set against any contact between the pair.

The next Friday, as were all Fridays in Muscatine, was Farmer's Night. The stores stayed open until nine. Some grocery stores stayed open until ten to catch the farmers on their way home. Sean was downtown on the south side of the street when he noticed Edie and Pete walking hand in hand on the opposite side. She seemed happy. He watched them for a while from a distance. Finally, they disappeared around the corner. He stopped at Eichenhaur's for a malt, then headed back to the south end.

CHAPTER 8: HALLOWEEN DANCE

The next big event was the Halloween Dance at the Masonic Lodge. It was the fall gala for the very wealthy young adults. Pete asked Edie if she would like to go. She said yes. She didn't like doing nothing and waiting for Sean was becoming futile. She had never expected to attend such to a high-brow event. "What do I wear?" asked Edie.

"I thought we'd go to the costume shop in Davenport and rent something," Pete answered.

"Zowie!" was her reply.

The next Saturday Edie and Pete drove to Davenport. Pete knew the lady who owned the costume shop. She took one look at Edie and said, "With her dark hair, I think you two would be perfect gypsies. I'll be right back. Let me see, miss, you're about a size six, right?"

"Yes."

They tried on several costumes. A couple of gowns were cut very low on Edie. Pete's eyes were everywhere as she changed her clothes. Once he pretended to walk into the wrong dressing room and caught her with her blouse off. He apologized immediately. Edie wasn't so sure he hadn't come in on purpose.

They rented their costumes and headed home after a nice dinner.

"I'll pick you up at—"

"Seven," Edie quipped.

"Yes, seven, next Saturday."

The week went fast, soon it was Saturday again. Edie hurried with her chores. Ralph and Ruth were partying also, but at a different place. Ralph had to use what was around home for his costume. Edie started at four to don her gypsy dress. Her mother helped. She wanted to make sure all the buttons and clasps were secure.

The outfit had two under petticoats which were heavily embroidered. They were covered by an over skirt which was quilted and embroidered. The petticoats and skirt stopped at mid-calf. The blouse was white with an embroidered bodice. It was topped by a colorful jacket. The costume was very heavy. Hattie let Edie wear a pair of her old dress shoes with heels. They were closed by hook and eyes and extended almost to mid-calf. Edie applied heavy makeup and eye shadow. She looked like a gypsy. When Pete showed up at seven, he stared at Edie.

He said, "If I hadn't known I was in the right house, I wouldn't know you. You'll be the hit of the dance."

The Masonic Lodge was full of young adults in many elaborate costumes. Some of the young ladies wore very low-cut dresses. One couple came as Greeks dressed in togas. The lady of this couple had slits up to her thigh and deep openings beneath her armpits. Evidently, her mother didn't know what she was wearing. The guys were all goggle-eyed.

Another couple came as Adam and Eve. They were scantily clad in large fake leaves. There were many animals and famous couples. Mae West made her appearance twice. Edie almost felt over-dressed. She had read about women in the East showing more leg and more chest. It seemed the women at the dance were trying to outdo each other. Supposedly, no one knew each other, but the secrets were quickly revealed.

Edie and Pete were guided by a ghost to a table of eight. Part of the night's entertainment was to try and guess who was sitting at the table. The conversation was mostly questions. Edie was the most difficult for the others because she was not from town and had not graduated from high school, although she had attended for three years. Pete was known for bringing new girls to the dances and this one was no exception.

Because some of the revelers were under twenty-one, they were required to give up their identity if they wanted any liquor. The rest stayed with tea or lemonade. There was a waiter at each table, some wore a costume and some did not. Their waiter started around the table. He wrote down each drink order. When he came to Pete, Pete looked at the waiter and said, "Sean, Sean O'Keefe, long time no see. How have you been?"

Sean gave him a puzzled look and didn't say a word.

Pete removed his mask and repeated, "Sean, it's me Pete McKillip. Don't you remember the kid who would bother you at the quarry? I'm Bruce's son. We went to Patterson school together."

Sean answered, "Yeah, I remember. Boy, you had me fooled. Your costume is great."

Pete replied, "I want you to meet my girlfriend, Edie Mohr."

Edie removed her mask and said, "Nice to meet you, Mr. O'Keefe."

All Sean could do was blurt out, "Edie, is that you?"

Edie and Sean locked eyes. Sean smiled. Edie smiled back.

Edie said, "Sean, I haven't seen you in years. You were in my brother's class at Patterson. Nice seeing you, Sean."

"Yes, Edie, it has been a long time."

Pete sensed there was more to this relationship than they were willing to tell. He watched Sean and Edie for the rest of the night. They didn't say much to each other, but their eyes told their story. He'd have to research their relationship further. Maybe he'd have to up his efforts or lose out. He'd never had competition before. It was always Pete who broke things off, seldom the girl.

The band played modern tunes and old timers. Pete could dance to the slow tunes, but his leg prevented him from doing the Black Bottom, Apache, Shimmy, and other novelty dances, plus the polkas and schottiches. Edie knew his reluctance to dance from earlier dances, so she found another girl for a partner. She loved to dance and learning new dances was easy.

The band started a set of slow dances and waltzes. There was a set of quick ball room dances like the foxtrot. Intermission was early, because it was revealing time. Everyone took off their masks. They were hot anyway. Some women retired to the powder room to repair their makeup. Edie wished she could remove her mask, but she wasn't wearing one. She was very warm under her costume. The band started again with polkas. Edie loved to polka, but she knew Pete could not polka. She sat beside him and watched. A tall young man approached their table.

"Would you care to dance, miss?" he asked.

Edie looked at Pete. He looked at the man and said, "Sure, Dan, go ahead. I shouldn't spoil her evening because of my leg. Oh, let me introduce my date. This is Edie Mohr. She lives out by me."

"My pleasure, Miss Mohr. I'm Dan Schottenmeir. I live in town. My dad is a lumber man, and my mother teaches dance."

Edie went to the floor and danced a set of polkas. Her heavy skirt kept slipping. She thought she would lose it during one of Dan's twirls.

"May I take a break, Dan? I have to adjust my costume."

Edie returned to their table and found one of the girls also sitting one out. She recognized her. She'd been in one of her classes when she was attending high school. Her name was Gloria. She was dressed as a lady of the court in England. Her dress had a high collar with heavy brocade fabric. She looked great, but her face was bright red.

Edie wiped her forehead and said to Gloria, "I'm cooking. This heavy skirt is sweltering and I can't keep it on my waist. It keeps slipping. I wish I could take it off."

"Me, too. I'm glad my mom told me to bring other clothes. My Dad is running the cloak room and has my other dress there. I need help changing. Would you help me?"

"Sure, I'm going to try and adjust this skirt. There are extra hooks on it to fit all sizes. Maybe you can help me."

The pair retired to the ladies' room. Edie helped Gloria out of her outfit. While Gloria was putting her dress on, Edie unbuttoned her skirt and took it off to see if there was anything she could do to adjust her skirt. She was standing in her petticoats and top.

Gloria suggested, "Why don't you just wear your petticoats? They are embroidered and fancy. You'd still have more clothes than most of the girls. Did you see Nelda Holdenberg? All she had on was a swim suit with leaves sewn on it. Heck, the suit is even nude colored. She looks like she is naked. I'll bet her father doesn't know it. He would be mortified. Then there's Shelia Cook with that toga outfit. I know she's not wearing a brassiere."

"But what would I do with my skirt?"

"You can put it with my stuff."

When Edie and Gloria returned, the band was playing some slow numbers. Pete gave Edie a Cheshire Cat smile. He liked the way she stripped down a bit. He hoped maybe he could get a little liquor into her and she would be more willing later. Pete rose from his chair and took Edie's hand. He could dance this set.

They were not on the floor five minutes and Pete tried to kiss Edie. He put his face close and Edie turned away.

Pete asked in a disgusted voice, "What's the matter now?

"You smell like liquor."

"Yeah, and so do most of the guys here. The bartender gets a little lax when there are so many customers. He doesn't have time to check IDs."

"Well, I don't like it. I'd rather dance with Dan."

"That homo, he's the biggest puss I know. He dances with his mommy and her girls. Go ahead. I'll wait for you at the end."

Edie danced with Dan the rest of the night. Her petticoats swirled and twirled. Once during the dance called The Black Bottom, she and Dan cleared the floor. Everyone watched. Edie caught Pete watching from the bar. He didn't return to the floor.

When the set ended Dan thanked Edie for a great time. He walked her to the door where she met Pete. Pete leaned heavily on the door frame. His speech was slurred. Edie gave him a disgusted look.

"How am I getting home? You're drunk!"

"I can still drive," he assured her as he stumbled forward.

Gloria's father stepped forward with Edie's extra clothes. "I think someone should drive you two home. I'll see if there is a volunteer in the kitchen."

He left and came back with, of all people, Sean.

Sean surveyed the situation. "Hi, Pete, looks like you need help. I can take you and Edie home. I know where you both live. Give me your keys."

Pete didn't resist. He recognized Sean. Sean helped him to the car. He put him in the back seat of the Studebaker. Edie climbed in the front seat with him. They hadn't made it to Weed's Lane before they heard Pete snoring. Sean and Edie small-talked the all way to her home. As they pulled up the lane, Edie noticed the living room light was on. She groaned.

"Daddy must still be up. You'll have to just dump me off." she sighed, "Say, how are you getting back to Muscatine?"

Sean answered, "There's a room in the barn at McKillip's. The tack man used to stay there when they had many teams. He slept there when the mares were foaling. I'll sleep there and leave early before Pete or anyone else wakes up. It's only two miles to the Pleasant Prairie station. I'll be fine."

Sean pulled up in front of the house. He shut the car off and looked at Pete sleeping in the back seat.

"I'd better walk you to the door or your parents will think you and Pete have broken up. How about I wear Pete's hat to walk you to the door. I can even limp a bit."

Edie laughed.

Sean helped her out of the car and walked her to the door. When Edie got to the steps, she turned and planted a kiss on Sean's cheek.

"Thanks for bringing me home, Pete," she said loudly, knowing her mother was on the other side of the door listening.

Sean returned the kiss on her lips. He gave a pat on her shoulder and whispered, "Take care."

He limped back to the car and drove away. Edie went inside. Her mother stood close to the window.

"Did you have a good time?"

"Oh yes, I had a great time. You should have seen some of the elaborate costumes."

"Was that Pete who drove you home?"

"Yes."

"I thought he wasn't that tall."

"Mother," Edie answered with disgust, "who else would drive me clear out here? Most of those people think we live in a log cabin. It was Pete in the car. Didn't you see his limp?"

This seemed to satisfy her mother, and she hurried to her room before there were any more questions. She hoped her mother would forget about tonight in the morning.

Meanwhile, Sean arrived at the McKillip farm. He pulled the Studebaker into the three-car garage. He checked on Pete, who snored loudly in the back. He went to the trunk of the car and found two blankets. Sean covered Pete with one and rolled the other for a pillow. Because he had worked for the McKillip's he knew the layout of the buildings. He headed for the horse barn. Sure enough, the cot was still there. He shook the covers to rid them of dust and lay down. It was a short night for Sean. At four thirty, he awoke and walked to Pleasant Prairie.

On the way, he wondered as he walked, "*When Pete wakes up, will he wonder how he got home? He certainly was in no shape to drive himself. How nice it was to see Edie again. I think it is better if I leave well enough alone and not interfere with her life anymore.*"

Pete woke with a pounding headache the next morning. He met his mother in the kitchen. She sighed and said, "Too tired to make it to the house last night?"

"Yes, Mother."

"Who drove you home? Because you certainly didn't! Did Edie drive you here then walk home?"

Pete looked at his mother with a sheepish grin. "You know, Mother, I don't have a clue who drove me home. All I remember is Gloria's dad took my keys away from me and gave them to someone." Pete paused, then added, "I think it was Sean O'Keefe who drove me home, but where is he now?"

"I don't know, but if he did, you owe him an apology and maybe money for his fare back to town."

"Yes, Mother."

Pete knew Sean was the driver. He also knew Edie and Sean could barely take their eyes off each other. What did she see in him? He was just a factory worker.

Pete started to think of how he could win the heart of Edie Mohr. The only way he could think was to shower her with gifts. He knew Sean would not have the funds to compete.

Pete spent Thanksgiving at the Mohr's. He took Edie shopping in Davenport and Cedar Rapids. On the second weekend of December, he took Edie, her mother, and his mother to Chicago. They spent a day on Michigan Avenue. Edie had never seen such big stores. If she didn't buy it, Pete did.

By Christmas, Edie's pile of gifts was huge. Edie's mother and father were impressed. Edie was grateful, but not really that enthused. She appreciated the gifts, but it was the sincerity she questioned. She felt Pete had other thoughts in mind. She'd tolerate him, since he was the best thing going at present. She hadn't heard from Sean since the Halloween Dance. He was disappointing her, too.

CHAPTER 9: OFF TO WAR

As the new year opened, the Great War in Europe grew. German U-Boats kept sinking ships supplying the Allies. President Wilson continued his pledge on neutrality. The British silently urged America to help. Many men from the U.S. went to Canada to volunteer to fight for the Allies. The war ground on.

February was cold and snowy. On Valentine's Day, Pete arrived with roses and a big heart-shaped box of chocolates. He took Edie to a Valentine Dance. He brought her a kitten from his farm. March came in like a lion with wet snow and cold. The roads became a quagmire. Highway 22 was graveled and the only passable road close to the Mohr home. Pete parked his car there and walked to Edie's, or he met her at the Kautz's in Blue Grass.

Edie was now a full-time employee of the Kautz family. When the children were in school, she cleaned house and did washing. On Fridays she would take the Interurban to Melpine Station and her father or Ralph met her in a buggy. Horses were better in mud than cars. Some weekends she stayed to babysit, and other times she would help with cooking and serving a meal for guests. There were times she and Pete went to Davenport for a silent movie or a vaudeville show at the Columbia Theater. He continued to be a gentleman, for Mr. Kautz was well-known and any improper action of Pete's would surely reach her parents.

Edie only thought of Sean occasionally. This relationship with Pete was temporary. She knew he would find another girl and their romance would be over. For now, Pete was entertaining and fun. He took her to places she had never been.

Sean moved up in Roach and Musser to assistant purchasing agent. He

117

continued to stay at Mrs. Kerchinske's. He paid her a little more rent, so she could afford indoor plumbing. She treated him like her son. He saw Edie occasionally, from a distance, but did not attempt to contact her. She seemed happy and that was enough for him.

He met a young lady who had a similar job as Edie. She was a Catholic, so there was no problem with religion. But she demanded attention and although not wealthy, she was an only child and spoiled. Sean knew she was not the end goal but just a link between Edie and another girl somewhere.

April roads continued to be muddy. There were some promising days, but as soon as the fields dried, it would rain again. The big news was the Germans started to sink American merchant vessels. Their strategy was to starve Britain into submission.

This angered the American public. The cry for war was heard across the nation even though the nation was not prepared for any conflict. On April 16, the United States declared war on the German-Austria-Hungary alliance. The nation had much to do before engaging into warfare. The first item of business was forming a viable Army. The call went out.

Ralph wanted to volunteer, but Frank wouldn't have it. He wasn't against the war, but he needed Ralph to help him with the farm. His reasoning was the country needed food more than men. Many of Ralph's friends were volunteering, but they either lived in town or had brothers to help in their absence.

The first contingent from Muscatine was given a big send-off. Their names were posted in the *Muscatine Journal*. On a Saturday, there was a gathering at the Courthouse. The mayor, the city council, and the county board of supervisors were all present. The young volunteers stood proudly as their names were called. Because one of her neighbors' sons was volunteering, Edie and her mother attended the ceremony. The list was fairly long. For the M's, there were six men; for the N's, eight. As the O's were announced there was O'Brian, O'Conner, then she heard Sean O'Keefe.

She stared at the red-headed man who stepped forward. She gasped and grabbed her mother's arm.

"That's Sean," she whispered.

"I know," whispered her mother. "Aren't you proud? You dated a soldier. I wish him well."

Edie had a sinking feeling in her stomach. Would she ever see Sean again? Would he come home safe? It would be a long wait.

Although America did not fight on European soil until December, the U.S. had to prepare many men. By July, the volunteers had slowed. A need to draft men into the service was evident. Pete's brother Harry was one of the first. Ralph was called with Pete in September. Ralph passed with flying colors. He would be going to Fort Leonard Wood in Missouri in two weeks. Frank was devastated. How was he going to get the harvest done?

Pete, on the other hand, went knowing he had the bad leg. When he arrived at the induction center at Fort Dodge, he made sure he limped even more. He was 4F and would not be accepted. He feigned remorse for not being able to go, but really, he was happy. Now not only was Sean O'Keefe out of the picture, but dozens of other men. He would have all the women to himself. The women would be competition for Edie. Maybe she'd be more affectionate.

Pete soon found out with his brother Harry gone, he had to take on more responsibility at home. One of the four hired hands was drafted. Another two quit to take jobs at the Rock Island Arsenal. They had shorter hours and better pay. Pete's father was now a county supervisor, which took him away two to four days a month. Despite his slight handicap, Pete no longer had time for courting every girl in eastern Muscatine County, especially Edie.

Edie was just the opposite. Despite her arguments and spat with her father, she forgave him. She pledged Ralph that she'd help her father. She'd help run the farm and Ralph should win the war. Pete would have to play second fiddle. In fact, he became third fiddle fast when one Friday evening on Second Street in Muscatine, Edie watched the flamboyant Pete drive down the street in his Studebaker with two women in the front seat and three in the back. She swore their romance was over.

Edie concentrated on helping her father. First, she had to convince her mother that she could do man's work, then she'd have to convince her father. If both agreed, she'd quit the Kautz's and stay at home. It didn't take long for her mother to agree. Frank was quickly becoming depressed. Her mother convinced Frank to give Edie a try.

The corn was in the field and not in the crib, and Frank was leery. Edie could do chores. She knew how to drive horses. If he taught her how to drive the T and the Wallis tractor, maybe she could be a great help. She wasn't very big, but she was tough and strong for her size. In the end, she was the only true answer to his dilemma.

Edie already had the work boots, it was the pants she lacked. Her mother bought some denim and made custom work slacks. She remade some of Ralph's work shirts. The problem came when Edie tried to find corn husking hooks or corn husking pegs small enough for her hand. They finally went to Tufell's Harness Shop in Blue Grass and had Elmer handmake a small hook to fit her hand.

Ralph returned home after his eight weeks of basics. He would be home for two weeks before he headed for New Jersey and then overseas. He and his dad started husking the corn. Edie quit her job at the Kautz's. Mrs. Kautz was sad to see her leave because she was so sweet and a such good worker, but she knew the war effort involved everyone.

Edie was determined to be Ralph's replacement. She rose early to milk so her dad and Ralph could start husking early. Although her hands ached from squeezing all those teats, and her back ached from pitching hay from the mow, she didn't complain. It didn't take her long to realize how out of shape she was physically.

The worst was filling the 55-gallon wooden slop barrel for the hogs. Hog slop contained skim milk, ground oats, and ground corn. It was a protein-laden hog feed. The hogs were fed fifteen three-gallon pails of the mixture. Once a week a pound of yeast was added to help with the fermentation. Edie had to dip the bucket into the smelly mess, then pour it into the troughs with a bevy of hungry hogs pushing and shoving her around. When finished with the feeding, she had to refill the barrel and add more oats and corn. The ground oats were dusty and itchy. They clung to her hands and crept inside her shirt. One time the slop bucket caught the edge of the slop barrel and spilled inside her blouse. She said a few cuss words and headed for the house. As she rounded the corner of the corncrib, Ralph was coming in with the first load of corn. He saw his slop covered sister and started laughing.

"What happened, Sis?" he chortled. "Take a bath in hog slop?"

Edie glared at him. She reached her hand down her blouse and pulled out a handful of oats and corn meal and threw it at him.

"Very funny," she answered. "If I wasn't a woman, I'd remove my shirt right here."

"Hey, tell Mom that Dad and I will be in at 11:30. With you helping with chores, we got out much earlier. Our wagons are full."

"Okay." Edie stalked toward the house.

Hattie met her at the door and took one look at her daughter.

"Whoa! Stop right there. You're not coming in here with those clothes. You go right downstairs and shower."

The two weeks went fast. Ralph taught Edie how to drive his used Willys Knight auto. He wanted her to be independent. He also tried to teach her how to crank the engine on the Wallis. Edie just wasn't strong enough. She'd get the crank to top dead center, but she couldn't get over it the hump. He did teach her how to drive the unwieldy machine. He had a wooden block attached to the clutch and brake pedal, so she could reach them. He strapped a steering knob on the steering wheel to give her more leverage when turning.

The day Ralph had to leave was tearful. Hattie hated to see her son go to a war so far away. Frank tried to be stoic. He shook his son's hand, then turned away so Ralph wouldn't see him shed tears.

Edie just hugged her brother and cried, "Please come home safe. I need you."

"I'll be back. Don't worry," was his answer before he boarded the train along with several other soldiers.

Those left behind waved until the train rounded the bend and out of town.

The Mohr's did not work on Sunday. They would go to church, come home, and rest. This Sunday was different. After dinner and a short nap, Frank asked Edie, "Would you husk a load of corn with me? It's down in the creek bottom."

Hattie got a shocked look on her face. "Frank, I thought you didn't believe in working on Sunday."

"Hattie, this is a special time for the nation. We may have to break the rules. Edie and I have a lot of work to do and without Ralph it will take a little longer. I think we should take advantage of all the good weather we can. Just don't let the neighbors see us."

The neighbors to the north worked Sundays. The day meant nothing to them if there was farm work to be done.

Edie hurried upstairs to change. She met her father at the barn and helped hitch the horses to the wagon.

"Edie, you take the team out. I'll drive the tractor out. It'll save the horses from pulling the full load back up the hill."

It took the rest of the afternoon to husk a full load. Frank unhooked the team and helped Edie on one of the draft horses. She grabbed the reins and headed off. The team could sense they were headed home, so they trotted briskly. Edie literally bounced her way home. Her father followed with the tractor. It was almost dark when they pulled into the farmyard. They had chores to do. Edie went to the shop for the kerosene lanterns.

"You start the milking, Edie. I'll do the outside chores and put the horses away. I'll help you finish later."

"Okay, Dad."

Edie started the milking and to her surprise, her mother appeared. She was dressed in her long skirt, but she had it pinned between her legs.

"Mom, I didn't know you could milk."

"It has been a long time, but when I was a girl I milked for my dad. I also milked when I was first married. I think my hands can still do it."

She grabbed a pail and a stool and took the cow next to Edie. The two women were half done when Frank arrived. He, too, was very surprised to see his wife. He carried the first full milk can to the cooler. When he came back he asked, "Edie, do you think you could help me shovel off our load yet tonight?"

"Frank, for heaven's sake, she's tired. Can't it wait until tomorrow morning?" scolded Hattie.

Edie quickly answered, "Sure, Daddy, I'll give it a try."

Frank and Edie headed for the corncrib. They hung their lanterns high on the rafters. Frank found Edie a smaller number ten shovel. It was after seven when they finished. Edie changed her clothes and helped her mother set the table.

"Edie, you sit down. I'll take care of supper."

Edie sagged into the big chair. She was exhausted. When her father arrived, they ate a supper of leftovers. Edie went to bed immediately. Tomorrow was Monday, and it was a full work day.

She was up at five and hurried to the barn. Her dad already had the cows stanchioned and fed. She grabbed her pail and stool and squatted behind the first cow. Soon her mother arrived. This time she was wearing a pair of Ralph's overalls and a pair of old shoes. She smiled at Edie as she started on the second cow. Frank disappeared to take care of the other animals. Edie and her mother chit-chatted while they milked. There were two cows left when Frank reappeared.

He said, "I'll finish up, Hattie. You go in and start breakfast."

After breakfast Edie and her father headed for the creek bottom. They had six acres to do. They could husk one acre before noon and one in the afternoon. At this rate, they had three days left. As Edie rode the team back to the barn, she found the wind at the top of the hill was much brisker than on the bottom. The temperature was in the forties. She dismounted at the water tank and let the team drink. Her dad pulled the wagon in to the driveway of the crib. There was lightning flashing to the northwest.

"You get your mother to help with milking. I'll shovel this load off right now," Frank ordered.

"Do you want me to help shovel, Daddy?"

"No, I'll get it."

The wind picked up. Frank shut the sliding doors on the crib. He hadn't scooped more than three bushels when he heard a knocking on the door.

"Daddy, it's me. Mom said I should help shovel before the storm hits. I brought another lantern."

Frank slid the door open just enough to let Edie in. For shoveling corn into the crib, he let Edie stand on the shovel gate while he stood on the ground. The crib was becoming full and ears rolled out.

"Edie, you're small. I'll lift you into the crib and you shove the corn further back."

At first, Frank didn't know where he should push his daughter. Edie could grab the crib slats but couldn't pull herself up any farther. Finally, Frank just placed his hand on her behind and gave her a shove. Edie went flying up on the pile of corn. She began to laugh.

"What's so funny?"

"I don't know. I guess it is the way you pushed me up here. Now how will I get out?"

"That's easy. Just jump I'll catch you."

It was one of the few times Edie had seen her father smile. He was always so serious. The pair shoveled and pushed the corn. They were done in thirty minutes.

"Suppose you mother is done milking by now or do we wait a little longer?" he quipped.

"Daddy! You should be ashamed of yourself," Edie answered, giggling.

Frank opened the door a crack. The wind was picking up. The flashes of lightning were getting closer. She squeezed through the crack and ran for the barn. The team was pulling at their reins. They wanted to be in the barn also. Frank quickly untied the reins and led the nervous horses inside.

The door had barely shut when big raindrops started pounding outside. The windows rattled as the barn doors strained against their hooks. Lightning flashed, followed by a thunderous boom. Edie found her bucket and started on the cow next to her mother's. The thunder made the cows nervous.

Edie had about a third of a bucket when old One Horn decided to kick. The pail went flying, covering Edie with a coating of frothy milk. Edie reached up and beat the cow with her stool. Not only had the old bovine kicked her bucket, but she had dented it and knocked it into the gutter. Now Edie would have to have a different pail. She was furious. All the cows strained to see what was going on. There was the sound of creaking wood and rustling straw.

"Edie, calm down or we will never get done," her mother warned.

It was another hour before they were finished. Frank appeared, soaking wet. Water dripped from the bill of his cap.

"I guess we won't be picking corn tomorrow, Punky."

Punky! He hasn't called me that since I was a little girl. Is he tired or is he happy to have me working with him? thought Edie.

It was nearly eight before all three made it to the house. Frank stoked the furnace so there would be some hot water for the kitchen. Hattie and Edie shoved some extra wood into the cook stove. They were all a bit chilly.

Hattie started to heat the skillet. She instructed Edie to mix up some pancake batter. Pancakes would be good on a cold night. They had their pancakes and bacon.

The weather sounded terrible. Frank stuck his head out the back door. The rain had turned to a heavy wet snow. It would be white in the morning. After washing dishes, Hattie helped Edie shampoo her hair, since she had taken a milk bath in the barn.

The snow subsided by six the next morning, but there was no hurry to milk. There would be no picking corn today. After chores, all three returned to the warm kitchen. Frank sank into his chair and fell fast asleep. Edie curled up on the love seat and dozed. Hattie found her knitting and rocking chair. She knitted and rocked and soon she dozed off. When she awoke, it was almost dinner time. She quietly worked at the sink peeling potatoes. Edie stirred and got up to help. She tiptoed by her father and went to the fruit cellar for some canned peaches and green beans. Hattie found a slice of ham in the icebox. The meat supply was getting low. Tomorrow they'd have to go to the Blue Grass Locker and retrieve some more cuts from their rented freezer box at the butcher shop.

It was four days before the snow melted from the stalks. It was now definitely November weather with muddy ground. On Sunday, there were still four acres to pick. After church Frank rode Sara, their only saddle horse, down to the creek bottom field. It was a mess. Many of the stalks had broken over. Some ears were on the ground. Picking would be slow and tedious. One load a day might be all they could pick. The worst part would be the mud. Early in the morning the frost would hold them up, but the ears and stalks would be wet and cold. Their hands would be the same. If they waited until afternoon, the frost would thaw and walking in the mud would be tiring. There wasn't an easy answer. He presented the dilemma to Edie.

"What if we start early and keep changing gloves?" suggested Edie.

"It would take too much time changing that often, especially on your peg hand."

"Well, I think cold hands are better than walking in mud. I say we do as much in the morning as we can."

"I was hoping you'd say that, Punky, 'cause that's what I think, too."

The next morning, they had the chores done by seven. Breakfast was put off until later. The horses snorted in the cold air. Their nostrils spouted steam. The Wallis was stubborn until Frank poured some straight alcohol into the carburetor. It popped and snorted to life. Frank decided he wouldn't shut it off until they were finished.

When he and Edie reached the field, the frost was still on the husks. In minutes their gloves were soaked and their hands were cold. As the sun warmed the air, the husks turned soggy. The ears on the ground were wetter than those on the stalk. By eleven both Edie's and Frank's hands were stiff from the cold. She could barely strip the ear from the stalk.

Frank told her he had had enough for one day. They were quitting. He unhitched the team from the wagon and re-hitched to the tractor. He helped cold Edie onto the horse and they headed home.

It was like this for the next six days, but finally they finished. Edie's hands were rough and swollen. Her face was tanned from the wind, but she was happy.

The next week or two was devoted to getting ready for an Iowa winter. The barns were cleaned for the last time. Frank belted the hand corn sheller to a stationary engine, so Edie and Hattie could shell corn for the chickens. They stuffed the cobs into a gunny sack. They would be used as fire starters in the cook stove.

CHAPTER 10: PETE THE MANAGER

Six miles away, Pete was busier than he liked. With his father as county supervisor, Pete was on his own. When two hired hands left for better jobs, he was faced with two hundred acres of corn to pick and little help with only two workers. All the young men, including his older brother, were serving in the Army. He was starting to panic. Pete was a playboy, but he also knew many people in Muscatine and Davenport, including those who worked as maids and servants to the high-class white people. His dad called them "darkies." Others had worse names, but Pete respected those with darker skin than his.

One was his barber, Earl. Earl told him there were young men in East St. Louis who were not employed. Even though the Civil War ended fifty years ago, African Americans were not accepted by the Armed Forces. Pete asked Earl if he would accompany him to St. Louis to find ten good men. Earl agreed.

By September, Pete had ten new employees. One of his hired hands quit because he wasn't going to work with "niggers". Pete quickly promoted the remaining hired hand, Jake, to assistant manager. He would teach the newcomers how to drive a tractor, how to husk corn, and how to clean barns.

His biggest problem was housing. His mother would not allow the new men in her house. To solve his problem, Pete remodeled one of the houses vacated by the departed hired hand. It was better than anything the men had in St. Louis, but they were poor cooks. Again, he turned to Earl. Earl found three young women from Davenport to cook and do washing. They were not to stay overnight with the men, but Pete found out later those rules were broken.

Pete agreed to pay their fare on the Interurban each day. The three women rode to Pleasant Prairie. Someone picked them up at six in the morning and returned them by five at night. The system worked fine. Pete had his corn husked before the November storm hit. He kept two men for the winter. He soon discovered two of the women became wives. Four men found jobs at the Rock Island Arsenal and the last four returned home. They had made more money in two months than they had in six months at home. They were happy. Pete had proved to his father he could manage the farm.

CHAPTER 11: NEWS FROM THE FRONT

Three days before Thanksgiving, a letter arrived from Ralph.

Dear Dad and Mom, I'm serving in the motor pool. I figured I got the job because I worked on tractors and engines at home. It also would keep me from the front lines. So, Mom, don't worry so much. I know the division is leaving December 7. While I'm waiting, I'm serving in the kitchen. Most guys hate KP duty, but I enjoy cooking and baking. They bake beans in a horse tank and stir it with a spoon the size of a two by four. One night I oversaw roasting the brats. I had to put 400 on a tray, then shove into an oven for ten minutes, then pull them out and turn them over and shove them back in for another ten minutes. Since I loaded the trays ten times, I was busy watching 4000 brats. Please tell Pete I met Harry. Harry is in the Artillery division. I helped load five hundred artillery pieces onto a ship. I love you all and Mom, don't worry, I'll be all right.

After reading the letter out loud, Hattie could not stifle her tears. She went upstairs to have her cry. Edie stayed with her dad. They talked about the war and its future. Edie knew her dad was trying to be brave, but his voice cracked a couple of times. Edie was disappointed she had not heard from Sean.

The next letter came before Christmas. Ralph was in France. He was taking training on Renault, Citroen, and Peugeot engines. They were the French motor trucks. He also was studying English-made motors. He would be closer to the action soon because they needed mechanics near the front lines. He ended again with *"Don't worry, Mom, I'll be all right."*

Edie and her parents went to Tipton on Christmas Day. As soon as they arrived, Aunt Helen motioned Edie to the kitchen.

"Edie, would you get the sugar for me? It's way up on the top shelf."

Edie knew the routine. She hurried for the step stool and reached high into the cupboard. Sure enough, there was a letter from Sean. It read:

Dearest Edie,

I arrived two weeks ago in Le Harve, France. After orientation, I was sent to the front lines. It is close to Christmas and the enemy is curtailing their actions. At present, it is a stalemate. Many of us crave some action. These trenches are cold and wet.

I received notice yesterday my wonderful mother had passed. I knew she was ill and in the care of my Uncle Billy. Now he is the only family I have in the States and he is eighty-nine years old. It has made me very lonely. You are my only family. I now miss you more than ever. I miss your smile and your touch. I dream of you every night. You pray for me as I pray for you.

Your friend, Sean

On New Year's Eve, Edie attended a Watch Party at Ruth Watts' church. Pete was there. He was the only man. He had his hand wrapped with gauze.
Edie asked, "How did you hurt your hand, Pete?"

"We were sorting cattle and one of men slammed the gate shut on my hand. Didn't break any bones though. Lucky, I guess."

"I bet you're glad it didn't happen during harvest."

"You betcha."

The night went fast. Pete soaked up all the attention from the women. The clock clicked down to midnight. Pete edged over to Edie and asked, "May I have a good luck kiss at midnight?"

"Sure, anything for a cripple," she teased.

Five, four, three, two, one. Happy New Year! Pete held Edie tightly and gave her a big kiss. He backed away and announced, "Thank you, Miss Mohr. Now I must go."

"Go home? You usually last till the sunrise."

"Not tonight. I talked my Mom into feeding the help and that includes the two black gals from Davenport. Mom wasn't too happy about it because she doesn't trust the darkies. She thinks they will steal everything. I've found them to be hard-working and honest. She's just prejudiced, like most white people. So, tomorrow morning I pick up the girls at eight in Pleasant Prairie. Take care, love you."

With that Pete, grabbed his coat and headed out the door. He threw a kiss. Edie waved good-bye. She was oblivious of the half-dozen other gals standing next to her. Each thought it was a kiss for her.

January was its usual cold self in Iowa. Chores were long and difficult. Edie's hands became chapped and rough despite coating them with udder balm. She hated the smell of the salve, but it healed the cracks and cuts. Hattie warned her hands would never again be lady's hands. Every night she would scrub her hands and apply some of her mother's Pond's cold cream.

The winter also made the basement shower very cold. Edie and her mother brought the old round galvanized wash tub inside and filled it with water from the cook stove. They bathed in the kitchen because the stove heated it faster. A couple of times, Frank used the warmer room for his weekly bath.

Another problem was keeping the water system functioning. The water tank sat uphill from the house and barn to get more pressure. Frank installed an oil heater in the pump shed underneath the tank. It would burn heating oil or kerosene, whichever was cheaper. Every night Frank filled the supply tank. If he didn't, the pipes would freeze and stop the flow of water. The worst scenario would be a broken pipe, which meant a major repair and loss of water.

The trio survived January. Every day Hattie hoped for another letter from Ralph. It was almost March before his next letter.

Dear folks, I have been transferred to the medic corp. They needed someone to assure the ambulances made it back from the front. I fill in as a driver now and then. It is horrible. The men I haul are burned and broken. Many suffer from mustard gas. It burns their eyes so bad, some may never see again. Yes, many have gas masks, but if you can't get them on quick enough you get burned. Sometimes the screams and crying from the back of the van scares me. I only hope I don't recognize anyone. It is better than fighting on the front, but not much. There goes the siren again. I must go. I am very tired, but I am alive. Your loving son, Ralph.

Hattie tucked the letter away in a shoebox and hid it in a drawer under the piano seat. She read them over and over, then she'd cry. Edie, although happy for Ralph's letter, was more interested in letters from Sean. Aunt Helen called her sister but made no mention of a letter from Sean. She had not

131

heard from him since Christmas.

Because of the severe winter weather in Europe, the war was at a standstill. Only skirmishes were fought. Everyone was waiting for the warmth of spring. The largest causality was due to health. Pneumonia was a big killer. The cold, wet conditions sent many men to the hospitals. Pete's brother, Harry, was one of the unfortunate soldiers.

Pete's mother received a letter from Harry the last week of March. His handwriting was feeble. He told her he was in a hospital in Orleans, France, and was expecting to be transferred to London, then he would be sent home. Pete expected to have Harry home for some of the spring planting. The McKillip family was excited.

On Easter Sunday afternoon, Bruce and Alma were sitting in the parlor when a military auto pulled up outside. Two men dressed in uniform came to the door. Bruce answered the door. The officer spoke. "Mr. McKillip?"

"Yes."

They handed him a telegram and said, "It is with great remorse to inform you that your son, Corporal Harry Andrew McKillip, has passed. He was recuperating in the St. Anne's Hospital in London, England, from pneumonia, but failed to recover. We are very sorry for your loss. The Department the Army will be in contact with you and your family shortly to arrange for internment."

Bruce was shaken but stoic. He thanked the officers and accepted their telegram. His next task was telling Alma.

Alma asked Bruce when he returned, "Who was that, Bruce? They looked very official. Did they have news about Harry?"

"Yes, Alma, they had news of Harry, but I'm afraid it is not good news."

Alma got a frightened look on her face. She screamed, "No! No! No! Not my Harry."

"Yes, my love, our beloved son, Harry, died in a London hospital last week. He will be coming home to rest. We must make plans for his funeral."

Bruce lifted Alma up and hugged her. He hugged her like he had never hugged her before. He was a man of little emotion, but this tore him to his core. Harry was the one to take over the farm. Pete was okay, but his wild and flamboyant ways worried his parents. They expected him to work anywhere but at the McKillip farm.

Alma struggled to help arrange Harry's funeral. They had purchased a family plot in Paar Cemetery just southeast of Pleasant Prairie for Mary two years ago. They never expected another child would be there before either of them. Harry's casket arrived six weeks later. The Rock Island Arsenal provided soldiers for a twenty-one gun salute. Alma received a new forty eight-star flag.

After the service, Alma wouldn't leave the site. It was Susan who convinced her to leave. The wake was short, for the neighbors were cognizant of Alma's sorrow. She told her family she would wear black for the next year. Her mourning became an obsession. Everything she did and everywhere she went, she told of Harry. After six months, she refused to go anywhere, even church.

Pete and his sister, Susan, were also shaken, but they knew life had to continue. The Mohr's attended the funeral and the wake. When they were saying their good-byes, Edie held Pete's hand.

She told him, "Anytime you need someone to talk to, come over. I am generally at home. Dad needs me until Ralph comes home."

"Thank you, Edie. I'll remember."

BOB BANCKS

CHAPTER 12: EDIE THE CELEBRITY

April was fast approaching. Planting season began, and the work load increased. Edie helped clean the lots and barns. Hattie worried about all the physical labor Edie was doing, but she knew Frank needed her help. In the back of her mind, she was proud of her daughter working so hard.

The first week in April, more bad news came to the community. Myron Hendricks was killed in the war. He was the Paul Hendricks' only son. Paul's wife, Myrtle, mourned so much, she committed suicide by cutting her wrists. Paul was so depressed because he lost both his son and wife, he rented the land and moved to Durant.

Paul's brother helped with the farm sale. Edie wanted to go, but her mother said it was no place for a young woman. It was man's territory. The sale started at eleven. Emil had small equipment, but it was well cared for. The crowd was large, mostly just lookers. The local men had filled their Spring needs already.

Frank returned around three. He walked into the kitchen all smiles. "Edie," he said, "could you come with me? I need some help getting some equipment home from Hendricks' sale."

"Sure, Daddy, just give me a couple of minutes to change."

"You'd better wear some of those overalls you wear for chores."

Hattie butted in. "Frank, she can't go to Hendricks' in those overalls."

Frank turned to Hattie, smiled a big smile, and replied, "Well, she can't drive her tractor home in a skirt."

Edie shrieked, "My tractor! You bought me a tractor?"

"Yes, I did, Punky. It is a small unit, but I think you can handle it. Nobody seemed to want such a small machine, so I bought it. Now I need you to drive it home."

"I'll be ready in a jiffy."

Hattie scowled at her husband. "Do you really think a young woman should be driving a tractor? What about her health? What about her having babies later?"

"Oh, come on, Hattie. That is an old wives' tale about women working tough physical jobs. Look at the Indians. Those squaws slaved in their villages. It was the braves who loafed. It won't hurt her a bit. Besides, I need another tractor driver. I'll make sure I start it and teach her how to drive. She drives a car now anyway."

Edie was back and ready to go. She and her father hopped into the T and headed for Hendricks'. An hour later, Edie came chugging up the lane on her 10-20 Fordson. Hattie came out with her Brownie camera and snapped a photo of her sitting on the rig. Edie thought she couldn't wait until the fields dried enough to plow. But before plowing there was oats to sow and alfalfa to seed. Her dad drove the big Wallis with the disk and Edie followed with the spike-toothed harrow. She harrowed it one direction, then cross-ways. She drove her little Fordson hitched to the wagon and seeder. Her father filled the seeder and kept the chain on the wheel. They worked until five, then home to help milk the cows. Most days they worked twelve hours or more. Her face and hands became tanned. She was so busy her thoughts of Sean were far and few between.

Her mother okayed a modern bob for Edie. She realized it was easier to wash and care for.

By mid-April, Frank started Edie out plowing some alfalfa ground. The cornstalks needed disking before plowing. Frank would do that with the Wallis. Edie found plowing was not difficult once you got the front wheel into the furrow. The most difficult task was reaching back and pulling the trip rope to bring the plow out of the ground or put it back into the soil.

She loved being outdoors. She would watch the birds dive after the worms and bugs on the surface of the newly turned soil. On the cool and windy days, she'd add one of Ralph's jackets and tie her felt hat down over her ears. As the month of May approached, the days became decidedly warmer. She'd let her hair blow. She'd roll her sleeves up like her dad and let the sun tan her arms. By five, her arms and hands would be tired. Her dad would stay and do field work while she went to the barns and started chores.

The story of Edie driving a tractor spread. One day a reporter from the *Muscatine Journal* called and asked if he could interview her. She agreed. He came out and took photos of Edie sitting on the Fordson. She made the front page because she was helping the war effort while her older brother was fighting. The story made the Associated Press wires and she became a celebrity. She received a letter from an Iowa Senator Wilbur Kenyon congratulating her work. The War Department awarded her a certificate of honor.

The fields were ready to plant by May tenth. Frank went out to check the warmth of the soil. He laid his bare forearm on the ground. If it didn't feel cold, it was okay to plant. Another test was the oak trees. If their leaves were as big as squirrel ears, you could start planting corn.

Now came the real test: if Edie could handle the big Wallis. She did fine except in the hilly fields where she would have to ride the uphill brake to help steer the tractor. Edie's arms and hands were so tired by lunchtime, she dropped her fork and her knife. Hattie winked at Frank and pointed to Edie. He took the hint and relieved her for the rest of the afternoon.

The days were long. Edie was usually tired and dirty. Hattie fashioned three pair of overalls for Edie. This way she could go three days before washing. Driving the tractor was not so dirty; it was the constant chores and muddy yards. Many days she'd undress partially in the wash house and dash to the house in her underwear.

Edie worked like a man, which in the rural world was not acceptable. Women had their place in the home, garden, and chicken house. They were to help milk the cows, take care of the children, and still go to church on Sunday. Edie was proving to her father and the rest of the world women were capable of very physical work.

BOB BANCKS

CHAPTER 13: THE ESCAPE

One warm Saturday afternoon, it rained. Edie was helping her mother sort seeds for the garden when they heard a car pull up. Before Edie reached the door, someone knocked. She opened the door and was surprised to see Pete. It wasn't the usual Pete. He was in overalls and flannel shirt. He was clean, but not the well-dressed Pete she knew.

"Pete, what brings you here?"

"Well, it rained, so I can't be in the field and I figured you couldn't be either, so I was wondering if you would like to go to see a movie?"

Edie looked back at her mom. She nodded her approval.

"Okay, but I have to do chores first."

"Fine, I have chores, too. Especially since I left most of the hired help off early. I'll be by about seven."

Edie started the milking early. Hattie helped her bathe and dress. She gave her a quick supper. Edie was combing her hair for the last time when Pete drove up the lane. It was his usual seven o'clock on the dot. They went to Muscatine for the movie. It was over by nine, so they went to Porky's Cafe. It was a little hole in the wall of a café, which many of the young adults patronized. They slid into a small two-person booth and ordered two hamburgers and two chocolate malted milks.

Pete heard someone yell, "Pete, Pete McKillip. Long time, no see, farmer boy. What brings you to town?"

Pete answered, "It rained."

"Come on over and sit with us and bring your friend."

It was Gregg Haskins. Gregg was known for being wealthy and flamboyant. His father was a banker and businessman in Muscatine.

Pete introduced Edie. One of the girls blurted out, "I know you. You're the gal on the tractor. You're a celebrity."

Edie smiled and acknowledged her comment but said nothing. These girls were much wealthier than Edie. They wore silk blouses and long tailored skirts. Everyone had earrings and bracelets. She felt a little out of place in her cotton blouse and skirt.

As the group sat at a long table, Gregg said, "How about everyone coming to my place? It's early and my folks are away. We can have a blast."

Pete looked at Edie. She shrugged her shoulders. It was still early. They left the cafe and journeyed to Gregg's. Pete drove his own car because Gregg's home was east of town and it didn't make sense to drive back to town before heading home.

They were almost out of town when Edie asked, "Pete, may I call my mother? I don't want her to wait up. This might be longer than we planned. I don't want Mom to stay up and wait."

"Sure. There's a phone at the next gas station. I know the owner. He'll let you use it. I'll stop."

On the way out, Pete explained, "The Haskins' home is large and just outside of town. Gregg is the son of a banker. His father influenced the draft board to keep Gregg from being drafted. He along with some of his rich friends used the excuse their sons needed to finish college. They promised after graduation their sons would volunteer. The fathers knew the war would be over by that time. Gregg has too much money and is used to getting what he wants and that includes women. If a girl doesn't come on to him like he desires, it is a one-and-done date."

"Sounds like a rich kid. How come you know him?"

"We were friends in high school. We both played baseball. I stayed with him because his car was a girl magnet. He asked me to go with him and some girls to Chicago for a Cubs game. The game was okay. It was the girls, Beverly and Janet, who caused the problem. We stayed at the Morrison Hotel in downtown Chicago after the game. We did a little bar hopping before bed. I didn't realize Gregg arranged to have adjoining rooms with the girls. Soon the door between the rooms was opened. Beverly was dressed in her nightie and robe. She told me to go to the other room and be with Janet. I could see I was not wanted there. I departed to Janet's room. She was fully dressed.

She asked, "I need to get more comfortable. Is that okay?"

I said, "I didn't care."

"She went into the bathroom and came out wearing a sheer nightgown, and I do mean sheer. She might as well have been naked. I could tell she was embarrassed. She wrapped a towel around her body. We sat and talked for a while. We heard love making sounds from the other room. I told Janet I'd sleep in the chair and she could have the bed. The next morning Gregg discovered we had not slept together. He was angry with me. It was the last time I saw him. I think it was at that time I realized maybe girls didn't want to have sex all the time. I know, you may not believe me by the way I pawed around on you our first date, but I have changed. I want to be your friend, Edie. We've been friends for a long time and I would like our relationship to continue."

"I would like to continue our friendship too, Pete. I almost think of you as a brother or at least a step-brother." Edie replied, "But I'll definitely stay away from that Gregg guy."

When they arrived, the three other couples were already there. Gregg was pouring drinks.

"You ever taste brandy, Edie?' he asked.

"No."

"Here, try some."

Edie took a sip. It burned her throat. She coughed some. He laughed.

"It only burns the first time. Here have another shot."

Edie did and agreed it was better, but she'd rather have ginger ale.

"Okay, little farm girl, ginger ale it is." he laughed again.

The party continued. Edie watched Pete. She noticed he would take a drink and hold it for a long while. One time she caught him throwing it into a potted plant. The others were becoming quite drunk. Pretty soon Lillian, Gregg's girl, said, "Zowie! It's warm in here."

"Well, take your dress off, we're all friends here." Gregg laughed.

Lillian faked a cough and replied, "Maybe later, sweetie, there's others here."

Then he asked, "Hey! Would you girls like to tour this mansion?"

"Sure," the girls chorused back.

Gregg said, "Well, follow me."

He led the four women through the kitchen. It was the biggest kitchen Edie had ever seen.

"How many people work in here?" she asked.

Gregg smiled and answered, "Well, little farm girl, Mom has two cooks for every day, but she hires a chef from Moline for big dinners. We feed as many as fifty people here sometimes."

"Fifty people! Wow!"

Gregg sensed he was impressing Edie. He took them up the servant's stairs to the second floor. As he led them down a long hall, Edie counted six bedrooms and three bathrooms. The girls followed him into a huge bedroom. It had a big bed with a canopy over it and off to one side was a master bath. The women oohed and aahed. Such opulence, even the rich girls were impressed.

"This is my room. I have my own bath and walk-in closet," boasted Gregg.

He led them down the grand staircase to the living room. To the right was a large ballroom. One of the girls commented, "This is huge. May we dance later?"

"Sure, I've got an electric phonograph. We've all the latest recordings. And guess what, below the dance floor is a swimming pool."

"A swimming pool! You have an indoor swimming pool?"

"Sure, my dad and mom swim almost every day."

"May we see it?"

"Sure, follow me."

They rounded up the men and all traipsed down to the pool. It was better than they expected when Gregg threw on the lights. It was all tiled with blue and white tiles. There were two lap lanes marked on the bottom. At the far end was a diving board. The water shimmered in the lights. One of the girls knelt and touched the water.

"It's warm!" she exclaimed.

"Oh, yes, Dad heats the water to eighty degrees. He likes to swim *au natural* as he calls it."

"Au natural? What's that?*"

"Naked, nude. Want to try it?"

"I've never done that before," said Gregg's girl.

One of the others giggled. "I didn't bring a swim suit."

"You don't need one as far as I'm concerned," replied Gregg with a mischievous grin. "I'll not wear one if you're willing. As I said, my dad does it all the time."

Everyone hesitated. Gregg announced, "Come on, we're all friends here. Guys to the left, gals to the right. Last one into the pool is a rotten egg, or..."

"Or what?"

"A celebrity farmer girl." said Gregg as he leered at Edie.

The guys hurried to doff their shoes and socks, next their trousers and shirts. Pete didn't follow the others as quickly. He feigned difficulty at untying his shoes. The gals quickly slipped out of their skirts and blouses. They kicked off their shoes and rolled their silk stockings down. Gregg's girl, Lillian, pulled her camisole over her head and slipped out of her half-slip. She was in her panties and brassiere.

Pete looked at Edie. He motioned her over to his side. He could tell she was afraid of what was about to happen. This crowd was too raucous for her. Yes, as a little girl, she and Pete had gone skinny dipping, but they were nine years old. This was way different.

"It looks like it is time for us to leave, Edie. What do you think?"

"Yes, most definitely," she answered.

They started for the door.

"Hey, where are you two going?"

"Home. We have to work tomorrow," explained Pete.

"Oh no, you don't. Grab Pete, guys. I want to see what this little farm girl is made of," sneered Gregg.

The guys corralled Pete. They slammed him into a chair and held his arms tightly behind the chair back. He winced in pain.

Edie hurried to his rescue and yelled, "You leave my friend alone. You, bullies!"

She began to flail one of the men holding Pete.

Gregg hollered, "Hey, you females, grab this wild cat before she hurts someone."

It took all three to pull Edie away. They held her against the wall. Gregg glared at the farm girl. He followed with a nasty smile.

"Hey, farmer girl, how much of a friend of Petey Boy are you?"

Edie didn't answer. She just glared back and waited.

"If two of you can hold her, I want Lillian to come over here a second."

The girls slammed Edie hard against the wall. Lillian sauntered over to Gregg.

"What do you want, Greggy?"

"Unbutton Pete's shirt and undershirt."

"Sure thing."

As she bent over to undo the buttons, Gregg patted her silk panty.

"Nice fabric," he said, "and nice fanny. I need to see more of you sometime."

Lillian looked up at him and smiled. Gregg lit a cigarette.

"Pull open his shirt." He looked at Edie. "Now, little farmer girl. We will see how much you care for this farmer boy. Let her go, girls."

"Now, farmer girl, come over closer. I want to tell you something."

Edie walked over and stood in front of Gregg.

"I'm going to tell you once and only once. I want you to strip to the buff or I will burn your friend with this cigarette. What do you say?"

This was getting ugly. The others were cheering Gregg on, even the women.

Lillian yelled, "Look at her hands and face. They are brown as a spic. I'll bet she's a spic."

One of guys yelled, "I'll bet two bucks her boobs are brown, too. I heard rural gals go topless in the summer."

Edie stalled. This was not like the incident in Muscatine. There the men forcibly stripped her. Now she was being asked to do something she didn't want to do. She thought, *Is Gregg bluffing? Surely, he wouldn't burn Pete.*

Gregg asked, "I'm waiting, farmer girl. Start stripping or Pete gets burned."

Pete yelled out, "Don't do it, Edie. He's bluffing."

Gregg whirled around and stuck the glowing butt in the middle of Pete's chest. Pete clenched his teeth. He strained against the two others. Edie decided to go slowly. Maybe one of the others would call a halt to Gregg's demands. She undid the clasp and buttons on the side of her skirt and let it fall. She stepped aside and slipped out of her shoes. She stood stocking-footed and stopped.

"Your top next, farmer girl."

Edie unbuttoned her blouse and took it off. Gregg took another swallow of whiskey. He knew he would win. He always won. Women who refused him wished they hadn't later. He had money. He had power.

Lillian laughed and said, "I guess she has white arms after all, but this skirt smells of barn. I think I'll wash it for her and maybe her blouse, too."

She picked up Edie's clothes and doused them in the pool, then tossed them to the side.

"Now your slip, country girl," said one of the girls.

Edie said, "I believe I've gone far enough."

"Oh, you think so. Well, I think not. I said to the buff. That means naked, nude, bare. You're taking everything off. I want to see tits and pussy," Gregg hissed.

Gregg didn't hesitate and rubbed another butt into Pete's skin. Pete swore at him. He looked at Edie and shook his head.

He said, "Don't do it, Edie. This guy's a creep. I should not have brought you out here. I didn't think it would come to this."

Edie backed away toward the women. She needed to stall and think of a plan. She had to stop Gregg from continuing to torture Pete. She glared at Gregg. She wanted to punch him, but she knew it would only aggravate the situation. When she was near the deep end she stopped. She slowly raised her slip over her head.

"Lookie, lookie, farmer girl does wear panties. I'll bet they're not silk, though. I'll bet she's hiding something. Maybe she's a guy," teased Lillian. "I bet her toenails aren't polished. Have her remove her hose next."

Everyone laughed.

Gregg leered at the small figure standing fifteen feet away. He puffed on his cigarette one more time, the end glowed red, and said, "Well, take off the hose."

Edie rolled down her hose. She placed them with her soaked skirt and blouse.

"See, her toes are plain. What a doof!"

"Okay, what's next? Top or bottom."

"Top, top," yelled one of the guys, "we want to see some tits. Maybe they look like cow tits."

Edie didn't move. She clenched her fists. She was not about to go any further.

Lilian stepped forward and said, "You girls hold her. I'll help her with her brassiere, then I'll do the panties."

Lillian stepped behind Edie and began to unfasten her brassiere. Edie had flashes of Muscatine. She wasn't going to become naked again in public, for men or women. She took control of her situation. She slammed her foot down on the arch of the girl holding her right arm. The girl crumbled in pain. Edie shoved her toward the pool. The girl stumbled and went headfirst into the water. Edie surprised the second girl by whirling around and grabbing the girl's brassiere and pulling her forward. Then she pushed her backward into the pool.

The men cheered. Lillian reacted by putting Edie into a choke hold. She was six inches taller and probably twenty pounds heavier. Edie struggled to free herself. She inched her way to the edge of the pool. She reached for the railing of a ladder coming up from the deep end. With one quick move she bent over, bringing the larger Lillian over her back. Lillian slid down over Edie's head and into the pool.

Pete yelled, "Run, Edie, run for the door."

Lillian surfaced and started splashing around. She shrieked, "I can't touch bottom. I can't swim. Help! Help!"

Gregg stopped his he-man charade and dove into the shallow end. He came up with his head all bloodied. He had hit the bottom. The other two dragged Pete to the edge and threw him in. They hurried to the distressed girls in the deep end.

Edie jumped in and helped the fully clothed Pete out of the pool. She grabbed her clothes and shoes. Pete guided her to an exit door. They ran outside only to find it was an enclosed patio. There was a fence about five feet high surrounding the area. Pete tried the gate. It was locked.

He panicked and cried, "How will we get out of here? We can't go back in there."

Edie didn't panic. First, she jammed a heavy lawn chair against the door to block the others.

"Come on, follow me."

She went to a low spot in the lawn. Throwing her clothes over the fence, she leaped up and grabbed the top board. With her toes finding cracks between the boards, she climbed over the barrier.

Pete was not going to let his girlfriend outdo him. He took a running leap and almost cleared the fence. He came down on his bad ankle. He heard a snap. He tried to get up.

"Edie, come help me. I can't walk."

Edie hurried back and lifted him. He leaned on her shoulder as he hobbled to his Studebaker.

"Get me to the other side. You'll have to drive."

Edie pushed Pete into the passenger seat, then ran around and slid beneath the steering wheel. She pushed with all her might on the starter button on the floor. The Studebaker answered with a roar.

The gang was at the patio gate yelling and shaking their fists. Edie put in the clutch and slammed the gearshift forward. The car lurched. She drove around the two parked cars ahead of her and headed for the gate. Quickly, she hit second gear.

The gate at the end of the lane was going shut. Gregg must have a switch to control the gate from the house. Edie floored the auto. She hit third and roared through the gate. They were on the road.

"Which way?" she asked.

"To the right, away from town. We'll lose them in the country. There is little dust because of the showers."

Edie floored the car. Pete turned on the headlights.

"I'm cold," he said.

"I'm not exactly warm," answered Edie. "I don't have much on and I'm barefoot."

"Drive to your place. I will stay there."

"I can't go home like this. I've got to put my clothes on and they are wet. What about your place?"

"My parents are having a party. Can't go there."

Edie noticed headlights in the rearview mirror.

"They're after us. Where should we go?"

"You drive. I'll direct."

Edie drove several miles. The sign said, "New Era, two miles."

"Stop and let the dust settle a bit. Now drive slow and turn right at the next driveway."

Edie slowed and turned into what she thought was a field. Pete doused the lights.

"Can you see the path in the moonlight?"

"Yes, but barely."

"I'll shine this flashlight ahead. I don't want the others to follow us."

"Where are we going?"

"We'll be there soon. It's my hunting shack. It used to be the manager's office when the mine was open. Dad tore down all the buildings and was going to tear this one down until Harry and I begged him to let us have it. We cleaned it up and used it for a hideout. Mom would come out here once in a while for peace and quiet. Pull up on the far side."

Edie followed the path. In a few feet a shed appeared. It was not painted and had a small porch. A metal chimney jutted out the back. She pulled around to the far side and stopped.

"Help me to the porch. I'll tell you where the key is."

Edie helped Pete out and started for the porch. He leaned heavily on her shoulder. She had her arm around his waist. He moaned.

"I'm not faking this, Edie, my ankle is really hurting."

"I know. I also watched you dump your drinks into the plant."

Pete tried to smile. "I'll bet it's the first drunk rubber plant around here. Here's the flashlight. The key is in the wood box."

Pete leaned on the porch post while Edie located the key. She opened the door and scanned the inside. It was just one room about the size of a chicken coop. There were two cots, one on each side. There was a small table and a couple of chairs. A pot-bellied stove was in one corner. On the table was a kerosene lantern.

"Why don't you light the lantern first? There's matches on the shelf by the window. I'll wait for you here."

Edie entered and took the glass chimney off the lantern, turned up the wick, and lit it. Once it was going she replaced the chimney and trimmed the flame. She returned to the porch and helped Pete inside. She sat him on a chair.

"Close the door, Edie. We don't want the light to show outside. If those headlights were really one from the gang, we don't want them to see us from the road."

Edie closed the door as ordered and pulled the curtains closed at the two windows. She turned and put her hands on her hips.

"Pete, you're a mess. We must get you out of those wet clothes and quickly. We also must get a fire going to warm this place up. What should I do first?"

"I think you should light the stove first, then we will talk about my wet clothes."

"Okay, I'll light the stove, then off with your wet clothes. Where is the wood and kindling?"

"Over behind the stove. There is some newspaper on the shelf."

Edie crumpled the paper, added some kindling and logs, and tossed in a small cup of kerosene, then lit a match. The fire was soon roaring away. She returned to Pete and frowned.

"You haven't done much."

"I know. Do I have to?"

"Yes, if you don't want to catch pneumonia."

"But. But..."
"But what? Are you afraid of me? Certainly, you have been naked with other women."

"Yes, but you're different."

"How, just because I'm a woman now and not a nine-year old girl?"

"Yes, and you're . . . you're Edie."

"So."

"You're my neighbor, my friend."

"All the more reason. Now let's get going. I don't want my friend to die."

Edie attacked his feet first. The left shoe and sock were easy. His right foot was the one hurting. She lifted it gently. He winced. She untied his shoe and inched his sock from his foot. Edie pulled over a little stool and rested his foot on it. Next, she attacked his shirt. She pulled it free and hung it up on a convenient wire strung across the room.

"Why the wire?"

"Harry and I hung our wet hunting clothes up there."

"Ok. Can you stand?"

"Barely."

Edie unbuckled Pete's belt. She put her arm under his armpit and lifted. With her other arm, she pushed his trousers down from his hips. She scurried around to his feet and pulled the pants off before he could change his mind.

"Boy, you are strong!" he commented.

Edie popped back, "I'm a farm girl, remember."

"That's right, you just beat three city girls single-handed."

"You got any blankets around here?"

"In the steel cabinet. Why?"

"Because you're going to need one after I take off your wet underwear."

"You're not going to do that, too, are you?"

"Yes, I am, then I'm going to wrap your ankle and tend to your burns. That is, if there is a first aid kit around here."

Pete sighed. He knew he better follow orders from this wisp of a farm girl.

"The first aid kit is in the cabinet behind Harry's cot."

Edie climbed upon the cot and found the kit. Next, she opened the steel cabinet and pulled out three blankets. She shook them out. They were small.

"What are these?" she asked.

"I forgot. Mom took all the big blankets home to have them washed.

Those are just lap throws and a baby blanket. I guess this is all we have."

"We'll make do."

Edie unbuttoned the top of Pete's underwear and slid them from his shoulders and down to his waist. She covered his bare shoulders with one throw. She motioned for him to try to stand. He steadied himself by putting a hand on her shoulder. She wrapped another throw around his waist, without a glance or smirk, and pulled his underwear to the floor. She noticed his teeth were chattering.

"Get closer to the stove. I'm going out to the car to fetch my clothes. They need to be dried, too. When I come back, I'll take care of your foot and chest."

She disappeared and scampered back in, being careful not to leave the door open for long. After she hung her skirt, blouse, and slip on the wire, she opened the first aid kit and found some elastic wrap.

Edie sat on the cot and said, "Put your foot in my lap."

Pete did as he was told. Edie began wrapping the sprained ankle. Pete watched her work. She was very efficient and precise.

She looked up and asked, "Now, is that better?"

"Yes, much."

"Now for your burns. There is some salve and gauze in the kit. I'll use that."

She removed the blanket covering his shoulders and back and had him face the lantern for light. Squeezing the tube of salve, she gently applied it to the burns. He gritted his teeth.

As she wrapped the gauze around his chest, she caught him staring at her bosom.

She glared at him and scolded, "You'd really like to see my boobs, wouldn't you?"

Pete didn't say a word.

"Well, I'm sure you have gotten an eyeful already. I must fetch some water to wash my feet. I can't put these dirty feet in my clean shoes. The pump at the well outside works, doesn't it?"

"Yes, it might have a mouse nest in the spigot, but just keep pumping and it will wash out."

Edie grabbed a small pail and headed for the well. Pete could hear her pumping the handle. Suddenly, he heard a shriek and some choice words from Edie. He hobbled to the door and glanced toward the well. There was Edie soaking wet.

"What happened?" he asked, trying not to laugh.

"Oh, there was a mouse nest all right. It plugged the spigot and the water squirted out the top. I got soaked."

She stomped into the little shack. Her panties clung to her like wet leaves. She pushed past him and turned to say, "Now what am I going to do? I'm soaked and have no dry underwear."

"I can see that," Pete mused.

Edie angrily shot back, "What are you staring at?"

"You."

"Oh, and I look terrible, don't I?"

"You look great to me. Why don't you join my blanket party?"

Edie calmed down, smiled, and said, "Good idea! Where's the third blanket?"

Pete handed it to her. She wrapped the blanket around her chest which barely reached her knees and tucked it in. Next, she reached under the blanket and took off her under garments.

"I guess now we're a pair. I'll hang these, then we can sit and talk until they are dry."

Pete watched as Edie stood on the stool to hang her undies. Her blanket was the smallest and covered the least. As Edie reached up, the split on her side showed much of her body. Pete wanted to reach up and give the blanket a tug, but he thought better of it.

Edie stuck another two logs into the pot-bellied stove. They moved their chairs as close as they dared. For the next forty-five minutes they talked. They talked about Harry and Ralph. They talked about farming. They talked about whether women should drive tractors and cars. There was a quiet moment.

Pete asked," Have you heard from Sean?"

Edie gave him a surprised look and replied, "Not since Christmas."

"Have you written him?"

"No."

"Why not?"

"Because my Dad won't allow it, since he found out that Sean is a Catholic."

"But he's fighting for all of us. The Army doesn't care what he is. Why should your father?"

"I know, but that's different, my Dad has a thing about Catholics."

"Do you still love him?"

'Who my Dad or Sean?"

"Sean."

"Yes, I do. I pray every night for his safe return. Why do you ask?"

"Listen, when we were at the Halloween Party months ago, I could see you two were still in love. Your eyes gave you away. I knew right then I had no chance. You love him."

"Really? Is it that obvious?"

"Yes."

Edie's face clouded. Tears welled in her eyes. Her lips started to quiver.

Pete reached over and took hold of her hand.

"Go ahead, Edie. It's all right to cry."

Pete moved closer to Edie and embraced her shaking body. She hugged him back.

He tilted her head back a bit to consider her face and said, "Edie, my friend, I love you and I will always love you, but until you love me back, I will just take care of you. In fact, I called Sean before he left and told him if fate does not let him return, I will then and only then court you. I hope Sean does come home. It is difficult for me to want that because of my feelings toward you. You and Sean should be together. God will take care of you and Sean and me until that time comes. I must admit you are a very attractive young woman. Any man should be willing to die for you. I know you were willing to do anything to save me from burns. You are a true, true friend."

He brushed back her hair and kissed her. Edie didn't resist. Her emotions were running high. She threw her arms around his neck and said, "Thank you, Pete. I will always be your friend."

The flame on the lantern flicker and died. The only light in the room was the glow through the glass on the stove door. Edie remembered the night Sean came to her room and sat all night and how in the morning he covered her with a blanket. Later, when she opened her eyes, he was there brushing her hair out of her eyes. The vision was so clear. Now she needed him again, but he was not here.

It didn't matter. Pete was with her now. They had survived a scary evening together, each sacrificing for the other. She gently touched Pete's face. It wasn't the same face from last October. He had changed.

Pete wanted to continue with the moment of passion. He wanted to throw their blankets on the floor and lie naked with Edie, but something made him stop.

He whispered, "I can't. It isn't right. I promised Sean. This is a moment of passion, not true love. Let's not do something we'd be sorry for later."

Edie was shocked, but she agreed. "You're right, Pete. If we are to remain friends, we must respect each other. I apologize for my passionate behavior."

"On the contrary, you are lovely, you are beautiful . . . and naked."

Edie began to giggle. She looked down at herself, her blanket had slipped.

"Do you remember the summers we played in the creek?" she asked looking at Pete.

"Yes, those were fun times."

"Remember the one day in August, just before school started? It was just you and me and our fishing poles. The ponies were grazing under the oak tree. You thought you saw a turtle. We waded into the water and discovered it was a turtle. The water was deeper than we could go with our clothes on, so we decided to strip. We were both a little embarrassed at first, but soon it didn't seem to matter. We played for about twenty minutes and forgot about the darn turtle."

"I'll never forget it. You were cute then and cuter now. Edie, you are a lovely young woman."

"I'll see if our clothes are dry. Maybe we should go home."

Edie re-tucked her small blanket and walked over to the clothesline and felt the cloth. She pulled some from the line and laid the almost dry clothes on the cots.

"Do you need help dressing?" she asked.

"No, I think I can manage. My ankle is much better."

Edie sorted her clothes and asked, "Do you know where my brassiere is?"

"Yes, it's over by the stove. I think it fell when you jiggled the clothes line."

"Oh, that's right. I remember. Say, how are we going to explain this event?"

"I got that figured out. We go to your place. It's almost morning. Your mom will question your mussed skirt and blouse. You tell her about the party and how we were thrown into the pool fully dressed because we refused to swim in our underwear. We'll tell her we went to my sister Susan's to dry our clothes, then came over to your house. I'll leave early saying I should go home for chores, which is the truth. On the way home, I'll stop at my sister's and explain the situation. She'll laugh, but she'll cover for us. I've covered for her many times."

"Sounds like a great plan. My mother will be suspicious, but if Susan will back us up, how can she be angry."

"Right, now let's get going."

Edie started to shake out her skirt. Pete untangled his underwear. They turned away from each other and dressed. In a few minutes, they were ready to go. Edie let Pete lean on her shoulder while he hobbled to the car. Edie slipped behind the steering wheel.

She turned to Pete and said, "You know, Pete, you're okay."

It was three in the morning. She helped Pete lie on the sofa, then headed to her room. Her mother stopped her at the top of the stairs.

She asked, "Who are you talking to?"

"Pete. He's napping downstairs on the sofa. The party was awful. We had some problems with the others."

"Why don't you have him sleep in Ralph's room? It will be better than the sofa. I'll go down and ask him."

"Mother! You must wear something more than a nightie."

Hattie smiled and said, "You're right, you go down. I'll turn the bed down. I'll get a pair of Ralph's pajamas out. We wouldn't want him to sleep naked, now would we?"

"No, Mother. That would be embarrassing. Oh, he also has a sprained ankle, so it may take a minute or so," Edie answered with a smirk on her face.

Pete gladly accepted Hattie's offer. He hopped on one foot as he ascended the stairs. In the morning, Edie heard her father head out for chores. Next, she heard her mother in the kitchen. She tiptoed to Pete's room in her nightie and woke him.

"Pete, I'm getting up. I must help Dad with the milking."

Pete opened his eyes and found Edie bending over him. She kissed him on the forehead and tiptoed back. Pete rose and quickly gathered his clothes. Before heading down, Edie poked her head into his room and said, "Have a nice day, Pete."

Pete answered, "Already have."

BOB BANCKS

CHAPTER 14: EDIE THE ORATOR

It was after Mother's Day when Hattie received another letter from Ralph. It read:

Dear Mom and Dad,

The Germans have attacked all along the front. We Americans are not yet ready. I carry many British soldiers back from front lines. Many soldiers die in the ambulance. I get so close I can hear the guns. The roads are muddy. Drive with chains all the time. I'm glad I don't have to fight. The cold and mud in the trenches must be awful. Tell Edie hi. Have her go to Ruth's and report I'm okay and will be home soon. Ruth writes every month. I hear we are going to attack, but in the Army, that may mean next week or next month. Say a prayer for all of us here.

Your loving son,
Ralph

Hattie cried a bit. She folded the letter and put it the shoe box. Edie hugged her mother and said, "Don't worry, Mom. Ralph said he'll come home and he will."

Planting began the next day. Frank had Edie drive the Wallis and disk. He would do the planting. Edie endured the hard-steering Wallis. Her arms ached, but she didn't let her mother know.

One day she wore her peasant blouse out in the field. Hattie warned her, but Edie ignored her. By evening she was sunburned. Her skin was red as red could be. Her mother didn't give her any sympathy. The next day was cooler so the regular blouse was proper because of her sore shoulders, she wore only a small chemise under her blouse.

By Decoration Day, the corn was poking through the soil. Pete arrived Sunday evening. He found Edie on the front porch.

"Would you like to come over to my place for a picnic? Ruthie, Connie, and Sandy will be there. Mom is having a gathering promoting women's right to vote. She says the women of America need to have the right to vote. With all the women working in factories and on farms, she says they should be able to vote. She even has Dad on her side. Mrs. Mohr, we'd like for you to come along, also. I think Carrie Chatman Catt is going to come."

"Carrie Chatman Catt, I loved to hear her," answered Edie, "Will you come Mom?"

"Sure. Does your mother need any help?" asked Hattie.

"I suppose. I'll pick you up at one. You know this right to vote thing is perfect. It snapped Mom out of her depression after losing Harry."

The next day Pete was there right on time. Frank said he would drive over later. He needed to clean up and shave first. When they arrived, there was a big tent in the yard.

"My goodness, how many people does your mother expect?" asked Hattie.

"I think more than two hundred."

"Pete, take me to your mother. I'm sure I can help."

Pete led Hattie and Edie to the kitchen.

Pete called his mother over and said, "This is Hattie, Edie's mother. Mrs. Mohr, this is Alma, my mother. Mrs. Mohr wondered if you needed any help."

Alma wiped her hands on her apron and reached out to Hattie saying, "Hattie, it's nice to see you again. I guess Pete forgets we cooked for the threshers many times. How have you been? It is a shame we don't get together more often. Yes, I do need some help with some last-minute fixings. The girls and I are becoming overwhelmed. The response we had was much greater than anticipated. Come, I'll find you an apron."

Pete looked at Edie and said, "If you don't mind, I have a surprise for Edie in Dad's office. We'll be back."

Pete led Edie into Bruce's office. It was filled with leather chairs, books, some trophy animal heads on the wall, and a big wooden desk in the middle. On the desk was an envelope and a piece of paper.

"Sit here, Edie," Pete said, pointing to the big chair. "Look on the desk."

Edie sat and viewed the desk. The paper and envelope were the kind you use to send letters overseas.

Pete continued, "I went to Mrs. Kerchinske's and got Sean's address. When you told me, your father forbade you to write him, I thought maybe you'd like to write him from here. I want you to write him, address the envelope, and seal it. My mother or I will make sure it gets mailed. Now I must help outside. You take all the time you need."

Edie was shocked. Tears welled in her eyes. She looked up at Pete and asked, "Why are you doing this?"

"Because you were willing to disrobe in front of all those ugly people just for me. That, in my eyes, was the bravest and kindest thing anyone had ever done for me. I thought I owed it to you to write your true love."

"Thank you, thank you, from the bottom my heart."

Pete winked and said, "I'll check back in an hour."

Pete returned to find Edie had written her letter, but she was still in tears. He returned to the kitchen and found Hattie. He explained what he had done for Edie. She went to her daughter and tried to console her.

"Mom," she whimpered, "I know you told me I had made my own bed and I had to lie in it, but I love Sean. I have never stopped loving him. Pete knows this better than anyone else."

Hattie looked Edie straight in the eye, "I believe you, my daughter, I just don't know how I can help you. You must continue praying and God will tell you show you the right path. Trust him and trust me."

When Edie calmed, she and her mother joined the group in the kitchen.

Alma hugged Edie and asked, "Edie, Carrie Catt is coming this afternoon to speak. She would like someone from the area to say something before she does. Sort of a warm up speaker. I would like you give us the honor of speaking first this afternoon?"

Edie's face went blank. She asked, "Me? Why me? I'm just a farm girl."

"All the better. You're doing work like a man because your brother is overseas. You are part of the new generation of women. You know how to work in a man's world. If men want us to work like men, then we need to be able to vote like men. We are one half the population. We need our rights. To change the way, men think of us, we need the right to vote. Please say yes. I have several important men in the audience and one very important woman. They need to hear you."

"But I've never spoken before a crowd. What would I say?"

"Just speak from your heart. It will come out okay."

The rally started at two. There were autos parked on the lawn, in the farmyard, and even in a pasture nearby. The crowd filled the tent. Some brought blankets and sat on the ground. Alma's crew were kept busy refilling the jugs of lemonade and iced tea. It was nearly two-thirty before Alma stepped to the podium.

"Ladies and gentlemen, I am so glad to see such a large crowd. We have gathered here to show our support for the nineteenth amendment to the Constitution of these Untied States of America. We women have been silent too long. We are working in factories, in the offices, and on the war front. We are as important as men. We need the right to vote."

A rousing cheer went up from the crowd.

Alma continued, "I have a young woman, my neighbor, who has replaced her brother on the farm. He is in France fighting for our freedom and the world's freedom. She works with her father driving tractors, doing chores, and milking cows plus helping her mother with her household work. She is a dynamo of energy. May I present Edie Mohr?"

There was a modest applause as Edie stepped forward. She eyed the crowd.
"I'm Edie Mohr, proud daughter of Hattie and Frank Mohr. I see many friends here in the audience. Yes, I am a farm girl. Look at my hands. They

164

are tanned. Ladies, I am asking everyone here who has gloves on to remove them immediately. Look at your white hands. They need the sun. Three years ago, scientists discovered we need to be exposed to sunlight to take in Vitamin D. Vitamin D builds strong bones. It builds strong women to have strong babies. We need to free ourselves of the ideas and false fables of the past. Who told us to dress the way we do. Men! Men design our clothes. Men sell our clothes. Men tell us how to eat, to dress, and to act. It is time we take hold of our own lives. We need to do what we want. How many of you work at the button factories in Muscatine? Why do the owners want women to work the button punches? Because we have small hands and are more efficient. We get more buttons from a shell. How many women work at Heinz? They want you because you know how to screw caps on bottles without breaking them. You know when the ketchup is ready.

"Those women who work in the sash and door factories are much more efficient than a man installing window panes. We are much better at typing and writing. We are better at many jobs. Now that our boys are fighting for us, we need to support them. The best way for us to do that is vote for better policies. We can no longer let men rule our lives. We must get things changed. To do that we need the right to vote. Wyoming, Idaho, and Utah women already have the right for state elections. We here in Iowa need the same right. The nation's women need that right. I say let's stand up and write your congressman, your senator, and our president to tell them we want it now!"

Edie stepped back from the podium. The crowd was silent, then a lady's voice yelled out, "You tell 'em, Edie. I'll write."

Then others hollered out. Soon the crowd rose to their feet and clapped and whistled. They rose in a chorus of "Edie, Edie, Edie."

The dignitaries in the front row, who were mostly men, rose and cheered. A single woman approached the small stage and spoke to Alma. Alma nodded her head. She led the woman to the podium. The crowd quieted and sat down.

The lady cleared her voice and said, "I am Carrie Chapman Catt. I have spent years championing the women's right to vote. I've heard many women speak, but this young lady said more in a few heartfelt words than all the speeches I have heard. She is what we are looking for, the new generation of women, women with new ideas, strong-willed women, women who see the future. This young lady although, as she said, is only a farm girl, will take our cause to Washington. Right now, we are embroiled in a war, but we will be victorious and after the war, we women will receive the right to vote. We will be victorious, because of women like Edie Mohr. Thank you for listening."

The crowd stood again. They gave Mrs. Catt a round of applause. Carrie Chapman Catt was a major national leader in the women's suffrage movement. She came to hear the grass roots movement. Mrs. Catt walked over to Edie and shook her hand saying, "Young lady, you did a terrific job. I commend you. How long did you work on your speech?"

"About thirty minutes. Mrs. McKillip just asked me when I arrived today."

"Oh, my goodness," answered Mrs. Catt. "In that case, I would like you to accompany me to Washington next week. If you are willing."

"I'd love to, Mrs. Catt, but we have hay to make and corn to cultivate. I couldn't leave my father with all that work. I must decline."

Mrs. Catt shook her head and said, "I admire you, Edie. You put your family before some silly politicians. Maybe some other time. This fight for our voting rights will take a long time. I'll be back when the war is won and your brother is home. Good-bye, my dear. It has been a pleasure speaking with you."

"Good-bye, Mrs. Catt. The pleasure is all mine, I assure you."

Mrs. Catt smiled back at Edie and replied, "Call me Carrie."

Mrs. Catt exited the stage. Many people shook her hand, including several politicians attending. Her entourage led her to her auto and off she drove.

Edie was immediately swarmed with reporters and well-wishers. She was really surprised when a tall, well-dressed young woman shook her hand and said, "Well, farm girl, I misjudged you. You are very articulate. You also are very strong. I know. You flipped me over your back like a twig. I hope there are no hard feelings." It was Lillian, Gregg's girlfriend. She gave Edie a hug and walked away.

The crowd was slow to disperse. No one wanted to go home. Hattie corralled her daughter and said, "Come, we must go home. Your father is waiting in the car."

The car was quiet on the way home. After Frank pulled into the garage, he helped Hattie out, then graciously helped Edie out. It was something he had never done before. He took Edie's hand and looked her in the eye.

"My dear daughter, I was lucky to arrive early and to hear your speech. I must tell you I have never been prouder. You were spectacular! You showed all those high-flutin' ladies from Mulberry Street that farm girls are just as smart as they are, only better."

Edie almost sank to her knees. Her father had never complimented her. Her eyes welled with tears.

Frank started to walk away, but he turned and said with a grin, "Now, farmer girl, we must milk those dammed cows!"

Edie smiled back at her father and replied, "Yep, I'll be right there pulling those teats."

BOB BANCKS

CHAPTER 15: EDIE THE FARMER

The week went fast. The euphoria of the rally dwindled. The weather indicated hay making. Frank discovered the Fordson was better mowing than a team of horses; it ran over less cut hay. He had Edie drive while he manned the mower. They could cut an acre an hour, much better than the slower horses. They finished in one day.

Three days later, it was time to rake and haul the hay to the barn. Because haymaking was very labor intensive, the Mohr's shared their hay-making chores with three other neighbors, the Peterson's, the Wetsel's, and the Watham's. The four families rotated by year who would harvest the hay first. This year it was the Mohr's turn to be first.

Frank also discovered the Fordson did a better job of raking than the horses, and Edie could do it. In the afternoon when the crew arrived, Frank found the tractor straddled the swath instead of tromping it. Edie was again called on to drive. She drove while two teen-aged boys loaded the loose hay from the loader. The boys loved to have a girl driving. Not only was it very unusual, but almost unheard of. She was witty and cute. She kidded the boys between loads. At lunch time, one of the boys asked his father, "Could Edie drive tractor at our place?"

Before Edie could answer, Mr. Peterson said, "I have your Grandpa Bill coming out for that job."

"Geez, Dad, Gramps is a terrible driver. He lets the clutch out too fast. He almost knocks us off the rack. Edie is so smooth."

The other teen added with a grin, "And she better looking, too."

Edie smiled and said, "I've got to cultivate corn tomorrow, but looking at you two young men would be better than looking at a pair of horses butts all day."

Everyone chuckled. Edie drove until six, then she had to leave to start milking. Frank took over for Edie. He decided to fill all the hayracks and unload them the next day. Still, it was seven thirty before the racks were filled. Hattie and Edie finished the milking. Frank told them he'd finish chores while they went inside and cleaned up.

He and his women had a supper of fried pork chops, boiled potatoes, and fresh peas. For dessert, Hattie retrieved some leftover cake from lunch. The next day was haying at Petersons. Edie would learn to cultivate. Hattie would go with Frank to help Mavis Peterson feed the crew at noon.

The next morning, the two young men drove in around nine. They manned the haymow, Frank stuck the hay fork, and Edie drove the pull-up with the Fordson. In an hour they were finished. Her father still thought horses were better than tractors when cultivating corn. He harnessed the team and showed Edie how to hook up the one-row cultivator. The cultivator was a simple machine with six V-shaped shovels in front of the axle nearest the corn plants and four V-shaped shovels behind the wheels to cover wheel tracks.

Edie started down the row. Frank instructed her how to turn and raise the shovels. He informed her the team, Rosie and Petunia, usually kept on the row. There was little to do until the end of the rows when she had to raise the shovels out of the ground. He told her every couple of hours the team needed a rest and water.

Edie placed herself in the steel seat and clucked to the team. Off they went. It was easy until she reached the end of the row. She tried to raise the shovels. Her father said it was easy, but he was much taller and stronger. The levers were long. Edie had to stand on footrests to release the pins to raise the shovels. She lifted the shovels easily when her dad was present, but that was with the shovels out of the ground. This was different. The team waited patiently each time.

By noon, she was ready for a rest along with the team. The afternoon was a little better on the lifting because Edie applied some oil on the levers. The sun beat down on her. The team kicked up dust which fell directly on Edie.

She rested the horses at three. Her mother was home and she walked out with a small lunch. She laughed at her daughter.

"You look like a coal miner," she said. "You've got rings around your eyes and your arms are black."

Edie replied, "I so tired, my arms feel like two logs. I'll sure be glad for a bath."

Edie quit at five. The team was tired and so was she. Edie unhooked the team in the field and rode Rosie bareback to the barns. The team trotted briskly for they knew it was the end of the day and there would be fed. Edie fed the team some oats and molasses before turning them out to pasture with the other horses. Next, she decided to wash her face and arms before milking. She drew some water from the barrel by the wash house. It was quite warm.

No wonder Dad thought this was a great shower, she thought.

After sweating through milking, she was ready for a shower. Her mother had fired the water heater before chores, so there was hot water. It felt so good. The dirt ran from her like mud down a creek. Hattie showered after her. The two women dressed in light house dresses. It was eight when the Peterson boys brought Frank home. This time he didn't have to ask for clothes. Hattie had already placed them on the bench by the outside shower. Edie lit the gaslights as Hattie finished supper.

Frank asked Edie, "How did your day go?"

Edie responded, "It was fine until I had to raise the shovels. That was almost too much. I oiled the levers, which helped a lot."

"Sorry, Punky, I forgot to oil them. Oil does help a lot. Glad you thought of it."

The next day was hay day at Wetsel's. Hattie did not have to help with dinner, so Frank drove the car himself. This way he didn't have to have transportation home.

The day was extremely warm. The temperature climbed into the nineties. The wind was infrequent. The dust from the team was heavy. Edie wore her wide-brimmed straw hat, but it didn't stop the heat. She stopped at noon for dinner with her mother. Hattie was not in much better condition. She had worked at the washing, which had piled up from Monday. Edie noted her mother's hair, generally piled on top of her head, was hanging down and stringy. The pair ate their light dinner on the porch.

Hattie remarked, "It's so hot you better quit early. If not for your sake, the team will be tired."

"I'll take them slow and give them more breaks. I'll be by the creek a couple of times. They can get a drink there."

Edie waited until one-thirty before returning to the field. The air seemed to stand still. The flies were biting, especially the deer flies. At three, Hattie brought some lemonade and cookies. She reminded Edie, "Now you quit early. I'm worried about your father, too. I hope he will drink plenty of water over at Wetsel's."

At four-thirty Edie rode Rosie back to the house. She was soaked with sweat. The team trotted back, ready for the pasture and shade. Hattie met Edie at the barn with some more lemonade. They sat on upturned buckets by the big elm tree next to the barn.

Edie was a bit surprised by what her mother was wearing, or not wearing. She had a blouse with cut-off sleeves and a gingham skirt without a petticoat. Edie knew this because when Hattie sat on the upturned bucket, she pulled her skirt up and revealed her bloomers. Hattie sensed her daughter's surprise and said, "This heat is almost unbearable. I'd take off this skirt if I thought it was proper. Now I see why the Indian women went bare chested in the summer."

"Yes, I thought the same. I almost removed my blouse out in the field," replied Edie.

"Well, it won't get any better. The cow barn will be terrible, the cows will be switching their tails batting at flies. No sense cleaning up."

The cows wandered in at five. Edie fed them while Hattie closed the stanchions. They retrieved their stools and began milking. Edie heard her mother grumbling as she poured the milk into the strainer. Next time she looked up, her mother was walking by in her bloomers. She had her blouse tied below her bosom.

"No men around, so why not get comfortable," said Hattie.

When they finished, there were four cans of milk to cool. The women loaded them onto the two-wheeled cart and pushed the cans to the pump shed. In the shed was a water tank. It took both women to lift the cans into the water tank. There was a slight breeze, thirty feet up. Edie pulled the lever down to engage the windmill pump. The cool water from the well filled the tank and then overflowed to the cattle tank outside. The system worked well. Hattie went back to the barn to retrieve their outer clothes. She started to dress when she exclaimed, "Oh, hell, it's just you and me. Why wear clothes from here to the house."

Edie smiled and almost giggled. She had never heard her mom use the word hell before. When they reached the wash house, Hattie looked at the barrel of water.

"Why don't we do like your dad and take our shower out here? There are bushes surrounding the area. Afterwards, we'll wash our hair in the kitchen sink."

"Sounds good to me," replied Edie. "If you're willing, count me in."

The pair stripped. Edie went first while Hattie turned the faucet on and off to conserve water. They acted like two children getting away with a prank. When finished they discovered they forgot the towels, so they just scampered giggling into the house and found towels in a wash basket at the top of stairs. After washing each other's hair, they put on their nighties. They knew it was just Frank coming home and not strangers.

Edie was lighting the kerosene lantern when her Dad chugged in. They had battery-powered electricity, but their efforts for saving batteries for later was always best. He was exhausted. He noticed the wet boards around his shower.

He called, "Did you leave enough water for me?"

"Yes, honey, but it might be a little cool. I had to add some water. Your towel and clothes are there on the bench. We'll eat on the porch."

Frank showered. It was cool and refreshing. He didn't say a word. On the porch he found his women waiting "How was the cultivating, Punky?" he asked.

"Hot and dirty."

"Well, just one more day and you can have a rest. Ken Watham didn't want to cut his hay. He said his knees told him it is going to rain. We aren't making hay till Monday. I hope it does rain. I need a break, too."

Hattie remarked, "I've just been upstairs. It's like an oven. I suggest we sleep on the porch."

"Good idea. I'll fetch the cot mattresses. Edie, you get the cushions from the couch and chairs. We'll bed down out here. The screens will keep the mosquitoes away."

By ten, the trio had their beds made, Hattie and Frank at one end and Edie at the other. Frank turned out the lights, took off his trousers, and climbed into bed in his union suit. They all were asleep in fifteen minutes.

Around two in the morning, Edie awoke. The air was cooler and a breeze had picked up. She pulled up her sheet. Her dad and mom were both snoring. It was horrible. Finally, she couldn't stand it. She picked up her sheet and headed to her room. It was still warm upstairs, but quiet. She lay on her bed without covers. Soon the morning sun was streaming into her window.

She heard a call from her Dad. "We'd better get going, Punky. Wessel's have a big day planned."

"Okay, Daddy, I'll be right down."

The day started off okay. Chores were finished early. Frank helped hitch the team to the cultivator. He watched Edie start for the field. "If it doesn't rain tonight, I'll hitch the other team to the two-row cultivator and we'll both work tomorrow," he called after her.

Edie waved the best she could with her hands holding the reins. The team seemed anxious to get going. By noon she had a couple of acres cultivated, but the sun came out from behind the clouds and began to bear down. The afternoon was hot and sticky like the day before. The flies seemed worse.

Hattie walked out around three. They stopped by the creek so the team could drink. Edie and her mother found a shade tree to eat a light lunch.

"You better quit early again today, sweetie. This heat is almost unbearable. I could see some thunderheads building to the west. You don't want to get caught out here in the rain."

"I'll keep a watch, Mom."

It was a quarter to four when Edie reached the end of the row. The clouds were building.

"I can do one more row. Come on, girls, let's get this done and then home we'll go."

They made the round. Edie had one set of shovels raised when a crack of lightning popped overhead. The team lurched forward, throwing Edie from her seat. Her foot caught between the front shovels and the foot rest. She struggled to right herself and grab the reins.

Another flash of lightning was followed by a loud crash of thunder. The team bolted for the barns, dragging the cultivator with one side still in the ground, and dragging Edie behind. The rough dirt clawed at her blouse. Soon it was pulled to her armpits. Her foot twisted and the back of her leg rubbed against the steel wheel. It cut her thin trousers. She hollered and hollered, "Whoa," but the team was not responding. They were hell-bent for the barn.

The horses powered through the first gate and onto the lane. Her pant leg, caught in a spoke of the wheel, began to wrap around the axle. With her shoes still caught, her pants began to rip. They tore to the waistband. There it stopped and began to pull Edie between the shanks which held the shovels.

The team wouldn't slow down. Edie was pulled double and her hips rubbed the wheel. She bumped behind the cultivator until the team hit the hard ground of the road, and this slowed them down. Her left leg was wrapped around a shank as the right pant leg and the waistband refused to tear anymore. She could barely breathe.

The team finally reached the gate to the barnyard and stopped. Edie managed to yell for help. Her mother, fortunately, was pulling radishes and cutting some lettuce for supper. She heard the screams and ran toward the noise. As she rounded the corner of the barn, she saw Edie pinned under the cultivator. She reached into her apron pocket and pulled out her garden shears. She cut the waistband and pulled Edie from between the shovels.

Edie gasped for air. Hattie ripped the left leg down the seam with her hands. Edie's leg slipped out. She was free.

The wind started rising and big drops of rain began to fall. Soon it was a downpour. Edie tried to stand, but her leg would not support her. Hattie swooped her up and carried Edie to the house. She somehow opened the door and made it inside. She lay Edie on the sofa. Edie moaned. Her left side was scraped raw, her tummy had a red band where the waistband squeezed her, and her leg was shooting pain.

Hattie ran to the telephone. She put the ear piece to her ear to see if anyone was talking. They had an eight-party line, which meant eight people could use the telephone. Wilma Johnson was talking to her mother.

Hattie butted in and said, "Wilma, may I use the phone for just a minute? I must call Dr. Wilson. Edie is badly injured. I need a doctor now."

Wilma replied, "Sure, Hattie. Call me if you need help."

Hattie called Dr. Wilson's office. His office assistant listened to her plea and immediately went to get Doctor Wilson.

She returned and said, "Doctor is with a patient, but he will come as soon as possible. Are you at home?"

"Yes, I have Edie lying down."

Just before Hattie hung up, Wilma butted in on line, "I'm sorry for listening in Hattie, but Jake is home early. He could stay with the children. I'm a practical nurse. I could come right over."

"Oh, please do. I am so worried I don't know what to do."

The driving rain was now a steady downpour. Wilma pulled in and rushed inside. She took one look at Edie.

"I think we should lay Edie face down. We also need a white sheet to reflect the light. I know Doc Wilson will appreciate it."

Edie was still conscious enough to raise her body as Wilma adjusted the sheet under her.

"Draw me some water. If it is warm, good, but cool is all right, and do you have some hydrogen peroxide? I'll try to wash her wounds and apply some peroxide. It will clean out the dirt."

Hattie rushed around and found the supplies. She slid a chair next to Edie and watched as Wilma gently dabbed Edie's back. Edie moaned in pain. Hattie knelt and held her hand. Wilma stared at Hattie for a second. Hattie's skirt and blouse were wet and muddy, and she hadn't removed her muddy shoes.

"Hattie, you better change out of those wet things or you'll catch a summer cold. I'll continue here. Doctor should be here soon."

Hattie disappeared into her bedroom and changed. She reappeared dry, but barefoot just in time for Doctor Wilson to knock on the door. She ushered him in. Wilma exchanged chairs with him. He cut off Edie's blouse.

"Hattie, do you have an electric lamp?"

"Yes."

"Good. Remove the shade so I have a bare bulb. I'll need all the light to clean the debris from these wounds. Wilma, you did a good job preparing her. I'm going to give her a sedative to lessen her pain."

Doctor Wilson gave Edie a shot of pain killer in her hip. Edie jumped. Doc examined Edie's injured legs while waiting for the sedative to take effect. He just shook his head.

Edie calmed. Hattie held the lamp while Dr. Wilson picked little stones and pieces of stems from her cuts. Wilma applied the peroxide and gently covered each cut with salve. He finished Edie's back and noticed her ear. It was torn in two places. He reached into his bag and pulled out a needle and suture. He had Wilma trim her hair away before he stitched her ear together. He fashioned an eyepatch for her right eye. Evidently, she had bumped her brow on one of the shanks. It was slowly swelling shut.

Frank arrived in the truck. He spotted the team standing still hitched to the cultivator. He stopped and muttered, "Why didn't Edie unhitch the team? She knows better than to leave the team standing in the rain."

He started to unhitch the team when he noticed one section of the cultivator was still in the ground and had dug a trench leading to the field. Seconds later he noticed a pantleg streaming behind the cultivator. He knew right away what had happened.

He quickly let the team loose and didn't bother to remove their collars. He hopped into the truck and drove around the corner of the barn. There was Doc Wilson's car and someone else's. He slid to a stop and ran inside. He kicked off his muddy shoes and entered the kitchen. He found Edie stretched face down on the sofa, bare to her waist. Doc was finishing up.

"What happened?" asked Frank.

Hattie answered, "I don't know for sure. I heard Edie scream and found her stuck between the cultivator shanks. Her trousers were tangled in the wheel. I had to cut her loose with my garden shears. She tried to walk, but she couldn't. It started to rain, so I carried her to the house. I don't know how I had the strength, but I just lifted her and ran."

"How is she, Doc?"

Dr. Wilson replied, "I don't think she has any broken bones. She does have a nasty ring around her abdomen. I would like to examine her abdomen. Now that you are here, I think it should be easier to turn her over."

Frank moved Edie's hip and legs. Wilma lifted her shoulders. They carefully turned Edie to her back. Wilma noticed Frank was also soaked.

"Frank, I believe you should change into some dry clothes."

Frank answered, "I will as soon as Doc finishes. I'm not leaving my daughter now."

He turned away when Doc poked and massaged Edie's stomach area. She had contusions and scrapes around her waist from the waistband.

Doc turned and looked at Hattie and Frank. He said, "I felt nothing injured inside. Only time will tell. X-rays do not work on soft tissue. I believe I have done all I can do. When she wakes, she will be in a great deal of pain. I'll leave some pain pills. You give them to her every four hours. Let me see. It is six o'clock now. The next will be at ten, then at two in the morning, and six again. If there is any change, call me at home."

"Thank you, Doc. We will do our best. She's the best daughter I have." replied Frank.

Doctor Wilson said, "Before I leave, I think we should turn her to her stomach again. Her back is the most painful."

This time Hattie helped. Frank stood and remarked, "Hattie, you stay with her. I'll do chores. I'm wet anyway. Wilma can go home."

"Okay," Hattie said.

Frank went to the barn. Wilma started to gather her things.

"Wait a minute," she said. "Let me call Jake. He can fix the children's supper. I will stay here until you folks get your chores finished."

"Thank you, Wilma, that will be a great help."

Hattie put on her long garden coat and headed outside. She found Frank in the barn leaning against the wall and looking out the window. He looked so sad.

"What's the matter, honey?"

Frank saw her coming and wiped a tear from his eye.

"What have I done to my sweet Edie? What if she has something ruptured inside? What if she can never have children? It's all my fault."

Hattie hugged him. "It isn't your fault. Something happened to the team. They bolted and dragged Edie. Thank God she's still alive. Now, we must move on. We have milking to do and chores. Wilma is staying here until we finish."

Frank kissed Hattie. It was something he hadn't done for a long while. They turned and did their chores.

"You know all we must do is the milking. The darn hogs can just go hungry. The chickens are in bed already. They'll only break a few eggs by tomorrow. Let's hurry," said Frank.

They rushed through the milking and returned to the house. Hattie started supper as Wilma left.

"See you in the morning. Doc wants me to bathe Edie's back again," she said as she closed the door.

Frank entered. He sat by Edie and stroked her hair.

"Don't you think you should change, Frank?"

"Yes, I suppose so."

He changed. They ate some supper. Frank settled into his big chair and watched Edie. Hattie cleaned the floor of mud.

"You know, it is almost ten. We are to give Edie her pills. You will have to hold her in a sitting position while I try to get her to take them."

Frank gave her a funny look and replied, "But she has nothing on."

"Frank now don't turn prudish on me. Just set her up. She'll be conscious enough to hold the sheet up. So, what, if you see her bosom, you've seen mine. There's little difference."

"But, she's older now and not a little girl anymore."

"Frank, she is still your daughter. Now quit stalling and help."

Frank relented. They gave Edie her pills. He told Hattie he'd sleep in his chair, so he could be close to Edie.

Hattie didn't argue. She was exhausted. The alarm went off at two o'clock. Hattie jerked awake. She hurried to the next room where she found Frank sitting by Edie. He was stroking her hair.

He looked up at Hattie and said, "She started to cry and thrash around. I rubbed her shoulders and neck. They're about the only places not injured."

Hattie stood silently for just a minute. She watched Frank stroke Edie's hair.

She thought, "*Frank, you old softy. There are days I can't stand being in the same room with you. You scold me and your children when we don't do what you think we should be doing. You hate Catholics, Jews and people with dark skin. Then you turn 180 degrees and are the sweetest man I know and love. I love the softer side.*"

Her parents woke Edie to give her the pain medicine. Edie went back to sleep. At five Frank slipped out for chores. The chores would be extra this morning.

At seven he noticed Wilma's car parked by the house. He would stay outside until Wilma and Hattie had treated Edie's back. His only miscue was when he opened the kitchen door to talk to Hattie. The women were giving Edie a sponge bath. He retreated in a hurry.

Hattie called for him at eight. Breakfast was ready. Edie was sitting up when he arrived. Wilma and Hattie had lightly dressed her. She opened her good eye and saw her dad.

"I'm sorry about the corn, Daddy. Did I plow a lot out?"

"I don't know, Punky. I'll check the field later. Do you need some breakfast?"

"Yes, I'm kinda hungry."

Hattie fixed some oatmeal. Frank held the bowl and started to feed Edie.

"Daddy," she cried, "I'm a big girl. I can feed myself. Just leave the bowl here and go eat some breakfast."

Frank smiled at his one-eyed daughter and said, "You're right, Punky. You're a big girl."

Doctor Wilson loaned Edie some crutches. Her right leg was injured the worst by the twisting of the pants. Her tummy turned black and blue. She moved slowly because every time she moved, it hurt. Nightgowns were her only attire.

Ten days later, Pete called. He wanted to visit. Hattie helped Edie dress. Pete arrived with flowers and candy. The young couple sat in the parlor and talked. Hattie tried not to listen from the kitchen, but she couldn't help but hear the conversation about Sean. It seems that Pete had become a close friend and not a suitor. Edie was confiding in him. It would be six weeks before Edie felt she could return to the barn. Her leg still hurt some when she bent a certain way, but her father needed help. She had seen times he was sore or ill and he still had to work. It is the way of the farmer. There is no one to fill in when you are ill. It was time to put her aches and pains aside.

CHAPTER 16: OLD FLAMES RE-LIT

The annual Fourth of July reunion of her father's family was approaching.

Edie asked her dad, "Could I skip the reunion this year? I don't want everyone looking at me and asking questions. My hair is still three different lengths and I still do limp some. If I stayed home, I could start some chores like bringing the cows in."

Frank replied, "Sure, Punky, I need an excuse to come home. Don't worry about the chores. I go because it is the one time I see all my brothers and one sister. The only brother I enjoy is Uncle Fred. He is the only one who finished high school and went on to college. My father was not in favor, but Fred insisted. He worked his way through Iowa State College and became an engineer for the Department of Transportation. He designs and builds bridges for the state. My other brothers are a disaster. Uncle Gary got the home farm, but he is so lazy, it is falling apart. I bet my granddad would turn over in his grave if he knew what Gary is doing. Uncle George works at Kohl's Packing in Davenport. All he does is complain about how little he gets paid and how hard he works. Uncle John works at the John Deere Spreader Works in East Moline. He spreads a lot of you know what. Last there is Aunt Freida. Her husband is a pure loser. I come home from the picnic and count my blessings. I have a wonderful wife, a son, who is fighting for this country, and a lovely, hard-working daughter, who I might add can drive tractors, drive a car, rake hay, cultivate corn, shuck corn, and many other things. If our country was made up of more young people like you and your brother, we'd be a great nation."

"Why, thank you, Daddy. I never knew you to say something like that."

"I should say it more often, especially to your mother."

Hattie walked into the kitchen. She heard the last bit from Frank.

She asked, "What should you say to me?"

Frank replied, "That I love you and all you do for me."

Hattie was shocked. She stood silent for a moment, then big tears started to well in her eyes.

"That's the sweetest thing you have ever said to me. I love you, too."

Frank rose from his chair and embraced and kissed Hattie right there.

Edie just smiled. It was the first time she had ever seen her father show any emotion.

Edie stayed home on the Fourth. She was sitting in the porch rocking chair when Pete drove in with Ruthie by his side. As they approached, Ruth was giggling.

"Ruthie, what brings you here?" asked Edie. "And Pete, too."

Ruth gasped, "Edie, you look terrible. I heard of your accident, but are you okay?"

"I'm feeling better. I can see out of my eye now. Doc took the stitches from my ear. The only place I hurt is my stomach. It is still very much black and blue."

"Gee, maybe I should have called first."

"No, I am all alone today. It's Dad's family reunion. He let me stay home."

Ruth handed Edie a letter. "I've got something to ask you, but first you must read this letter. It's from your brother."

Edie opened the letter. The first few sentences were about his job in England and how he liked the people there. It told how he could live with the townspeople instead being on base. He needed to be closer to the hospital. It was the last two sentences which were the most important. They read, *Ruth, I want to tell you how much I enjoyed your company all these years. I figured some day we would marry. I want you to be the first to know. I fell in love with a British nurse. Her name is Marcie Halsted. She is the sweetest girl I've ever met, besides you and Edie. We are getting married next Sunday. I plan on bringing her home in a couple of months. I wish you and whoever you meet to have a joyful and fruitful life.*

Your friend always,
Ralph

Edie looked at Ruth and said, "I'm so sorry, Ruthie. He never told any of us."

Ruth shot back, "Don't be sorry for me. That's what I came to tell you. Pete and I have been going together since June. Last night he asked me to marry him and I said yes. We're getting married on September fifth. I want you to be one of my bridesmaids. Will you?"

"Sure! My hair should be grown out by then."

Edie looked at a beaming Pete and said," Congratulations, Pete. I trust you will take care of my best friend."

"Oh, I will, Edie." he replied, then added, "but I won't forget the good times we had together."

Ruth glared at him and said, "And what were those good times?"

Edie interrupted, "Oh, we had some good times when we were little. My dad worked for Pete's dad. We played together often. We are the same age, you know."

"Yeah, we often went fishing in the creek and other things."

Ruth sensed there was more than they were telling. She asked, "What other things?"

Edie wished Pete had kept his mouth shut, but she answered, "Well, Miss Nosy, when we were nine we went skinny dipping once. That's all."

Ruth seemed satisfied. The conversation changed. Ruth told Edie about her wedding plans. Pete and Ruth were about to leave when Pete reached into his pocket and gave Edie a newspaper clipping. Edie unfolded it and began reading out loud.

"Master Sergeant Sean O'Keefe of Muscatine, Iowa, will be receiving the French Legion of Honor Medal in Paris, France, on Thursday, July 1. It is the highest medal of honor the French government can bestow on a foreign soldier. It is equivalent to the Medal of Honor in America. Sergeant O'Keefe risked his life several times rescuing six French soldiers and one German soldier during the Battle of Argonne Forest while being injured himself. He will receive this honor on Bastille Day in France. He also will receive the Distinguished Cross from the United States Armed Forces. When asked how he felt, he answered that it was his duty, and he couldn't wait until he returns home to his girlfriend, who lives on a farm in Iowa."

Edie tearfully said, "Where did you get this?"

"The *Des Moines Register*. It will be in the *Journal* tonight. Dad says the city is planning a big parade on Labor Day. All the men who will be home will be honored. Sean will be Grand Marshal," Pete said.

"Then Daddy will find out tomorrow?"

"I would think so."

"Isn't this great, Edie? Sean will be home. Probably Ralph, too," added Ruth.

"I don't know what to say. I'm happy Ralph is coming home. I don't know about Sean."

"What do you mean, Edie?" asked Pete.

"You wouldn't understand. You're a man."

Ruth eyed Pete and said, "Pete, don't you have to wipe the windshield on your new car?"

"No."

"Yes, you do, sweetie, now go."

Pete received a glare from Ruth, then he caught on. "Oh yes, I've got to polish the headlights."

Pete walked slowly away. He could hear Ruth ask, "Let me see your tummy, Edie?" When he got to the car, he saw Ruth peeking around the corner. He knew her question was just a ploy to get rid of him.

Ruth turned to Edie and asked, "Whatever do you mean? You love Sean, don't you?"

"Oh yes, very much."

"Then, don't you want marry him?"

"Yes."

"Then what is your problem?"

"My Dad, you see, things have been going swell since Ralph and Sean entered the Army. Dad worked harder, but he also had mom and me. We did things he never thought a woman could do. He not only had a good work crew, they took care of him, fed him, washed his clothes, and one even went to bed with him every night. He really was loving his little women crew. Now that Ralph will be home, I'll probably have to go to town for a job. With Pete, Dad never questioned me dating him. He wasn't a Catholic. I don't know how he will react to Sean this time."

"Maybe he will change? I hope for your sake, he will."

The next day *The Journal* arrived. Edie waited for her father's comments at the supper table.

"I see your old boyfriend is a hero. He's going to be the Grand Marshal of the Labor Day Parade. I suppose you would like to go to the parade."

"Yes, I would, Daddy."

"I suppose the Irishman will want you to ride with him."

"I doubt that. He's the hero, not me."

"Well, don't get any ideas of meeting him. I forbid it. He's a Catholic and they control their women. They think the Pope is God."

Edie shot back, "And I suppose you don't think you control your women."

Edie stared at her father, then pushed her plate away. She didn't say a word, as she rose from the table and went upstairs. After supper, Hattie checked the stairway. She could hear Edie crying.

"I'm going to check on Edie," she said.

"Leave her alone. She'll get over him. I'll not have a Catholic for a daughter."

"You won't let your daughter marry a Catholic. Keep it up and you won't have a daughter. I'm going up."

Edie did her chores every day. She said very little.

Ralph returned the first week in August. He had his new wife, Marcie. She was a peach. Her nursing degree would allow her to find a job quickly, but first she needed to become accustomed to the Americans, especially the Iowans.

Sean arrived in Muscatine mid-August. Edie knew because his picture was all over the front page. Muscatine had a hero. Edie waited. She went to the parade with Ruth and Pete. She didn't try to meet Sean. Instead, as soon as the parade was over, she boarded the Interurban for home. When she reached home, she hurried to her room and cried. Finally, she could cry no more. Her tears stopped. She decided she'd have to get on with her life.

She thought, *I must live the best I can. I will never marry. I will work in town until I can make enough money then I will become a teacher and move far, far away. As for now, I'll work for Dad.*

After the big Labor Day Parade in downtown Muscatine, there were speeches and music held at city hall. The mayor introduced Sean, along with other honorees. All the time, Sean scanned the crowd for a glimpse of Edie. Sean asked the mayor how long the celebration would last.

"I imagine another hour or two," he replied.

Sean asked Ralph, who was one of the honorees, "How long are you and your folks going to stay?"

Ralph looked at his pocket watch. "Dad told me to meet him at the corner of Iowa and Second Street at five. It's just two-thirty now."

Sean sat nervously. The mayor dawdled and went on and on. He praised all the men. He started to ask some of the soldiers to come forward to speak. Sean got up first and said, "It was an honor just to fight for my country. I know I was protecting the freedom of the world and all my fellow Americans."

The crowd applauded. The next soldier rose to speak. Sean didn't return to his seat, but instead walked from the stage. He ducked down the alley and headed for the Interurban station. In twenty minutes, he was at the Melpine Station. He ran down the road to Edie's house. He knocked on the door.

Edie pulled her robe together and thought, "*Who could this be?*"

"Who's there?' she called.

Sean tried to disguise his voice as he answered, "Just me a little old lady from down the road."

Edie suspected it was a gypsy. She grabbed a broom and opened the door, "Get out of here . . . Oh, Sean! How did you get here?"

"The same way you did, the Interurban."

"But you are supposed to…"

"Be with you."

He grabbed her and kissed her.

"Oh, Sean. I missed you so much. Do you remember how I look?"

"I remember being with you in Olga's bedroom."

"Sit here on the swing and tell me all about the War."

They talked between kisses and hugs.

Finally, Sean said, "I must be going. Your parents will be home soon."

"I know," sighed Edie, "but I have missed you so. How can we meet again?"

"We'll work something out."

"Help me bring in the cows before you go. I want all the time I can have with you," she said.

Edie dashed to her room and changed into her chore clothes. Sean and she walked hand in hand to the pasture. The cows were just starting to gather for the trek to the barn. It was easy to herd them home. Just as they were coming over the hill, they heard the T slowing down.

Edie whispered, "It's my parents. Now what will you do?"

"Don't worry, my pet, I know my way home through the pasture. I will go back to the creek and follow it upstream to the Interurban tracks and then to the platform stop."

"Will I ever see you again?"

"I hope so. Give me a kiss good-bye."

"I'll contact Pete or Ruth. Maybe they will help us."

They embraced and kissed. Edie's couldn't hold back her tears. Sean hugged so tightly she could barely breathe. Just before he left he reached inside his shirt and pulled out his dog tag from the Army.

"Here I want you to wear this until we see each other again." Sean said. He slipped it over her head and Edie tucked it inside her blouse. Sean turned and headed back to Pine Creek.

CHAPTER 17: BACK TO MUSCATINE

The celebration was over. Ralph was home. The next big celebration was Pete and Ruth's wedding. Despite Pete's dismay, it was small. Ruth told him her family couldn't afford a big wedding. Seven months later, Sophia was born.

Ruth's mother, Dottie, commented, "She'll never be able to do that again."

At the Mohr house it was a bit crowded with Marcie and Ralph. There were now three women in the kitchen. Marcie tried to help, but it just wasn't her home. Edie sensed the tension and applied for a job at the Pleasant Prairie Savings Bank. The owner, Mr. Baker, knew the family and hired her immediately. She could easily ride the Interurban the five miles to Pleasant Prairie. Some days, when Ralph and her father were working, she'd drive the car to work.

Mr. Baker liked Edie's work ethic and discovered she never completed high school. He suggested she attend night classes and receive her diploma. He told her it would really help her later in life. Classes had already started, but he used his influence to help her become accepted anyway. Her classes happened to be Friday night and Saturday morning. Edie contacted her old friend Louise. She was married but readily invited Edie to stay overnight in her home on Hershey Avenue. Edie cautiously asked her mother if it was all right with her.

"Of course. Sometimes I wish you would have finished high school, but your father was against it."

"What do you think he will say now?"

"I don't know. I suspect he will pooh-pooh it and say it isn't necessary. But if you are paying for it and you are over eighteen, he really can't stop you. Can he?"

"I'll ask him anyway."

That evening at the supper table, Edie asked Frank, "Dad, Mr. Baker says I could get my high school diploma by going to night school and some Saturday classes. I'd like to do it. What do you think?"

Frank swallowed a swig of coffee and answered, "I think women going to high school is a bunch of wasted money. They don't need a higher education. All they need is to stay home and learn to cook and clean house from their mothers. I suppose your mother already said it was okay."

"Yes, I did," answered Hattie. "I think if she wants an education, she should have it."

"Well, I suppose, but I'm not paying for it."

Edie shot back, "I knew you'd say that. You won't have to, Father. Mr. Baker said he'd pay for it and take a little bit from my salary each week until I have it paid it off. Sort of like a loan. Last year I was okay to work for you. Now, because the War is over, it is back to a man's world. You want women to serve you men. You just wait until we get to vote. I think you are afraid of what might happen. You just want to be king."

Frank lambasted her, "There will be no talk like that in this house, young lady."

"I think I can take care of myself."

Edie rose from the table and stomped out of the room. Ralph and Marcie said nothing. The next morning Frank was outside before Edie left for work. Hattie drove her to the platform.

"Go ahead with the classes. Your father will not change his mind. Tell Mr. Baker thanks."

Friday afternoon, Edie hurried home, grabbed her suitcase, and headed for Muscatine High School. It was only three blocks from the station in

Muscatine. She started with a test to evaluate her level of education. She tested well. The instructor told her she could graduate in less than a year if she studied hard. The best benefit was Edie had a reason to be in Muscatine on Friday night. Classes were over by seven. She would take a trolley to Hersey Avenue and walk three blocks to Louise's house. She tried to study, but Louise's two children wouldn't allow her. They wanted her attention. She took a chance and called Olga.

"Olga, this is Edie Mohr. You know, Sean's old girlfriend. I am wondering if I could come over and study at your house."

"Why, sure I remember you, child. Sean talks about you all the time. Where are you now?"

"I'm over at my friends' house on Hershey. I'll walk down."

Suddenly, a male voice spoke on the phone. "Edie, you stay put. I'll be up and walk you down. I don't want another episode like a couple of years ago."

"Sean, Sean, is that you? Oh, sweetie, I'll wait, I'll wait."

Sean arrived in ten minutes. Louise understood her dilemma. She promised she would cover for her if her mother called.

The system worked well. Edie stayed at Louise's Friday evening. Sean would meet her and walk her to Olga's. She did her homework before she and Sean would do something late Friday night. They avoided downtown because of the risk someone might see them together.

On the second Saturday of every month, there was a dance at the Moose Lodge. Edie told her mother she was attending it with a friend. On Sunday morning, she'd be home before church. She'd tell Hattie who was at the dance and how much fun it was.

Edie was a star student. By May, she would receive her high school diploma.

At home, Frank claimed he was okay with Marcie, but really having another female in the house was not his cup of tea. He could parade around in his underwear with Edie, but Marcie was different. She wasn't really from his family. Her accent was difficult for him to understand. There were times Frank went outside to get away from her.

On the first of November, Emil Staker drove up the lane at the Mohr's. He was met by Ralph at the back door.

"Emil. How are you doing? Dad and I were just thinking about you this morning. Is there anything we can help you with?"

Emil looked at Ralph. His eyes began to tear. He leaned into Ralph and hugged him.

"I'm so glad you're safe and home. My Allen thought you were a great friend when you were in the service with him."

"Yes, he and I were in the same outfit for a while. He transferred to artillery. He told me he wanted to be closer to the action."

"Someone said you drove the ambulances from the Front."

"Yes, I did for six months, then they transferred me to South Hampton Hospital in England."

"Did you know my Allen died there?"

Ralph stared at Emil. He didn't know what to say. "No, I'm sorry, I didn't know. I was there October and November. When was Allen there?"

"He died there in May. I guess you wouldn't have been there." Emil took a handkerchief from his overalls and wiped his tears and blew his nose. "Sorry, my memories keep coming back."

"That's quite all right, Emil. Would you like to come in and sit a spell? Marcie will fix us some British Tea."

"I would like that very much. I have something to ask you and your English wife."

While they sat at the table. Marcie fixed some tea. Hattie arrived from town. Frank was over at Watts helping Hank fix a broken axle on a wagon.

Emil started, "Ralph, when Allen died, I thought I could survive. My Mamie, of course, was devastated. She wanted to go to town immediately. I said no. Well, it hasn't gotten any better. The other night she was hysterical. She tried to kill herself. I tried my best to reason with her. Finally, I conceded. She would be better in Durant where her sister lives. Yesterday, I applied for a job at the elevator. I got it. They told me they needed me right now. I told them I had corn to harvest. We worked it out that I could work four days there and have a three-day weekend. I was wondering if you and your father could help me with the harvest."

"Yes, Emil. By all means. I certainly will do all I can. What about the livestock?"

"I don't know yet. I thought maybe you and your pretty wife could move over there. If you want, I'd like to rent the farm to you next year."

The three Mohrs looked at each other. Hattie was the first to speak.

"Emil, don't you worry. We'll help you get your corn out. I assure you Ralph will take care of your livestock. When are you and Mamie moving to Durant?"

"Next week. Mamie and I are staying at her sister's for a while. If you want, I'm sure Ralph and his bride could stay over at our place right away."

They talked for another half hour before Emil looked at his watch and said, "I must be going. I must pick Mamie up at her sister's. I must not leave her alone. No telling what she might do."

Emil left. The trio watched as he pulled away and waved. Ralph turned to Marcie. He hugged her and said, "We will have our own place, Muffin. No more checking the door at the privy. And you won't have to dress before you leave our bedroom."

"Oh, honey, do you think I can do the dishes in just my knickers?"

"Yes, definitely. You can do them without your knickers if you like."

Hattie had to ask, "What are knickers?"

"Well, mum, they are what you Americans call underpants or panties. Sometimes at home I didn't want to soil my dress, so I'd strip right down to me knickers to wash the dishes or dust the furniture. It made me feel free." Marcie snickered, "Of course, I had to be sure the blinds were closed. You should try it sometime."

Hattie smiled and replied, "I already have."

Ralph and Marcie planned on moving December tenth. Ralph made a deal with Emil to buy his hogs and beef cows. Frank purchased the dairy animals. Emil sold his two teams at the sale barn. Ralph was determined to be horse free. Tractors were the wave of the future. Emil gave Ralph one third of his crop for helping harvest. Ralph applied for a loan at the Tipton Bank to buy a new John Deere GP tractor. Ralph and Marcie were independent. Fortunately for Ralph and Marcie, but unfortunately for Emil, Mamie somehow found a gun and shot herself the day before Thanksgiving. Emil gave all his furniture to Ralph. He moved into a furnished apartment above the office at the elevator.

With Ralph and Marcie gone, Edie and her parents were quickly back to their old ways of living. Frank no longer had to check before entering the kitchen in his long johns. Conversation at the table was always about the day ahead and supper was about tomorrow. Frank never asked about Edie's job or her schooling. He refused to acknowledge the need for a high school education. Hattie would ask Edie about her day while Frank was in the other room reading the newspaper. He was always about the farm and his work.

CHAPTER 18: CAUGHT

The Mohr household was somewhat back to normal. Edie was home for five nights during the week. Friday and Saturday nights, she would stay at Louise's.

It was a rainy Saturday night when Edie returned home. She had walked home from the station and was soaking wet. At first, she wondered why her mother or father were not there to pick her up. She thought maybe they had forgotten or there was something more important happening at home. When she opened the door, she saw her mother crying at the kitchen table.

"What's wrong, Mom? Did something happen to Dad?" she asked as she took off her wet coat and shook it out on the porch. The next time she looked at her mother, she saw a red welt on the side of her face. Her mouth was bleeding.

"Mom, what happened? Tell me."

Her answer was a racket upstairs. She went to the stairwell and was met with a shower of clothes and shoes. Edie gathered the clothes and recognized they were hers. She slowly climbed the stairs and entered her room. Frank was throwing her clothes, her shoes, and her cosmetics in to a gunny sack.

"Dad, what on earth are you doing?"

Frank turned and screamed, "You . . . you . . . little wench. You disobeyed again. You are nothing but a bitch. I will not have a bitch in my house."

Edie ran toward him and grabbed his arm. She tried to stop him. He turned and slapped her across her face, then pushed her down on the bed.

He scowled at her and yelled, "Herman Brus said he saw you dancing with . . . with that . . . that Catholic Irishman. He said not once but several times at the Moose Lodge. I told you not to see him again. You are no daughter of mine anymore. Get out!! Get out now, tonight."

Edie held her hand on her face and replied, "But where would I go?"

"I don't care. Just get out of my sight. Go live in the barn with the rest of the bitches. I don't care, but you better be gone when I go to milk in the morning."

Frank turned and stomped downstairs. Edie gathered what she could. She threw her clothes on her bed and wrapped them in a ball with the bedspread. When she returned to the kitchen, her mother was standing by the stove.

"Mom aren't you going to do something?"

Hattie faced Edie. Her eyes were red and swollen, and her cheek was already turning colors. She said, "Edie, I protected you the last time because you were only seventeen. Your father warned you. Now, you are nineteen and you disobeyed your father, again. I cannot continue to protect you."

"I see I'm no longer needed here. Ralph comes home and Edie is no longer needed. She is just a bitch. Good-bye, Mother. I love you and I always will."

"Where will you go tonight?"

"I'll walk to Watts'. I'm sure Mrs. Watts will let me stay overnight. I'll go to Louise's tomorrow night. Is it okay if I borrow a slicker tonight or do I have walk in the rain?"

"Sure. You should wrap your clothes in a slicker, too."

"Okay, Mom. I can't carry everything tonight. I'll put my things in the wash house and maybe Marcie will deliver them to Watts'. Tell Marcie I'll call her tomorrow."

Edie gave her mother a long, sorrowful hug and put on the slicker. She opened the back door and walked out into a drizzling rain. It would be a long walk to Watts', but she'd make it. She was on her own now. By the time she made it to the Watts' back door, Dottie was standing with open arms. Hattie had called ahead and explained what had happened.

"My land, girl, you are soaked clear through. Come in and get out of those clothes. Leave those shoes and boots on the porch. I'll clean them up later."

"I'm afraid I have no dry ones to wear. They are all soaked." Edie sobbed. "Mrs. Watts, what am I going to do?"

Dottie answered, "Well, first thing, as I said, is to get you out of those wet things. Elmer is still in the barn. He won't be in for a while. You take your wet things off. I'll get one of Ruth's robes, then I'll fix some hot cocoa."

Edie was sitting at the table when Elmer arrived. He was surprised, but sympathetic. He told her she could stay as long as she needed. He'd take her to the station every morning if need be.

The next day Marcie delivered Edie's things to Watts. Dottie washed and ironed Edie's dresses. At night, she was glad to have another woman to talk with in the evenings since Ruth's marriage to Pete.

When Sean found out Edie was kicked out of her home because him, he became more attentive. So, what, if someone saw them together. Edie went to church with Louise and her family, then spent rest of day with Sean. She encouraged Sean to work for a high school diploma. Even though he had never graced the halls of Muscatine High, when he tested to enter, the principal said because of his service education all he would need were some science classes and two math courses to receive his diploma. Sean told the principal he would like to attend classes the following Fall semester.

Hattie called Edie often. She knew if Frank caught her, she would switch to Dottie. Edie continued her schooling, spending Friday night and Saturday in town. She took the final exam and passed with flying colors. She graduated with honors. When her mother called she invited her parents to attend the graduation ceremonies the twenty-ninth of May.

Her mother said, "I will come, but I doubt your father will."

"Well, he can be his stubborn old self. Mr. Baker said he'd come." Edie sighed. "I'm sorry, Mom, that I caused you all this heartache. I will still call you and try to see you if you want."

"Of course, I want to see you, Edie. I still love you."

"Mom, Sean is going to be there, too."

"I kinda suspected that."

The graduation was small, just the night class students. Ralph, Marcie, and Hattie attended. Aunt Helen and Uncle Bill came from Tipton. Uncle Bill and Mr. Baker knew each other from the Iowa Bankers Association. Sean walked in all alone. Edie met him at the door. She introduced him to her aunt and uncle.

Aunt Helen shook his hand and remarked, "So this is the young man who wrote you so many letters. I am glad Ralph interceded for Edie and I got to become a part of your romance."

Sean replied, "It is a pleasure to meet you. I often wondered what happened to those letters I sent to Tipton, Iowa. I see now they were in good and lovely hands."

Aunt Hattie almost blushed as she replied, 'Now I know why Edie loves you. You are quite a charmer."

Uncle Bill asked, "Where is Frank? Isn't he coming?"

Hattie started to speak but Edie interrupted. "Daddy was too busy. It's been a late spring. He's still planting some corn."

"Oh, I see. Too bad he couldn't take time off to see his daughter graduate from high school."

The ceremonies lasted about forty minutes, after which Uncle Bill announced, "Let's all go down to the Muscatine Hotel and have a late dinner. We need to celebrate with this new graduate. Tell you what, it's on me. Sean, you come, too."

Edie's life changed very little. She continued to work at the bank. She figured she owed Mr. Baker her loyalty for a while. The only difference was she no longer had to attend classes. She'd go to Louise's on Friday evenings and wait for Sean. They would walk Second Street with no worry about being caught. According to Frank Mohr, she wasn't his daughter any more. On Saturdays the pair would go to a dance or movie, or sometimes stay at Olga's and play Gin Rummy with her. Sundays she attended a church on Oregon Street named Musserville Methodist. Louise's Episcopalian church was not Edie's style. Many times, Sean attended with her, then he'd drive her to the

Watts'. Ruth's father loved to reminisce with Sean about the war.

May flowed into June, June into July. The threshing season was upon them. As soon as that was over, it was fair season. The McKillip's showed their Angus cattle at all the major fairs. It was when Bruce made most of the farm's sales. Pete usually headed up the show herd, but this year, because of the new baby, he decided he should stay home and run the farm. He was a little disappointed, although he knew his husband duties overruled his fair exploits.

The winter of 1918-19 was one of the coldest and snowiest of the decade. It forced Edie to miss several days of work. She told Mr. Baker she thought she should try to find a job in Muscatine. Mr. Baker was disappointed to see her leave, but he understood. He told her he knew the president of Hershey State Bank and would recommend her.

She started working right away. Edie located a women's boarding house on Iowa Avenue just three blocks away. She made six dollars a day, plus an extra four if she worked on Saturday morning. The best benefit was being able to see Sean every weekend.

The winter subsided. Spring arrived late. Mrs. Catt wrote Edie that she wanted her to come to Washington D.C. Edie wrote back she could not come because she had just started her new job at Hershey State Bank.

The very next week, Mr. Hershey called Edie to his office. He said, "Miss Mohr, I have just received a telephone call from a Mrs. Carrie Chatman Catt. She asked if I supported the women's right to vote and the Nineteenth Amendment. Of course, I said yes. Mrs. Hershey is one of the state's leaders in the movement. Next, she asked if I had a Miss Edie Mohr as an employee. I'm now very embarrassed that I had to say I didn't know because we have many employees. She pressed me more, so I asked Mrs. Catt to hold while my secretary, Mrs. Hartman, checked the names of our workers. She assured me you were an employee and a very good one. I told Mrs. Catt yes, you were here. After which she asked if you could be allowed to come to Washington, D.C., and speak before the Congress of the United States. Miss Mohr, I readily agreed and told Mrs. Catt I would pay for the trip if my wife could come as an escort. She agreed to those terms. So, if you agree, Edie--may I call you, Edie?"

"Yes, sir."

"On July 30 if you are willing, you and Mrs. Hershey will travel to

Washington by train for you to speak before a congressional committee. This is a very great honor for any young lady to have. What do you say?"

Edie was flabbergasted. She blurted out, "Yes! Yes! I'd love to go. But where would I stay and how do I dress?"

"Everything will be taken care of by Mrs. Catt."

Edie was so excited. She couldn't wait to tell Sean and her mother. She was about to leave Mr. Hershey's office before she turned and asked, "Mr. Hershey, do you suppose my mother could join us on the trip?"

"By all means if she wants to go, you let me know tomorrow before I purchase the train tickets. In fact, if she agrees, I believe I will go also. Have a good day, Edie."

When Edie got to her rooming house, she immediately called her mother. Hattie was hesitant. It would be a long trip, and what about Frank? She'd have to ask him first.

"I have to know by tomorrow. So, call me tonight," Edie told her.

Next Edie called Olga. She asked her have Sean call her as soon as he got home. Edie was so excited she could barely eat her supper. The other women in the home were happy for her and a little envious. They all waited for the telephone to ring.

The first call was from her mother. She said, "I asked Ralph and Marcie before your father. Marcie said she would feed and take care of your father. Ralph would also help.

"When I approached your father, he said, 'Who does she think she is? Some celebrity. If you want to go with that woman, you can.'"

"Great, Mom, I will tell Mr. Hershey tomorrow morning."

Sean called next. He was happy for her. "I'll save my surprise for you until you get back."

"What surprise?"

"You'll see, but now you have to wait."

The next two weeks were a blur. Edie was given a crash course on etiquette in Washington. She was informed she would be introduced to many senators and their wives. There would be fantastic tours of the Capitol. There was even a chance she would tour the White House. She would speak before a committee of Senators. Edie reviewed her government representatives. Sean helped her with her speech. Mrs. Hershey took Edie and her mother on a shopping spree in Cedar Rapids.

It was a two-day trip to Washington D.C . Mrs. Catt had some of her staff greet the Iowans at Union Station. They were taken to their hotel and told Mrs. Catt expected them for dinner at seven in the hotel restaurant. Edie and Hattie dressed in their new frocks, but they were careful not to outshine Mrs. Hershey. At dinner, Mrs. Catt outlined the agenda. Her staff would take care of almost everything. The next day was Edie's presentation.

In the morning, Edie was so nervous, she couldn't eat. Her mother tried to calm her. Mrs. Catt insisted she be called Carrie. Senator Donovan and Kenyon both invited Edie to their offices. Their staff coached her on the procedures of a Senate hearing. It was half past ten when Edie entered the chamber. She was seated with Carrie at a table in front of several Senators. An introductory statement was read. Carrie spoke first. She spoke of the inequalities for women in the United States. The Senators questioned her. Carrie introduced Edie. Edie was about to read her statement when Senator Kenyon spoke.

"Miss Mohr, I am wondering if you could tell us in your own words how you feel. I found out through Mrs. Catt your speech at a rally in Iowa was spontaneous. I would like that same spontaneity."

Edie paused, then folded her papers in front of her. She surveyed the panel of Senators sitting in front of her.

"Senator Kenyon, I have come all the way from Iowa to speak to this committee. As you know, the State of Iowa is mostly farmers. If you and your fellow Senators lived on a farm, you would realize women work with their husbands or fathers and have been doing it for years. Women worked in factories during the war and replaced many men. We women are fifty per cent of the population in America, but we have little say about our government. I sit here today and view a panel of distinguished gentlemen before me and see not one woman. I hope in my lifetime I will see that changed. I assume most of you have or have had wives and daughters. Don't you think they are intelligent enough to vote? I do. I want to vote for my congressman or congresswoman. I want to vote for my senator. I want my voice heard. It is well past time I get to do just that. Senators, I strongly urge you to pass the Nineteenth Amendment to the Constitution of these United State of America and give all of its citizens the right to vote."

The room was silent for a minute as though the people were stunned by this small country girl. It was Senator Kenyon who started something which was rarely seen at a hearing. He stood and applauded. Soon the whole room stood and erupted in an applause. Carrie rose and encouraged Edie to rise.

She whispered to Edie, "Turn around and acknowledge the rest of the room with a wave of your hand and nod. You were quite impressive, my dear. Your statement will certainly help our cause."

Later in the day, Carrie called on Edie. "You have been invited to meet President Wilson this evening at the White House. It is a white tie and evening gown affair. Do you have a gown with you?"

"Heavens no, I don't even own one. What do I do?"

Carrie smiled and said, "Don't worry. There must be someone on my staff who is your size. I'll see if they have a gown. I will be back with you in a few minutes. You are a size six, aren't you?"

"Yes, if I don't wear a corset, which I don't have either."

Carrie chuckled, "Well, my dear, that is something else we will have to rid ourselves of. I wish I could say I never wore a corset."

By three, a gown was found for Edie. It was an exquisite silver silk gown, long enough to hide her not-so-stylish shoes. Mrs. Hershey loaned her earrings and a necklace. Carrie sent Edie to her personal hair stylist. By six, she was ready to meet President Wilson. She and Mrs. Catt arrived at the White House in a limousine. She and Carrie lined up in the hallway. There was a long line of guests. Edie shook hands with the President, then Mrs. Wilson.

Mrs. Wilson eyed Edie and commented, "You must be the young woman from Iowa who wowed the senate hearing this morning. Now, I wonder if it was your speech or your beautiful looks which caught the attention of those old farts."

Edie was shocked at Mrs. Wilson's words, then Mrs. Wilson gave her a wink and added, "We'll get that amendment passed. I know a lot of powerful senators. We Edies must stick together. You do realize my name is Edie, also?"

All Edie could say was, "Yes, Mrs. Wilson, and thank you, Mrs. Wilson. I am so glad to have met you."

They toured the city the next day, then caught an early train for the long ride home. Edie was met by the *Muscatine Journal* reporters as she disembarked from the train. They said her speech at the hearing was fruitful because the Senate passed the Nineteenth Amendment and now it must be ratified by at least 29 states. The process would probably take a year since many legislatures would not meet until next January.

The train arrived in Muscatine at the Rock Island station on Front Street. The press was there also. Edie had now become a celebrity in Muscatine. Mr. and Mrs. Hershey beamed at their famous employee. Her life would change because of them.

Ralph and Marcie were there to pick up Hattie. Marcie gave Edie a hug, then hugged Hattie.

"Got a surprise for you, Mum. You're going to be a grandma."

"A grandma? Oh my goodness, when?"

"Next February or early March."

Edie butted in. "Then that means I'll be an aunt. Congratulations to the both of you. Have either of you seen Sean around?"

"No, but don't you think he might still be at work?" stated Ralph.

"Oh, I suppose so. It is only two o'clock. I'll see him later. He said he had a surprise for me and I'm anxious to see what it is."

Marcie led the foursome down to the levee where the car was parked. Three got into the car. Edie waited outside. Hattie stuck her head out of the rear window and said, "I had a wonderful time. Tell Mrs. Catt and the Hershey's thank you."

"I will, Mom, and say hello to Dad."

CHAPTER 19: THE FARM

Edie walked to her boarding house on Iowa Avenue. The girls were excited to hear Edie's stories of Washington, D.C. Edie talked as fast as she could, all the time hoping Sean would appear at the door.

Finally, she asked, "Has anyone seen Sean?"

Most shook their heads. Amy raised her hand and said, "Sean O'Keefe? I heard he's been promoted and is now the lumber buyer. He's in Wisconsin right now. He'll be back on Saturday. At least, it's what my boyfriend, Titus, said."

"Gee, he didn't tell me," responded Edie, then she thought, *"Maybe his promotion was the surprise. I'll act surprised when he tells me."*

By Saturday, Edie was a basket case. She hadn't heard from Sean. Saturday morning, she volunteered to work overtime at the bank. She felt she owed it to Mr. Hershey. When she walked out the bank door at noon, there was Sean, dressed for a picnic. Edie jumped into his arms and kissed him.

"Sean, why didn't you tell me you were going to Wisconsin?" she scolded.

"Because I didn't find out until the day after you left for Washington. I was going to telegraph you, but I didn't know where my celebrity girlfriend was staying. I trust you had a great time."

"Oh, Sean, it was wonderful. I'll never forget it for as long as I live. I'll tell you later. Now, what's my surprise? It's been driving me crazy."

207

"Oh yeah, the surprise, well, follow me, my Muscatine star. We will go there pronto."

"Shouldn't I change?"

"No, I stopped by your house and had Amy get what I thought you might need. It's all here in this bag."

Sean took Edie's arm as he led her to his new Chevrolet Roadster. It was a sharp-looking two-seater. He helped her in and set the bag in the trunk with the picnic basket. "I had Olga pack us a basket," he said, smiling.

They drove out to New Era, down to Pine Creek Mill, across the iron bridge. He stopped just past the bridge. There was a lane leading up the hill. He opened the gate and drove to the top. There was a small white clapboard house, a red barn, a chicken house, and a pig pen. Edie looked around. There was no one there.

"Whose place is this?"

Sean now was grinning ear to ear, he replied, "Mine. I just bought it. I hope someday it will be ours."

With that, he knelt on one knee and opened a small box containing a shiny ring. It wasn't very large, but it was sparkly. He said, "Edie, will you marry me and be my wife?"

Edie put her hands over her mouth. She was speechless. She surprised Sean by kneeling, looking him straight into his eyes, and saying very calmly, "Yes, Sean O'Keefe, I will be overjoyed to be your wife."

He smiled and placed the ring on her finger. Kissing was difficult because they were both kneeling. It didn't stop Edie. She sprang forward and knocked Sean over onto the grass. They embraced, kissed, laughed, then embraced, kissed, and laughed all over again. Finally, they lay quietly and gazed into each other's eyes.

"I love you, Sean O'Keefe," whispered Edie.

"I love you, too," answered Sean. "Now let's have our picnic on our front lawn."

"How will you farm and keep your job at R & M?"

"That's the second part of my surprise. I mean we, do not get possession until March first of next year. You see, this place is an estate. It has been rented for several years by the neighbor, who just happens to be Bruce and Pete McKillip. When they found out I had purchased it, they were not angry at all, but glad for me. The next day Bruce called and asked if I would manage their farms. Bruce is becoming very active in state politics and Pete has another outside venture he would like to pursue. He didn't tell me what, but it will take him away from the farm. So, on March first of next year, I'll quit R & M and become a farmer. Until then we will fix up this house and barn, have kids, and get married. Oops, I got that backward. You know what I mean."

Edie was smiling so much it hurt her face. Her dreams were coming true. She was going to be with Sean and a farmer's wife and live close to Ralph and Marcie and her parents.

"May I see the inside of the house?"

"Sure."

Sean had the key to the front door. They walked in. There was a small front room, a bedroom or parlor next to it. The kitchen was in the back of the house. There were some steep stairs leading up to two more small bedrooms. On the porch was a big door which had to be lifted to reach the basement. Edie carefully stepped down. The last step broke and down she stumbled into a dark damp basement. She screamed as she landed on her hands and knees. Sean threw the door back and jumped down after her.

"Are you hurt, Muffin?" he asked.

He helped Edie stand. She brushed the cobwebs out of her hair. The front of her dress was very wet.

"I'm all right except I think I sat in a puddle of water."

She moved her foot and could feel water running inside her shoe. Sean struck a match. The light showed a basement with about three inches of water flooding it. The walls were limestone and wet.

"I guess this will be one of my first projects. Now, let's get out of here. I'll go up first and pull you up."

They made it out safely and headed outside. Edie looked at her dress. It was streaked with mud.

"What kind of clothes did you bring me?" she asked.

"I don't know, I just told Amy something for an overnight stay."

"You were planning on staying out here?"

"No, I thought we might stay at Olga's like you did before. She likes you, but I bet she's going to get tired of you coming in with soiled dresses."

Edie giggled a bit. "Well, I can't stay in these things."

She dug into the bag and found a short nightie, a skirt and blouse, and some underwear. She shook them out.

"What do you want me to wear right now, my future husband?"

"Either one will be okay. Why don't you try on the nightie? It will be cooler. I'll spread the blanket under the tree."

Edie smiled back and cooed, "You devil, you, it is broad daylight and you want me in a nightgown."

Sean shrugged his shoulders and replied, "Okay, put on the skirt and blouse, then. You'll look pretty in either one."

Edie disappeared behind a bridal wreath hedge to change. Sean spread out the blanket and opened the picnic basket. By now, it was two in the afternoon and the day was warm. Sean removed his jacket and shirt as he waited for Edie. She was taking a long time. He took off his shoes and socks. Edie appeared wearing the skirt and blouse, but as she walked toward him she let the skirt fall to the ground. Beneath it was the skirt of the nightgown. She stopped right above him and slowly unbuttoned the blouse and let it fall from her shoulders. There she stood in the thin cotton nightie. It was light blue and tied at the shoulders with soft cords. She was barefooted and looked so innocent. The sunshine outlined her legs. She bent over and kissed his forehead.

"How close is the nearest neighbor?" she asked.

"I'd say about a half a mile away."

"Good, because I wouldn't want people to talk. I'm not wearing much."

"I can see that."

They ate lunch. Edie's gown kept slipping down her shoulder. Sean had trouble eating. His eyes were focused on Edie and her state of undress. After they finished eating, Sean lay back. She tickled his toes. He laughed and told her to quit. She wouldn't so he sat up and pulled her to his chest. She laid her head down on his shoulder and they gazed at each other.

"I love you," Edie repeated. "I love your face, your eyes, your mouth, even your ears."

Sean looked at her lying on his shoulder. He caressed her bare shoulder. Edie closed her eyes as if she were dreaming. She smiled as she enjoyed his caresses. He petted her neck and arms. Edie shifted her body. He stopped.

"Don't stop, Sean, it feels so wonderful," she said in a very soft tone.

"Do you want me to rub your back?"

"Sure."

Edie slid from his shoulder and lay face down on the blanket. She turned her head to one side. Sean got to his knees and began massaging her back. He worked up to her shoulders and back of her neck. She closed her eyes again. He took a chance and untied the shoulder ties. Her lips formed a slight smile. He worked the back of the gown down as far as he thought he could without moving her. He started all over, now working on bare skin.

Edie whispered, "My lower back is killing me. Could you massage it also?"

"I can try. Raise your hips some so I may slip your gown lower."

Edie obliged. He slid the gown below her waist. He began again. She sighed.

"There, how do you feel now?" he asked.

"Wonderful and half-naked. Have you ever done legs?"

"No, but I can try."

He moved down her body and began massaging her feet, then her calves, and finally, her thighs. By now, the gown was covering just Edie's hips. The sun on her skin, which began as warm, now was hot. She opened her eyes and noticed the other side of the blanket was in the shade.

Edie whispered as if someone might be close by, "Let's go over in the shade. Close your eyes."

"Why?"

"Because my gown is to my waist, I need to pull it up."

"Why?"

She turned her head and smiled at him and said, "Please."

Sean loosely covered his eyes while she pulled up her gown and moved. She lay on her side in the shade and motioned Sean to follow. He crawled over and propped himself on his elbow and gazed at Edie. Edie let him gaze. She adored the look in his eyes. She'd like to satisfy his longings. She propped her body up on her elbow.

"You like what you see?" She giggled as she held up her finger.

"Very much," was the answer.

They lay side by side and gazed into each other's eyes. Nothing was said.

"Aren't you warm?" Edie asked.

"A little bit. Why?"

"Well, here I am with almost nothing on and feeling comfortable. You're fully dressed. You must be hot."

Sean eyed her as she slowly unbuttoned his shirt. He sat up and removed his shirt.

Propping himself on one arm and ran a finger down Edie's side. She giggled. She coyly dropped the one side of her gown.

"I love you, Sean. I will be the best wife I can. We will have children. We will have a farm with chickens and ducks and cows and pigs and cats and dogs." Then she added, "And we'll have sex every day."

Sean smiled and said, " When we are married, it will be such a dream. Now, I think you and I should get dressed. Olga will have a supper waiting."

Edie rose, gathered her gown to her neck, and disappeared behind the bridal wreath shrub. After she had changed, she helped Sean pack up the basket and fold the blanket. By five, they were headed for Olga's. As soon as Edie burst through the door she held out her hand to display the ring.

"My, my, I see my boarder has made up his mind who to marry. Of course, I don't think he ever had anyone else in mind. My best wishes to you both."

Edie hugged her. Sean came in carrying her bag. He unloaded the soiled dress and other things.

"What's this?" asked Olga.

"I fell down the basement steps at Sean's farm and the bottom was flooded. I had to change."

"Can you wear what you have on tomorrow? I don't do wash on Sunday."

Sean and Edie both laughed.

The next morning, Edie came to breakfast in Olga's robe. Olga was in her Sunday-going to-meeting clothes. She eyed Edie and asked, "Aren't you two going to church?"

Edie answered, "Yes we are, Olga. Sean and I are going to Musserville Methodist. I tried his church several times and just don't feel comfortable there. He agreed to try my church. I have been going there since I moved to town."

"I see, but why way down here? There's a Methodist church almost next door to you."

"Oh, I went there a couple of times, but my boss was there, plus other wealthy people. Their daughters wouldn't accept me. My roommate, Amy, went to Musserville. I decided to attend with her. I like it down here. Sean also likes it because a lot of his fellow workers go there."

Olga finished her breakfast and said, "I must be going. It takes me an hour to get to Zion Lutheran. I don't walk as fast as young people."

Sean staggered down before Olga left. He said good-bye. Olga scolded, "Now you two get to church and not to bed. I don't want any shenanigans while I'm at church."

"Okay, Olga," they both answered. As soon as Olga had cleared her backyard gate, Edie doffed the robe. She could work better in her nightie. Sean liked it better, too. Edie poured Sean some coffee and made some oatmeal. They decided to ask Pastor Ray if he would marry them.

It was late when they arrived at the services. They found seats near the back. Afterwards, they asked the Reverend if he would marry them. He said yes but on one condition. The had to counsel with him before the actual date. The next Wednesday they met with Pastor Ray. He listened to their dilemma. He asked Sean how he felt about Edie and would he demand she convert to Catholicism. Sean answered he would not.

"Good, because my next statement is what I tell all my couples who are not of the same religious background, especially Catholics and Protestants. I ask them to choose one or the other, because I have found if they don't, one will support the church while the other never returns to the church. I would rather you convert to my religion, but I do not support split families. It is not good for the marriage or the family."

"Pastor Ray, I enjoy your church and your congregation. I have told Edie I am willing to change. My parents would not be happy, but they are both deceased. I know many of the people here since I work with them at Roach and Musser. What is required of me before I can become a member?" Sean replied.

"Not much. I know you are baptized. The only other questions I will ask you now and you will be asked before the congregation is: Do you believe Jesus Christ is the son of God? The second is: Do you believe Jesus Christ is your Savior? If you can say yes to those two questions, you may become a member of this church."

"I can."

"This is good news. Now, when do you plan to get married?"

Edie spoke quickly. "Would the end of September be too soon?"

"Let me check my calendar. The last Saturday in September is open. Shall I reserve the date?"

They both answered with a resounding, "Yes."

The next problem was telling her parents. Edie's mother would not be a problem, but her father would. They drove out unannounced, so Frank could not disappear. Hattie was shocked when Edie opened the door.

"Is Dad around?"

"Yes, he is in the living room."

"Good, I need to talk to you both. I told Sean to stay in the car until I signaled him."

Edie followed Hattie into the living room. Frank was reading the paper.

"Dad, I need to speak with you and mom."

"If it's about that Irishman, I don't want to hear it."

"Okay, but I'm going to tell Mom. Mom, Sean and I are engaged to be married. I know you do not like him because is a Catholic, but he has left his church. We have been going to Musserville Methodist Church together. Sean is going to join next Sunday."

"Did I hear you say he is going to leave his church?" asked Hattie.

"Yes. We had a talk with Pastor Ray. He will marry us on September 29."

Frank put down his paper and growled, "I suppose you want me to come."

"Yes, Dad, I want you to walk me down the aisle and give me to Sean. He is out in the car. He wanted to ask your permission, but I forbid him to come in until I told you."

"It sounds like you already have things settled, so why ask me? No is your answer. I will not give my daughter to a Pope-worshiping Catholic. That's it."

215

"Oh, Dad, please don't say that. I want you, not Ralph or someone else. You're my father."

"Nope, and that's final. If you marry that man, you must never darken my door again."

Hattie got into the conversation. "For Pete's sake, Frank, she is your only daughter. She worked hard for you two years ago. You'll never get to do it again. Can't you soften your stance for just one day?"

"Then I would be a hypocrite. Wouldn't I? Nope, I will not walk you down the aisle. You can tell that red-headed fish-eater to stay in his car and don't come back," Frank snapped. He folded his paper and left the room.

Edie was in tears. She said to her mother, "How can he be that way? Sean is a good person and I love him."

"I know, honey. He might soften someday, but for now he is hurt. Truthfully, I'm a little disappointed, too. I thought someday you would find a nice Protestant boy."

"But I did find a Protestant boy, Sean is leaving his church. Sean and I are meant for each other. I can feel it. He loves me, and I love him. I hope you will come to my wedding. I think Ralph and Marcie will bring you. And, by the way, Mom, Sean just bought the old Parham place, so we will be farming close by. Sean will be the McKillip's farm manager. He starts next March. If we have children, I hope I you will come see them."

Edie left crying. Sean helped her in the car. Through her tears she told him what happened. He wasn't angry or disappointed, since he suspected Frank would reject the marriage. He turned the Chevrolet around and headed back to town.

The wedding was small. Ralph walked his sister down the aisle as best man and Ruth was matron of honor. Several of Sean's friends from work were there. Hattie came with Ralph and Marcie. She was pleasant, but seldom cracked a smile. Olga was seated in the front row on the groom's side. Mr. Hershey and his wife attended. The ceremony lasted twenty minutes followed by a small reception in the church basement.

Mrs. Kerchinske presented a package to Edie.

"What's this?" asked Edie. "We said we didn't need any gifts."

"I know, but this is special, and I wanted you to have it."

Edie remembered Olga's promise the night of her attack. She excitedly tore off the wrapping paper. It covered a well-worn box from Batterson's Department Store. Inside the box was Olga's nightgown.

Edie hugged Olga and said, "Thank you, thank you, Olga. I'll wear it tonight."

Olga replied with a sly grin, "I'll bet not for long."

As Mr. and Mrs. O'Keefe left for their very short honeymoon, it began to rain. It was a cold September rain. No one was told where they were going. In twenty minutes, they were at the farm. They had cleaned the house enough, so they could stay there. As they walked onto the porch, Edie pointed to the oak tree where they spent the day when Sean asked for her hand.

"I'll remember the day you asked me to marry you forever."

Sean swooped her up and carried her across the threshold.

He carried her to the bedroom downstairs. The upstairs had not been cleaned yet.

He plopped Edie on the old bed. Edie stopped him from unbuttoning her wedding gown.

"Wait a minute. I have a surprise for you, but you must leave the room for just a minute."

Sean reluctantly went to the kitchen.

"Okay, you may come in." Edie cooed.

Sean entered, Edie was wearing the nightgown Olga had promised her. Sean just stared at her. The gown was very sheer, and Edie made sure she was standing between Sean and the window. Her curves were very visible. She liked Sean's stare.

"Do you want me to take it off?" she asked.

"No, I will take it off."

Sean quickly slipped the gown over her head.

She shivered in the cool night air.

"Hurry get undressed. Let's hop into bed before I freeze to death."

It didn't take them long to be lying in bed.

After their first go around, Sean asked, "Isn't it great we waited. I hope you loved having sex as much as I did."

"It was better than I dreamed. Lets' do it again."

The next morning the sun was shining with a cool northwest wind moving the leaves. Edie left her exhausted Sean in bed. She slipped Olga's nightgown on underneath her robe. After firing up the small stove, she began to make coffee. The smell of coffee awakened Sean. He plodded to the kitchen in his shorts.

"How are you feeling, hon'?" she asked.

"Drug out and a bit chilly. What did you do to me last night?"

"I put every move I could think of on you."

Sean sipped a cup of coffee as Edie scurried around to mix up some pancake batter. He grinned as her robe flew open to reveal her skimpy nightgown when she spun around. She tossed in some bacon to grease the pan, then tested it with a sprinkle of water. It was ready. She made several cakes and placed them on a platter, then set them on the table and returned for more coffee. As she was pouring his cup, Sean pulled on the bow that held the robe together. It fell open, revealing her thin lacy nightgown.

He said, "Fair lady, pray tell, what are you wearing under your robe?"

"Why, kind sir, do you ask?"

"Because as a man of Irish descent, I enjoy fair ladies clothing or the lack there of."

"Oh you, charmer. I believe a lady should be careful of your desires."

"All I desire is you."

"Is there a possibility I could satisfy your desires?"

"Yes, and quite easily."

"And what would that be, my prince."

"I believe it would be seeing you without your robe."

Edie smiled at Sean and replied, "It is finally warming in here especially near this stove. I will accommodate your desires."

Edie slipped from her robe and continued to work at the stove in Olga's nightgown.

When the pancakes were finished, she slapped them on his plate and set them in front of him.

"You're drooling. Are you that hungry?"

"Hungry for you."

"Well, maybe if you are a good boy, I can help you satisfy your hunger."

As she swirled around, the sun popped out from behind the clouds and shone brightly through the bare window.

Edie looked out and said, "It looks like it's going to be a nice day."

Sean grinned and asked, "Perchance, would you remove Olga's gown? I know you would not want to soil it with breakfast."

"You want me to eat breakfast naked?"

"Yes, and I want you naked all day."

"But it's cold, silly."

"Don't worry, I'll keep you warm."

Edie slowly slipped out of her gown and laid it over the back of her chair.

It was the first time she felt a little conspicuous. She could feel Sean's eyes studying her.

"You're beautiful."

"Why, thank you, kind husband. I think you're pretty handsome yourself."

"Let's go back to bed right after we wash the dishes."

"My, my, my, I thought you were too tired."

"I am, but you invigorate me. I figure we have today. Tomorrow it's back to work and the same old grind with one exception."

"What's the exception?"

"We will sleep together every night."

Edie exclaimed, "Did you hear a car?"

"No. you must be hearing the wind and maybe a train down by the river."

"No, I swear it sounded like a car."

They played around all afternoon. At nine, they readied for bed. They were exhausted. Edie put on her nightie and Sean the bottoms of his pajamas. They fell into bed and had barely shut their eyes when the loudest noise came from the front lawn. There were saw blades banging, horns honking, and whistles screaming. Sean threw on a shirt and opened the front door. There were a dozen people or more standing and shouting. They were clapping and laughing.

"We want Edie. We want Sean. We want fed."

Sean hurried back to Edie and said, "There are bunches of neighbors outside. They want to see us. They want to be fed."

Edie smiled and said, "Sean, honey, this is a chivaree. It is just a custom among rural folks. We just go out and meet them half dressed. They think it's funny. Come on."

"But what about the food? How did they know we were here?"

"They brought their own food, don't worry. I suspect Ralph figured where we were. I wouldn't be surprised if he wasn't over here sometime today to make sure."

"Do you think he saw us?"

"Maybe, but remember he just got married, too. He knows what we were doing. Come on. Enjoy the fun."

Edie grabbed her robe and padded barefoot onto the porch. Sean pulled on some trousers and followed her. They presented themselves to the crowd.

"Kiss her, kiss her," they shouted.

Sean grabbed Edie and gave her a big, back-bending kiss. Her bare leg showed from the slit in her robe. The group roared their approval.

"Bring on the food," they shouted.

"I got the food," called Ralph, "but I need some help."

Soon there were cakes and pies lining the porch. Ralph and another man carried two ice cream freezers to the porch. Soon everyone was eating cake and pie covered with homemade ice cream. They had a good time. When the crowd started for home, each neighbor shook Sean's hand and hugged Edie. They welcomed them to the community. Ralph was the last to leave.

He hugged Edie and said, "Mom wanted to come, but Dad forbid her. Give him time, Edie. He will come around. Sean's a good man. He'll turn Dad's heart. You just have to be patient."

Edie started to cry. He patted her shoulder, then turned and winked at her.

"How does it feel eating breakfast naked?" he said with a wink.

"Ralphie, you spied on us?"

"Yep, it was quite a show."

"Ralphie, shame on you. Don't ever tell anyone."

"Don't worry, sis. Only Marcie will find out."

Edie took a half-hearted swing at her brother as he walked away.

Their honeymoon lasted two days. On Monday afternoon, they returned to town. Sean was right. Tuesday was the same old grind. Edie hopped a ride to the trolley uptown. Sean started work at seven. The newlyweds lived with Olga until March. Before he left, Sean built Olga an indoor bathroom with a tub, lavatory, and toilet. He also installed a kitchen sink with running water. The city promised sewer and water to their south end residents by the following year. He asked if she wanted some help finding a new renter. She said no. He would be her last.

CHAPTER 20: SEAN TO THE RESCUE

On Christmas day, Edie announced she was going to have a baby. Sean was elated. When Edie told her mother, Hattie hugged her.

She said, "I'll help you when I can. Your father will probably ignore the baby, but that is his decision, not mine."

The first of March came too quickly. They had worked on the farmhouse most of the weekends all winter. It still needed some finishing touches. Sean said good-bye to Roach and Musser. He started at McKillip Farms on Monday. Edie quit her job, for she was too far away to commute. She had plenty to do at the farm. There was a garden to plant, grass to mow, rooms to paint, and curtains to make. She ordered some baby chicks from the hatchery. If she needed groceries, she drove to the New Era Store. Edie saw her mother when she visited Marcie. Edie's baby was due in late August.

Sean's job required more hours than planned. He had to learn the many facets of farming, but the hired men were patient. They had to get everything ready for planting. Mr. McKillip purchased two new Farmall tractors with narrow front ends. The units allowed the men to cultivate two rows at a time. The farm would be fully mechanized by Fall. The only use for draft horses was to pull a balky tractor to get it started. The first year Sean borrowed equipment from the McKillip's to put in a crop.

Edie gave birth to a girl. They named her Francine. As predicted, Edie's father would not acknowledge the newcomer.

The McKillip farm prospered. People in town had money. They wanted beef, which was considered better than pork or chicken. Sean wanted to cash in on the demand. He thought he could improve the McKillip herd through better genetics. He suggested Bruce go to Scotland and acquire some fresh bulls. Bruce loved the idea. He quickly headed for England with Alma. He bought four of the best bulls in England. The McKillip Angus line became sought after throughout the Midwest.

Pete and Ruth built a new home on the bluff overlooking the Pine Creek valley. Pete had his own office at the house. He always had business in Chicago or St. Louis and seldom came to the farm. Expensive autos arrived at The Bluff House. He wined and dined the rich people. Edie helped feed the larger crowds. Her dishes were raved about by the guests. Soon she was the main cook for his sumptuous banquets.

In October the next year, Edie delivered a boy. They named him Luke. Her mother drove over to help Edie, but Frank refused to acknowledge the little leprechauns, as he called them. Ruth entered the hospital ten days later.

She and Pete had a boy they named Wade.

In the spring, Ralph bought a used John Deere A. He and his dad were resetting the right rear wheel for cultivating. It had been moved closer to the frame for plowing. The right rear wheel ran in the furrow. Now they couldn't raise the wheel high enough to slide it out on the axle. Ralph went into the shop for another jack. Frank decided he could get one more pump out of the jack by himself. Ralph heard a thud, a clank, and a sickening scream. The tractor had rolled from the jack and crushed Frank's upper leg. He was pinned beneath the iron wheel with one of the lugs pressing on his hip. Ralph tried desperately to reset the jack, but to no avail. He ran to the house and called Marcie. They both tried. Frank stoically laid quietly. He seemed numb from the pain. Ralph ran back to the phone and called his closest neighbor, Sean. Sean just happened to be in his office.

Ralph excitedly said, "My dad is pinned under the tractor. I need help. Can you come?"

Sean replied, "Sure, I'll bring Ross and send Jake out to fetch Ernie. We'll be there in a jiffy."

Sean ran out of the office and found Ross and Jake in the shop. Ross was a huge man. He was 6'6" and three hundred pounds, strong as an ox. Sean explained the situation. Jake went to get Ernie, who was cultivating the early corn. Sean and Ross hopped into the old truck and roared to Ralph's. The old truck skidded to a stop followed by a cloud of dust.

Ross surveyed the situation and said, "Ralph, you pull your dad out while Sean and I lift the wheel."

Sean and Ralph both looked at each other. It seemed impossible, but Ralph crawled under the tractor and steadied his father. Ross told Sean to grab hold toward the outer edge of the wheel. It would give them more leverage. Sean and Ross grabbed the spokes on the yellow wheel. Ross said, "On the count of three, one, two, three." Both men let out a roar and lifted the wheel. Ralph slid Frank away from the tractor.

Sean looked at Ross and yelled, "Now what?"

Ross yelled back, "Drop it!"

They let go. The John Deere fell with a thud.

Jake and Ernie arrived in Sean's old beater car, a model T. Ross turned to Jake and joked, "What took you so long?"

Jake shot back, "Ernie just had to have another cigarette. No, he didn't. I'm kidding."

Sean brought them back to reality. "We must get Frank to the hospital and fast. Ralph, go tell Marcie to call Edie. Tell Edie her father has been injured and she should bring the kids over in the Chevrolet. Ross and Ernie, see if you can find a couple of planks or an old door we can use for a stretcher. Jake, you help me slowly move Frank and find some small boards for a splint."

The men moved quickly. Jake took Ralph and Marcie's children to the porch. He had four children himself, so he was capable of babysitting until Edie arrived. Ralph helped Marcie straighten Frank's leg. He screamed in pain. They had heard it before in the war. They didn't flinch as they attached the splint.

Ross ripped a wooden door on the corn crib from its hinges. They carefully slid Frank onto it. Marcie held the injured leg. Ross and Sean carried Frank to some shade. They placed him on a bench and waited for Edie.

They didn't wait long. Edie came roaring up the drive with the children sitting in the front seat of the old truck because she couldn't find the keys to the car. She pulled alongside the group and leapt out. She knelt beside her father.

"Dad, Dad, it's me, Edie. I'm here. We'll take care of you," she cried, then looked at Ralph. "Does Mom know?"

"No. Who's going to tell her?"

Sean interrupted, "Okay, here's what we'll do. Frank will fit across the back seat of Ralph's car. Marcie, since you're a nurse, you ride with him. There won't be room to sit on the seat, so someone get her a bucket to sit on. Jake, you and Ernie stay with the kids. Edie, you go get your mother. Ralph, you come with me. We're going to Muscatine to a hospital."

Ross asked, "What about me?"

Sean looked at the big man and said, "You drive Edie over to Frank's in the truck. I'm sure Hattie will be upset so you may have to help her to the car. Then you drive Edie and her mom to Muscatine. Everybody understand?"

"Which hospital?" asked Edie.

"Hershey."

A groan came from Frank. Everyone looked at Frank and started their assigned tasks. Soon the big car was headed for Muscatine. Sean didn't waste any time. He reached the city in fifteen minutes. Luckily the police were elsewhere, because Sean had broken the city speed limits.

They pulled into the emergency lane. Marcie in her lovely British accent described Frank's condition to the attendants. They carefully lifted Frank out and rushed him to Emergency.

Meanwhile, Ross jumped into the truck and fired it up. Edie ran around to the other side. She pulled on the handle. It wouldn't open. Ross started to move.

"Wait for me. I can't get the door open," Edie yelled.

Ross reached over and popped the door open with one smack of his huge hand. Edie hiked up her skirt and jumped in. She slammed the door shut.

"Move this wreck, Rossy," she yelled.

Ross let out the clutch and the truck lurched forward. He smiled at Edie. He liked his boss's petite wife. She had spirit.

They were at Hattie's in five minutes. Edie hopped out and ran to the house. Over her shoulder she called to Ross, "Get the Velie. It's in the garage."

Edie threw open the door and cried, "Mom, Mom, Dad has been injured. Sean is taking him to the hospital. We're to meet him there."

Hattie was washing dishes. She tore off her apron and started to pick out the proper hat.

"Come on, Mom, we haven't time for any hats. Ross will drive us."

Hattie followed Edie to the car. Ross helped her into the back seat. He lumbered around to the driver's side and squeezed under the steering wheel. He shifted into gear and roared off.

"What happened?" asked Hattie.

"The rear wheel of the tractor rolled back on Dad's leg. Marcie knows it is broken. She rode in with Sean and Ralph."

"Who has the children?"

"Jake and Ernie."

"Who's Jake and Ernie?"

"They're hired men at McKillip's. Jake has four kids and Ernie has three. They know what to do. I wouldn't be surprised if they take them to one of their homes. Don't worry."

Ross delivered his passengers to the hospital entrance. Ralph met them at the door.

"Dad is in for x-rays. We should know something soon. The doctor said it could be a multiple fracture."

They were ushered to the family waiting room. Shortly. Dr. Harper appeared with a set of x-rays. Holding them up to the window, he pointed with his finger at the negatives.

"Your husband has a triple break. It will be difficult for my team to set. I suggest you take him to the University of Iowa Hospital in Iowa City. I have already spoken with the staff up there. They can be ready if you authorize the move. If you stay here, we can try, but his leg is in three pieces and some small fragments are floating away from the bone. I don't know if it will heal properly. We can move him to Iowa City in an ambulance."

Hattie looked at Ralph. Ralph looked at Edie. Edie set her jaw, then said, "Come on, this is simple. We take Dad to Iowa City. Sean will drive us. Ross, you take Marcie home, so she can take care of the kids. Dr. Harper call Iowa City. Tell them we're on our way."

The doctor nodded and left. Sean drove the Studebaker around front. They headed for Iowa City. The ambulance led the way. In a little over an hour they arrived at the big hospital.

Frank was in surgery for six hours. It was nine o'clock in the evening when a surgeon, Dr. Gladstein, met with the family.

He said to Hattie, "Your husband is resting well. We placed a stainless-steel rod in his leg. When he wakes, he will probably experience a lot of pain. I would like you to be with him when he is brought to his room. It is hospital policy no visitors are allowed after nine, but tonight you will be an exception and allowed to stay the night, if you want."

Hattie turned to Edie and said, "I have no clothes or makeup. Where will I sleep? What will I do?"

"Don't worry, Mother. You can sleep in a chair for one night. I'll make sure someone will be here early in the morning. Visitor's hours are from one to three, but someone will be here much earlier. The staff will notify you. You take care of Dad and don't fret about how you look. I'm sure they have seen much worse. Now, we must to go home, but you don't be afraid to call me long distance."

Hattie survived the night. She was surprised to find her sister was the first one there in the morning. Edie had worked her magic. Aunt Helen brought a large bag of cosmetics and some clean clothes. She attended to Frank's needs while Hattie changed.

Frank was confined to bed with a huge cast from his waist to his ankle. When the doctor visited, he said Frank would be hospitalized for a couple of weeks in Iowa City, then he could be moved to a Muscatine hospital. Hattie visited Frank every other day. She got brave enough to drive to Iowa City alone.

One afternoon, Hattie walked into Frank's room to find a priest seated by his bed.

The priest rose and spoke. "Mrs. Mohr, I presume. I'm Father Joe Halligan."

"Good afternoon, Father Joe. Is there a problem with my husband?"

Frank answered, "No, Hattie, I'm fine. Father Joe stopped in several days ago. We have been discussing my questions about Catholics. He has been very enlightening."

Hattie remarked, "Well, Father Joe. I'm shocked. My husband usually throws all Catholics out."

"On the contrary, Hattie, Joe and I have hit it off quite well. Haven't we, Joe?" interrupted Frank.

Father Joe chuckled, "Yes, Mrs. Mohr. I came in one morning to ask how he was feeling. He groaned. I really don't think he knew who I was at first. Then I started to pray for him and he awoke. He really told me to stop, but in his condition, he couldn't do a thing. So I started to talk. I believe we are good friends now. You agree with me, Frank?"

"Yep. He didn't try to convert me, but I understand my Catholic neighbors better. He also told me I am missing out on my family by being so hard-headed. Hattie, I got grandkids I've never met, and they live next door to me. Then there's my own daughter, she slaved for me when Ralph was off to war. She became a spokesperson for women's suffrage. I rejected her. I've been a fool."

Hattie had to sit down. She couldn't believe what she had just heard. Her Frank was visiting with a priest. She thought, "*I suppose a nun will arrive next.*"

She didn't have to wait long. Sister Ann Marie entered the room. She looked at Father Joe and said, "Father, we must be going. We must get ready for mass tomorrow. You remember the bishop is coming."

"Yes, Sister, I know." he turned to Hattie and said, "Nice to have met you, Mrs. Mohr."

Father Joe and Sister Ann Marie returned to their visiting schedule. Hattie scooted her chair close to Frank's bed.

She held Frank's hand. "I never thought I'd see the day you would even speak to a priest. Maybe this accident was God's plan."

Frank scoffed a bit and replied, "Hattie now you sound like a Presbyterian. No, I am just glad Father Joe came in to check on me. If it is God's plan, it's a good one."

Hattie smiled at her husband. Maybe he was going to change.

The next Monday the doctors took x-rays. The x-ray showed his bones were healing, but he would have to wear a cast, a smaller and lighter one, for several more weeks. They told him he could go to the hospital in Muscatine to finish recuperating. After he was transferred, Frank remained at Hershey Hospital for three more weeks. Each week more cast was removed. He was under the care of Doctor Wilson. Finally, two weeks later, Doctor Wilson released Frank on the condition there would be no steps or pets at home.

Ralph and Edie had anticipated these requirements. Frank was to come home July thirtieth. It had been eight weeks since the accident. Sean had his men build a ramp to the porch. They moved the bed downstairs to the parlor. Sean built a small closet for a commode, so Frank could have some privacy.

When Frank came home, Marcie checked on his progress. She helped Hattie bathe him, which embarrassed Frank. Marcie assured him she'd bathed many soldiers. It was routine for her.

Edie kept in touch with her mother but didn't visit her father. Sean would come to help Ralph but avoided the house. He'd talk to Hattie on the porch. Ralph stopped every morning and helped with his father's exercises. Edie supplied many meals and took washing home.

One morning in late August, Frank said to Hattie, "Is there a possibility Edie would bring my grandchildren over?"

Hattie was surprised, but answered, "I think she might. I can ask. Are you sure you want to see her and your grandchildren?"

"Yes, and I want her husband to come, too. As I told you at the hospital, Joe said I was missing out on an important part of my life."

Hattie hurried to call Edie. Edie was surprised, but overjoyed. They could be over when Sean got home from work.

Edie and Sean arrived after seven. Edie went to Frank in the living room. Sean stayed in the kitchen. Frank was in his usual chair. His leg was stretched out and rested on a foot stool. Hattie had fashioned some trousers with one leg short and baggy to accommodate the cast. He had a clean shirt on and Hattie had helped him shave.

Little Luke hid behind his mother's skirt. He'd never met his grandfather. Francine slowly approached Frank. She touched his rough hand, then crawled up to his lap. She looked into his eyes and asked, "Why are you crying?"

Frank smiled and through his tears he answered, "Because your grandfather is so happy to see you."

He looked at Edie and said, "Edie, will you come to me?"

Grandma Hattie held Luke while Edie walked to her dad. She sat beside him on a stool. Leaning over, she kissed her dad on the forehead. He drew her to him and held her tanned hands.

"I'm glad you came, daughter. I discovered I was wrong about you and your husband. I heard it was his men who saved me, and he has helped Ralph all summer. I owe him a lot. And you have taken care of me and your mother. You could have shunned me as I have shunned you. What a fool I have been! You worked like a man while Ralph was in the Army. I cannot apologize enough for my actions. I want you to know I appreciate all you have done. Did you bring Sean? I want to shake his hand and apologize to him."

Edie replied, "Sean is in the kitchen. He didn't want to spoil our reunion, just in case it didn't go well. I'll get him."

Sean walked into the living room. He was very nervous. Frank reached for his crutch and started to rise.

"Please, don't get up for me," said Sean.

"Oh, but I do. I must rise to meet the man who is better than me. You, my red-haired Irishman, have every reason to punch me in the mouth. You have made me eat my words. You could have walked away, but you forgave me and never thought for one minute not to help Ralph, Hattie, and me. Thank you. I apologize for my actions."

"There is no need for that, Frank. You are my neighbor and my father-in-law."

"I suppose you and Edie are wondering why I saw the light."

Edie replied, "Yes, Dad, we are wondering."

"Well, during my stay at the hospital in Iowa City, Father Joe visited me. Yes, I know, he was a Catholic priest. He and I visited for hours. He could tell I was opinionated, but he never wavered. He told me about how people lose their families and friends because of prejudice. He said if I didn't change, I would lose you and Sean and my grandchildren. I learned not to judge people by their faith or origin. It's not God's way. Now, God bless you both and you are welcome here at any time." He tousled Francie's curly mop of hair and added, "Of course, you must bring my grandkids with you."

Edie laughed. "Thank you. Don't worry, Dad. We'll bring them over. They've got a lot of catching up to do."

"No, Punky, I should be thanking you and Father Joe. I feel as if a great weight has been lifted."

The next months were great. Edie brought the children often. Frank never recovered completely. He always walked with a limp. He could work for about four hours, and then the pain in his hip would drive him inside.

CHAPTER 21: PETE TAKES OVER THE MINE

Sean's duties became taxing. Pete was away more and more. He told Sean his business in Chicago was becoming quite profitable and taking much more of his time. He indicated a cheese-making firm needed a place to store and age some cheddar cheese. The old sandstone quarry fit the bill perfectly. He was going to refurbish the mine.

Sean asked, "May I be of any help? I worked there with my father in the summer."

Pete replied, "No Sean I do not want you to be involved or ever to be involved, because there will be no mining or quarrying."

Sean accepted his boss's orders. Farming was more to his liking anyway.

Soon the old quarry site was bustling. Trucks and construction workers flooded the site. They were all imported from Chicago. The only thing that didn't change was the entrance. It remained covered with trees and brush. The gravel at the gate was left minimal. Fifty feet inside the field, the road was well graveled. The trees covering the old mine were not disturbed. They provided cover to the mine entrance. To the passers-by it appeared as nothing had changed.

By March, cheese packed in barrels began arriving. The former mine office was electrified along with the mine. Pete was busy finding housing for the workers and entertaining investors from Chicago and St. Louis. The investors would overnight at the Bluff House, tour the mine, and return to Chicago by evening. The beautiful bluffs of the Pine Creek Valley attracted some high rollers from the big cities. Pete planned on building some vacation cottages for his investors. At present, the investors staying at the Bluff House dined there also. Soon Ruth was overwhelmed with the responsibility of preparing the meals. She hired two women to help. Still, some meals were difficult to prepare. The hired women were more adapted to cleaning. Ruth called Edie to see if she would be interested in cooking. Edie loved to cook. She accepted. On the days she was needed she took the children to Marcie's or her mother's. One day, she prepared roast beef, potatoes, and green peas followed by apple pie. After the meal, a man entered the kitchen.

He asked in a gruff voice, "Who did the cooking today?"

Edie spun around and answered, "Who wants to know?"

"The Boss."

"And who might be the Boss?"

"Tony Rondario, and who might you be?"

"Edie, Edie O'Keefe. I am the cook today."

The big man was, at least, six foot plus and 280 pounds. He had dark black hair and deep brown eyes which were outlined by big bushy eyebrows. He was impeccably dressed in a brown suit. As he approached Edie, he stared at the petite five-foot, four-inch woman in a light blue print dress covered partially by a full apron. She was bare-legged in black strapped shoes. Her hair was short with a slight wave on the side of her head. She met his stare and raised a big butcher knife for protection.

He raised his hands and exclaimed, "Now, now, little lady. I mean no harm. I just want another taste of that delicious pie."

Edie put down the knife and grabbed a pie and dish. She cut the man a huge slice of apple pie. He devoured it.

Starring at Edie again, he said, "Do you live here?"

"No, I just work here when Ruth has to entertain her guests. What's your name?"

"Giuseppe Romono. I work for Tony."

"You look like you have a family."

"Yes, ma'am. A wife and four kids, but she can't cook like this."

"Thank you."

"The boss wanted me to find out if you can cook Italian dishes?"

"A couple, but I seldom get the call for them."

"Well, next time we come over, could you fix one?"

"I could try if I have a day or two's notice."

"Okay, I'll tell the Boss to let Pete know. Is the lady wearing the green dress relation of Pete's?"

"Yes, she's his wife, Ruth. Why do you ask?"

"Well, she is pretty, but not as young as the others."

"Others? What others?"

Giuseppe coughed and answered, "Oops, I think I just spilled the beans. Sorry, ma'am. Please don't tell Mr. McKillip I said that and, definitely, don't squeal to Mrs. McKillip or the Boss will kill me. I mean, he will literally kill me."

Edie could tell the big man was shaken. She quickly replied, "Don't worry, Giuseppe, I won't let your secret out."

Giuseppe wiped his forehead with his hankie. He pushed the plate away and smiled.

"That was some piece of pie, ma'am. Is it possible I could have another?"

"By all means why you don't eat the last piece right out of the pan?" she replied as she shoved the pan toward the big man. He finished it, wiped his mouth, and slid away from the table.

"I better get back to the meeting. I'll be in contact before we come next time."

"You do that, Giuseppe. Nice knowing you."

Giuseppe left. Edie cleaned the kitchen. She was about to leave when Ruth arrived.

"How's the chef?" she asked.

"Okay, I guess."

"What do you mean. I guess?"

"Well, one of your guests stopped by and had some pie and requested an Italian dish next time."

"Oh, and who was that?"

"Giuseppe."

"He is such a nice guy. I hope Tony never gets rid of him."

Ruth sighed. "I suppose I should tell you, Edie, but don't be surprised if you notice some young women around here. They're Pete's. He claims they are for the guests, but I suspect he spends time with them, too. I don't like it, but I hope he will tire of them and come back to me. I suppose I should divorce him, but I still love the little stinker."

"I'm so sorry for you, Ruth. I just hope you are right."

Edie headed home. She picked up the children at her mother's. They were tired and needed supper. Sean would be home in an hour. She pulled some noodles out of the cupboard and cut up some of the leftover roast beef to flavor the pasta. She pulled out some snickerdoodle cookies. Francine had just finished setting the table when Sean walked in. The children all rushed to hug their father. Sean gave Edie her kiss and washed up for supper.

He came back all smiles and said, "Guess what? Bruce liked my idea of purchasing a mechanical corn picker. I had suggested the idea to him a couple of weeks ago. I told him how much more efficient a mechanical picker was. He said he'd consider it and today he told me he ordered, not one, but two two-row pickers. He also ordered a chain elevator to unload the corn. I figured with this efficiency we could do all the McKillip corn and ours. How was your day?"

Edie replied, "It was fine."

During supper Sean explained the merits of corn pickers and how they were going to improve the operation. He went so far as asking Bruce if he could use the pickers on their farm.

Edie's only comment was, "Why are you always talking to Mr. McKillip and not Pete?"

"Cause Pete is seldom here," was his reply.

"Speaking of Mr. Pete . . . he's . . . "

Edie turned and looked at the children and said, "Francine why don't you and Luke go upstairs and get ready for bed."

"But Mommy, it's still daylight out," she protested.

"You're right. It is early. Well, why don't both of you go and put your bed clothes on and we'll catch lightning bugs later."

"Did you say I can wear my nightie outside?" queried Francine. "Do I keep my underpants on?"

"I don't care. Whatever you feel comfortable in. Go naked if you want," Edie said with a grin.

"Oh, Mommy, you don't mean that, people might see us."

Edie replied, "Who, your daddy? He wouldn't care, but maybe you should wear something."

Sean leaned back in his chair and chuckled. He knew Edie was playing with his daughter.

Sean spoke." I'll tell you what. It is very warm upstairs. Why don't we camp out on the porch tonight? You change and then help your mother and me drag out pillows and cushions for our beds."

"Are you and Mommy going to sleep out there, too?"

"Sure, we'll sleep right beside you."

Francine let out a squeal of delight. She hurried upstairs to change into her little nightie. She brought down her pillow and blanket from her bed. Luke followed with his teddy bear. Soon the beds were made. Sean helped Edie with the dishes. He noticed something was eating at her.

"What's the matter, honey? Have a bad day at Pete's? You were about to say something about him earlier."

Edie kept washing dishes and didn't turn to him. She said, "I just found out that Pete has other women. I didn't say anything to Ruth., but she brought it up. She knows he is playing around. She hopes he is just going through a phase. Unless it gets worse, she will stay with him because of the children. I'd be gone in a flash. What makes men do that, hon?"

"It doesn't surprise me about Pete. He has always played around. I think there is more going on in Chicago and St. Louis than what he's telling his dad or me. There are too many trucks going in and out of the quarry to be just hauling cheese. Some night I'm going to sneak over there and look for myself. I know the back ways to the site."

"You keep out of his way, babe. I don't want you to get fired, or worse, shot."

"I'll be careful, but that is later. Right now, let's enjoy the evening with the kids."

"Okay, right after we finish, I'm putting on my nightie and enjoying the outdoors with the children."

Sean got a big grin. "Put on the old short one that shows some skin. The kids won't notice."

Edie gave each child a jar and off they ran, chasing lightning bugs. Edie sat in the swing in her nightgown. Soon Sean came with just his pajama bottoms on. He had gone to the water tank and poured water over his head and body to cool off and clean up. His skin glistened in the setting sun.

Edie could hear the children laughing and giggling as they chased the flying insects. They were further and further away. She decided to seek them out. She was at the yard gate when she heard Luke scream.

"Mommy, come quick. Francine fell into the horse tank."

Sean heard the screams, too, and dashed across the farmyard to the big concrete tank. He could see Francine's nightie under the tank heater. He jumped into the water and ducked under the planks covering the one side and quickly pulled her free and to the surface. Francine was lifeless. Sean thought quickly. He held her by her feet and slapped her back. She sputtered, coughed, and spit water out. Sean lay her on her on the ground. He lightly tapped her back again. She spat more out.

Edie arrived and knelt by Francine. She stuck her finger into Francine's mouth and removed some green tank moss.

Francine opened her eyes and cried. "Mommy, Mommy."

Edie and Sean gave a sigh of relief. Sean scooped his daughter up and headed for the house. The rest of the family followed. Once inside, Edie grabbed an old kitchen towel and wrapped the wet Francine.

She asked, "Honey, do you think there might be enough hot water in the heater?"

He answered, "Yes, there should be if I go to the basement and drain it direct. I'll fetch a couple of pails full, then I'll bring the wash tub from the back porch."

"Luke, you find your sister a dry nightie and some underpants, then go into Mommy's bedroom and in the third drawer in the chest find Mommy a dry nightgown. Mine is soaked through. I think there is a pink one on top."

Within minutes all the tasks were accomplished. Sean poured two pails of warm water into the tub.

"Sean, I forgot to have you bring some bath towels from the basement. Would you please get two?"

"Okay."

Edie turned to Luke and said, "You may go outside while I give Francine a bath. She was covered all over with moss and mud from the bottom of the tank."

Sean added, "Unless you need me, I'll take care of Luke."

He and Luke went outside to the porch. Edie stripped the wet nightie and underwear from her daughter and sat her in the tub. It took a while to remove all the moss in her hair. Finally, she was clean as a whistle. Edie rubbed her dry and helped her dress. Francine waited for her mother to change her nightgown.

It was after ten by the time the family got bedded down. Francine was still frightened from the ordeal, so she slept with Edie on the big mattress. Sean took Francine's three sofa cushions and tried to make do. His feet hung over the end.

Old Rodger Rooster crowed. Edie and Sean awoke. That rooster crowed way too early. Edie was pulling on her dress when the phone rang. It was Ruth.

"Edie, Mildred is sick and cannot help me this morning. Could you come over? I have four of Pete's guests. They're the same men you cooked for a month ago. You know, Giuseppe and Mr. Rondario. I need you desperately."

Edie paused, turned to Sean, who was just putting his shoes on, and said. "It's Ruth, she needs me to help cook this morning. What do I say?"

Sean replied, "I can stay home with the kids until ten. If it gets late, I'll drive them over to Marcie's or your mom's. You'd better go. She's my boss's wife, you know."

Edie spoke into the phone. "I can be there in a half an hour."

"Oh, thank you, Edie. What should I start preparing?"

Edie thought a minute and replied, "Brown some pork sausage and get some eggs out of the icebox."

"Okay, but Edie, I have a refrigerator, remember."

Edie held her tongue. It was just Ruth's way of telling her she had money. It was the only reason she stayed with Pete.

By the time Edie finished dressing, Sean had the car ready to go. She waved good-bye as she headed for the McKillip's. She entered the back door and found Ruth still in her robe, trying to brown some sausage.

Edie said, "I'll take over. You get dressed, only this time in your house dress because I will need you. How much time do we have?"

"About an hour. Pete likes his breakfast at seven. I'll try and be quick with my clothes."

Edie knew better. Ruth always took her time dressing. She'd be alone most of the time. Fortunately, after feeding this crew earlier, she had looked up Italian breakfasts. She'd cook one up with an Iowa flavor. She rolled out a pie crust and filled it with scrambled eggs, sausage, tomatoes, cheese, and peppers, brewed some strong coffee, and cut some bread into squares topped with creamed cheese. Pete showed up at seven. He was surprised to see Edie.

"Where's Ruthie?" he asked.

"Upstairs, getting all prettied up. She couldn't serve breakfast in a robe."

"Oh! Well, the men and I are ready when you are. You don't have to dress at all. Oops! That didn't come out right. You know what I mean."

"Yes, Pete, I know what you mean. Tell your guests breakfast will be served in about ten minutes."

"Okay, Edie. If your breakfast is anything like your dinner two months ago, it will be worth waiting for."

Edie pulled the Italian casserole from the oven just as Ruth arrived.

"My, that looks fabulous, Edie. Tell you what. You take off your apron and serve the casserole yourself. I'll just take credit for calling you this morning."

"But I just wore my old housedress. I didn't have time to comb my hair or put on any makeup. I look awful."

"Oh, you look sweet with the flour in your hair and a smudge on your cheek. The guys will be understanding. They have families, too. Oh, I must tell you something, so you won't be surprised. There's a woman out there. Her name is Minnie. She's young and pretty. Sort of dumb. All the guys think she's cute, including Pete. I'm not angry with him. I married him for better or worse. I hope this is his worse."

"Okay, I'll smile my best. Here, take out the coffee and biscuits. I already have the jelly on the table."

Edie carried out the breakfast. The steaming casserole was a hit. Minnie claimed she was allergic to eggs and ate very little. Edie offered her some oatmeal and served Mr. Rondario his second helping. As she bent over his shoulder, he turned and grinned. He touched her hand as she laid the portion on his plate.

"This is delicious, young lady. My compliments to you. I would like to invite you to my home and cook for me. I would pay you very well."

Edie was surprised at his offer. She pulled back and looked him in the eye.

She said, "Mr. Rondario, I have two children and a husband to take care of. My father is handicapped. I'm needed here. I appreciate your offer, but I must decline."

Edie turned and walked away, leaving the boss man flabbergasted. No woman had ever refused an offer from him. He glared at Giuseppe and pointed his finger at the kitchen. Giuseppe immediately rose and headed for the kitchen.

Edie was filling the dishpan with hot water when he entered. He stood silently and waited until Edie acknowledged his presence.

"What may I do for you, Giuseppe?" she asked.

"Mr. Tony is disappointed with your answer. He doesn't like being turned down, especially by a woman."

"Well, you tell your Mr. Tony I was flattered by his offer; but my family comes before money or his stomach."

Giuseppe just smiled and returned to the dining room. Ruth entered the kitchen. She scurried over to Edie and said, "You just turned down Mr. Antonio Rondario. He's the big boss of the syndicate on the north side of Chicago. He controls everyone. You mustn't say no to him."

Edie answered, "Well, I did and I will. No man rules me. Not even the biggest mobster in Chicago. Now, if you will excuse me as soon as I get these dishes finished, I'll be heading home. I have my own home to take care of."

Ruth sensed Edie was miffed. She returned to the dining room and brought Minnie back. Minnie was dressed in a very low-cut dress which only came to her knees. Edie couldn't help but eye her ample bosom, which were mostly uncovered. Her eyes were made up and she wore oodles of lipstick on her lips. She eyed Edie and the kitchen.

She said, "This kitchen looks just like my mother's back in Kentucky. She has electricity but still uses a cookstove like this. I'll bet it's difficult to cook in this kitchen. Tony has everything electric. You'd love it."

"I suppose I would, but I will not change my mind."

"Okay, but Tony doesn't like to be turned down."

Edie watched the young hussy walk out, then turned to Ruth and said, "I don't mind cooking for you, but don't try running my life. I must ask you to refrain from ever asking me to cook for Mr. Rondario again. I will not be bought."

Ruth snapped back, "Listen, you little snip. You're just an employee here. I could have you fired."

"Go ahead, and next time see who you can find when you need an instant cook."

Edie took off her apron and stomped out.

Sean was loading the children into the truck when Edie pulled up to the house. She walked right past him and into the house. Sean and the children followed.

"What's going on?" asked Sean.

"Oh, honey, I just had a fight with Ruth. It was all over that Mr. Rondario and this cheese storage. He asked me to come to Chicago and cook for him. I refused. I guess no one refuses Mr. Rondario. Ruth got all upset. She said she could fire me, I said go ahead, and walked out. I feel terrible. We need the money."

Sean replied, "Now, sweetie, you know she needs you. As for Mr. Rondario, he doesn't know you. He's just used to getting his way. It will blow over."

"I think I should call her and apologize."

"If it will make you feel better, go ahead. I'll bring the children in and head to work. State fair is next week. Bruce wants every bull and heifer ready. With the city people getting richer, they all need more beef to eat."

"I'll call her right away. Say, couldn't you ask him for a raise?"

"Maybe after the fair?"

The phone rang. Edie stood on her stool to answer.

"Edie O'Keefe."

"Edie, this is Ruth. I'm so sorry for what I said. I don't want you to go. I'll make sure Mr. Rondario doesn't ask you for anything again. Please accept my apology. You're my best friend."

"Ruthie, I'm so sorry, too. I shouldn't have spouted off like that, but that hussy Minnie just burned my skin."

"Edie, the funny thing is when Giuseppe came to the kitchen, he wanted to express Mr. Rondario's apology to you. He was impressed with your devotion to your family. When he found out I had called you just this morning, he gave me some money to help pay for your work on such short notice."

"That was nice, but you pay me enough, Ruth."

"Edie, I peeked inside the envelope. It's a fifty-dollar bill! I'll have Pete run it over later. Now, I must go to town and buy some new clothes. When you left, I was so mad I backed into the table and spilled the tomato sauce you made all over me."

"I'll be home all day. Say, why don't Sophia and Wade come over. She and Francine can babysit the boys."

"Sure, I'll do that. They love coming to your place. I guess it's better than going to Grandma Alma's."

Edie was glad that their little rift was over. She an Ruth were always best friends , but trying to control her life just cut her wrong. But Mr. Rondario was a person who thought he could buy anything or anyone, was not buying her. She was independent.

CHAPTER 22: SIX YEARS LATER

In December of 1926, Sean and Edie became parents of twin girls. Edie had a full house and a busy one. When she arrived home from the hospital, Luke looked at his new sisters and said to Edie, "Mommy, do you think you could have a boy next time? I need a brother."

Edie answered, "We'll see, my little man. We'll see."

Pete's cheese business prospered. He expanded to St. Louis and a couple of sales in Kansas City. High rollers continued to visit the Bluff House. They were accompanied by several young women named, Betty, Carmen, Peaches, Flo, and so on. Some came once, some several times. Ruth claimed she should have kept a guest book. The women all slept in a room adjoining Tony Rondario's room.

The depression in farming country was worsening. Many people were out of work, but the demand for liquor never slowed. Despite the efforts of the Justice Department to rein in the mobs, crime bosses flourished. Edie became quite the accomplished chef and cooked for Ruth several times during the next five years. With the farm struggling, her income was a welcome help for her family of six. Tony Rondario wrote her a personal letter and wished she would continue to furnish the meals for his men when he came to Muscatine. Guiseppe made sure she received bonuses for her excellent meals.

Pete's father was unhappy with the bull sales after the fair. No one had any money to buy. The crop prices were a disaster. There were no government programs to bail farmers out or payment for not planting extra acres of wheat. The wheat country farmers didn't cut back; they just plowed up more ground to grow more bushels. Wheat competed with corn for animal feed, and the corn market collapsed. The depression in rural areas was a forbearer of very difficult times ahead for America.

Things were beginning to change at the McKillip farm. Alma McKillip was diagnosed with stomach cancer. She required almost all of Bruce's time. Pete's "cheese" business flourished. He spent little time at the farm. Sean's management decisions increased. He cleared all major decisions with Bruce. They took the marginal ground out of production and seeded it to pasture or hay. Sean searched farm sales for good used equipment and moved Jake to top mechanic. They converted the large horse barn into a shop. The only horses used on the farm were for working cattle.

Alma's health deteriorated, and she needed around the clock care. Bruce seemed helpless. Ruth helped in the mornings and Edie took the afternoons until the children came home from school. Marcie checked in and helped bathe Alma every other day.

Sylvia was the last young woman to visit with Mr. Rondario. On one visit, Giuseppe asked Ruth if Sylvia could stay behind in the Bluff House. It seemed Mr. Rondario had found another "girlfriend" for his Chicago home and he wanted Sylvia in Muscatine. Ruth wasn't happy with the setup, but Pete explained it was for the business. He assured Ruth that Sylvia was not his. Her staying had benefits because she could stay with Alma during the night and was glad to help. Just lounging around Ruth's home was not what she desired, but quitting Antonio was out of the question. Other girls who had tried sometimes just disappeared.

Sylvia stayed close to Alma's bed during the night. Often, she would wear her more comfortable lounging clothes. One morning, Ruth was delayed in relieving Sylvia. Sylvia thought she heard Ruth coming to the back door. It had been a long night. Alma was moaning and groaning all the time. Sylvia had little sleep. She went to the door in her short nightie with the deep plunging neckline. When she opened the door, it was Ross, their hired man, not Ruth. Sylvia was shocked. She tried to cover herself.

"Ma'am," he said, "Ruth asked me to tell you she is on her way. She had a flat tire and Ernie is fixing it. Is there anything I can do to help?"

"Yes, just get out of here. Can't you see I'm not dressed?"

"Yes, Ma'am, and you look mighty fine."

Ross started to turn away, but Sylvia realized she was the one at fault.

"Wait a minute! This is my fault, not yours. Who are you anyway?"

"I'm Ross Kennedy. I work for Mr. McKillip. Sean O'Keefe is my boss. May I ask who you might be?"

"Sylvia, Sylvia Henderson. I guess you might say I work for Mr. McKillip, too. I take care of Mrs. McKillip at night. That's why I'm not properly dressed."

Sylvia dropped her arms. She smiled at this huge man. He smiled back, but he seemed uncomfortable speaking to a woman in a nightgown, especially one as revealing as Sylvia's. Sylvia thought this man was genuine. She'd ask more about him when Ruth arrived.

Ross surprised Sylvia when he asked, "Would you care if I sat with you until she comes? I mean, we could sit on the porch and talk. I don't have to be at work until seven."

"Okay, but I must get my robe. It's a bit chilly out."

She dashed inside and grabbed her robe. She found Ross sitting in the swing-armed rocker, and she sat beside him. They talked about their lives and where they came from. It was only fifteen minutes before Ruth arrived.

"Well, I better get to work. Here comes the boss's wife."

"Thanks for the chat, Ross. Maybe we'll meet again."

"I'd like that. How about tomorrow morning? I could be here at six."

"Okay, I'll brew some coffee and fry an egg or two. I'll dress, too."

"You have a date. I'll be here at six on the dot. May I say I like the gown you're wearing. It really makes you look cute."

"I'll see what I can do," Sylvia said with a smile.

The next two weeks, Sylvia served breakfast to Ross. Several times Bruce ate with them. Sylvia enjoyed both men's company and she was becoming fond of Alma, too. Soon she was staying there twelve to fourteen hours a day. Most nights Bruce could tend to Alma and Sylvia stayed at Ruth's. She gave Ruth and Edie the needed breaks to be with their own families.

One day Bruce told Sylvia he had to go to Des Moines. He'd be away for two days. He wondered if she'd be okay by herself.

"Sure, Mr. McKillip. I think Mrs. McKillip is stable. I'll sleep in her room tonight. If you want I stay all day."

"That won't be necessary. Ruth and Marcie come in the mornings."

Sylvia prepared Alma's supper and helped her eat. Alma was so weak, she could barely talk. Sylvia helped her into bed. Before leaving the room, she asked, "Alma, is it okay if I asked a friend over tonight?"

Alma perked up and answered, "Is it a man friend?"

"Why, yes, it is."

"Is it Ross?"

"Yes, how did you know?"

"Bruce told me you were fixing breakfast for him and Ross. He thinks Ross is a very good hired man. You know the men call him Ross, the Hoss, but Ruth refers to him as the Gentle Giant. To answer your question, yes please invite him over. I'd like to meet the young man."

"I'll call him right away."

Sylvia ran to the phone and called Ross.

"I'm all alone with Alma tonight. Mister McKillip is in Des Moines. Do you want to come over?"

"Sure, I can be there in fifteen minutes. Should I bring anything?"

"Heavens no, I'll pop some popcorn and maybe we can play some cards."

Sylvia hurried back to Alma and told her the good news.

Alma perked up and said, "Sylvia, get my good bed jacket and comb my hair. I must be presentable to the young man."

Sylvia smiled. She was surprised at Alma's enthusiasm. It was the perkiest she had been all week. Sylvia fluffed Alma's bed pillow, then combed her own hair and applied some lipstick.

When Ross arrived, Sylvia said, "Mrs. McKillip would like to meet you. Do you mind?"

"No, I'd be glad to meet her. I've heard a lot about her."

Sylvia led him to Alma's bedroom. She could tell Alma was surprised at Ross's size.

"I hear you are sweet on my nursemaid?" she asked.

"Yes, ma'am, I think she is a very nice young lady."

"Well, come here and sit by me. I need to ask you some questions. I think highly of Sylvia and I don't want her to be hurt."

Ross pulled a chair next to Alma's bed. Sylvia sat on the other side. Alma asked Ross about his family, where he came from, how he liked working for the McKillip's, and so on.

Finally, she stopped and glanced at Sylvia. "Sylvia, would you go and fetch the cribbage board? Let's see if Ross can play cribbage. You can tell a lot about a person by the way they play cribbage. Ross, if you could bring that table over here by my bed. I think I can sit on the edge if you would prop some pillows behind me."

When Sylvia returned with the cribbage board, she found Alma sitting up, all smiles. She and Ross pulled their chairs to the table. The game began. They played for two hours. Alma proved to be a sharp cribbage player. She won several games. The clock struck ten.

Ross said, "I must be going. I have to work tomorrow, you know."

"You're coming for breakfast?" asked Sylvia.

"You betcha'. See you in the morning."

Ross departed. Alma sighed.

"Are you okay?" asked Sylvia.

"I'm fine. That's the most fun I have had in years. I hope I didn't spoil your evening?"

"No, I had fun, too. Now you should go to bed."

"Did you know Ross sews his own clothes?"

"No, really!"

"Yes, he says he has a difficult time buying clothes his size, so he makes his own. I think he can cook, too. I think you should hang on to him, girl. He's a good man."

Sylvia smiled back and replied, "I'll try, Alma, I'll try."

CHAPTER 23: SYLVIA'S SURPRISE

In mid-May, school let out. Ruth and Edie were busy. Sylvia became a twenty-four-hour helper for Alma. Marcie helped with the bathing. Ruth and Edie brought in meals. The only time Sylvia was away from Alma was when Mr. Rondario arrived in June for three days. Ruth's mother and Hattie watched Alma. Sylvia returned to the Bluff House. Her first obligation was to spend time with Tony, as she called him. He always showered her with new clothes and gifts, which she displayed at the meals. Sylvia's room was next to Tony's with adjoining doors, at his request. The evening before he headed back to Chicago, Tony knocked on her door.

"Would you come over to my room? I have something for you."

"I'll be there in a minute," she replied.

When she entered, Tony was sitting in a small sofa with his feet on a hassock.

He smiled at her and said, "Sit down by me, my pretty one."

She sat by his side. He placed his hand on her knee. She leaned over next to him. He moved his arm around her shoulders. His fingers lightly stroked her breast. Sylvia knew she must endure his fondling.

She looked at him and asked, "Tony, is it all right with you if I take care of Pete's mother? She has cancer and needs care. I have plenty of time when you are not in Muscatine."

Tony answered, "I see no reason you shouldn't. I do not need you in

251

Chicago. You have my blessing."

"Thank you, Tony." She planted a kiss on his forehead.

"Sylvia, I am very fond of you. I brought you something special from Paris. Would you try it on for me?"

He handed Sylvia a package. Inside was a negligee. She held it up.
"Oh, Tony, it is lovely, but a bit sheer. Thank you. I think?"

"Try it on. I believe the French women wear nothing underneath."

Sylvia went back to her room and slipped on the gown. It was pale pink and very sheer with sequins in critical areas. The back of the gown dipped to her waist. A thin cord kept the little cap sleeves from slipping from her shoulders. She entered Tony's room again. He motioned with his hand for her to turn around. She followed his request and slowly turned for him.

"No, spin faster, like a dance."

She spun more quickly. The gown flared out. It swirled around her legs when she stopped. From the side, the sheerness of the fabric revealed Sylvia's shapely curves. She could tell he was pleased.

He leered at her and ordered, "Take it off!"

Sylvia turned and started back to her room.

"No, I mean take it off right here and now, for me."

Sylvia slowly slid the shoulder straps down. As she did, Tony unbelted his robe. He was stark naked. Sylvia gasped as her negligee fell to the floor.

"Get on the bed and put your hands over your head."

Sylvia was shaking, but she did as she was told. Tony secured each hand to a corner post on the bed with a necktie. She lay with her legs close together. Tony hovered above her and grinned. He kissed her with a vicious kiss and proceeded down her neck to her breasts. There he sucked and bit until she screamed. He slapped her and quickly put his hand over her mouth.

"Don't scream, you'll wake the household." He reached in the drawer in the bedside table and pulled out a handkerchief which he stuffed in her mouth. He continued to molest her. Finally, he moved down and split her legs. He shoved them wide, then drove into her with such a force her head rammed into the head board. He didn't stop but kept ramming like a piston on a steam engine. This went on for five minutes. After he was spent, he rolled away and groaned. Reaching above her head, he untied the neckties. Sylvia brought her arms down and spit out the rag. She was starting to roll over when he put his foot on her back and pushed her out of bed onto the floor.

"Get out of here!" he growled.

Sylvia crawled into her room and shut the door. She hurt everywhere. She pulled herself up into her bed and cried herself to sleep.

In the morning, Tony arrived at the breakfast table all bright and cheery. He shook Pete's hand and complimented Ruth on her nice dress. When Edie entered with an egg casserole and a big heap of bacon, he complimented her.

"Where's Sylvia?" Edie asked.

"I believe she is going to sleep in this morning. She seemed awful tired last night," answered Tony.

Edie didn't say another word, figuring Tony was speaking the truth. She did notice Tony ate at a faster pace. He seemed impatient with Giuseppe.

"Hurry up, Giuseppe. We've got to catch the ten o'clock train. I have a meeting this evening. Go get my bags. I'll meet you in the car."

Giuseppe wiped his mouth, rose, and said thanks to Ruth and Edie. He disappeared upstairs.

Tony rose from the table and said, "Sorry we can't stay longer, but we've a train to catch."

He turned and walked briskly to his car. Giuseppe threw the bags into the rear seat and off they roared down the drive.

Pete looked perplexed. "I wonder what that was all about? He's never in a hurry."

Ruth added, "He did act strange. I'm going to check on Sylvia."

Ruth went upstairs and down the hall to Sylvia's room. She knocked.

"Sylvia are you okay?" It's nine and your breakfast is getting cold."

"I don't want any breakfast," came from the other side of the door. "Go away."

Ruth heard a moan. She turned the knob and opened the door. She found Sylvia curled in a ball on her bed. She pulled back the sheet covering the woman. The bottom sheet was covered with blood.

"Sylvia, what happened?"

Sylvia rolled over and with blood-shot eyes, said. "Tony raped me. He sucked my breasts until they bled. Then he slapped me for screaming. I hurt all over. What am I going to do, Ruth? What if I'm not here when he comes back? He'll kill me. I know he will. It's what happens to all his former girls."

Ruth lifted the distraught woman up, hugged her, and said, "No one is going to kill you. We'll figure something out. First, we must make sure you are okay. I'll call Marcie. She'll know what to do. Don't you worry."

Ruth helped her put on a robe. Sylvia sat on a chair while Ruth stripped the bedding.

"You stay here, I'll send Edie up with some breakfast."

As soon as Ruth stepped into the hall she stormed down stairs to confront her husband.

"Pete," she screamed, "your so-called business friend just raped Sylvia. What kind of people are your clients? Only crooks would do what he did to Sylvia. I want some answers."

Pete didn't say anything at first. He just looked at the floor as if to collect his thoughts.

He raised his head and said, "Ruth, Sylvia is an adult. She may not have known what was expected of her when she joined Tony's harem. Tony is a rich man. He can have as many young women as he wants. He uses them as trinkets. If they get in his way, he disposes of them. There are many more available to him. I told you we need the money with the farm prices as they are. I do not want to lose his business."

"Just what kind of business is he in?"

"He is the crime boss of north Chicago. He is very powerful."

"Does this mean he deals in booze?"

"Yes."

"And you're saying you supply him with the booze."

"In a way, I store and distribute product. I have fifteen distillers working independently. I buy their liquor and sell to the highest bidder. I split the profits with the distillers. I also sell equipment to the distillers."

"Distillers, ha. They're bootleggers. It is all illegal and you know it."

"In a way, but Ruth, if you want to continue living the way you are, you will say nothing."

"I'll say nothing on one condition, you get yourself out of this business in a year or I'll turn you in."

"You wouldn't."

"I would."

"Give me two years and I'll be out completely. I swear."

"Deal. Now you come with me and help me figure out a way to save Sylvia from Tony."

"We'll have to have some kind of story for Mom."

"The truth, Petey Boy, tell her the truth. She will be appalled, and you know it. I suspect what I agreed to will be liberal compared to what she will say."

Sylvia returned to Alma's. Pete told her to be honest. He'd be over to explain later.

Pete arrived late in the evening, because he knew Sylvia would be with Ross. Both his parents were there. He explained how he got where he was, how he wanted to help the farm, and how he planned to escape the Chicago mob. He also promised to be free in a year. Alma listened and then exploded. Even from her death bed, she scolded and threatened. Bruce told him how disappointed he was. He advised Pete to pay off his suppliers and have them leave the state. Pete assured his parents the farm would never be held responsible.

He told them the Muscatine County Sheriff knew of his operation but was reluctant to prosecute until the Federal agents told him. The Government Agents wanted to arrest some of the big players, not just a small supplier.

CHAPTER 24: MIDNIGHT AT THE MINE

The leaves were beginning to change color. Business at the Cheese Cave was brisk. Trucks were moving barrels in and out. Sean suspected the cheese cave was something more from the beginning, but Pete told him to stay away. Sean honored his boss's wishes until now. There would be a half moon tonight. Grandma and Grandpa Mohr asked to have the children stay over for the evening. They were going to have a wiener roast at Ralph's. Edie and Sean were invited, but they saw it as a chance to be home alone.

"Let's go for a horse ride, sweetie. I'd like to check the back pasture," said Sean. "There will be enough moonlight to see objects."

Edie was excited. She hadn't been on a moonlight ride for years. She changed into her riding pants and white blouse.

Sean took one look and said, "Why don't you put on your dark blue top? It won't be so visible."

Edie wondered what Sean had in mind, but she changed into her blue blouse. When she got to the horse barn, Sean was strapping on the garden scarecrow, a blanket, and an old pillow on the back of his saddle.

"Don't you think it is bit cool for some romantic adventure?" she asked. "And what's the scarecrow for?"

Sean didn't say a thing but turned to help Edie on her horse. Soon she discovered why the darker clothing and all the extra gear. Sean was headed for the cheese cave. They rode quietly.

Sean whispered, "I told you I wanted to see what is actually going on here. I don't think it is only cheese. I figured two would be better than one."

They were a hundred yards from the cave when they dismounted. Sean reached into his pants pocket and pulled out a sack with oily black kerosene soot. Smudging Edie's face with the black soot, unfolding the black cape, and he wrapped it around her shoulders. He instructed Edie to smear the soot on his face him.

They walked quietly up the slope to the entrance of the cave. The opening was completely boarded with three windows, two walk-in doors, and one big sliding door. They heard men's voices inside. Sean crept to the lighted window and peeked in. The room was full of paraphernalia for stills. Pete was supplying bootleggers with equipment. Two men working in the dim light had a cask on a stand with a tube attached to the bung. The tube fed six other smaller tubes which filled the bottles. One of the men filled the bottles. The other man applied labels and packed them into empty cases. On the other side of the room was a huge receiving tank. Below it stood empty casks waiting to be filled.

Sean moved to a darkened window. Luckily, it slid open. Now he could check on the inside. He motioned Edie over.

"I'm too big to fit through the window. I'm going to help you through. I want you to check the barrels marked cheese and the barrels behind them. I think they contain booze and not cheese. Here's a pencil flashlight," Sean whispered.

"How will I know?"

"The cheese will smell. If you tip one of the others, they should slosh. Just don't tip one over. If you hear someone coming, hide somewhere until I can cause a diversion."

Edie nodded she understood. Sean lifted her through the window. Edie landed on a barrel. She jumped down to the floor. She rocked the first barrel. No slosh. The barrel she landed on sounded solid. She smelled the top. It was definitely aging cheese.

Next Edie moved to a row of barrels behind the front row. She rocked the first barrel. It sloshed and smelled of liquor. She crawled on her hands and knees and counted the barrels in the row. Next, she stood and flashed the light across the room. It was crowded with crates and crates of liquor marked Wild Cat. She counted twenty long rows of wooden racks holding barrels stacked four high, plus some short rows. She estimated there were a hundred plus barrels in the cave and somewhere between 1000 - 2000 crates of filled bottles.

She tip-toed back to the window. Just as she was about to climb on the cheese barrel, she stepped on a board or stick. It snapped.

"Who's there?" came a holler from the next room.

Edie froze. She ducked below the barrels. A flashlight searched the room. Sean ran down the hill and leapt on one of the horses. He rode away. The man searching the room ran to the window and shot the light out. He spotted Sean riding away. Edie was right below his feet, about three feet away. She slipped the cape over her body and almost invisible in the darkened room.

"Clem, there's a guy riding away on a horse. Get your gun!"

The man ran from the window and out of the room. Edie heard them running away. Three shots rang out. She jumped out the window. The fall was further than expected. She twisted her ankle and almost cried out.

The men heard her fall and returned inside. They shouted and cussed. As Edie crawled away along the base of the sandstone cliff, she spotted a dark cedar bush. Ducking behind it, she discovered a hole in the sandstone wall. Edie squeezed in, hoping there weren't any critters inside. There were the usual cobwebs. A field mouse dashed out. She pulled the bush limbs across the opening.

The men with the flashlight approached. They shone the light into the bush, but all they saw was a black hole.

One said to the other, "Let's check inside and see if there is any damage. It could have been just a local idiot trying to get some free booze."

Edie waited until they were inside before crawling out of her hole and down the slope to her horse. She tried to stand and mount when she heard a noise. She turned and there was Sean. He and his face were so dark she could barely see him. His horse was probably home by now.

He whispered to his injured wife, "You didn't think I'd leave you stranded, did you? We can't ride out of here, so I have a plan. I'm going use the scarecrow and have him ride out on your horse. That's why I brought the pillow and blanket. Meanwhile, I'll carry you home the other way."

Sean tied the scarecrow in the saddle. He slapped the horse on the behind and yelled. The horse leapt away. The two men emerged from the cave again, this time with shotguns. They fired toward the fleeing horse. Fortunately, they were too far away to hit the animal. Sean carried Edie at a fast trot for about a quarter mile the other direction.

"Put me down," ordered Edie. "I think I can walk."

Sean let her down. He was puffing.

"I guess I'm not as young as I thought."

The pair walked slowly home. It was two in the morning. They were quite chilled.

They went to the basement clean up. The lampblack was difficult to remove. Finally, Edie tried cold cream. It seemed to work. She had a difficult time with Sean. Each time she stood on the stool to reach his face, he'd tickle her ribs. They removed most of the black from each other, raced for bed, and fell asleep in each other's arms. Next morning would be a discussion on how to handle what they had discovered the previous night. Pete was storing illegal booze and selling illegal equipment.

Edie was at the stove making breakfast when Sean came down.

"How is your ankle?" he asked.

"Much better. I think if I soak it in Epsom salts a couple of times, I'll be fine. What are your plans for our escapade last night?"

"I believe we should be very quiet about it. We weren't supposed to be exploring the mine. Pete has told me many times to mind my own business and keep away from the mine. I had suspicions he was dealing in liquor. Mr. Rondario is a crime boss in Chicago. He may be nice to you out here in Iowa, but be careful, he may turn on you like a snake. As for, Pete, I say give him enough rope and he'll hang himself."

"You think Pete will hang himself?"

"No, it's an old saying. Give a crook enough rope and he will hang or catch himself. It means Pete will get caught in his own dealings and we won't have to do a thing. I just hope it doesn't kill him."

"Changing the subject, what are you doing today?"

"I'll check in over at the farm and see how Ross is doing. It's his day for chores. Next week we start picking corn. It is the last off day I'll have in a while. Why?"

"The children are at Ralph and Marcie's till evening. I thought we might go to town for some shopping. I need some new things."

"What do you mean, things?"

"Oh, I need a different nightgown and a bigger dress."

"Why, you're not getting fat?"

"There are other reasons."

Sean eyed Edie. She had a mischievous smile. He asked, "Are you pregnant again?"

"I might be. I missed two periods. If my calendar is correct, the baby should be born some time next spring."

Sean grabbed and hugged her. He picked her up and spun around. When he stopped, he let Edie slide slowly through his arms. As she slid, her gown rose to her tummy. Sean knelt down and kissed her bare skin.

"This is great news, honey."

CHAPTER 25: SHUTTING DOWN?

Corn harvest started in mid-October. Sean had Jake help Bruce search out ears of corn for next year's seed. They would need several bushels for seed. The ears were collected and stuck on spike-like drying racks hanging in the corn crib driveway. Reid's Dent had been the new variety this year. It produced big ears which were easy to shuck from the stalk. Sean and Jake serviced the tractors and added alcohol to the radiators. Ross cleaned the final ears out of the cribs and shoveled them into pile in the machine shed. This would be ground for feed until the new corn was ready.

Pete checked at the shop and asked some questions, then saddled a horse and rode out to check the cattle. Sean sensed something was bothering Pete. The entire farm family, which included the hired help, knew about Sylvia's ordeal with Tony. Pete had commandeered the farm's trucks several times. They would be gone for three or four days. Sean said nothing. He noticed Bruce quietly standing on the porch, watching Pete.

The first weekend in November, a big Cadillac arrived at the Bluff House. A little man got out, carrying a satchel. Pete met him at the front door. They hurried into his office. Ruth was summoned.

"Would you please bring us some coffee, honey?" Pete asked.

She asked, "Who is your friend?"

"Oh, sorry, this is Ted Chapman. He is Tony's CPA. He's here to check on the supply?"

"What would you like for lunch?"

263

"Just some sandwiches. Ted wants to leave early enough to catch the four o'clock back to Chicago."

Ruth fixed coffee and added some homemade cookies. She was about to open the office door when she heard the conversation.

"No, you can't quit."

"Well, I am. You tell Tony I have enough booze for him to last him a year, if he wants it. He takes about eighty kegs a quarter. I have over four hundred. Tell him I will give him a discount of ten dollars a barrel, but he must have it out of the mine before March or I will sell it to the highest bidder. The Feds are getting too close. Our county sheriff says he can't hold them off much longer. I have already warned my suppliers and helped them move. Plus, I gave each one three hundred dollars to find a new location. I suggested Missouri or Arkansas."

"But I can't do that. I can't tell Mr. Rondario what to do!"

"You can and you will."

"Is there an earlier train to Chicago?"

"I believe so. Why, are you leaving?"

"Yes."

"Won't you stay for coffee?"

"No, I'll get my coffee at the station."

"Okay, then, thanks for the money. I see you have it already counted. I trust Tony . . . this time."

Ruth backed away from the door just in time. Ted threw the door open. He glared at Ruth and headed for the front door.

"Good-bye, Mrs. McKillip. I'll take a raincheck on the coffee and cookies."

He disappeared outside and jumped into the Cadillac.

Ruth stepped into Pete's office.

"Well, that was a vivid conversation. I am proud you stood up to Tony for once. Do you think there will be any repercussions?"

"Might be, but I doubt it. I'm giving him time and a good deal to buy me out. I think he will do it. I've made a deal with Sid and Clem. I have told them as soon as the suppliers leave, they could finish the bottling and move on. They didn't like the idea, but agreed to it. Old Herman over in Sweetland Township is staying until his supply of rye runs out."

"Sounds like a good plan. I'm so proud of you for quitting. The kids will be in school until four. Let's celebrate," remarked Ruth.

"What do you have in mind?" asked Pete.

"Give me a minute and I'll show you."

Ruth disappeared down the hall. Pete went back to his desk. Hearing soft footsteps, he turned and there was Ruth, barefoot in a dressing gown. She coyly untied the sash. The gown fell open, revealing that she had nothing on underneath. He smiled. They had not had sex for many months. Ruth let the garment fall to the floor. She saucily sauntered to Pete and began to undress him.

"Shouldn't we go to our bedroom?" he asked.

"No, let's do it right here, right now. It will be more daring. I've never had sex on a conference table."

They started on the table, but ended on the floor with its plush carpet. They lay on the floor looking into each other's eyes.

Ruth cooed, "This is the reason I married you, Pete McKillip."

Pete hibernated in his office for another day. Early the next morning, he was at the farm. Sean was mildly surprised. He had seen the Cadillac parked at Pete's house a couple of days ago. Generally, it meant he was headed for Chicago. This time Pete was not frowning. He was smiling.

Pete met Sean in the farm office, which was a converted horse stall. Sean reviewed the condition of the farm. He told Pete his father had not been out of the house for days because of Alma's cancer. Sean wondered if Sylvia could manage for a few hours alone while the two of them checked the cattle. It would do them both good.

Pete replied, "I'll make it a point to see Dad takes a ride out with me. I need to see the cattle for myself. Despite what others think, I miss farming, and Sean, I'm getting out of the cheese business. I'm finding the cheese smells a little like whiskey. It has been very profitable but working with the mob in Chicago is scary. The sheriff has looked the other way. He has let me alone. I do think at some time he must tell the Feds and shut me down. I just thought I should get out before anything happens. Now, what do you think about this hybrid corn? I've read many articles about a Dr. Henry Wallace promoting the concept. He has done a great deal of research."

"I've read about the corn. Yes, I think we should give his corn a try. We could plant it alongside what we use presently and compare. Sort of a test plot. I think your dad will have to be convinced before he switches."

"Yes, he will be skeptical."

"We could plant the seed down on the creek bottom, away from our neighbor's eyes."

"Good idea. I also thought maybe down the road we could grow our own seed. Maybe even sell some seed. I think this is a major breakthrough in agriculture. Someday, everyone will plant hybrid corn. I can see yields approaching a hundred bushels per acre."

"Boy, you really bought into this concept. I agree with you, but right now we must walk the fields for some old-fashioned ears," Sean said with a grin.

"Right. I know Dad and Jake like to do that. This year I'll take Dad's place. Now, I'm going over to my folks. It's time I check in with my Mom."

As Pete drove away, Sean wondered if Pete meant what he had said. If he did, maybe this depression in agriculture would be tolerable. Maybe with the Chicago people out of the picture, Edie could be a mother again, especially when the new baby arrived.

Pete showed up for work almost every day. He called Sean if he wouldn't be at work.

Ridding himself of the liquor business was not easy. Clem and Sid didn't want to give up their jobs. They each had a lady friend depending on them. In fact, several times the ladies helped with the bottling. Pete sold them the business, but he kept ownership of the existing liquor. When it ran out, he was out. He would rent the mine to Clem for bottling. Everyone seemed satisfied.

One day Pete returned to the Bluff House. Someone was playing the piano. He walked toward the sound and discovered it was Sophia playing. "That's beautiful, baby. How long have you been doing that?"

Sophia turned and said, "I have been taking lessons for three years, Daddy. You just haven't been here to listen."

"This old piano sounds tinny? I think you need a new one."

"Really, Daddy. I'd love different piano. Mrs. Barton, my teacher, has a baby grand. She told me there are used baby grands available in Davenport. I can manage with this one, though, because I know grands are expensive."

Later in the evening, Pete was reading the newspaper. Ruth was listening to the radio. Pete put down the paper and asked, "How long has Sophia been playing the piano?"

"Why I believe it has been three years."

"Hmm, that's what she told me. She sure plays well."

"Mrs. Barton claims she is a natural. She has an ear for music and thinks maybe Sophia could have a career in music."

"I'd buy her a better piano, probably not a new one, but I think there will pianos for sale soon. This depression is difficult for many people. The farming community is already in trouble. We must tighten our belts. I've made a lot of money, but it is going to stop soon. Next year we will depend on the farm to support us."

"We can do it, Pete. I am so glad you are quitting. I hate that Mr. Rondario."

Christmas was more subdued than normal. Pete bought Sophia a used baby grand at an estate sale. Wade was matched with a sled and bicycle. Pete bought Ruth a new dress.

Christmas season was also the time for parties. Ruth paid Edie to cater her galas. Edie stayed in the kitchen since her tummy was growing and she didn't have proper maternity dresses. Ruth invited Sean and Edie to her New Year's Eve bash. They were to come as guests and not workers. Ruth gave

Edie one of her dressy maternity frocks. The women worked together to make it fit Edie.

Ruth's children went to the O'Keefe's for a party with Grandma and Grandpa Mohr.

At the Bluff House, Pete broke open some of his choice wines. He had some harder stuff from Canada which he had received from Tony earlier. By twelve, most were very tipsy except Edie and Sean. They abstained from the alcohol.

Sean commented, "Somebody has to drive the revelers home."

Instead, many of the guests decided to stay over. The Bluff House had many bedrooms. Edie and Sean left around one. Edie said the party was becoming too rowdy for her.

Four days later, Sean received a call from Pete. Alma was much worse. Pete and his sister, Sue, were staying with their parents around the clock, because Sylvia had traveled home for Christmas in Indiana. Doctor Wilson said Alma was very close to death.

Alma died January seventh. She was buried in the Patterson Cemetery beside Mary and Harry. When Sylvia returned, Bruce asked her if she'd stay until spring.

She said, "I'd be happy to, if Ross can continue to have breakfast here."

"He may have all his meals here as far as I'm concerned. Maybe I can get him to marry you," Bruce replied.

Sylvia moved in permanently. She did all the housekeeping plus fed Ross. Ross never stayed over, but according to Bruce he might as well have. He seldom left before ten.

January flew by. February was snowy. Pete enjoyed it all. He was glad not to be traipsing to Chicago and St. Louis. Sophia enjoyed her piano and Wade, his sled. Ruth just enjoyed Pete.

March arrived and no word from Chicago. Pete waited until the fifteenth before he contacted Luigi in St. Louis.

Two days later, Ted, the accountant, called and said, "I hear you contacted

Luigi in St. Louis. Tony would like to deal."

"Fine. I was hoping he was still interested. His allotment for March hasn't been touched. St. Louis is interested in the rest, if Tony doesn't want it."

"He says he needs more time."

"Can't do it. The Feds are getting close. Sheriff Kerns said he would hold them off for one more month. The mine must be empty by April."

"We'll send a truck tomorrow. You must keep the rest until June."

"You tell Tony I won't do it. If he won't take it all, it will go to St. Louis."

"He won't be happy."

"Well, he can shove it. Next time contact me in person."

Ted hung up. Three trucks arrived the very next week. They loaded about half the inventory. Pete contacted Luigi for the rest. He would be out of business by June first.

BOB BANCKS

CHAPTER 26: MUD, MUD, MUD, BABY

The month of March was its usual self. Rain and more rain. The dirt roads became impassable. Sean hoped for drier weather, so Edie could make the trip to the hospital. Edie was eight months pregnant. She was miserable. This was her fourth pregnancy. Doctor Wilson recommended bed rest.

She refused, saying, "I've got a family to take care of. I can't rest."

"Do the best you can," the doctor told her. "Could your mother help? What about your husband?"

Hattie gratefully helped. She dragged Frank with her. They rode over in a horse and buggy through the fields. Sean returned from work early in order for cooking supper and putting the children to bed. He moved a bed downstairs. He slept on the sofa, so he could be near Edie if she needed any help. Marcie checked in every other day. She'd call in Edie's condition to Doctor Wilson.

Grass started to turn green and crocuses poked their heads through the warm earth. Every time the ground seemed to dry, it would rain again.

"Why don't you move to town?" Hattie asked.

"Where in town, Mother?" Edie asked.

"How about the Steinbeck's?"

"No way. I'll just have the baby here at home. Jake's wife, Wilma, is a midwife. She lives a mile away. Marcie is a nurse. One of them should be able to make it. Sean could get them on a tractor or horse and buggy. Heck, who knows, maybe the roads will dry."

"In April! Ha!"

The roads didn't dry; instead, they got worse. The problem with country roads was they were frozen solid in winter, but in the spring, ground would thaw above the frost. The layer of frozen ground would not let the water pass through. This layer of soil would become extremely soft. A person could barely walk on the surface let alone drive a car on it. The more it rained, the more of a quagmire the roads became. Many became impassable.

Sean joked about building an ark. He took the children to school in the horse and buggy through the fields. Edie's delivery time was getting near. Her bold statement about having the baby at home seemed too bold now. She wished she could be in town.

"Maybe I could stay at Louise's?"

"But didn't you say she moved to West Liberty?"

"Oh shucks, that's right. Can't go there."

"If you give me enough warning we can go in a buggy. Horses seldom get stuck in the mud," he said.

The only way to Muscatine was over the bridge by Pine Mill. The river road was only partially graveled and getting up Wyoming Hill was treacherous. The road through New Era was probably their best bet except the small bridge over Sweetland creek was under construction. All they could hope for was dry weather.

April sixth, Marcie walked over to O'Keefe's to check on Edie. Marcie brought her stethoscope to check he baby's heartbeat. Everyone seemed fine.

Edie asked, "Are you in a hurry to leave? I have this funny feeling. Maybe I should call Sean."

In her condition, Edie could not reach the phone, let alone get close to it. Marcie tried calling the McKillip's, but Sean was out. Bruce answered the phone. He said Sean and Pete were mending flood gates. He knew Jake was in the shop. He'd send him out to fetch Sean.

As Marcie hung up, she heard a scream from Edie. She ran into the parlor where Edie's bed was temporarily housed. There was Edie standing in a pool of liquid. Her water had broken.

"The baby's coming, the baby coming," screamed Edie. "What will we do?"

Marcie in her calm British accent replied, "Well, Luv, I guess we'll have it right here."

"Right here? I can't do that, I've had all my others in Muscatine." said the panicking Edie.

"Sure you can. I'll call Wilma. I'm sure she will come over and help."

Wilma rode a horse through the pasture. She arrived just as Sean rode up on his horse. They walked into the house together and were met by a distraught Edie, who Marcie was trying to undress.

Edie wailed, "Sean, the baby is coming. Marcie says we won't make it to the hospital. She says I will have to have the baby here."

Marcie butted in and said, "Now don't you worry Edie. Wilma and I will take care of everything. It will be a piece of cake."

Sean dashed to his wife, took her hand and said, "You'll be fine. I'm here."

He looked at Marcie and asked, "What can I do?"

"First, we must get her back to bed. I'll need your help."

Edie burst out, "I'm not having this baby in my bed. It's too messy. I'll never get the stains out. Can't I have it on the floor?"

"What about the kitchen table?"

"Heavens no, not on my kitchen table."

Marcie gave Edie a frustrated look and asked, "Where then? In the barn?"

Sean answered, "Why don't I bring in the washtub bench? It is about two feet high and three feet wide."

"Good," said Wilma. "Get it."

Sean dashed to the wash room and carried the bench inside. He set the bench endwise against the wall.

"Now get some cushions or pillows to prop Edie up. Do you know where she keeps the sheets and towels? We'll need plenty."

"They're in the closet next to the stairs. Do you need hot water?"

"Yes, by all means, draw some from the cistern. I'll stoke the cook stove," answered Wilma. "I'll need some clean scissors. Sewing scissors will do if you put them in boiling water first."

Sean ran around as fast as he could, taking orders from the two nurses. Wilma covered the bench with a sheet. Marcie undressed Edie. They propped her on the bench with pillows. Sean helped Edie sit on the bench. She looked at him and winched. Sean was bewildered. Men were never invited to a birthing. Edie moaned again and said, "It's coming! It's coming!"

Marcie took over. She positioned herself.

"Sean, you take this wet washrag and mop Edie's forehead. She'll need you to hold her hand also. Don't be surprised if she crushes it."

"Edie, now when I say push, you push with all your might. Okay, one, two, three, push."

Edie pushed and screamed. She squeezed Sean's hand until her fingers were white. She pushed again and again.

"I see the head," announced Marcie. "One more big push, Edie. Wilma be ready to receive this baby."

A minute later Marcie held up a wet, unhappy baby boy. Wilma grabbed him and wrapped him in a baby blanket. Sean kissed his worn-out Edie.

"You did it again, honey."

Wilma washed the baby, then placed him on Edie's chest. He had a head of dark brown hair and brown eyes. He was not the redhead like his sisters and brothers. Marcie washed Edie and helped Sean put her to bed. The children would be home from school soon. Edie wanted to look her best.

Jake brought the children home. He told them they had a new brother or sister, but he didn't know which. The girls were the first to see their mother, followed by Luke. He was happy, since he really wanted a brother.

"What shall we name him?" asked Edie.

The children had all kinds of names. Finally, Sean said, "You know I really wanted a boy, so how about Michael Franklin. We could call him Mike."

"That sound good to me."

Sean called Hattie and told her the news. She and Frank came over immediately. She was appalled to see Edie standing by her bed. Edie explained that Wilma was a matter-of-fact woman. She didn't believe in modern medicine's view which states a woman should stay in bed after birthing. She believed it just caused infections and other problems. Wilma got her views from her Native American grandmother. She asked Sean to help Edie sit up, then stand. Marcie held Mike while Hattie helped Edie with a robe. Edie shuffled a couple of steps. They helped her to a chair in the living room. Marcie brought little Mike to her to nurse. Soon mother and child were asleep.

Hattie stayed for three days. Frank went to Ralph's. Marcie checked in every morning. She made Edie walk some every day. Hattie was not in agreement, but since Edie seemed to be responding well, she said nothing. In two weeks, with Sean and the girls' help, Edie was independent again. By May her figure had returned to somewhat normal. She was the good-looking woman Sean adored.

BOB BANCKS

CHAPTER 27: CHICAGO VISITORS

May finished warm and dry. The crops got planted just a little late. The corn emerged along with the weeds. The first week in June was a combination of cultivating corn and making hay. Pete was content. His lifestyle was going to change, the worry about the Feds was almost over.

One evening, he and Ruth were enjoying the view of the Pine Creek valley from the porch swing. They heard a car crunching gravel as it slowly came up the lane. It was the sheriff's car. Pete walked out to greet him. Sheriff Ken looked at Ruth and asked, "Could we go somewhere and talk?"

"We can talk right here, Sheriff. If there is any trouble, Ruth needs to know, also."

Another man exited the right side of the car. He tipped his hat to Ruth and reached for Pete's hand.

"Pete, I'm Agent John Albright. I'm with the Justice Department. I've come to talk about your business."

Pete's face changed from a smile to a frown. Ruth went inside.

The G-man spoke. "We know of your distributing liquor enterprise. The sheriff tells me you are retiring. I'm afraid retiring won't be enough. You have been breaking the law for several years."

"Are you going to arrest me?"

"I could, but I'd like to suggest a proposal which would work well for you in court. If you agree to help us catch a couple of gang bosses, I could speak in court of your efforts."

"What's the proposal?"

"I know you have dealings with Luigi Luciano of St. Louis. I also know you deal with Antonio Rondario of Chicago. I would like you to bring both men here. Have them purchase some liquor. We, meaning the government, would wait until they have left your property and would then take them into custody."

"Do you need both of them here at the same time?"

"No, that would never work. It would definitely raise their suspicions. Crime bosses seldom are friends, even from different locales. If it is okay with you, I would prefer Mr. Luciano first. I'll let you work out the details. Sheriff Wright will be your contact."

Pete looked at the sheriff, then the ground.

Sheriff Ken said, "Pete, I've given you a long rope. I can't go any further. This is a chance to redeem yourself. If you chose to cooperate, I believe the judge will go easy on you. Jail time could be less than a year."

"Well, gentlemen, I guess I have little choice. I was to call Mr. Luciano this week. It was going to be my last sale to him. I'll entice him to come and view my operation himself. As for Mr. Rondario, we have strained relations. I now go through his accountant. I'll see what I can do, but I can't promise anything."

"I understand, Mr. McKillip. One will be better than none. I appreciate your help."

After some more small talk, the men shook hands. Sheriff Ken and Agent John drove away. Ruth reappeared.

Ruth returned to the porch and asked, "What was that all about?"

Pete explained the deal. He told Ruth the consequences of not setting the trap. He told her it could be dangerous, but because it might lessen his sentence, he agreed. Ruth hugged and kissed her husband.

She said, "Honey, I'd go through hell with you. This will be a piece of cake. You get Luigi to come. I can entice Antonio with some of Edie's cooking."

The next day Pete called St. Louis and set a meeting date. Before he could contact Chicago, Tim, the accountant, called Pete. He would come to Muscatine next week. He had some business to discuss. Next week, Tim arrived. Pete had Ruth hire Edie to help prepare a meal.

After the meal, Tim announced, "Mr. Rondario is getting a divorce. He would like Sylvia to return to Chicago."

Ruth blurted out, "That won't happen. She's engaged to one of our men. They're getting married in August."

Tim had a surprised look on his face.

"Is this true, Pete?" he asked.

"Yes, I believe it is. Tell Mr. Rondario he'll have to find someone else. I would also like to invite him to come and settle accounts. I hope you told him as of June 30, I am out of business. He'll have to deal with Clem and Stub. They are renting my warehouse and developing some suppliers. They also bought all my remaining rye, so the quality should be the same."

Tim looked at his pocket watch. "I believe I better be going. I'll see if Mr. Rondario will come. I have been taking care of his business, but I do not involve myself in his romantic life."

"But the train to Chicago doesn't leave for four more hours," Ruth said.

"I know, but I have some other work to do. Maybe I should contact this Clem and Stub? I heard they are nearby."

"Yes, they are less than two miles away. You turn right out of our drive. It's the second gate on your left. The lane runs along the cliff. I could ring them and tell them you are on your way if you like. They don't like to be surprised."

"That would be much appreciated, Mr. McKillip."

Tim left the table. His warm attitude had turned to a frosty one. Pete called Clem to warn the pair not to shoot the incoming car.

Pete received notice Mr. Luciano would accept the invitation. He would come June 30. There would be six in his party. Pete replied his driver would meet them at the station in Muscatine. They would be treated to a delicious meal before any business was transacted. Mr. Luciano's assistant confirmed the plan. Pete drove to Muscatine to inform the Sheriff. He did not trust the party phone lines with this important business.

Ruth called Edie. She offered her double pay if she would cook an Italian meal. Edie prepared lasagna smothered in Alfredo sauce. She called a bakery in Davenport to buy some Italian bread to fill with Italian beef. For dessert, she baked four Dutch apple pies and homemade ice cream. She knew they weren't Italian, but no one could turn down her pies.

It was late morning when the entourage arrived in Muscatine. Pete hired a limousine to drive the five men and one woman, named Collette, to his home. Unknown to the guests, the chauffer was Sheriff Ken. After Edie's sumptuous meal and delicious apple pie, Luigi and Pete conducted their transactions. His entourage had second servings of pie. Luigi was saddened to hear Pete was going out of business. He was relieved that Pete had rented his warehouse to two of his former employees and they would continue supplying him. Pete suggested Luigi visit with Clem and Stub. Pete cranked the little lever on the side of the telephone, but instead of calling Clem he phoned a deputy waiting at the farm.

"Hello, Clem. This is Pete. I'm sending a Mr. Luigi Luciano from St. Louis over to talk to you. They are leaving here in about fifteen minutes . . . so don't shoot them. They're driving a maroon Dusenberg . . . Okay, I'll talk with you later. Good-bye."

Pete turned to Luigi and said, with a grin, "Clem is anxious to meet you. Be easy on him. He's a little back-woodsy and trigger happy. He almost shot one of my employees who was just checking my beef herd."

The deputy put the plan into action. Pete received his settlement in cash, as always. Ruth suggested Collette stay behind and wait for the men to return. She was happy to do so. Riding around on country dirt roads with a bunch of men was not her piece of cake.

The entourage drove to the county road and turned left. A half mile down the road the limo was blocked by a road crew. Sheriff Ken told the passengers he would see what the delay was. As he got out he turned the ignition off and the limo died. It was a signal for several deputies and G-men, who were posing as road workers, to surround the car. Mr. Luciano meekly got out with his hands in the air and ordered his men to do the same. He wanted no bloodshed. He surmised his lawyers could outsmart any of these hick lawyers in Iowa. They were loaded into a truck and hauled to the Muscatine County Jail. The Sheriff drove back to Pete's and met Pete and Ruth on the porch.

"Pete, we got them, no shots fired. Tell the lady I would like to question her. If she refuses, I'll get a warrant for her arrest."

Pete replied in a loud enough voice for Ruth to hear, "This is good news. I'll have my wife tell her."

Ruth knew "good news" was a code for her to return to Collette.

"Collette, I'm to inform you your escorts have all been arrested. The sheriff would like to question you. You have two choices. You may go to Muscatine quietly and be interrogated or escape by way of the back door. Honestly, you have nowhere to escape to. You don't know the country. In a few hours, you will need to give yourself up."

Collette thought for a minute. She reached into her purse and pulled out pistol. Ruth was about to scream when Collette put the weapon in her mouth and pulled the trigger. She was dead in an instant.

Ruth was aghast. Pete and Sheriff Ken ran into the room and found Collette dead on the floor. They looked at each other, then at the dead woman.

Pete said, "Well, Sheriff Ken, evidently she knew more than she wanted to reveal. Poor woman."

Although the sting was successful, the next one would be more difficult. Pete hoped Tim could convince Tony to come.

He didn't have to wait long. That evening, Pete received a phone call.

"He wants to come the Fourth of July? But that's a holiday . . . Yes, I suppose the cops will be busy with parades. It might be safer . . . Ruth says she will have lunch fixed . . . Yes, we can have the little lady cook come over. I may have to pay her more . . . Don't worry, I'll take care of it . . . Okay, we will see you at eleven o'clock on the Fourth of July."

Pete turned to Ruth and asked, "Do you think Edie can fix a meal on the Fourth?"

"I'd doubt it. Maybe she could prepare it the third and I would just have to finish it. I'll call her. How much do we offer this time?"

"A hundred dollars."

"A hundred dollars! Wow! You're very generous."

"This is my last time. Why not throw some of Tony's cash around?"

Ruth called Edie. Edie couldn't turn down an offer of a hundred dollars. She'd miss the parade and send the children with Sean. They were going with Ralph and Marcie anyway. Later she would find them in Weed Park.

Edie went to town to purchase her supplies Tuesday, then delivered everything to the McKillip kitchen on Wednesday. Since the Fourth was on a Friday, she told Ruth she'd be there early Thursday to start.

Pete called Sheriff Ken. He was disappointed in the timing. He said he would tell Agent Albright. They would work out some sort of a plan. He'd check back Thursday.

Pete was up early Thursday morning. Because the day was going to be a very warm day, he sat barefoot and shirtless on the back porch going over the plans. He wanted all his ducks in a row for the next day. A motor vehicle pulled up front, Pete walked down the connecting hall to answer the knock on the door. The door flew open before he reached it. In came a huge man, followed by Giuseppe and three others. Behind them was Antonio Rondario.

"Tony, we were not expecting you until tomorrow," exclaimed Pete.

"I know. I just thought maybe you had a little party for me and I didn't want you to go to any trouble. So, me and the boys came early. I want you to meet my assistants. You already know Giuseppe. This is my enforcer, Bruno, the butcher." Pointing to the thin man, he said, "This is Marco, and lastly this is Deano, my driver. His wife runs a second-hand ladies clothing shop. He likes to pick items up along the way for her. So, we have nicknamed him 'the scavenger'. You see, I have found that instead of killing people, we embarrass them to death. People with few clothes on die in cold weather and in warm weather they just take longer to work free while they are swimming. It's also more difficult to identify a naked body."

Pete nodded. A shiver went up his spine, he didn't like Tony's cold-blooded comments. "Nice to meet you all. Now, what may I do for you?"

"I came to settle accounts. First, I would like to talk to Sylvia. I hear she's engaged. You know she's still my employee. I own her. Next, I heard my competition from St. Louis has purchased your good stock. All I got was hog slop."

"You have to speak to Clem about that."

"We already have. They are secured in your former warehouse."

"My former warehouse?"

"Yes, the boys captured them watering down some brew. I decided to burn the place. We tied them and their lady friends to a pole in the middle of the room. The boys poured some of the contents from your barrels around the building. If you don't believe me, follow Bruno. He'll show you the smoke coming from your former establishment."

Bruno roughly grabbed Pete's arm and led him outside. He pointed at the smoke rising about a mile to the east.

"Too bad about them two fellows and their ladies. I had to tie them to a post inside before I set it on fire. I'm sure they are plenty warm by now," Bruno said with a smirk.

"You burned them alive!" exclaimed Pete.

"Let's say, I roasted them. It sounds better," Bruno answered with a grin, "but first, Deano gathered the women's dresses and shoes before we doused them with booze."

"Now," added Tony, "I feel I'm entitled to Luigi's stash. I'm sure you still have it somewhere in the house. I'm thinking maybe I deserve Mr. Luciano's loot because he received my liquor. You do have a safe?"

"Yes, come to my office and we can discuss this further."

The four men followed Pete to the office. When they entered, they found Ruth dusting the trophies and other items. Her back was turned, so she didn't know who opened the door. She was wearing her new silk silver pajamas which were the rage of the rich set. Tony and his men smiled at Ruth's figure outlined by shiny fabric. Bruno grabbed Pete and twisted his arm behind his back.

Thinking Pete was the only one entering, she said, "Sweetie, Sylvia is bringing us some red, white, and blue bunting and several small flags. She had extras and wondered if we would like them. I told her yes. She'll be here around ten. Is that okay?"

"That would be just fine, Mrs. McKillip," Tony announced.

Ruth turned with a jerk and exclaimed, "Mr. Rondario, you weren't supposed to be here until tomorrow."

"I know, and I see I came at a better time. You look lovely this morning, Mrs. McKillip," answered Tony.

Ruth glared him. He smiled back. His eyes were locked on Ruth's chest. The silk pajamas revealed she wasn't wearing any under garments.

Ruth calmly said, "If you gentlemen will excuse me, I need to dress."

Tony replied, "On the contrary, Mrs. McKillip, you need to stay."

Ruth started for the door, but Marco blocked her at the door. He grabbed her arm and led her to one of the office chairs. He pushed Ruth down, then secured her with a rope around her shoulders.

"Open the safe," he bellowed.

"I can't it is on a timer," replied Pete.

"No, it isn't. I know better than that."

"Yoo hoo, is anybody home?" called a voice from the kitchen.

Sylvia appeared at the office door. She was startled to see Tony and his men standing there.

She coolly asked, "Tony, Ruth told me you weren't coming until tomorrow. If you are conducting some business, I can come back later."

"Sylvia, I need to talk to you. Please have a chair next to Mrs. McKillip."

Sylvia walked quietly to the second office chair. She sat with her hands on her lap. Marco was about to secure her also, but Tony waved him off.

Tony sat on the front of the Pete's desk and eyeballed Sylvia.

"Stand up, please, Sylvia."

Sylvia stood.

Tony asked, "I hear you're engaged to be married."

"Yes, to Ross Johnson. We are to be wed in August."

"Sylvia, you are still my employee. You answer to me. I need you back in Chicago. I forbid you to marry anyone."

"Well, I'm sorry, Mr. Rondario. I can't go with you. If it is a problem, then I quit."

Tony slapped Sylvia hard across her face. She staggered and put her hand on her face.

Tony glared at her. He asked, "Who bought you those earrings?"

"You did."

"Take them off. I want them back. I want that necklace also. I'm sure I paid for it."

Sylvia removed the jewelry and handed it to Tony. Tony scanned her body.

"I'll take the dress and shoes, too."

"Right here?"

"Yes, right here. Do you need any help? Deano is very skilled at undressing women."

"No, thank you, I can do it myself," she answered in a trembling voice.

She stepped out of her shoes and handed them to Deano, who had now stepped forward. Sylvia unzipped the side zipper of her dress.

She reached down to the hem, pulled her dress up over her head, and handed it to Deano, then readjusted her slip.

Sylvia glared back at Tony and said, "I suppose you want me to give you my underwear, too. I used your money to buy it."

Tony paused and replied, "No, that won't be necessary. I'm sure the men would like it, but for now, you little slut, sit down."

Marco secured Sylvia to her chair. He tied a handkerchief around her head to gag her.

Tony turned to Pete and said, "Open your safe and give me my money."

Bruno shoved Pete across the room. He knelt by his safe. He spun the dial and unlocked the safe. Inside was a shoe box. Bruno grabbed it and spilled the contents on the desk. There were two banded stacks of bills, some coins, and jewelry.

"What the hell is this?" demanded Tony.

"That's all I have in the safe." answered Pete. "There is no more. Look for yourself."

"There's more someplace, you little wimp. Luigi paid more than two G's for that booze. I'm saying it should be more like fifty G's. Now tell me, where is the money?"

Pete responded, "I have no more. That's it."

"You @&*+@&%# punk operator, tell me or I'll have Bruno find out."

Pete was silent. Tony nodded to Bruno. Bruno punched Pete in the stomach. Pete doubled over. Next Bruno hit Pete on the back of his head. Pete crumpled to the floor. Bruno kicked him in the ribs as Pete tried to crawl away. Blood started to flow from his mouth.

Ruth screamed, "Stop it. He doesn't know where it is."

Tony turned his attention to Ruth and asked, "Maybe you know where it is, Mrs. McKillip. Would you like to tell me?"

Ruth realized she was in trouble. She answered, "Maybe I do and maybe I don't."

Tony said, "Bruno, let's help Mrs. McKillip remember."

Bruno lit a big cigar. He puffed on it twice, then screwed the fire end into Ruth's palm. She screamed. Before Ruth could speak, Sophia and Wade burst into the room.

Sophia cried, "Mommy, what's going on?"

Ruth replied, "Get out of here, Sophia. You and Wade go to Grandpa Bruce's. Run as fast as you can."

Tony spoke, "Deano, stop the kids. Put them in a closet."

Deano and Marco slammed the door shut and captured the pair. They forced them into the office closet. As soon as they shut the door, Wade started pounding on the door. Marco pulled his weapon and shot three rounds high into the closet. The pounding ceased.

The interrogation continued. Bruno moved to Sylvia. He reached inside his coat and pulled out a hook knife, the kind carpet layers use. He pulled Sylvia's hair straight up and began sawing away close to her scalp. He cut deep enough to cut her scalp. Blood started to flow down the sides of her head. She jumped and wiggled in her chair, her eyes filled with terror. In seconds Bruno had almost scalped her. He turned his attention to Ruth, who was watching in horror. Bruno grabbed her hair.

Tony stopped him. "Mrs. McKillip, will you tell us where the money is, or do we continue with the questioning? I must warn you of the consequences. Bruno will first scalp you, then he will return to your friend and remove an ear or something else. Bruno loves to slice women's middles."

Ruth paused. Bruno started to cut. Ruth screamed, "It is in the brown suitcase in the hall closet."

"Thank you, Mrs. McKillip. Deano, will you check the hall closet?" said Tony.

Deano left the room and returned with a brown suitcase. He laid it on the desk and popped it open. There were bundles and bundles of cash.

Tony smiled and ordered, "Marco, take it to the car. We must be going."

"Boss, what about my take?" asked Deano.

"Oh, I almost forgot. What do you want?" answered Tony. He needed

Deano for driving. He was an expert. He had gotten the gang out of many scrapes by his crafty driving and knowledge of automobiles.

Deano answered, "Boss, I'll bet there are some nice rags in the missus' closet."

"Okay but be quick. As soon as Marco returns, we're leaving."

"Thanks, Boss, I'll be quick as a bunny."

Deano scrambled upstairs. He pulled armloads of garments from Ruth's closet and threw them on the bed. He wrapped the bedspread around them. When he returned, he had a huge sack of Ruth's clothes plus most of her jewelry. He dumped it by the door.

Deano said, "Man, she had some good stuff. It'll bring top price in Chicago. Thanks, Boss."

Marco returned.

"What next, Boss?" asked Bruno.

"We must leave soon. We haven't much time. I don't like being at killings. I say we secure everyone for at least an hour. It will give us time to get to Illinois."

Marco suggested, "What about taking a hostage?"

"Good idea! But which one?"

"Sylvia?"

"No, we take the girl. Go get her." Tony ordered.

Deano opened the closet door and pulled Sophia out slamming the door shut before Wade could escape. Sophia meekly followed the skinny man. Ruth glared at him. She pulled Sophia to her. Sophia stood on one foot and tried to hide behind her mother.

"Okay, let's go," Bruno growled.

He grabbed Sophia and started to leave. There was the sound of a screen door slamming in the kitchen. Tony put his finger to his lips, indicating silence. Bruno put his hand over Sophia's mouth. Marco threatened Ruth with his gun. Pete was basically unconscious.

The sound was Edie arriving. She had Luke with her on the promise that if he worked well in the morning, he could play with Wade all afternoon. He could help carry water, peel potatoes, and clean vegetables.

As she entered the kitchen, she noticed a pan of oatmeal still simmering on the stove. The coffee pot was set from the stove, but no cups poured. It seemed unusual. She ordered Luke to bring some potatoes from the cellar. It seemed too quiet. She tied a scarf around her forehead to keep the sweat from her eyes. Edie knew it was going to be hot baking her rolls and cakes, so she dressed lightly. Pete seldom entered the kitchen, so she wore just a cotton camisole under her dress.

The clock on the kitchen wall chimed ten. Edie thought she should check with Ruth and headed for the office. She was shocked to see Mr. Rondario, three other men, and Giuseppe. Pete was lying in the corner of the room. Ruth and Sylvia were tied in chairs, their faces bloodied. Sylvia's hair was almost gone from her head. Bruno held Sophia under his arm like a sack of potatoes.

Ruth bit into Bruno's hand. He pulled it away for a second, just enough time for Ruth to yell, "Edie, get out of here." Bruno slapped Ruth. Her head hit the wooden back of the chair. She received a cut on the side of her face.

Giuseppe countered, "No, my little cook, you must stay here."

Edie retreated to the kitchen. Giuseppe and Bruno chased after her.

Edie yelled, "Luke, run and get your dad. Tell him Tony's here today."

Edie ran to the phone and started to scream into the mouth piece. Bruno knocked her away and ripped the earpiece from the phone, but he didn't flip the hanger for the ear piece up to shut off the phone. A switch board operator in Muscatine heard all the sounds coming from the kitchen.

Luke ran out the door and across the field toward the woods. He knew a short cut through the Brandt land.

Bruno bellowed, "Giuseppe, get the kid. Shoot him if you have to."

Giuseppe ran after the fleeing boy. Fortunately, for Luke, Giuseppe was overweight and slow. He was almost in the woods before the older man had even crossed the meadow. Giuseppe hollered, "Stop or I'll shoot."

He fired a couple of rounds. Luke fell to the ground and crawled the rest of way. The meadow grass was tall and hid him. Once inside the timber, he ran again.

Soon he was at the cliff. He knew he could climb down, but it would take time. Just a few feet away was Steamboat Rock. It was a formation which had split from the main cliff years ago. The gap was about four feet. If he jumped the gap, he knew the other side was an easy climb down. He and Wade had played there many times. He would also be protected from Giuseppe's gun.

He stepped back six feet and took a running jump. He made it. He turned to see where his assailant was. Giuseppe was getting close. Luke hid behind a small bush. Giuseppe stopped at the edge of the cliff. He looked up and down the thirty-foot cliff. He called Luke's name, next he swore at the boy. Luke hunkered down close to the ground. He placed his hand down, and it touched something soft. It was a coiled bull snake.

Luke had an idea. He grabbed the coiled reptile and jumped up.

He yelled, "Hey, Mr. Giuseppe, here I am."

He had the snake by his tail. He twirled the hapless reptile around his head once and let him fly. The snake wrapped around the man's head. Giuseppe screamed and pulled at the snake. He took one panicked step backwards into space and fell thirty feet to the base of the cliff on some rocks. He moaned. Luke looked down from above. He scampered down the far side of the rock and ran to the farm. Near the cow yard, he saw his dad and Ross fixing a fence.

"Dad, Dad! Mr. Rondario is at Mr. McKillip's. He's got Mom. She said you should call the sheriff."

Luke was so out of breath he collapsed into his father's arms. Sean scooped up Luke and ran to the main house. Ross headed for the garage and the truck. Bruce was sitting on the porch.

"Bruce, call the sheriff. Pete is in trouble. Luke said Rondario is there. He's a day early. Ross and I will head up there. You take care of Luke."

Ross met Sean with the truck. He had acquired an axe handle and a post tamper, a six-foot wooden rod with a steel cap, used to pack soil around wooden posts.

Back in the kitchen, Bruno was trying to corral Edie. She was quicker than he. She dashed for the knife drawer. There she grabbed a butcher knife and meat cleaver. The cleaver flew across the room. Bruno ducked it easily.

"Oh, you want to play tough. Here, catch this," he boomed as he threw a chair.

She ducked and ran around the table toward the back door.

"Oh, no, you don't. You're not escaping me, my little rabbit."

He shoved the table against the wall, blocking her path. He cornered her behind the cook stove. She grabbed the simmering oatmeal and threw it at him, hitting him in the chest. He growled and threw the pot across the room.

Edie raised her knife, but he was too quick and strong. He caught her arm and spun it around her back. She cried in pain as she dropped the knife. He marched her to the office. She kicked back and hit his shin. He cussed and pulled her head by her hair.

Marco looked at Bruno and laughed. "What happened to you? Did you spill your breakfast?"

"No, this witch threw her cauldron on me. This is a hundred-dollar suit. She's gonna pay. I'm gonna' skin her alive."

Bruno turned Edie around and rubbed her face in the oatmeal. Next, he slammed her into the desk and pinned her down. He whipped out his hook knife and sliced the back of her dress. The hook knife sliced her dress and skin. He pulled the back of her dress down below her waist. Blood was flowing from the four long, deep cuts. Edie screamed. The pain was excruciating. She turned her face toward Tony. Bruno was about to do more damage when Tony stopped him.

"Enough, Bruno. Don't kill her."

Bruno shoved Edie to the floor. The back of her dress was split open and covered in blood.

Tony barked out orders. "Marco, you and Deano lock Pete and the women in the closet. Then go in the kitchen and start something burning. There must be some kerosene someplace. By the time the fire department gets here there will nothing left but a few ashes. Bruno, you grab the girl. Let's get out of here."

"What about Giuseppe?"

"Evidently the boy got away. He might have made it to his father. We'll leave him."

Bruno reached for Sophia. She struggled and cried out, "Daddy, save me."

Pete tried to stand. Marco stopped him with the butt of his revolver alongside Pete's ad. He crumpled again to the floor. Ruth started to run to his side. Marco stopped her and pushed her away. He kicked the crumpled Pete into the corner as if he was a dog. Deano opened the closet door. Out dashed Wade. He took one quick look and ran out the back door. Deano started after him.

"Let him go," barked Tony, "We'll be far away before he finds anyone. Find the kerosene."

Marco made Ruth and Sylvia drag Edie into the closet. Deano placed a chair against the knob. The women immediately began to pound on the door. Marco fired three shots high through the door. The pounding stopped. Tony and Bruno, who held Sophia under his arm, headed for the front door. Bruno was about to open the door when it came flying inward.

It was Ross. He slammed the iron end of the tamper into Bruno's jaw. It broke several teeth and cracked his jaw. Bruno dropped Sophia. She scrambled away and hid behind a door. Bruno growled and charged Ross. He was met again by a flailing six-foot rod. It caught him alongside his head. He staggered and sat against the wall. Ross emptied a large flower pot and jammed it on Bruno's head. He turned his attention to Tony.

Tony put his hands up and stuttered, "N-n-n-now, c-c-c-c-an we settle this peacefully."

"Sure, Tony, my good man, you go to hell and tell Satan that. I'm sure he will accommodate you."

Tony reached inside his jacket pocket and pulled out a small revolver. He fired. The shot caught Ross in the thigh. It enraged Ross more. He charged

Tony. He slapped Tony with such force, the gun fired into the ceiling and rattled in a chandelier. Ross grabbed Tony and lifted him high over his head. He spun around, looking for a place to throw Tony.

Leaning against the wall was Pete's prized elk head with its five-foot spread of antlers. He tossed the handsome Tony onto the rack like a hot dog on a stick. The first prong caught Tony in his neck and severed his carotid artery. A second prong punctured his belly and ripped his thoracic artery. A third stuck into his leg. He died instantly.

Marco heard the commotion. He raised his gun and slowly approached the hallway. He did not hear the tall red-headed Irishman sneaking through the kitchen door. Sean brought the axe handle down on Marco's wrist with such force he broke it. Marco screamed in pain. He turned to meet the axe handle crashing down alongside his skull. He crumpled to the floor. Sean turned to Deano, who trembled and fell to his knees.

"Don't hit me, please."

"Where are the women? You scumbag."

"In the closet."

Sean kicked the chair away and opened the door. Ruth was the first out. Ruth ran to Pete, who was unconscious. She knelt beside him and kissed his cheek. The blood from her head wound was dried. She gingerly raised Pete's head and placed it in her lap, then stroked his hair with her unburned hand.

"Petey, Petey, don't die. I couldn't live without you," she cried. Pete moaned.

"Where's Sophia?" she asked.

A little voice came from behind Ross. "Right here, Mommy. Is Daddy okay?"

"No, sweetheart, Daddy needs a doctor. He is badly injured."

Sylvia helped Edie stagger out. When she started to fall, Sean caught her. She cried in pain when he placed his hand on her back. He felt the torn fabric of her dress and turned her around. The gown was shredded from her shoulder to her waist. There were four ugly cuts down her back. Her camisole was covered with dried blood. She was bleeding again because of the twisting of her torso. Sean picked her up and held her face down.

"Where should I lay her?"

Ruth was occupied, so Sylvia answered, "Carry her into the parlor. Sophia, pull some cushions from the couch and lay them on the floor like a bed."

Sophia led Sean to the parlor. They tried to make Edie comfortable. Now it was Sylvia's turn for help. Ross limped over to her. She was a mess. Her eyes were swollen and discolored. The blood from the scalping was drying, but the top of her head was very tender. Ross looked down on his fiancée and noticed a small flap of skin lying loose. Evidently, she hadn't felt the top of her head.

"You'd better sit or lie down yourself," he suggested.

Sylvia screamed. "Rossy, my pet, you're hurt. I see blood on your pants. Let me see."

"I'll be okay, Syl, it's just a bullet wound. I think it went clear through. I'll be okay."

"I'll be the judge of that. Sophia, would you please bring me the ugly knife Bruno left on the table."

Sylvia sliced Ross's pant leg. She examined his thigh and said, "Yep, you're right. It went right through. I see two holes. You'd better have Marcie look at it, though."

Ross gently took Sylvia's fingers and placed them on the top of her head. She moved the loosened skin.

Blood began to flow again. She put her hand up to stop it only to notice how tender her eyes were. She walked to a mirror and nearly passed out. Ross caught her.

She whined, "My hair. I have no hair. I'll never be pretty again."

He whispered, "You'll always be beautiful to me."

Sirens were wailing out front. Sheriff Ken and Agent Albright burst in the door. They scanned the mess.

Agent John commented, "I believe we're a little late. Is anyone hurt?"

"Yes, my husband," cried Ruth. "He needs to get to a hospital quickly."

Sheriff Ken said, "I anticipated there might be some causalities. I already have an ambulance on the way, but I didn't expect this. Someone here left the phone off the hook and Lorraine at central had another operator call me. I contacted John and we came as quickly as we could. Is there another phone in the house?"

"Right here on the floor, Sheriff. It was knocked off," answered Ruth.

Ken picked up the ear piece and found Lorraine still listening.

"Lorraine, I'll need two ambulances at Pete McKillip's. Will you also contact Freer Funeral? We have one deceased out here. Hurry . . . Thanks, I know I can count on you. . . Okay, you may call the *Journal* . . . Yes, I will find the other phone and hang it up."

Sean called out, "Someone call Marcie. She's a nurse."

"What's her ring?"

"Two long and a short."

Sheriff Ken turned the little crank. Marcie answered along with three other women.

Marcie said, "I'll be right over. Tell Sean not to move Edie, if possible."

Another voice came on the line. It was Wilma. "Could I be of any help? I'm a practical nurse."

"Sure, come on over. There are several injured."

To Ken's surprise, Bruce butted in. "I'll be up in five minutes. Tell Ruth and Edie I will bring the boys."

Ken and John handcuffed the two alive men.

"Where's the little guy?" asked Ken.

"Right here." came a voice from the kitchen. Deano stumbled into the office. His face was bleeding. Jake was right behind with a pitchfork."

"I tripped him up just as he came running out the door and hit him twice with the handle, then I threatened to stick it where it would hurt the most. He surrendered."

Albright, who had first aid training in the Navy, attended to Pete. Pete's pulse was fine. The agent stretched out his legs and elevated his knees to get more blood to his head.

Marcie arrived, followed by Wilma, Gertie, and Myrtle. The women quickly warmed some water. Someone had called Doctor Wilson, who was busy, but he had a new intern, Doctor Heidi Kimball. He sent her out.

At first everyone was skeptical of a woman doctor, but she put everyone at ease with her skill and knowledge. She clipped all of Sylvia's hair from her head and stitched the flap of skin. It took thirty stitches. She had Ross apply some ice cubes for Sylvia's eyes and gave her some pain medicine, which made her sleepy. She treated Ross's wound with some hydrogen peroxide and wrapped a bandage around his huge thigh. He was a tad embarrassed to have her cut away most of his pant leg. Ruth's scalp was not cut as deep as Sylvia's. Dr. Kimball sheared her head also and fashioned a skull cap to keep it clean. She told Ruth Pete should be treated at a hospital.

Edie was a much larger task. Marcie cut away most of the back of her dress. She and Wilma bathed the wounds. Two were not deep and wouldn't require stitches. The other two were deep into the muscle. Dr. Heidi, as she liked to be called, gave Edie a shot of morphine to deaden the pain as she stitched. One cut required fifty small stitches, the other one hundred and two. It would be a long time before Edie would be back to normal.

Gertie tried to dress the groggy Sylvia because she thought men should not see a woman in her undergarments. Myrtle was more concerned about cleaning the house. She swept the hair clippings and dirt on the floor from the flower pot. Both women had good intentions but were in the way most of the time.

Soon there were four more agents and three deputies swarming into the room. They attended to the wounded gangsters. Deano was handcuffed to a chair. Ruth glared at him.

"Where's my clothes, you little rat?"

"In the bag. You can have them back. They weren't worth much anyway."

The G-men were leading the thugs outside when Bruce arrived. Luke followed him and ran straight to his dad.

He said, "Giuseppe is lying at the bottom of the cliff. I think he is dead. I couldn't tell."

"Where this cliff, son?" asked Sheriff Ken.

"Over on the Brandt place. Wade and I play there a lot."

"Would you take me there?"

Sean said, "You take the Sheriff. I'll stay here with Mom."

The sheriff and two deputies headed across the pasture. They found Giuseppe alive. He had landed on several rocks and had broken his back. Sheriff had deputies help the Montpelier Fire Department carry Giuseppe out. He was paralyzed from the waist down and had several broken bones.

The ambulance arrived and transported Pete and Ruth to Muscatine. Bruce assured Ruth he would take care of the children. Ross said he would help Bruce and stay to care for Sylvia. While Dr. Heidi attended to Edie, Sean and Ross helped pry Tony from the antlers for the mortician. The mobsters were jailed in Muscatine for a while. All had criminal records and were extradited to Illinois.

Edie needed special help if she was to return home. Marcie called Hattie and explained the situation. Hattie came over immediately with Frank in tow. She would help care for her daughter.

Bruce phoned at five and asked Sean if he'd accompany him to the mine. He saw the smoke and was curious about the damage. He and Sean drove to the still-smoldering mine. Sean parked his truck in front of the office building. He heard someone holler when he shut the engine off.

"Help us! We're behind the office."

Sean hurried around back. There were Clem, Stubby, and two women handcuffed together in a circle. They had escaped the burning interior of the mine. Clem had burns on his hands and face, but otherwise, the four were just dirty and scared.

"Can you get us apart?" asked Clem.

"Not here, but I could haul you to the shop and cut them with the metal shear," Sean answered.

It was quite a task loading all four onto the truck bed. Sean backed the truck up to the front porch. Since they were handcuffed together, the men carried the women aboard. Bruce went inside the shack and found two blankets for the women.

On the way back to Bruce's, he asked Sean, "Do you suppose we should contact the sheriff or one of those government agents before we turn these four loose? I know they are lucky to be alive, but they were distributing booze."

Sean replied, "Good idea. You go to your house and phone while I cut one of the links. Two couples will be better than the circle they are in now."

While Sean ushered the circle of crooks into the shop, Bruce went to the house to telephone the law. He returned carrying his shotgun.

"Sheriff said he'd would like to talk to all of you folks. You are to stay here until he arrives. I just thought I will make sure."

Clem said, "Now listen, Mr. McKillip, we don't plan on going anywhere. We're just glad to be alive. If that old post in the center of the mine had been more solid, we'd been roasted like wieners."

"Well, I think I'll just make sure anyway."

Sean paired the couples and cut the chains. He ordered them outside where Bruce calmly sat on the end of the truck bed.

Sean eyed the four and said, "Each of you give me one shoe."

"What!" exclaimed Stubby, "What in tarnation for?"

"I figure you'll have a difficult time running away with one shoe and one bare foot."

Bruce and Sean waited about an hour for some deputies. Ross wandered out with his leg wrapped and relieved Sean, so he could return home.

Ruth stayed in Muscatine. She seldom left Pete's side at Hershey Hospital, where he stayed until August. The doctor said there was nothing else he could do. Marco's blow hit his right temple. He lost most of the sight in his right eye and his memory was in and out. Some days he was fine, but other times, he couldn't remember his name.

Sylvia asked if she could go home. She wanted to be married at home. She made it clear it was only temporary. She and Ross belonged here. To everyone's surprise, she returned in one week with her little sister, Amy, who was Sophia's age. She thought Amy might be good for Sophia, who was having a difficult time recovering from her traumatic experience of her parents being victimized. Also, to everyone's surprise, the sweet Sylvia was not the Indiana country bumpkin they thought. She was the daughter of a prominent lawyer in her hometown of Hendersonville, Indiana. Her family was wealthy. Still, they accepted Ross and encouraged the marriage of their wayward daughter.

BOB BANCKS

CHAPTER 28: LUKE THE HERO

Ruth and her children moved in with Bruce. The memories at the Bluff House were difficult to forget. Bruce was happy to have his family back home. He started to take more interest in the farm. When Ross and Sylvia returned from their wedding, he gave them the eighty-acre Irwin farm as a wedding gift. They were overjoyed and promised to help at the McKillip farm when needed.

Sean and Edie were also rewarded by a gift of eighty acres next to their present farm. Bruce suggested Sean go on his own. This was the way of the agricultural ladder: hired hand, renter, and owner. Jake moved from hired hand to farm manager. He and Wilma said they planned to stay with Bruce for as long as he needed them. The McKillip farm was reduced to a manageable three hundred sixty acres which was mostly pasture and woods.

Pete returned home the twentieth of August. His inability to easily use steps or stairs hampered his mobility. Sean and Jake built a ramp to the front door. Pete was content to sit on the porch and watch the operation. His father conferred with him on daily decisions. Some days Pete understood, and others he just looked blankly ahead. Pete became deeply depressed. Bruce depended on Ruth to help make important decisions.

Edie and Sean were now land owners. Most of their ground was pasture and woodlands, but it was still theirs. Edie was admiring her farm when Sheriff Ken arrived. Two other men exited the sheriff's car. Sheriff Ken introduced the men as two Muscatine County Supervisors.

"Is Luke around?" he asked.

"Yes, I believe he's with his dad. They're in the barn. Do you want him and not Sean?"

"Luke."

"I'll call them."

Edie let out a yell. Soon two red-headed men appeared from the barn. The small one was barefoot and wearing bib overalls with no shirt. He had a grin and a face full of freckles. The other one was also in bibs but wore shoes and a shirt.

Sheriff Ken extended his hand to Luke and said, "Mr. O' Keefe, I'm Sheriff Wright. These two gentlemen are Mr. Stiles and Mr. Howe. They are supervisors for Muscatine County. I believe they would like to speak to you."

Mr. Howe shook Luke's hand and said, "Luke, Mr. Stiles and I are so proud of you for your bravery. It was because of your escape the sheriff was able to capture some ruthless criminals. We have been authorized to give you the county award for bravery. If it is all right with your parents, we would like to present the award at the county court house on Labor Day."

Luke didn't know what to say, so Edie butted in. "He'd be glad to be there. Sean and I are both very proud of him. We know because of his brave effort, his father would have never reached McKillip's in time and I would be dead."

"It is agreed, we will see you at the ceremonies. They will be held at ten o'clock on the front steps of the court house." Mr. Howe replied.

He shook Luke's hand again. Luke smiled and nodded his head. The men left.

Edie grabbed her son and squeezed him tight. His father smiled a big smile and shook his hand.

"Well done, son. I'm very proud of you."

"We must buy you some new clothes. Can't have you looking like a hick," remarked Edie.

The word spread quickly in the neighborhood. Bruce came over and congratulated Luke. He gave him ten dollars for a new pair of shoes.

He also praised Luke for his bravery. He asked, "Luke, what made you think of throwing the bull snake?"

Luke answered, "I guess I didn't think. Mr. Bullsnake was not happy with me in his nest, so I thought, let's see if you can fly. Mr. Giuseppe thought he was a rattlesnake. It was sort of funny the way he screamed and danced around over a silly bull snake."

It was hot on Labor Day. Picnics were planned at Weed Park. At nine, Luke and his family arrived at the courthouse. It was festooned with red, white and blue banners. Luke and Sean were seated on a temporary stage. Luke was smartly dressed in a white shirt and necktie along with neatly pressed new trousers. His bright red hair was neatly combed.

The ceremonies started right on time. Mr. Howe, the chairman of the Board of Supervisors, spoke first. He spoke of the people of Muscatine County and how they were such talented and industrious workers. He praised the educators for providing such excellent students. His speech lasted for thirty minutes. Luke started to fidget. Edie, seated in the front row, raised her finger and shook it. She was not going to have her son embarrass her. Finally, it was time for the award.

Sheriff Ken approached the podium and said, "Ladies and gentlemen, it is my pleasure to introduce to you a young man of exceptional bravery. Following his mother's orders to locate his father, he ran for over a mile while being chased by a Chicago mobster. The mobster fired a pistol at him several times, but he dodged the bullets. He ran into a wooded area and hid. The only problem was there was a bull snake curled where he hid. Instead of panicking, he grabbed the snake and threw the reptile at his pursuer. It wrapped around the man's neck. The mobster panicked and stepped over a cliff. He survived but is now confined to a wheelchair. Luke proceeded on and warned his father, who is also a hero. For he and his employee rushed the gang of mobsters at the Peter McKillip home. They disarmed the gang and held them until Agent John Albright and my deputies arrived. Mr. Luke O'Keefe, would you please come forward."

Luke rose and went to the podium. Edie watched with pride. It was several years ago when she stood at the same site and watched a tall red-headed man receive commendation for volunteering to serve America. He was later the Grand Marshal of a Homecoming Parade. He'd received medals for his bravery. Now her son was showing the same traits.

"Luke, I am pleased to present you with this plaque for your bravery. I, along with the citizens of Muscatine County, am proud of you. Along with this award, the county would like to present this check for fifty dollars."

Luke had his photo taken with the sheriff. He walked to the podium, but it was too tall, so he stood beside it and said his practiced speech.

"I want to thank Sheriff Wright and the Board of Supervisors for this award. I also want to thank my parents."

He stopped for a moment and looked directly at his mother. His voice cracked as he said, "Mommy, it was for you I ran so hard. I love you."

The crowd clapped and cheered. Edie stood and walked to the stage. She gave Luke a big motherly hug. Sean took out a handkerchief and handed it to his tearful wife. Most women in the crowd were also sniffling. Even some men were blowing noses. It was a very touching moment.

The next day school started for everyone except little Mike. The O'Keefe's had their picnic with Ralph and Marcie's family plus Edie's parents. The boys played a pickup game of baseball. The girls headed for the swings. By four o'clock the picnic was over because all families needed to go home for chores.

By seven, Sean, Francine, and Luke finished milking the cows. Edie had the twins help with supper, which was picnic leftovers. The tub was brought up from the basement for baths. Since it was so warm, Edie gave the twins baths on the back porch. Francine and Luke decided they were old enough to shower in the basement by themselves. After the baths, Edie treated everyone to milk and chocolate chip cookies. She fed Mike and put him in the crib. The children were tired and were asleep quickly.

CHAPTER 29: THE END OF BLUFF HOUSE

Edie and Sean sat on the porch and watched the storm clouds gather. Lightning flashed brilliantly. The cool breeze which proceeds a thunderstorm forced Edie and Sean inside. They rushed around closing windows. A flash of lightning and an immediate crack of thunder shook the house. The twins were scared and ran to find their mother. She held them tight.

The crack of thunder also woke Luke. The whole family sat on Edie and Sean's bed. They watched out the window. At first Sean thought he was seeing things. On the ridge where Pete's home was built, there was an orange glow. Soon there were flames leaping above the trees.

Sean exclaimed, "Pete's house is on fire. I must go and help the fire department."

He rushed out into the driving rain and drove the truck to Pete's house. When he got there the small fire truck from Montpelier was trying to douse the flames, but with their meager water supply, it was hopeless. Ruth, Bruce, and the children were there, huddling in the garden shelter. Ruth greeted Sean with a hug.

"I came as soon as saw the flames above the trees." Sean said.

"I knew you would come, Sean. The fire was so far advanced the rain doesn't help." Bruce assured him.

Ruth said, "Sean, will you tell the firemen to let it burn. I will never rebuild. It brings back too many memories, good and bad."

Sean spoke to the fire chief. The men backed away and watched the mansion crumple into a pile of ashes. An era was over for the McKillip's. It was 1931.

CHAPTER 30: TROUBLE AHEAD

The Great Depression deepened. Farmers suffered from low, low prices. They didn't lack work, only money. Edie and Sean would joke later that at one time they had just eighty-five cents in the jar at home. Edie learned how to barter eggs for sugar at the Pleasant Prairie store. Francine taught the twins how to milk cows. They and their mother did chores while Luke and Sean worked the fields.

Sean helped Ruth and Bruce as a friend, not an employee, knowing getting paid would be much later. Ruth sold most of her fancy clothes and jewelry. She commented that she came from a farm and now was returning to her roots. Pete's health was expensive. Health insurance didn't exist. Ruth pledged Jake that he would always be paid. She needed him as much as he needed her. Jobs elsewhere were non-existent.

Jake and Ruth managed the farm. Bruce complicated the management by being trampled by a cow while checking the herd alone. He became just an advisor. Sophia turned sixteen and was a great help around the house. She continued her music by paying her music teacher in eggs and chickens.

Wade turned thirteen. He and Luke were active in a new youth organization named 4-H. They showed beef animals at the West Liberty Fair. Wade always chose the best calves from the McKillip herd. Luke and Jake's son Barry chose second. Although Wade placed higher in the classes, the boys never were jealous. It was in 4-H where Luke met another cattleman's son, George Maas. He lived north of Muscatine in Bloomington Township. Later they became great friends.

The mid-Thirties brought drought. The Great Plains of the West were blowing apart. The temperature baked Iowa to 103 degrees. The corn plants shriveled in the sun. Cinch bugs and grasshoppers ate anything which was green. Farmers cut willows and other saplings to feed livestock. Walking across the lawn was like walking across paper.

The nights never cooled. Edie made beds on the porch. Her beautiful brown hair was beginning to show wisps of gray. The ordeals of her life caused her some aches and pains, but nothing she couldn't tolerate. Her husband was always there for her. As she looked up at the golden sky of an Iowa sunset, she gave a sigh of contentment over her growing family.

The phone rang. It was Ralph. "Come quick to Dad's. Marcie thinks he has had a stroke. Mom needs you." he said.

Sean and Luke were just coming in from chores. Edie ran to them and cried, "Ralph just called and he thinks Dad has had a stroke. I must go right over. You feed the children, then come over. Francine and Luke can babysit for a short time."

She rushed over and found Marcie holding Frank's wrist. Frank was sitting in his lounge chair. His eyes were closed. Hattie was holding his other hand.

"How is he?" asked Edie.

Marcie answered, "All I can say is he has lost control of his right side. His words are slurred. Ralph called for the doctor. He should be here soon."

It was Dr. Kimball who arrived, she quickly determined Frank's condition.

"He has had a severe cerebral stroke. The blood vessels in his brain area have ruptured. We can only hope they heal, otherwise, the pressure of the fluid will cause more problems. Can we get him into a bed?"

Sean arrived in the nick of time. He and Ralph helped Frank to his bed. Dr. Kimball gave him a sedative to help him rest. Hattie and Edie would take turns sitting by the bedside. They would report Frank's condition to Dr. Kimball in the morning. Sean and Marcie returned to their homes.

Hattie took the first shift until midnight. Edie relieved her and sat in the chair beside her father's bed. She held his hand. Many thoughts were going through her mind.

Edie remembered her younger days with her father and how she disobeyed him. Her memories of the day, she and Sean brought the children to see Frank for the first time. Yes, he was prejudiced and a tyrant at times, but she loved her father.

Edie was sleepy, and she laid her head on the edge of the bed. She awoke a little before two. In the dim light she noticed her dad was extremely quiet. She rose and put her hand below his nose and felt no breath.

"Mom, Mom, come quick."

Hattie rushed into the room. She saw Edie's panicked look.

"I......think ... he... died, Mom. I don't feel any breath."

Hattie put her head on her husband chest. She heard no heartbeat. She rose and hugged Edie.

"Yes, he is gone. He is in a better place with Jesus. Help me cover him. We must call Ralph and Sean."

Two days later was Franks funeral. Hattie stayed at Edie's for a week before deciding to return home. Her house was very quiet, but it would be her life from now on. She had her family and grandchildren. She would survive.

CHAPTER 31: DEPRESSION WOES

The election of 1932 brought a change of government. Prohibition was repealed. Government intervention was accepted by all. Congress formed the Civilian Conservation Corp and Works Progress Administration to provide jobs for the unemployed. The Great Depression not only affected the United States, but the whole world. The Far East was being gobbled up by Japan. A radical group named the Nazis was headed by a radical named Adolph Hitler and gaining control of a depressed Germany. By 1935 farm life was improving. As people had money to buy food and clothing, they provided a market for farm products. Farmers had funds to purchase equipment, thus provide jobs for their city cousins.

Pete's health was an issue. He required many extra hours of care. Bruce tried to help, but his encounter with the cow limited his ability. Ruth had Edie help prepare meals. Marcie volunteered to help on her off days, since she worked three days a week at Belview Hospital in Muscatine.

1936 was a year of heavy snow and blizzards followed by extreme heat and drought in the summer, but that is another story. In January of 1937, Ruth reviewed the books with Bruce. The farm was in trouble. Pete's health was a burden. The pair decided to sell part of the herd. It was their only alternative. What they didn't realize, Pete was listening in the next room.

On Valentine's Day, Pete called his sixteen-year-old daughter to the parlor. He dictated a letter for Ruth. His words were slurred, and it was difficult for him to talk. Sophia would write a few words and read them back. She enjoyed writing his love letter to her mother. When he had finished, she read it back to him.

My dearest Ruth,

You have been the light of my life. You stuck with me through thick and thin. We have two beautiful children. I cannot imagine my life without you. I know I have been a burden to you and our children, but I feel my life is quickly coming to an end. I just want to tell you how much I love you.

Your loving husband,
Pete

He signed the letter with an X. He had Sophia seal it in the envelope and had her promise not to give it to her mother until Friday. With tears in her eyes, she did as she was told.

On Wednesday, Edie dropped Mikey at her mother's. She and Ruth were responsible for lunch at Thursday's Farm Bureau meeting. They planned to bake some brownies and make ham sandwiches. She arrived at Ruth's around nine-thirty. As she walked into the kitchen, she found Pete sitting at the table.

"How are you doing today, Pete?" she asked in a cheery voice.

"Oooookkaaaay," he answered.

Ruth cut in, "Pete, honey, we are baking brownies and cookies for Farm Bureau. If you are a good boy, we'll let you try one later."

Pete nodded his head. He turned and hobbled away. His pace was deliberate. One step with his right foot, move the cane, and drag his left foot. Once Pete was out of the kitchen, Ruth sighed.

"How about you?" asked Edie.

"I don't know. This week it seems nothing pleases him. I can't get him to eat. I can't get him to bathe. I'm almost to the end of my rope."

Edie gave her a hug. She knew Pete was not only a financial burden, but also a burden on Ruth's physical and mental being. She turned and mixed the batter. Ruth sat and cut bread for sandwiches. The conversation quickly changed to everyday events. In less than an hour, the first batch of brownies was finished. Edie cut the first row. She placed two on a plate and poured a glass of milk.

Edie said, "You stay put. I'll take these to Pete."

When she entered the parlor, Pete was not there. She checked the living room and his downstairs bedroom. As she crossed the hall, she noticed the front door was ajar. She stepped outside. There was a light dusting of snow. Edie saw footprints going down the ramp and across the lawn.

She glanced back at Ruth. Her head was on the table. She was catching a quick nap. Edie tip-toed in, retrieved her coat and followed the tracks across the farmyard to the basement barn. The old barn was a relic of the past. Its foundation was of sandstone quarried from the mine. Pete's tracks led to the big sliding door which had a smaller walk-in door built in. She opened the little door and called Pete's name. He didn't answer.

She stepped inside the dimly lit drive way. On the floor was a coil of half-inch trip rope. She noticed it had been recently cut. Midway through the barn was the ladder to the lower level. On one of the rungs was tied some of the rope.

"Pete, Pete, where are you?" Edie called out.

She looked down the ladder and gasped. There hanging from the ladder was Pete. She ran outside and around to the lower level, into the alleyway. Grabbing Pete's legs, she tried to lift him.

She screamed, "Ruth! Ruth! Jake! Come quick! Help! Help!"

Ruth woke and heard Edie's terrifying screams. She grabbed her coat and ran toward the barn. Jake came from the shop. He found Edie holding Pete by his legs. Jake rushed to the haymow and cut the rope. Pete's body fell across Edie's, knocking her down. Ruth rushed into the barn and loosened the noose. Jake dropped down and turned Pete over to pump his chest. He tried to revive him. Edie held Ruth. Jake worked and worked. Finally, Ruth patted Jake's shoulder.

"Jake, it's time to quit. Pete is gone. All the pumping in this world will not revive him."

Tearfully, Jake looked up at Ruth and said, "I'm sorry, Ruth. I promise I will stay here and keep the farm going."

Ruth gave him a hug.

"Do you want me to call the funeral home?" Jake asked.

"Yes, please do. Could you have them hurry. I'd don't want the children to see him."

Jake replied, "I'll take care of it. You and Edie go back to the house."

Ruth and Edie walked out with their arms around each other. Edie pulled the last tray of brownies out of the oven. They were burnt badly.

Bruce hobbled into the kitchen and said, "I smell something burning."

Then he noticed both women with red eyes, sniffling.

"What's the matter, Ruth? Is there something I can do?"

"No, Bruce, there is nothing you or I can do. Edie just found Pete in the barn. Somehow, he tied a rope to the haymow ladder and hung himself. I'm sorry."

Bruce hugged his daughter-in-law and said, "I was afraid of this. Pete's been acting strange lately. Two days ago, he asked if there was a way we could send some of the herd to other cattlemen and have them raise our calves. I think he sensed we were having money problems. This was his way of relieving you and me. I know he would like us to carry forward. He wanted Wade to inherit this place. We must hold it together until he is old enough to do so."

Ruth dried her tears and replied, "Yes, I suppose you are right. We must move on. Will you help Jake with the hearse? He called them for me. They should be here soon. I want Pete's body out of the barn before the children get home. Edie, could you call Sean? I'll need his help. Maybe Ross would help, too."

"Don't worry, we are here for you. I'll call right away."

Sean and Ross arrived about the same time as the mortician with his hearse. They carried Pete's body out of the barn.

Wade and Luke were walking home as the hearse pulled passed them.

Wade looked at Luke and said, "I wonder who the dead wagon picked up now?"

They both snickered.

Wade turned up his lane and said goodbye to Luke. He entered the house and started to change his clothes for chores.

"Wait a minute, Wade. I have something to tell you."

"Okay, Mom, but my calves are hungry, and I have some homework to do. Is Dad around? I need his help with my math."

"Come here and sit down, son. Your father killed himself this afternoon. He is dead. Edie found him in the barn. Jake tried to save him, but he was too far gone. Now he is with Jesus. He suffered here for a long time."

Wade was shocked. First, he didn't say a word, then he burst out crying. Ruth hugged him as he sobbed. She knew it was difficult for a young boy to understand death, especially, his father.

Sophia arrived from high school in Muscatine. She and Francine drove to school in good weather. Today was Sophia's day to drive. She had already dropped Francine at her home. She noticed quickly something was wrong because of all the vehicles in the yard.

"Did something bad happen?" she asked her mother as she entered the kitchen.

"Yes, your father hung himself in the barn this afternoon. Edie found him. We tried to revive him, but we were too late."

Sophia turned and ran to her room. She returned with the letter from her father.

With tears streaming down her face she said, "Dad asked me to write this and he made me promise to not tell you until he was gone. I figured I wouldn't have to give it to you for many years."

Ruth read it and sat down and cried. She gathered Sophia and Wade and hugged them.
"We must keep this farm going for your father. It was his wish, I know," she said.

Wade said, "I will help Jake. I know we can do it."

The funeral was set for Friday with visitation on Thursday. Rural Iowa visitations are well attended. It was well past the closing time before the visitors were gone. The services were at the little Presbyterian Church in Pleasant Prairie. The crowd filled the sanctuary and the basement of the small building. As the crowd filed by the casket for the last time, Edie stopped. She reached in and touched Pete's cold hand.

She thought, "*Petey, boy, you have been my friend for a long time. We played and fished in the pasture. You told me you and Sean made an agreement you would take care of me until he returned. You were a gentleman and did just that, even when we were chased by those rich snobs and we ended up at the shack. Thank you from the bottom of my heart. Be a good boy in Heaven.*"

Pete was buried in the family plot in the Patterson Cemetery. Edie and Marcie organized the wake in the New Era Gym basement because the Pleasant Prairie Church had no running water. As in all rural funerals, mountains of food poured in. Ruth encouraged Edie and Marcie to take some home for it was more than her family could ever eat or keep.

With Jake's help, Ruth managed the farm. Bruce, despite his age and injuries, became more active. Wade entered high school and enrolled in vo-ag classes. He was determined to make his father proud. Sophia received a music scholarship to attend Augustana College in Rock island. She met a young man from Burlington, Iowa. He also studied music. They married and moved to Cedar Rapids.

Edie and her brood prospered. Luke became interested in hybrid seed corn. He worked for a new company named Pioneer Hybrid Seed Corn in the summers. They offered him a scholarship to Iowa State College, but before he was able to go, war broke out. Luke and many young men were sent to fight.

The O'Keefe farm supplied the war effort. Sean put in extra hours helping other farmers who had their sons in the service. He received an award for his efforts. Edie baked and sewed to send items to the troops. It was a time when everyone had one goal: win the war. It didn't matter whether you were rich or poor, old or young, everyone worked as one. The O'Keefe's, the Mohr's, and McKillip's worked together. Their sons were deployed to fight. Letters became treasures. Edie helped her neighbors who lost their sons. She cried their tears. She dried their tears. She was the leader in Montpelier Township.

Fortunately, Luke came home from the service a grown man. He used the GI bill to attend Iowa State. After graduating he worked for Pioneer Seed until his father was elected to the Board of Supervisors of Muscatine County. Luke's knowledge of corn and soybeans grew into an off-farm business of chemicals and seed.

Francine attended Iowa State Teachers College in Cedar Falls. She taught several years at Muscatine High School and married the Vo-ag instructor, Leon Butler. Because of her marriage, she could no longer teach in the Muscatine system. It was the school system's policy, no married women were to teach in the secondary schools. Maybe the rule was okay, for she and her husband provided Edie with four grandchildren. Leon later became a partner with Luke in his seed enterprise.

The twins married the Pace twins. Edie kidded them as "double trouble". Mike married a beautiful Catholic girl, whose father needed help with his farm. Her father, unfortunately, had no sons so Mike fit right in. They had six children.

Hattie lived to be ninety-three years old. She had seven grandchildren and twenty-one great grandchildren and three great-great grandchildren.

Sean and Edie were forever in love. Sean kidded her about her scarred back. He claimed he could play tic-tac-toe on it. She told to go ahead since he was the only person to see it.

The life of Edith Mae Mohr O'Keefe, who was affectionately known by everyone as Edie, continued for many years. She became a grandmother and a great grandmother and hoped to be a great-great grandmother before going to heaven.

ABOUT THE AUTHOR

Bob started writing after he retired from 48 years of farming. He and his wife, Jane, of 55+ years raised three sons on their 600 acre Iowa farm. His many years of farming in Eastern Iowa gave him the basis for his many stories. Others were dreamed up while spending many long hours in the field planting and harvesting. When asked why he writes, his answer is, "I just enjoy telling stories."